# ENERGIZED

# EDWARD M. LERNER

# ENERGIZED

A TOM DOHERTY ASSOCIATES BOOK  NEW YORK

ENERGIZED

An earlier version of this novel was first published in *Analog Science Fiction and Fact* in 2011.

A Tor Book
Published by Tom Doherty Associates, LLC
175 Fifth Avenue
New York, NY 10010

www.tor-forge.com

Tor® is a registered trademark of Tom Doherty Associates, LLC.

ISBN 978-0-7653-2849-6 (hardcover)
ISBN 978-1-4299-4750-3 (e-book)

First Edition: July 2012

Printed in the United States of America

0  9  8  7  6  5  4  3  2  1

*For Katie,*
*May your future always be bright.*

# CONTENTS

# DRAMATIS PERSONAE

*NASA (including contract employees), Earth-based*

MARCUS JUDSON  Support contractor; assistant to government program manager, Powersat One (PS-1) program

PHILIP MAJESKI  Kendricks Aerospace engineer; PS-1 program manager

ELLEN TANAKA  Government program manager, PS-1 program

BETHANY TAYLOR  Kendricks Aerospace engineer; PS-1 chief engineer

*NASA (including contract employees), Phoebe-based*

DINO AGNELLI  Kendricks Aerospace engineer, PS-1 program

THADDEUS STANKIEWICZ  Kendricks Aerospace engineer, PS-1 program; deputy station chief

IRV WEINGART  NASA manager; station chief

*National Radio Astronomy Observatory (NRAO), Green Bank*

PATRICK BURKHALTER  Onetime principal investigator, *Verne* space probe; radio astronomer

SIMON CLAYBURN  Valerie's son

VALERIE CLAYBURN  Radio astronomer

AARON FRIEDMAN  Radio astronomer

IAN WAKEFIELD  System administrator

### PS-1 Independent Inspection Team

OLIVIA FINCH  Professor, Caltech; quality assurance engineer

SAVANNAH MORGAN  U.S. Air Force civilian employee; computer security engineer

REUBEN SWENSON  Department of Energy employee; power systems engineer

### U.S. government, non-NASA

DEVIN GIBSON  President of the United States

GERALD HENDERSON  Director, Central Intelligence Agency

CARLOS ORTIZ  Colonel, U.S. Air Force; computer security engineer

TYLER POPE  CIA analyst

CHARMAINE POWELL  CIA analyst

VONDA RODGERS  General, U.S. Air Force

### Russo Venture Capital Partners (RVCP)

KAYLA JORGENSON  President, Jorgenson Power Systems (an RVCP-backed company)

LINCOLN ROBERTS  Technical adviser; electrical engineer

DILLON RUSSO  Principal partner, Russo Venture Capital Partners

FELIPE TORRES  Technical adviser; communications engineer

JONAS WALKER  Technical adviser; software engineer

### Other Americans

ROBIN BRILL  Socialite; sister of Thaddeus Stankiewicz

GABRIEL CAMPBELL  First geologist to explore Phoebe; deceased

### Russians

YAKOV NIKOLAYEVICH BRODSKY  Deputy trade representative, posted to the Washington embassy; undercover agent of the Federal Security Service (in its Russian acronym, the FSB)

IRINA IVANOVNA CHESNOKOVA  Yakov's longtime assistant

DMITRII FEDEROVICH AMINOV  FSB station chief, posted to the Washington embassy

ANATOLY VLADIMIROVICH SOKOLOV  Ambassador to the United States

PAVEL BORISOVICH KHRISTENKO  President, Russian Federation

# Earth and Vicinity, 2023

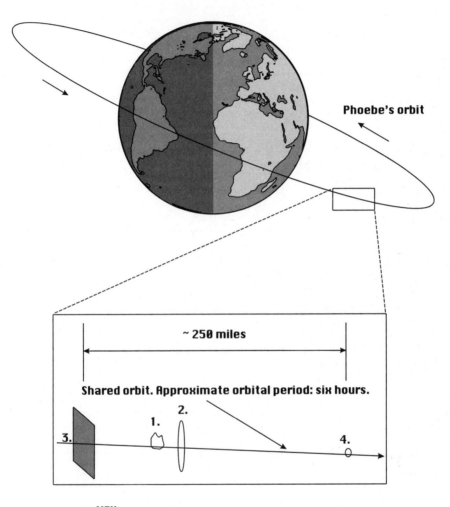

Phoebe's orbit

~ 250 miles

Shared orbit. Approximate orbital period: six hours.

1.
2.
3.
4.

KEY
1. Phoebe
2. Free-flying sunshield
3. Powersat One (PS-1)
4. The Space Place

Notes:
- Object sizes not to scale.
- Ground track of orbiting objects shifts.
- The sunshield maneuvers to keep Phoebe in shade.

PROLOGUE | 2020

Earth hovered, almost at full phase, breathtakingly magnificent. Distance concealed the works—and blights—of man, and the globe seemed pristine. Its oceans sparkled. Its cloud tops and ice caps glistened. And it was *huge*: the natural moon, had it been visible, would have appeared only about one-hundredth as wide.

Earth seemed close enough to touch through the exercise room's tinted dome, but Gabriel Campbell held firmly to the handles of the stationary bicycle. Not that he relied on the strength of his grip: he wore a seat belt, too, and straps bound his feet to the pedals. *This* world had too little gravity to notice.

His eyes alternated between the vista overhead and the image of Jillian, his fiancée, which he had taped to the bike's digital readout. Strawberry blond hair cascaded down her neck and shoulders. Freckles lay scattered across that most adorable, pert little nose. Her clear green eyes—and more so, her smile—all but outshone the Earth.

He was here, on Phoebe, to make a future for both: the Earth and the love of his life. In just one more month, he would go home. Then he and Jillian would marry and they would never be apart again.

Basking in earthlight, his legs pumping furiously on the bike, Gabe was pleasantly tired, professionally fulfilled, emotionally satisfied—

Unaware that before two hours had passed, he would be dead.

\* \* \*

Phoebe completed an orbit around the Earth in just less than six hours, and as Gabe pedaled darkness crept across the face of the world. The changing phase of the Earth told him he had been working out for almost two hours.

Sweat soaked his Minnesota Twins T-shirt, and still ahead of him was a stint on the not-quite weight machine: the resistive exercise device. Without exercise, muscles atrophied and bones lost mass in Phoebe's miniscule gravity. Four hours of daily workout were mandated, but he would have worked out anyway. He patted Jillian's picture. "I'll be plenty fit for you when I come home." Fit, and horny as the devil.

And with no way up here to spend a dime, he would have banked six months' salary with which to build their future. The pay was damned good, too, much higher than anything he could get on the ground. He tried not to think of the premium as hazardous-duty pay.

The bike whirred. A damper rattled in the ventilation system. Voices, indistinct, blended with dueling music players. And then, from the comm unit clipped to his sleeve, soft chimes. Gabe tapped the unit. "Campbell."

"We've got a bot in trouble," Tina Lundgren said, her voice throaty. She was deputy station chief of Phoebe base and in command on the night shift. Not that day or night had any meaning here. The station followed Eastern time for the convenience of folks on the ground. "In sector twelve."

"And it's my turn to go outside." Hell, Gabe was happy to go out. Only a handful of geologists had ever left Earth, and *he* was one of them. Had there been any way to get Jillian up here, he would want to stay forever. "What's the problem?"

"Stupid bot tangled itself up in a rock jumble. Otherwise, it's healthy."

Likely a thirty-second task, after an hour or so to suit up and trek halfway across the moonlet. Good deal.

Tina contacting him meant that he was in charge of the excursion. But no one went outside alone—too many things could go wrong. Gabe asked, "Who else is on call tonight?"

"Thaddeus and Bryce. Shall I give one of them a holler for you?"

"I'll take Thad. Newbie could use the practice." Gabe eased off his pedaling. "And no, don't call. I'm in the gym. I need to cool off first." Outside was not the place to get stiff and inflexible.

After winding down for a few minutes, Gabe unstrapped his slippers from the pedals, unbelted, and, carefully dismounting, firmly planted a slipper on one of the deck's Velcro strips. Trailing damp footprints he crossed the exercise room, the Velcro pads on the soles of his slippers *zip-zipping* with each step.

At the hatchway he took hold of the handrail that ran along the corridor ceiling. The Tarzan swing was the quickest way through the station. Many of his crewmates would be asleep, and he kept a Tarzan yell to himself.

Thaddeus Stankiewicz was not in his quarters, the tiny common room, or the even tinier sanitary facilities. When Gabe tried the machine shop, the hatch squeaked on its hinges.

Thad was new to Phoebe and micro gee; his surprised twitch launched him from his stool and scattered whatever he was working on. Gabe saw cordless soldering pistols, metal tubes, metal rods, wire coils— and, writhing free at the end of its oxygen and acetylene hoses, a cutting torch tipped with blue flame.

Gabe leapt, catching the torch by a hose and with his other hand giving Thad a firm shove clear. The push—equal and opposite reactions— brought Gabe to a near halt at mid-room, above the deck. About a foot: call it thirty seconds hang time. That was plenty long to give Thad a tongue-lashing for his carelessness.

Newbie looked so flustered that Gabe relented. He killed the torch and merely glared as Thad, who by then had grabbed a bench edge, began gathering parts (of what?) and cramming them into his pockets. Stankiewicz was short, broad shouldered, and intense. His thick black eyebrows and deep-set eyes made him seem perpetually brooding. He wore a standard station jumpsuit, the royal-blue version, with its integral Velcro slippers.

Finally touching down, Gabe slid his foot until it engaged a Velcro strip. "What are you working on?"

Thad shrugged, looking uneasy. Embarrassed? "Personal project."

The station offered precious little privacy, so Gabe let it go. "A surface rover got stuck. You and I are up to extract it."

"Okay." Thad kept grabbing and stowing the scattered pieces of his project. "Almost done."

"Leave that, Newbie. We have a job to do."

They made their way to the main air lock. The closer they got, the more dark streaks and splotches marked the gray metal panels that lined the corridor. You couldn't help but track Phoebe's dust and grime into the station, and once inside the stuff found its way everywhere. The crew vacuumed endlessly, but it was a losing battle.

Their spacesuits were filthier than the interior halls and no longer permitted in most of the station. Once you couldn't change in a closet-sized cabin, bracing yourself between opposing walls, the best place to suit up was inside the air lock.

In the air lock, back to back and studiously ignoring each other, the two men stripped. Even more studiously they ignored jostling and brushing into each other.

The body suits fit snugly against bare skin. Donning a very elastic body suit in the all-but-nonexistent gravity was like squirming into a sausage casing—underwater. Every nudge and bump sent them careening off bulkheads and decks and each other. Still, these mechanical counterpressure suits beat the hell out of bulky, pressurized space-suits. Gabe had tried an old-style suit once in training. It was easier to get into, but *way* more massive. Inertia varied with mass, not weight, and fighting that much inertia was exhausting.

Gabe finally wriggled into his suit and helped Thad finish getting into his own. "Check me out," Gabe said. He launched himself, with a bit of practiced footwork, into a slow, midair pirouette.

"You look fine," Thad said.

The answer had come too quickly. Anywhere that the suit failed to settle securely into place, fluid would pool beneath. Gaping was the major issue with the skin suits, with the crotch area especially problematical. It wasn't as if Gabe wanted another guy checking out his crotch, but he wanted even less to have blisters down there from an ill-fitting suit. "Check it again," he snapped.

Done properly, spacesuit checkout took time. Eventually, though, their suits were wrinkle-free and without sags or pouching. They mounted and sealed the compression neck rings to which their helmets would attach.

They slipped on their backpacks and checked readouts for everything: oxygen, heating, sensors, radio, batteries. Their helmets and air hoses were locked into place.

They stowed their indoor clothes, Thad's pockets clanking, in lockers near the air lock, buckled on tool belts and tether reels, stuck emergency maneuvering guns in their holsters, and pulled on gloves and boots. Ready at last, Gabe configured the air-lock controls for surface access.

"Oscar, end-to-end system check," Gabe said. Status messages, the text all green, scrolled down the inside of his helmet visor. He had named the voice-activated user interface Oscar as a nod to the suit in *Have Spacesuit, Will Travel*, a book he had loved as a child—and because, crammed into this suit, he knew how a sardine must feel.

"Comm check, Thad," Gabe radioed on the public channel.

"Back at you," Stankiewicz said.

Gabe called, "Tina? Two robot wranglers set to go outside."

"Happy trails," Tina answered, yawning. "Stay in touch."

"Roger that." Gabe tapped the air-lock control panel. Pump noises faded as air was sucked into holding tanks. He felt the first stirrings of warmth from the heating elements in the thermal layer of his suit. Light poured inside as the outer hatch opened. Shrunken to a crescent, the Earth still shone more brightly than a full moon. For now, the moon itself remained hidden behind the Earth.

Newbie gestured at the ladder. "Age before beauty."

"Pearls before swine."

Gabe grabbed the ladder rails and climbed. He paused on the third rung, with only his head and shoulders above the surface. The horizon was freakishly close. Despite earthlight, the landscape was only a dim presence, less reflective than asphalt. Without its coat of rocks, soot, and hydrocarbons, Phoebe's ice—the ice they were here to mine, the ice that could change *everything*—would have streamed off as a spectacular comet tail.

His grandparents still talked about where they were, what they had been doing, when they first heard that President Kennedy had been shot. For his parents' generation, and even for some of Gabe's own, the event seared into the collective consciousness was 9/11. The World

Trade Center towers crashing down had marked Gabe, too—he had been sixteen that day—but the news that had *truly* marked him, had changed everything for him, even more than 9/11 or the Crudetastrophe, had come a mere five years ago.

As though it were yesterday, he remembered: a rumor at first, run rampant on the blogosphere, then the hastily called presidential address. A space rock, a *big* one, was headed Earth's way. It was not dinosaur-killer-sized, not quite, and the likelihood it would hit Earth was only one in a thousand—but no sane person would leave home against those odds, let alone bet the future of civilization. The rock had to be deflected, and despite its many woes only the United States had the capability to tackle the job.

But the excitement, the game changer, was this: rather than deflect the rock *away,* NASA would undertake to aim it more precisely *at* Earth. To ensure capture of the object. To exploit its resources and forever change space exploration.

And to hell with whether anyone else thought this was a bad idea. Gabe had never encountered much in the way of presidential leadership. It was exhilarating.

He had long ago lost his youthful interest in the space program. Decade after decade of pointlessly circling the world, scarcely skimming the top of the atmosphere: what was the point? No one cared anymore.

But suddenly there *was* a reason. Saving the planet. Maybe, in the process, pulling the country out of an economic abyss. And to be honest—adventure. Faster than the president could finish speaking that night, Gabe had vowed he would be an astronaut. Somehow.

That rock—only it had turned out to be far more complex and interesting, a dormant comet—was now Earth's second moon. Was Phoebe. And once again, *he* was about to explore its ancient surface.

"The view here is less interesting," Thad radioed from the bottom of the air lock.

"Sorry." Gabe unreeled four feet of tether, clipping its carabiner around the staked cable labeled SECTOR TWELVE. He clipped a second tether to the guide cable before grabbing handholds outside the hatch and pulling himself up and out. He waited ten feet along the cable until, gopherlike, Thad's head and shoulders appeared.

"*Two* tethers," Gabe reminded the newbie.

It was easier by far to fall off this toy world than to cross it. Phoebe was roughly a sphere a mile and a quarter across—where *rough* better described the body than *sphere*. It was round in the sense that a popcorn ball was round, with stony lumps taking the place of popped kernels and veins of frothy ice—and in spots, only vacuum—taking the part of molasses. And in the sense that a popcorn ball remained a ball after it had been whacked a bit, dented here, flattened there. Phoebe was less a single object than a rubble pile loosely bonded by its mutual gravity. If its orbit had dipped much lower, the tidal forces from Earth's gravity would have ripped the little moon to shreds.

"Two tethers," Thad repeated. "Done. After you, Pearl."

Gabe pulled himself hand over hand along the cable, coasting above the inky surface. His eyes insisted he was soaring up a cliff face. Gravity's feeble tug told his inner ears he was falling *into* the cliff face. His gut wished eyes and ears would come to some agreement.

After twenty yanks Gabe stopped pulling. "Coasting," he radioed the newbie.

"Thanks. The view from behind is unattractive enough without climbing up your butt."

Gabe slowed with gentle hand pressure against the cable at the first glint ahead of a piton anchored in the rock. Carefully he unclipped one carabiner and snapped it back onto the cable on the opposite side of the ring. He did the same with his second tether. He made sure the newbie followed the same fail-safe procedure before resuming the trip to sector twelve.

The surface lights, antennae, and trash dump of the station dropped behind the too-close horizon. But a status icon in his HUD shone a steady, reassuring green, confirming connectivity with Tina and the command center. The metal guide cable did double duty as an antenna.

Every hundred or so feet a piton interrupted their glide, and in such short increments they made their way toward sector twelve. After ten minutes Gabe checked in with Tina. Twice he saw survey robots—their silvery, octopoid shapes unmistakable—creeping along the surface. The second bot's instrument suite must have sensed a buried ice seam, because the machine was staking a radio beacon. Had Gabe cared to tune to the proper frequency, he would have heard soft beeping from the marker.

Ice meant water. Water meant oxygen and hydrogen. And water, oxygen, and hydrogen already in near-Earth orbit—not lofted from Earth's surface or the permanently shadowed polar craters of the distant moon, in either case at the cost of thousands of dollars per pound—were dearer than gold or platinum. So, too, whatever mineral wealth could be wrung from the rocks of Phoebe. On scheduled outings, he continued to survey for exploitable resources.

It was said: Low Earth orbit is halfway to anywhere in the solar system. That was a metaphorical truth, almost poetic. Half the work of going anywhere in the solar system *was* expended fighting Earth's gravity. Building powersats with Phoebe's mineral resources, beaming down solar energy to an energy-starved world, would be only the beginning. Phoebe would be the gateway to the planets.

Away from the station the moonscape dissolved into a shadowy sameness. They passed the pilot distillery sited at a safe distance from the habitat. Parallel glints revealed pipes snaking across the dark surface, delivering water, oxygen, and hydrogen to the base.

Gabe played tour guide, pointing out the little world's interesting features. "On our left, the thermal nuclear rockets that nudged Phoebe into orbit." He glanced at his Geiger counter, even though workers had long since recycled the uranium fuel rods in the base power plant. No matter how many powersats got their start here, Phoebe, forever behind its sunshield, would stay nuclear. "And on our right, the Grand Chasm. It's no great shakes by Earth standards, but relative to Phoebe, it's huge."

"Uh-huh," Thad said.

Newbie had been moody since they left the station. As for what preoccupied him, Gabe could only guess. Maybe no more was at work here than that Thad—like most of the crew—was an engineer, without interest in Phoebe itself. When Thad deigned to interrupt the travelogue, it was always with practical questions. About pressure suits, their related gear, and how soon anyone would come after them if comm should break down. . . .

Fair enough. Knowing the limitations and vulnerabilities of the equipment could save a person's life. Although Gabe wished he could share the excitement of discovery, the rocks were not going anywhere. Maybe Newbie would lighten up after he got more comfortable with his equipment.

They glided past the infrared telescope. Good, Gabe thought, we're halfway there. About all he understood about IR astronomy was that hot objects emitted infrared, so you wanted your infrared instruments kept cold to minimize their own intrinsic thermal noise. Behind its sunshield, Phoebe was about as cold as anywhere in Earth's neighborhood ever got. The 'scope's cryocooler, powered by the base nuclear reactor, kept the IR sensor colder still.

He slowed or stopped whenever a surface feature caught his eye, but even a cursory look said most of these rocks were yet more carbonaceous chondrites and silicates. Two bits of stone he could not immediately identify went into his sample bag, for tests back at the station.

*He* was curious about this tiny world, even if there was no point in discussing it.

Isotope dating of previous samples said Phoebe was more than four billion years old. So why did it still exist? Its desiccated, rocky crust was not *that* impressive as an insulator. Had it always followed the orbit in which it had been discovered, swooping inside Earth's own orbit, Phoebe's ice would have sublimated long ago, its rocky remains dispersed into a short-period meteor shower. Of course if it had always followed that orbit, the Near-Earth Object Survey would have spotted Phoebe years earlier. Or Phoebe would have smacked Earth before anyone even knew about death from the sky.

So: Phoebe had had another orbit, an orbit more distant from the sun. Planetary astronomers had yet to work out Phoebe's original path and what planetary close encounter might have sent Phoebe diving at the Earth. Gabe guessed there was a Nobel waiting for whoever figured it out.

As the Earth waned and the landscape faded into darkness, he had Oscar project a topo map on his HUD. The blinking red dot had them most of the way to the green dot representing the stranded bot. Pits and ravines, ridges and rocky jumbles leapt out of the map image. He tugged his tethers once, twice for reassurance.

"Let's stop for a minute," Gabe called. New Earth was imminent, and Newbie was in for a treat. "Watch the limb of the planet."

Earth's crescent became the thinnest of arcs, then disappeared.

A pale, shimmering arch—part rainbow, part oil slick—emerged from the darkness. Phoebe's sunshield. The free-flying Mylar disk that hovered above Phoebe warded off the sunlight that might yet boil away precious ice as boots and robot tentacles and, eventually, mining operations scraped through the insulating surface layers. The shield's sun-facing side reflected most of the light that hit it. What little sunlight penetrated the shield—the bit they could see—was scattered by the backside's granular coating.

For an endless moment the arch, large but faint, was the brightest object in the sky. Then the trailing edge of the shield, too, slid into the Earth's shadow, abandoning the sky to stars like chips of diamond.

Now the sole clue to Earth's presence was a hole in the star field. Even with eyes fully adjusted to the darkness, from this altitude Gabe could not spot any city lights. He could pretend that all was well below, that the world was not divided between energy haves and have-nots.

"Show's over," Gabe said. He switched on his helmet lights. An instant later, Thad activated his own. "Pretty cool, though, don't you think?"

Thad only grunted.

"So, Thad. What *were* you making in the shop?" Gabe was just making conversation. Skimming the pitch-black rock face in the near darkness was eerie.

He felt a tap-tap on his calf and twisted around. Thad had only one hand on the guide cable, waggling his other hand. Two fingers were raised.

"Oscar, private channel two," Gabe ordered. "Okay, Thad. What's going on?"

"Private channel two," Thad repeated. Finally, he added, "You'll keep this to yourself, right?"

"If that's what you want."

Hand over hand, they went. A rim of sunshield reappeared just before the Earth returned as a new crescent. Gabe doused his helmet lights.

On his HUD the red and green dots were converging. Another few minutes and they would veer from the guide cable.

Eventually Gabe prompted, "Well?"

"Okay. I put my life in your hands." Thad sighed. "I have a thing for Tiny."

Tina Lundgren was big for an astronaut, even a male astronaut. The nickname was inevitable—and you used it within her earshot at your own peril. Gabe had to admit that, in an Amazonian kind of way, she was sexy. And she was one of only two women, and the only unmarried woman, on Phoebe. Gabe understood Thad wanting this conversation on a private channel.

Having bared his soul, Thad went on and on about Tina's womanly charms.

"Uh-huh," Gabe finally interrupted. "And you were cutting pipe as an outlet for your unrequited love?"

"Not exactly." A rueful laugh. "I'm making a still. Whether or not homebrew appeals to her, I figure it won't go to waste."

"Does she know how you feel?" Gabe asked.

"Not from me! Not yet. Frankly, the woman scares the crap out of me. Maybe that's why I have to have her."

To their left, a ghostly plume: an ice pocket flashing to steam bursting from the ground.

Behind its sunshield Phoebe should be colder than the night side of the moon: for two weeks out of four, every part of the moon but a few deep polar craters felt sunlight. But shield or no, some sunlight *did* reach Phoebe. No software was perfect, and occasionally the sunshield—tugged by Earth, moon, and Phoebe; pushed by the solar wind and by sunlight itself; balancing the many conflicting forces with its own feeble thrusters—drifted out of position. Whenever that happened, sunlight beat directly on the surface. Even when the shield balanced perfectly, the traces of sunlight penetrating the shield scattered in unpredictable ways. Earthlight and moonlight were, in the final analysis, echoes of sunlight. And heat leaked from the underground base and its nuclear power plant. All that energy mingled, meandered, and reradiated in unpredictable ways.

And so, seemingly at random, little geysers. The vapor was too diffuse to do any harm. Most times. If you were unlucky, a geyser could sweep you right off Phoebe.

"A still," Gabe repeated, his thoughts divided between the plume, already trailing off, the topo map on his HUD, the landscape sliding by inches beneath his visor, and the conversation. Ethyl alcohol boils at a lower temperature than water, so alcohol fumes waft up a still coil before water vapor. You separated out the early condensate. But *up* comes of having gravity. "Will a still even work in Phoebe's grav—"

Too much happened at once, the sequence unclear:

—A sharp tug on Gabe's backpack.

—Thad saying, "Wrong answer."

—A power alarm.

—A second yank.

—Helmet lights and HUD going dark.

—A hard shove forward.

Gabe twisted around. Earthlight showed Thad a good twenty feet away, receding. Just staring. And bulging from the mesh pouch of Thad's tool belt: two battery packs.

Without power for his suit's heating elements, Gabe would freeze within minutes. Already the cold seeped into him, body and thoughts turning sluggish. He got his feet beneath him, even as he ripped lengths of tether from their reels. He leapt.

His right foot slipped on loose gravel and he sailed far to the side.

The shorter tether pulled him up short. Its yank started him spinning even as the tug started him back toward the surface. Too slowly. He took the maneuvering pistol from its holster—but it slipped from fingers already numb with cold. As he drifted down he managed to grip a rock outcropping.

All the while, maintaining his distance, Thad watched. Stared.

"Why?" Gabe screamed. Not that his radio worked without batteries. Not that his shout could cross the vacuum. "Why are you doing this?"

Maybe his murderer read Gabe's lips. Whatever the reason, Thad shrugged.

Gabe advanced. Thad retreated.

As cold became all, as consciousness faded, the last thing Gabe saw was the waxing crescent Earth.

Earth no longer seemed close enough to touch.

* * *

"He just went *nuts*!" Thad said once more.

With minor variations the words had become his mantra. First with Tiny, when he had called in from across Phoebe about the "accident." Over and over with Bryce Lewis and Alan Childs after they joined Thad on the surface. And now hopefully for the last time, in the station's comm-gear-packed command center, with Lyman Hsu, the dour station chief.

"Details, please." Hsu rubbed his pencil-thin mustache as he spoke.

Thad ignored the request. "You should have let me go with the other guys. You can't imagine what it was like." I damn well hope you can't imagine it. *He* struggled to understand it.

"You'd been outside long enough for one day. You know the rules."

Because their utility craft were little more than flying broomsticks: compressed-nitrogen bottles, saddles, and minimal controls mounted to latticework frames. A counterpressure suit was your only protection.

"But I don't have to like the rules," Thad said. Which, emphatically, he did not. What if he had overlooked something? Joining the rescue team might have given him a chance to cover his tracks.

"Details," Hsu prompted.

"You heard Gabe switch to private channel two." It had all come down to Gabe taking his cue, because everything on the public channel got recorded. Sooner or later, he would have figured out what Thad was building. Certainly the bullshit about Tiny and making a still for her would not bear scrutiny. That fable was all Thad could come up with on the spot, blather to occupy Gabe's mind until they got farther from the station. "When I linked in, Gabe was already mid-rant. He missed Jillian, unbearably. He knew—but couldn't explain how—that she was cheating on him. He loved her and needed her and couldn't bear for anyone else to be with her. He would show her. And then"—Thad paused dramatically—"he unclipped his tethers."

"And you . . . ?"

"What do you *think*, Lyman? I tried to talk sense into him, damn it."

"And not a word of this reported to base."

"I didn't dare switch channels! There was no telling what Gabe might do if I wasn't on. If I didn't respond when he expected an answer."

"And he jumped anyway."

"As I keep telling you," Thad said.

He had never been much of a basketball player. On a good day, his vertical leap was two feet. On Phoebe, that was more than enough leg strength to vault two men and their gear past escape velocity. He had let go of the body, untethered, before coming to the end of his own fully unrolled tethers. After the ropes pulled *him* short with a jerk, Thad had watched the corpse recede into the darkness.

Hsu tipped back his head, staring through the command-center dome. "He had second thoughts."

"What do you mean?" Thad asked.

"When Tina and Lewis found Gabe, the suit heater was on. He must have been in late-stage hypothermia by then, half delirious. It's a marvel his suit still recognized his voice." Hsu sighed. "By then it was too late."

The heaters kicked back on once Thad replaced the batteries. Not done till Gabe was, unequivocally, dead.

But Hsu hadn't finished. "The flight surgeons suspect that the suit heater kicking back on was the coup de grâce. Evidently the human body resists hypothermia by constricting blood flow to the extremities, conserving warmer blood for the vital organs. The rush of heat would have dilated the blood vessels in Gabe's arms and legs—and flooded his heart with cold, oxygen-poor blood. That afterdrop likely triggered a fatal arrhythmia. We'll know more once the docs groundside get a look at the body."

*He'd left Gabe* alive? *With a working* radio? *Jesus!* "Arrhythmia?" Thad managed to get out.

"An abnormal heart rhythm. After a little while Gabe's heart would've just stopped."

"It's a shame," Thad said, meaning it. Gabe was not a bad guy, only in the wrong place at the wrong time.

"A damn shame."

Silence stretched awkwardly. After a while Thad said, "It's been a hell of a day. I'd like to . . . hell, I don't know what." Except that he knew damn well. He had to finish what Gabe had interrupted, and get everything stashed away. At least then the man would have died for a reason. "Something other than relive this disaster."

Hsu nodded. "Sounds like a good idea. Get some sleep."

"I will," Thad said. And wondered if he could.

CONVICTION | 2023

**M**arcus Judson slipped into the back of the downtown Balti-
more hotel ballroom, more than an hour late. Though the
room was packed, it did not seem like anyone was having a ball. Certainly not his colleagues huddled at the speakers' table at the opposite
end of the room.

He surveilled from behind a freestanding sign that read: THE POWER
OF POWERSATS: A TOWN MEETING. From the way Jeff Robbins, one of the
EPA representatives on the dais, blotted his face with his handkerchief,
the townsfolk bore, however metaphorically, torches and pitchforks.

The PowerHolo orientation spiel (of which Marcus was thoroughly
sick, after many such gatherings) ran about thirty minutes. That meant
the Q & A session had just begun. It did not bode well to find Jeff already wound so tight. Plenty of head-in-the-sand types in the crowd,
then. Damned Luddites.

Marcus hated being such a cynic—but he was more this way every
day.

This could have been any public meeting room anywhere. High
ceiling. Cheap carpet and cloth-covered walls to muffle the audience
noises. Sidewalls comprised of narrow segments that, folded into accor-
dion pleats, would open into other, similar rooms for additional space.
Recessed ceiling lights. Amplifier and loudspeakers deployed across
the foot of the dais. Holo projection console.

Men and women filled the rows of chairs, and yet more people had queued up in the aisles for turns at the audience microphones. At the right-hand mike, a tall, balding man, his sleeves rolled up, was gesturing grandly. Marcus had arrived too late to catch the man's point. If he *had* a point. They often didn't.

". . . would be a better use of public land," the balding man finally concluded.

"Thank you for your comment," Lisa Jackson began. As she—as all the panelists—had been trained. "We agree that parks are important. That said, so is a sufficiency of electrical power. We at the Department of the Interior must consider both."

The novelty of powersat town meetings was long past; the room's lone tripod-mounted camera might feed only the municipal Internet server. With *no* media visible the protocol would have been the same, because half the audience sat holding comps or phones or datasheets. Any slipup would be on YouTube within minutes. So all panelists were trained in changing the subject. Better a nonanswer than an impolitic one.

*If inconvenient questions were to be evaded, what was the point? Why hold these town meetings at all?* Marcus had asked, and his question, evidently, was also impolitic. "It's policy," a long-ago boss had once told Marcus in similar circumstances. "It doesn't have to make sense."

But coaching by a NASA spin doctor was not what had made Marcus a cynic.

He half listened, half pondered how and when to move to the front of the room. On the dais, behind the long, skinny table and its billowing, ruffled skirt, sat eight chairs: two places each for Interior, Energy, the EPA, and NASA. The lone unoccupied seat was Marcus's.

With Lisa expounding from five chairs away from the empty seat, this seemed as good a time as any for Marcus to claim his spot.

He edged through the least crowded aisle, murmuring apologies as he went, answering dirty looks by tapping the NASA ID badge clipped to his suit lapel. I'm with the government. I really *am* here to help.

Once through the crowd, he slid into the empty chair at the speakers' table.

Ellen Tanaka, NASA program manager for the powersat—and Marcus's boss—looked weary. They all did. Her eyes, too myopic for LASIK, were owl-like behind thick, round lenses. She covered her mike with a hand. "Good of you to join us," she whispered.

That he had texted ahead changed nothing. Everyone had made the drive that morning from somewhere in metro D.C. She would not want to hear about the rain, the line at the gas station, or signals flashing red throughout Fairfax County because the traffic management system had crashed or been hacked. He would not have, either.

"Car trouble," he mouthed. "Sorry."

Lisa was still answering the balding man. "We'll be using property already dedicated to power generation, in this case for ground-based solar power. In particular, we'll retrofit selected solar farms with arrays of short antennas suited to receiving power downlinks. Land recycling, if you will, very environmentally correct. The antennas will be vertical, scarcely blocking any sunlight from the solar cells on the ground. So, you see, the powersat demonstration does not preempt any parkland."

"But that land *shouldn't* be wasted on—"

"Thank you for your comment," Ellen interrupted. "I'm afraid that's all the time we have with so many others still waiting." She pointed to the head of another line, where a middle-aged woman, rail thin, her face tanned and leathery, clutched a folded sheet of paper. The woman wore the judgmental expression of a Resetter. "Yes, ma'am?"

Marcus and Ellen took turns moderating these meetings, because NASA's part of the solar-power-satellite project drew the fewest questions. Public comments mostly concerned public safety, energy policy, and land use. Never mind, Marcus thought, that Powersat One, the full-scale demo system nearing completion, would be the largest structure ever built. Or that NASA was constructing PS-1 in space, where neither night nor weather could interrupt the sunlight streaming onto its solar cells.

But all that dependable—and desperately needed—solar energy became useful only when it reached the ground. And once brought to Earth, the power had to be distributed far and wide. Terrestrial solar farms already had connections to the national power grid. Siting the downlink antennas amid the ground-based solar farms just made sense.

To Marcus, anyway.

"About that downlink," the thin woman began, frowning. "'Downlink' sounds like an Internet connection, and that's more than a little disingenuous. *Your* downlink is nothing so benign. You're talking about microwaves. A *gigawatt* or so of microwaves. If you turn on that satellite, it'll roast anyone unlucky enough to encounter the power beam."

"No, it won't," someone muttered from down the table—and a mike picked it up.

Marcus leaned forward to see who had gone off script. Apparently Brad Kaminski, from DOE. He was clutching his mike stand, and a bit red in the face.

"Um, thank you for your comment," Brad backtracked. "Yes, downlinks from the power satellite will use microwaves. That's for a good reason: Earth's atmosphere is transparent to microwaves. By beaming microwaves, we can harvest most of the power on the ground.

"But as for safety, ma'am, there is no cause for concern. The beam is strongest at its center. By the edge—"

"How strong?" someone in the crowd hollered.

"About like direct, overhead sunlight," Brad said. "By the edge of the—"

"Like a second sun beating down on you," the woman at the mike said. "*That* should be healthy."

Brad persisted. "By the edge of the collection area, a zone miles across, the beam has attenuated to well within public safety standards."

The woman laughed humorlessly. "You expect the birds to mind your fences?"

From deep within the crowd, a snort. "Lady, do you have any idea how many birds get chopped up by wind generators?"

"Forget the damned birds!" someone shouted back from across the ballroom. "Just keep the lights on and my car charged."

Taunts and insults erupted, on every side of the issue. Cameras big and small pointed to memorialize the chaos. It took Ellen several minutes to restore order—

In order that more decorous criticisms could resume. That powersats were: unsafe, unnecessary, or poor investments. That if only everyone conserved, instead of wasting resources on foolishly audacious projects, it would be better for the United States and the entire Earth, too. That the country could extract additional energy from the tides, or build more wind farms, or reshingle more roofs with solar cells, or grow more biomass, or . . . do *anything* other than the powersat project.

And from the opposite end of the opinion spectrum: That the wind did not always blow when people need power. That—duh!—the sun did not shine at night or do much for snow-covered roofs. That sunlight beating down on Arizona did nothing for New England. That people shrieking "energy sprawl" against a few square miles to be used for East Coast microwave downlinks fooled no one by suggesting new high-voltage power lines could be built across the continent from solar farms in the southwestern deserts. That the NIMBYs had even less credibility proposing huge new storage systems to save solar power for exploitation at night. And that if the tree-huggers did not wise up, civilization would grind to a halt. Shivering in the dark.

Since the Crudetastrophe, oil was scarce and painfully expensive. That did not make gasoline any less essential. There simply was not enough electrical power generation to cope with the hurried—and ongoing—switchover to plug-in cars; if there had been, the over-burdened power grid could not reliably distribute the added load. Marcus did not bring up any of that. No one on the panel did. They were not permitted to say anything verging on politics, geo- or other.

*Do it all!* Marcus wanted to shout, but that was yet another truth no one on the panel was permitted to speak. Any other means of power generator, distribution, or conservation was someone else's project.

From time to time it was his turn to field a harangue. He dutifully thanked whomever for their comment and, all too often, parroted some preapproved, eminently inoffensive platitude. And began to wonder if there was any way he could not have become cynical.

If he hadn't been already.

A young woman in a Johns Hopkins sweatshirt reached the front of a comment line. An engineering student, Marcus suspected, because she asked about the radiation environment in space gradually degrading solar cells. When he thanked her for the question, he really meant it. *He* was an engineer, too.

He talked about radiation hardening, on-orbit repair methods, and opportunities for in-space remanufacturing. He reviewed the deleterious effects of weather on *terrestrial* solar cells. This, finally, was a question he could answer without breaking protocol—not to mention an interesting topic—and he pretended not to notice his boss's sidelong glances until she tap-tapped her mike to cut him off. It was almost noon and they were, "regrettably nearly out of time."

Two more danced-around questions and the ordeal was over. Until two days hence, in another city. Marcus forgot which, and it hardly mattered.

This was no way to save a country.

*   *   *

Long after Marcus and his colleagues had collected their things and were ready to hit the road, many of their audience still milled about in animated clumps, arguing. The stragglers showed no sign of clearing the aisles.

The wall behind the dais had two camouflaged service doors. Marcus opened one a few inches and peeked out. He found the service hallway empty and, apart from the distant, muffled clatter of pots and pans, quiet. "Shall we?" he suggested to his colleagues.

No one disagreed.

In the austere corridor, her shoes clicking on the tile floor, Ellen limped along beside Marcus. She had not quite recovered from a skiing accident the previous winter. Ellen was tall to begin with; in heels, she was almost his height. "Not fun, Marcus, but we need public support. It's going to be a big change."

"Understood," he said. And still a waste of their time.

"Not everything can be as fascinating as radiation hardening techniques for solar cells." With a laugh, she changed the subject. "What's the car problem?"

"The circuit breaker in my garage tripped overnight." The overtaxed grid, sagging and surging, was beyond anyone's ability to predict—and with every new electric car on the street the load became a little greater, a bit more mobile, and that much less predictable. "The breaker must have popped right after I got home and plugged in the car, because I had about zero charge this morning."

"And you had to buy gas this morning? Ouch. Well, you must have had ration credits left. That's something."

Double doors swung open into the service corridor, the kitchen noises swelling, and waiters rushed toward them bearing lunch trays. Marcus stepped aside.

Twenty bucks and change per gallon. That ridiculous line at the pump. Ration credits he had been saving for a vacation. None of it bore thinking about.

"And Marcus . . ."

The pregnant pause. Her charcoal-gray power suit. Heels. She was *way* overdressed for the morning's public flogging. "Where are you off to, boss, and what do you need me to cover for you?"

She grinned. "Clearly we've worked together too long. The administrator called last night. He wants a program update today. Hence, you'll be taking my place at this afternoon's interagency coordination session. I'll mail the minutes from the last session."

When the administrator of NASA called, you went. Still . . . "Isn't that task force all career civil servants?"

Which Marcus was not. He was a SETA contractor: systems engineering and technical assistance. Fortunate SETA contractors got involved in everything their government counterparts did. Unfortunate SETA contractors took meeting minutes and fetched coffee. Lucky or not, they spent most of every workday stymied and snubbed by the contractors from the big aerospace corporations who did most of the actual R & D.

If you had to have a supervisor, Ellen was as good as they came. Kendricks Aerospace, prime contractor for the demonstration powersat, balanced the scales. Most Kendricks engineers on the project detested Marcus. Not personally, nor even professionally—they would have hated *anyone* looking over their shoulders. Asking questions. Making suggestions. Auditing their work. Highlighting risks. He got the disdain they would not dare exhibit toward Ellen.

When had he last been able to *do,* not merely review?

"Trust me," Ellen said. "You won't be the first support contractor to sit in."

"What's my goal?"

"Answer questions and take notes. Beyond information exchange, these meetings don't have specific goals." She paused. "If anyone tries to pin you down to something uncomfortable, you can plead lack of authority."

Because he *had* no authority. God, he loathed meetings.

They exited the service area into a carpeted corridor. A wall sign pointed the way to the main lobby. They continued walking. "Okay," Marcus said, "where is this meeting?"

"DOE in Germantown. Nancy Ramirez's office."

Reflexively, Marcus began guesstimating the miles added to today's commute. He must have winced.

"I'd reimburse you for the gas if I could," Ellen said.

But more than that, she had the look that said *I wish there were something I could do for you.* At least she had stopped asking if he "wanted to talk about it." Because he really, *really* did not.

As for NASA reimbursing him for the gas, he understood: her hands were tied. Space Systems Science, Marcus's direct employer, had bid for the SETA contract at Goddard Space Flight Center without reimbursement for local travel. Shifting local travel costs onto the staff kept the hourly rates a few cents lower. It hadn't much mattered, when Marcus took this job. He had lived only a couple of miles from GSFC then. He told himself he might not have a job if SSS had pursued the work less aggressively.

He told himself lots of things. Other things he just refused to think about.

"But maybe," Ellen added hopefully, "your car charged up during the meeting."

"I wouldn't complain." Even at the hotel's exorbitant parking-plus hourly rates.

But in the two hours he had spent at the town meeting, *his* car would not have taken much of a charge. The Jincheng was overdue for a battery pack replacement—which would run him about half of what a new car would cost. New car or new battery? He would put off buying either for as long as he could, rather than support the lithium cartel. Bolivia and Chile, curse them, controlled half the world's lithium supply. Every lithium-ion battery bought anywhere propped up prices for the cartel.

Supporting the Russian oil cartel this morning felt just as crappy.

In the hotel garage, the eight panelists fanned out toward their various vehicles. Coming straight from home, only three had managed to carpool. "Have a good meeting," Marcus said as he and Ellen paused by his car.

"You, too," she said. "And don't do anything I wouldn't."

"You should have thought of that earlier."

Smiling, she kept walking.

Marcus's car had accepted scarcely a tenth of a recharge, about what he expected. The car would switch to its little gas engine well before he reached his meeting.

"Destination: Department of Energy, Germantown complex," he announced, backing out of his parking spot. The console beeped and a reasonable-looking map appeared in the main dashboard display. He tapped the ACCEPT key.

Once he merged into the clotted traffic of I-695 he activated auto-drive, and the car guided itself to the rear of an auto platoon. He found himself nose-to-tail with a late-model blue Toyota. Seconds later, a white cargo van filled his rearview mirror. The van was too close to make out the company logo on its hood.

He had more pressing things to read than logos. Marcus dismissed the map to check e-mail, and Ellen had already forwarded the information he needed. But he had driven for too many years before auto-drive to concentrate while cars not two feet apart joined and departed the platoon, and when to both sides, bumper to bumper, eighteen-wheelers blotted out the sky.

With only the ride to prepare, he opaqued the windows and began skimming.

He had *also* been around long enough to expect recession to *reduce* traffic. Not since the Crudetastrophe. Without funding for maintenance, highways crumbled faster than traffic diminished.

Marcus began reading Ellen's annotated meeting minutes. He stopped noticing swerves (around accidents? potholes? the chicken crossing the road? Through the opaqued windows, he could not tell) and ramps from one freeway to the next. The traffic noises faded . . . .

A pop-up usurped the dashboard screen. Blinking red letters

announced: *Power alert.* Smaller text, scrolling, gave the particulars: a high-voltage line severed from the Nantucket Sound wind farm. Terrorism neither indicated nor ruled out.

Marcus rapped the screen to acknowledge and again to retrieve a list of related headlines. The list expanded faster than he could tap through to even a smattering of the articles. Scattered secondary outages across Massachusetts as generators, distribution stations, and power lines overloaded and shut down. Sporadic blackouts predicted throughout New England, possibly rippling down the East Coast, while the grid rebalanced, or until the wind farm's underwater high-voltage line could be repaired. The schedule of preemptive brownouts. Talking heads blathering about unsafe, indefensible infrastructure. Resetter groups saying the same, more nastily. Predictions, into the tens of thousands, how many cars would fail to recharge overnight. The certain spike tomorrow in East Coast gas prices, a buck or more per gallon, when all those cars headed for the pumps. The stock market tanking.

Multiple groups and causes claimed responsibility.

Cursing them all, he went back to Ellen's notes. Too soon, the dashboard trilled: time to disengage autodrive. He took back control and made his way to the DOE parking lot. The charger-equipped slots were all occupied.

Sighing, Marcus got out of his car. Another damned meeting. He wondered if ever again he would get to *do* something.

G ood afternoon," Dillon Russo told the latest earnest entrepreneur to pass through his office that day.

They were all earnest. It took more than *earnest* to set oneself apart. He had been merely earnest once. Then he had gotten savvy. And shorted a portfolio of mortgage-backed securities before the markets realized that subprimes were toxic. And so, became very rich.

And so, here he was . . . .

Who is this woman? Courtney something. One more engineer and MBA, yadda yadda yadda. Dillon had already forgotten her last name. If it mattered, he could find the name in her leave-behind or on his calendar. He did not foresee it mattering.

Speed dating, venture capital-style was a lot like speed dating of the social kind, only even more demeaning. Dillon allotted each petitioner a half hour: fifteen minutes for the pitch, ten for Q & A, and five alone, afterward, to organize any notes he had taken. The lone note for Courtney read *Not on your life*, jotted down before, earnestly asserting her appreciation for his time, she all but backed out of his office.

He dropped her leave-behind into a drawer. She had brought the day's fifth pitch for enhanced cellulosic biofuel production. Her process involved platinum nanoparticles, lots and lots of them, employed as catalysts. As though, even in a world starved for energy, *that* could make any kind of economic sense.

It hardly mattered. Fail or succeed, anything anyone could hope to accomplish with biofuel synthesis was mere tinkering at the margins. He only cared about opportunities that *could* make a real difference.

Another make-us-both-a-pile-of-money pitch would come through his door in about four minutes. He used a half minute to get out from behind his desk and stretch. The rest he would spend admiring Central Park, thirty-eight stories below.

At least the biofuel types had done enough homework to know that his interests lay in eco-friendly opportunities. Ditto Noah, the gangly, pinch-faced man pitching virtual-reality tools for high-end telecommuting and Suresh, with a new wrinkle in fuel cells. Those who had not done their homework, who wasted his time with trivial visions for the next big social network or junk food, got the hook. Fast.

Dillon watched a line of mounted police watch a mass gathering down in the park. In theory demonstrations were legal in Central Park, but permits remained hard to come by and the crowd swirled and surged in a pretense of spontaneity. He never could judge crowd sizes, not even from his bird's-eye view. A thousand? Two? It did not help his estimating that the crowd shifted restlessly. When, all but inevitably, the cops dispersed the demonstrators, a new flash mob would simply converge elsewhere in the park.

Permit or no, frequent arrests notwithstanding, the Resetters demonstrated daily in the park. Applauding, if not the Crudetastrophe itself, the resulting economic slowdown—and, with it, the reduced use of fossil fuels—as benefits to the environment and the planet. Opposing new energy infrastructure as only repeating past environmental insults.

Dillon could sympathize with their opinions. But to expect civil disobedience and petty vandalism to change anything? Such naïveté sadly amused him.

Someone rapped firmly on his door.

"Come in," he called.

A blond woman strode in, wearing a severely tailored dark-blue suit. She was short, compact, and very serious. "Mr. Russo," she began, speaking quickly, not yet halfway to his desk. Very focused. *Focused* beat the hell out of *earnest*. "I'm Kayla Jorgenson, of Jorgenson Power Systems. Thanks for seeing me. You won't be sorry."

I'll be the judge of that. "Have a seat, Kayla."

Handing him a brochure she launched into her pitch. "What the world needs, more than anything, is clean, affordable electrical power generation. We had sporadic petroleum shortages *before* the Crudetastrophe. Electric cars—not that anyone can produce them fast enough—help only to the degree there is electricity to recharge their batteries. Too often, there isn't."

Focused *and* aware. Dillon began leafing through her brochure.

She did not let his page flipping distract her. "Why I'm here, in a phrase: ocean thermal energy conversion. OTEC is conceptually very simple—and a vast untapped resource. Any heat engine turns heat energy into mechanical work by exploiting a temperature differential. Steam engines are heat engines, the high temperature that drives them coming from fire heating a boiler.

"Now consider the ocean. The tropical ocean's surface can approach human body temperature, and yet around a half mile below, where sunlight never penetrates, the temperature is scarcely above freezing! Tremendous power-generating potential exists in the differential between the hot and cold layers of the ocean—and with no energy source involved but sunlight.

"I would guess you've been pitched concepts for harvesting wave power. The energy OTEC can theoretically harvest is greater by an order of magnitude. The challenge is in efficiently and affordably . . ."

Did Kayla ever stop for air? His wife, while playing her French horn, did something she called circular breathing. What, exactly, Crystal did eluded him—surely the windpipe worked in only one direction at a time—but somehow she could sustain a note indefinitely.

Just as, somehow, Kayla kept up her patter. ". . . and while the theoretical efficiency of a heat engine operating with such a small temperature difference is about seven percent, past OTEC trials have achieved only one or two percent. With our proprietary technology, we can . . ."

Dillon took down his first note. *This could be real.* He did not begrudge Kayla her full fifteen minutes. "So you're going to save the world," he probed.

"Hardly. We need many ways to generate power, Resetter fanatics notwithstanding. OTEC can be one method. It *should* be one, in the tropics, anyway." She rattled off more of OTEC's virtues. Finally, she took a breath. "Will Russo Venture Capital Partners back us?"

"I'll have to touch base in-house." That was a stall, because as principal partner Dillon's was the only opinion that mattered. He only took aboard investors cowed by his reputation, being especially partial to the pension funds of small towns in flyover states. Well, there was one exception, but Yakov's interests were . . . different. *Yakov* was different: fascinating and worldly-wise. If Yakov sometimes demanded more involvement than Dillon's usual partners, he also brought resources none of Dillon's other partners could offer.

Kayla persisted. "If you have further questions . . . ?"

"But I will admit to being intrigued." Dillon spared her the briefest of smiles. "Perhaps sometime I could tour your prototype."

"Absolutely!" Her discipline finally slipped. With a grin, she whipped a folded datasheet from her jacket pocket. "Let's set that up now."

"We're about out of time," he countered. "I'll be in touch."

She all but floated from his office—at the last, as naïve as any of the day's supplicants. As naïve, in her own way, as the Resetter activists whom she disdained.

Nodding welcome to yet another earnest entrepreneur, Dillon thought: That's how I can do what I do.

**V**alerie Clayburn glowered at her datasheet. Neither it nor the wildly colored globe it projected deserved her wrath—but they were *here*. Telecommuting was fine in its place, but much of her job demanded the personal touch.

And with that moment of resentment, she felt rotten, as though she were shortchanging the sick little boy in the next room.

Not that Simon *sounded* sick. He was making the deep-in-his-throat, revving and growling noise that all little boys make—to the amusement and consternation of their mothers—whether playing with cars, G.I. Joes, or toy dinosaurs.

She had three sisters. None of *them* ever made sounds like her son and his friends did.

She had once found Simon galloping in circles "flying" a toy stuffed rabbit, its floppy ears bent sideways like wings, making those same annoying/adorable noises. Something she and her sisters would never have thought to try. He had been about three. Smiling at the memory, she went to check on him.

She found him deep in his toy box, playthings strewn about his bare feet. From the doorway to his bedroom, the little-boy noises sounded a bit different than usual. Deeper. Phlegmy. "Back in bed, kiddo," she commanded.

"But *Mom*, I was only—"

"Doesn't matter," she said. "Pick a toy and get back under the covers."

He emerged from the toy box, one hand clutching little cars and the other action figures. Testing the limits. She let it pass. "Bed. Now. Move."

He dumped his double handful of toys on his blanket. "I have to go to the bathroom."

Predictable. As he passed her in the doorway she felt Simon's forehead: still warm. His blond hair was dark with sweat. The jungle-camouflage pajamas (little boys!) he wore were snug and inches too short, but he would not give them up until she replaced them. If he would only *stay* in bed, the bare ankles and wrists would hardly matter.

Heading off an "I'm thirsty" stall, she topped off the orange juice in the glass on his nightstand while he dawdled in the bathroom.

With a struggle, she got him into bed. "Tuck me in?" he asked.

"Sure, pumpkin."

Simon made a face. He was *nine*, too old and rough and tough to be anyone's pumpkin.

Not so. She half tucked, half tickled until he giggled. "Now *stay* in bed," she ordered.

She returned to the kitchen. Elbows on the table, chin in her hands, glower reemerging, she resumed her staring contest with the slowly turning globe.

Saturn's largest moon: Titan.

This was not how any human would—or could—behold Titan, its dense atmosphere all but opaque to visible light. Only radio-frequency waves pierced the perpetual shroud to reveal the tumultuous surface of one of the most interesting—and, in some ways, most Earth-like—bodies in the solar system.

The holo orb was all swathes, indeed layers of swathes, like a world made of papier-mâché. Each strip was a separate radar study, some undertaken from Earth, others from flybys years earlier by the late, lamented Cassini probe. Swathes varied in color, a distinct hue assigned to represent each radar wavelength. Dark and light shades showed what polarization had been used, the choice optimized for sensing smooth or rough features.

Despite appearances, the mosaic was not constructed from photographs, because radar did not "see" as a camera would. Behind the imagery lay complicated mathematics, embodied in even messier software, that reconstructed topographic features from Doppler shifts, the slightest differences in round-trip signal delays, and echo strengths. (Not that the echoes *were* strong: at their closest, Earth and Saturn were about eight hundred million miles apart.) Fortunately she had reached the stage in her career when grad students handled the programming scut work.

All those swathes and the riot of colors would have suggested to most people that Titan had been well mapped. Not so. Valerie was no casual observer, and her eyes went straight to the problem areas, mostly adjacent swathes that failed to align. Oh, nearby swathes might appear to match, were meant to overlap, but that could not just be assumed. Scanning a particular bit of Titan from across the solar system was tricky.

Stuck home for the day, if not the rest of the week, eyeballing strips for common features was something she could do. And deucedly difficult.

Titan was a dynamic place, its surface sculpted by erosion and weather, its methane lakes ever shrinking and expanding, its orbit tweaked and tugged in a complex dance by sixty-plus lesser moons, the entire *world* tidally flexed by Saturn's immense gravity. Software tried, with mixed success, to align radar images. Human eyes were still the best at matching multiple views of a canyon or lakeshore or hill captured at different resolutions, at different times, from different angles. Nor did the hills always stay put between radar studies. Dunes hundreds of feet tall and hundreds of miles long—dunes not of sand, but of exotic hydrocarbons, looking, the one time a probe had landed *to* look, like wet coffee grounds—drifted with the seasons. The marvel was that Valerie and her grad students had stitched together even this poor semblance of a topo map.

Here and there, maddeningly, areas remained pitch black. Not yet scanned. Titan Incognita.

Water bottle in hand, she stared at the tan layer—what there was of it. The latest survey had produced hardly any data. *No* data she might have chalked up to bad aim, but the bit that had come in confirmed proper aiming, and diagnostics confirmed correct operation of the receiver.

So what had happened? A software glitch that somehow discarded the radar echoes? Always possible, but she had seen nothing indicative of mishandled data. Radio interference that perfectly canceled the signal but did not reveal itself? Very implausible.

It took a while for the penny to drop. It took an hour of calculations, punctuated by two quick peeks in on Simon, asleep amid a jumble of toys, to work out the geometry and confirm her suspicions.

There had been interference, all right: the signal bleeping *blocked*, after a round trip of almost two billion miles. By Phoebe's sunshield.

Of course the moon, the first-and-real moon, sometimes got in the radio telescope's way—but on *its* stately orbit Luna crossed the plane of the ecliptic, potentially blocking the line of sight to other targets in the solar system, only once every couple weeks. Phoebe and its sunshield whizzed around the Earth in less than six hours! Damnation, she *knew* that. Phoebe and its shield were small, but her luck was bound to run out.

As it had.

Valerie sighed. She could plan future observations around them, but what a nuisance. Long term, the observatory needed to reprogram ASTRID—astronomer's integrated desktop—to keep Phoebe-compromised observations from ever getting scheduled. And—

And it had not been a penny that had dropped before. Wrong metaphor. A *shoe* had dropped. No, a big honking boot. And now, so did the other one.

Phoebe was not the big problem. The big problem was everything that Phoebe portended . . . .

* * *

Marcus loitered in a vending room, sipping a cup of lousy coffee, savoring the break from an interminable meeting. Sunlight streamed through the room's window wall, which offered an otherwise uninspiring view of an interior courtyard.

A predisposition to fog from off the Potomac had given this neighborhood its name, but diplomatic obfuscation was what preserved the label. To most of the world, Foggy Bottom meant the State Department, in whose blocky headquarters Marcus had unhappily spent his afternoon. Ellen had gotten a call just as the meeting started. She left, giving him only a you-know-how-it-is shrug for explanation.

Today was nonetheless a change of pace, because this meeting involved *international* whining. As the demo powersat approached completion, more and more countries were objecting to powersats as weapons of mass destruction.

And so Marcus had gotten to explain microwave downlinks to a roomful of Foreign Service Officers. Yes, the beam carried a lot of power. That was the project's *purpose*: bringing power to the ground. And of *course* the beam was concentrated, to minimize the dedicated collection area on the ground.

Then it had been on to safety interlocks. Every collection station had a guide beacon that the power satellite used as its target. If a collection station detected the power beam slipping off center, off went the beacon and the satellite ceased transmission.

"Target?" an FSO had repeated.

"A poor choice of words," Marcus had answered. *He* wasn't a diplomat. *Aimed* would be no better. "Directed. The satellite directs the beam at the collection station."

"And beams only at collection stations?" another FSO had asked. "My online identity has been hijacked twice, and you wouldn't believe what a pain in the posterior *that* was. So you'll understand that I'm just a tad skeptical about how secure any system is."

"Yes, only at collection stations." In his mind, Marcus had added an exclamation point. And speculated about birthdays and children's names used as passwords. "Downlink coordinates are hard-coded into the powersat. By design, we can only update coordinates physically, on PS-1 itself. To update the list of authorized collection stations, we'll dispatch a robot probe."

"Switchable on and off. The downlink point commanded from the ground."

Who wants a system that *can't* be turned off? "The idea," Marcus had explained, "is to deliver power where it is most valuable, and that varies. It could be the D.C. area in summer, and maybe only in the hottest part of the day when the use of air conditioning peaks. It could be Fargo in winter, during a cold snap, when the demand surges for heat. Or filling in when some wind farm lacks wind. Or anywhere an equipment failure creates a power shortfall. And by beaming to the downlink station nearest the point of need, we reduce stress on the national grid."

"If I may summarize," the first FSO had jumped back in. What the hell? Were they tag-teaming him? "A gigawatt of focused energy 'directed' at the ground. Steerable beams. It *could* be a weapon."

"And any satellite launch *could* become a ballistic missile aimed at the ground," Marcus had snapped in frustration, only to be told he was not being helpful.

To the degree Marcus had ever had control of the session, that was when he lost it. From then until the break, the FSOs had revisited, with painful circumlocution, perhaps every criticism anyone ever made about the U.S., back to those (idiots, in Marcus's opinion) who had objected to American unilateralism in the capture of Phoebe. Diverting a space object, let alone using a nuclear-powered thruster for the dormant comet's final orbital insertion, could be construed as a violation, at least in spirit, of the Outer Space Treaty. (Excuse me: the Treaty on Principles Governing the Activities of States in the Exploration and Use of Outer Space, including the Moon and Other Celestial Bodies.)

In what universe was doing nothing, and maybe having Phoebe *hit* Earth, the preferred course? The same universe, evidently, where one listened to members of the energy cartels, and the cartels' most dependent and coercible customers, and Third World ankle biters who did not care how bad things got for them as long as they could get in a dig at the United States, and—

Marcus stopped himself mid-mental rant. Reliving the experience accomplished nothing. His geopolitical opinions were doubtless as well founded as the engineering opinions of a roomful of diplomats.

"Hey, Judson."

Marcus turned around. One of the FSOs stood in the break-room entrance. Somebody Ryerson. No, Ryerson Smith. "Yes?"

"We're ready to resume," Smith said.

Oh, joy. "Okay. I'll be right—"

When Marcus's cell rang, the caller was not in his directory. He did not recognize the number that came up instead of a name. Not even the area code. "I should get this," he said.

"You know where to find us." Smith headed down the corridor.

Taking the call, Marcus did not recognize the face projected from the cell display. She wasn't someone he would forget, not with those high cheekbones, chiseled features, hazel eyes, and full lips. Her hair, a rich brown, worn shoulder length, nicely framed her face. Forty-ish: about his age. And she looked *mad*.

Mad about what? he wondered. He said, cautiously, "Hello."

"Marcus Judson?"

He nodded.

"Valerie Clayburn. I'm calling about the powersat."

While she spoke he had queried her area code. West Virginia? "Did you see me on the 3-V news?" he guessed. Damn town meetings.

"Hardly," she snipped. A bit of glower added, *Aren't we full of our-selves*. "I Googled 'powersat NASA program manager' and got your boss. She gave me this number."

"I'm due back in a meeting, Ms. Clayburn. May I ask what this is about?"

"It's Dr. Clayburn, and I'm calling to schedule a meeting."

Doctor of what? But Ellen had vetted the woman, supposedly, and he had a flexible day coming up. "I have some time open next Monday morning. Will fifteen minutes suffice? Telecon, or will you be coming to my office in Maryland?"

"Fifteen minutes?" She laughed. "Not even close, and anyway, you need to come out here. But Monday works."

"Why there—and where is that, by the way?"

"*Here* is the Green Bank Observatory. And *why* here? Trust me, it'll make sense when you see the place."

Could she be any stingier with information? He had neither the time nor the inclination to play twenty questions. "I've got to go," he told her. "I'll get back to you."

"I'll be here," she said, and broke the connection.

* * *

His datasheet folded in quarters because that took less effort than clearing the table, eating (and trying not to taste) a nuked frozen dinner, Marcus sampled the news. In one window headlines scrolled, an all-too-familiar litany of scattered blackouts, spot gasoline shortages, and layoffs. The Russian-led cartel had announced a production cut, sending oil futures up ten dollars a barrel. A credit-rating service and a large hospital chain were the latest to disclose that hackers had compromised their customer files. Across the Middle East and Central Asia, more terrorist bombings and sectarian slaughter. In a streaming-video window—for the third day, but still telegenic—squadrons of Resetter activists disrupted construction of a new offshore liquefied-natural-gas terminal near Newark.

Enough, he decided. A few sharp taps on the periphery of the datasheet banished the depressing news and put a virtual keyboard in their place. He started to surf.

The Green Bank Observatory was in Green Bank, West Virginia, which was in the middle of nowhere. Deeper into the middle of nowhere, nonsensical as that was, than he had guessed. Run by the National Science Foundation.

And Valerie Clayburn, Ph.D.? He found her, too. More than enough to beg the question what an up-and-coming astronomer wanted with him. Presumably not for any insight he might offer into distant galaxies or dark energy, or whatever was the hot topic in radio astronomy these days.

Marcus went for a walk to clear his head. The evening breeze was pleasantly cool. Lawn sprinklers muffled the drone of traffic. In most front yards, the cherry trees were in bloom, just past their peak. Even in the many yards with FOR SALE and FORECLOSURE signs. And overhead . . .

Urban glow and the crescent moon had all but washed the stars from the sky. Phoebe was too dark to see even during the rolling blackouts. Phoebe's sunshield was for the moment essentially edge-on to him, and so also invisible. But The Space Place sparkled, the brightest "star" in the sky; it put even Venus to shame. The orbiting hotel complex, its surface silvered for cooling, was its own best advertisement.

When he won, say, two lotteries, or struck oil in his backyard, he would be sure to book a stay.

As for the nearly completed powersat, Marcus searched in vain. Alas. He would have welcomed some evidence that his life entailed more than meetings and talk.

When he had called Ellen from his car to ask about her curious referral—and to vent about that afternoon's waste of time at State—his boss, in very few words, speaking more in sorrow than in anger, had shocked Marcus into silence. Hours later, her rebuke still stung: "Have you considered the possibility that someone else might know something?"

Yeah, he had. Only cynic that he had become, it had been a while. Since Lindsey.

By the dim glow of a neighbor's post lamp he texted the enigmatic Dr. Clayburn. *CU Monday a.m. around 11.*

The road trip to Green Bank began painlessly enough, the morning warm and sunny. The observatory banned electric vehicles because they might cause interference, so Marcus had a government motor-pool car and full tank of gas. The car's data link kept dropping out. After twenty miles he gave up on his e-mail.

The first half of his drive, more than a hundred miles, was Interstate, and autodrive did all the work. Leaving behind the D.C.-area sprawl the scenery was gorgeous, especially as he crested the Blue Ridge, the Shenandoah Valley, lush and green, stretching before him. The sky was a beautiful clear blue. Radio blasting, he drummed on the dashboard to the beat of the music, trying to ignore the many tasks he could, and perhaps should, be attending to at the office. He wondered what he would do when he arrived early.

He got off I-81 near Harrisonburg. Almost at once he encountered the billboard: not digital, but an old-style, ink-and-paper signboard, sun-faded.

The sky, the Tower,
We lust for power.
The Flood, the Burn,
We never learn.
Reset.
Repent.

*The Burn* was not bad—poetically speaking—for the Crudetastrophe. Marcus could not come up with a biblical-sounding term for powersat, either. *We never learn* rang all too true, although his take on the lessons to be learned and the poet's clearly differed.

U.S. 33-W narrowed to two lanes, soon ran out of embedded sensors for autodrive, and lost its shoulders to narrow some more. Sturdy trees crowded right up to the pavement. He slowed way down, and his fretting changed to showing up late. The "towns" along the "highway" became smaller and smaller, and the houses scattered between towns ever shabbier.

Until there were no towns. He guessed he had missed the West Virginia border. By then he was well into the Appalachians, deep within the George Washington National Forest. Negotiating switchbacks. Up and down steep grades, many of them miles long. As were—whenever gaps opened among the trees—the luxuriant wooded vistas. Stunning. Fantastic.

The Blue Ridge? By comparison (at least where he had crested it), that was a speed bump.

And despite Marcus's best intentions, he thought: Lindsey would have *loved* this drive.

\* \* \*

For a long time, he and Lindsey had been great together.

Almost always they had fun. Even when they didn't, when the world made one of them sputter, the other would find the silver lining, or the amusing absurdity of it all, or a way to put matters into perspective. They both liked scenic drives and country inns. They liked hiking and canoeing, classical music and experimenting with exotic cuisines. Together, they learned how to scuba. They mocked the same bad movies.

More than anything, she always knew the right thing to say.

"*I* know your brother is a slacker," she had once said, driving home from a miserable dinner out with his parents.

Had Marcus not already loved Lindsey, those few words would have done the trick.

It was nothing against Sean. His older brother was who he was. Sliding through life on charm and modest ambitions somehow worked for him.

But growing up, "It's not what you know, it's who you know," had suited Marcus about as well as, "Why can't you be more like your brother?"

As a kid, Marcus could never understand why their parents tolerated Sean's mediocre grades and goofing off. The folks did not much like their jobs, but they were far from lazy. Dad was a lawyer and the Washington lobbyist for a national association of rural electrical utilities. Mom was a Realtor and had an MBA. Not until well into high school had Marcus seen the bigger picture. Wheedling legislative favors, unloading money pits onto unsuspecting buyers, and coasting through school had something in common. All were ways to game the system. And *that* apparently, was what impressed his parents.

Marcus could never bring himself to see things their way. He wanted to learn, not just make good grades. To make a difference, not a living. To change the world, not game it.

Sean put in four years in general studies at a party college. He went on to become the one-man HR department at a small company—gloating, to parental approval, that the position lacked quantifiable responsibilities.

Marcus earned a math degree at the University of Virginia and a master's degree in systems engineering from MIT. He went on to do contract work at NASA where, with luck and if he did things right, maybe he could change *more* than one world.

What he could not change was his parents' attitude. Their only feedback on Marcus's choices was that he worked too hard, that he let Space Systems Science and NASA take advantage of him. Sean said the same, only more bluntly: "You're a sucker, bro."

But *Lindsey* got him. He thought he got her.

Ready to move in together, the big question had been: where? His apartment was in Greenbelt, Maryland, near Goddard. Hers was in the City of Fairfax, Virginia, near the insurance company where she worked (and not far, as it happened, from the house where he had grown up). Neither apartment was big enough for two, not unless at least one of them shed a lot of possessions. Nowhere in the middle appealed to either of them.

He suggested they find a place near her work, and she countered with moving near his. She was *so* solicitous about what his commute might become, so sympathetic, that it drove him to insist on northern Virginia. Together they found the town house in Reston, a beautiful place with a private dock on Lake Anne. He bought a canoe. It was going to be her moving-in present.

Reston would mean an easy twenty-minute commute for Lindsey, and he was thrilled for her. "To return the favor," she insisted that he buy the town house solo. The equity growth would all be his—the slow, grinding decline in house prices had to end *someday*—and she would spare him the complications of entwining their finances. Though he did not follow her logic—there was no hurry, but marriage was the obvious next step—he went along. That Marcus should own the place was obviously important to her.

Because for Lindsey, moving in together had become Plan B. Because she was in the running to open and manage a new regional office, in *Seattle*. She kept that possibility to herself until, two days *after* closing on the town house, her promotion came through. By the end of that week she was off to the Left Coast, for the opportunity she "couldn't not take."

You understand, Marcus. Right? And you own a house now, so be glad.

It hadn't helped Marcus's newfound cynicism that Lindsey's manipulations impressed Sean. As in, "You're a sucker, bro."

＊　＊　＊

West Virginia Route 28, when Marcus finally came to it, was as isolated and unused as the crumbling road that had preceded it. For no discernible reason the national forest he had yet to leave had changed names from George Washington to Monongahela.

He knew he was close when radio reception went to hell. Guessing what he would find, he checked his cell: no service. So he must have zipped past a second road sign unawares: announcement of the National Radio Quiet Zone.

GPS satellites paid no heed to a terrestrial ban on transmission, though, and his nav system worked fine. He spotted the modest sign for the National Radio Astronomy Observatory where he expected, just before the unincorporated town of Green Bank.

A few low buildings clustered near the observatory entrance. Passing the Science Center, the two cars and one yellow school bus in its parking lot seemed forlorn. He parked outside the L-shaped building Valerie Clayburn's acknowledging text message had indicated.

He was a half hour early.

Bright white dish antennas, one after another, receded into the distance. None stood close enough to offer any sense of scale. So how big were they? Rather than kill time at the Science Center among grade schoolers, why not find out? He could not have asked for a nicer day for a stroll.

His first stop: the trio of signposts abutting the parking lot. Ambling over, curious, Marcus found placards for the sun, Mercury, and Venus. Earth had a sign not far away. Touring the scale model of the solar system would take him out to the big antennas. He walked to Mars, only a few steps from Earth.

Past Mars he came to a tollgatelike barrier across the road. Boldly lettered signs announced DIESELS ONLY BEYOND THIS POINT and TURN OFF YOUR DIGITAL CAMERAS. A well-trodden footpath circumvented the gate and he kept going. By the time he spotted the Jupiter sign, the first big antenna had caught his interest. It had a descriptive sign, too. The dish was forty-five feet across! How big were the antennas in the distance?

Marcus understood the scale of the solar system—intellectually. Hiking it, even at a 1:3,000,000,000 scale, was something else again. Pluto and the last of the big dishes were still more than a mile away. He turned around without ever seeing the sign for Uranus.

*    *    *

Valerie's office in the Jansky Lab overlooked the parking lot, and she glanced out her window whenever she heard a car. First-time visitors tended to arrive very early or very late. No one's intuition about the drive was any good until they had made the trip once. Twice cars came, and both times technicians she knew got out. A third car brought one of her grad students.

Rapt in her work she must have missed a car, because the next time she checked outside a man wearing a suit and tie was striding toward the building. Looking down from the second floor, she could not see his face, but it had to be Judson. No one but govvies dressed so formally, and then only on a first visit.

Scientists dressed casually. Today she wore jeans, a random T-shirt, and a plaid flannel overshirt. When the Nobel Committee called, she would shop for a dress. Maybe.

Shutting her office door behind her, Valerie bounded down the stairs. The man with the charcoal suit was in reception, signing for a visitor badge. "Marcus?" she called out.

The man turned, and she recognized the face from last week's conversation. Judson, all right.

He had clear blue eyes, wavy black hair (at the moment wind-stirred) gone gray at the temples, a strong jaw, and, despite the early hour, hints of a five o'clock shadow. A bit guarded in his expression, perhaps, but fair enough: she had been less than forthcoming. Forty or so, she estimated. Not Hollywood handsome, but handsome enough. Not that that mattered. He was about six two and broad shouldered. Maybe a few pounds over his ideal weight, but he carried it well. Other than overdressed, he seemed, all in all, like an everyday sort of guy.

"I'm Marcus," he agreed, extending his hand. "Hello, Valerie."

"Thanks for coming." She hesitated. This was a person in front of her, not some bureaucratic abstraction.

But neither were powersats abstractions.

"Valerie?" he prompted.

"Right." She took his hand, casting off her doubts. "Welcome to the National Radio Astronomy Observatory, NRAO. We'll start with a tour. The things we need to discuss will make more sense with some background."

"What else have you planned?"

"The weekly technical lunch discussion among the professional staff, always fascinating, and we'll wrap up with a quiet conversation in my office." A long and pointed conversation.

"Okay. Lead on."

Following her outside, he seemed surprised at her beat-up old Volkswagen Jetta.

"Because it's a diesel model," she explained. "We only take bikes and diesels near the dishes. Anything else would mean RF from spark plugs or electric motors. And the older the car, the better. New cars have electrical everything, from locks to clocks to seat positioners. Makes them noisy."

"The instruments are that sensitive?"

Wait till you see the dishes up close, she thought. A short drive brought them to the internal gate. She got out of the car to swipe her ID badge through the reader. Just past the gate, she pulled onto the shoulder. "That's one of our smaller telescopes. Forty-five feet across."

"I know. I walked around for a bit."

"How far did you get?"

"Half past Saturn before I turned around. Any farther and I would have been late."

She pulled the Jetta onto the shoulder near each telescope to share some of its background. Near one dish, bikes leaned against a trailer: the mark of grad students at work. She took Marcus inside the cramped maintenance trailer for a peek at the equipment—and at the quarter-inch steel walls shielding the dish from the electronics.

Back in her car, as she started to describe the first eighty-five footer, the Science Center's white diesel tour bus lumbered past. "This is part of a three-telescope interferometer. An interferometer—"

"Synthesizes data from multiple instruments into one image. The composite has the resolution of an instrument the size of the separation between instruments. Same principle as synthetic aperture radar." He grinned. "I'm an engineer, and I come prepared."

Valerie knew the former. She had hoped for the latter—and that he would be open-minded. Only then did it occur to her to ask how open-minded *she* was.

It was not the time to second-guess herself. And anyway, he would get much the same message from many of the staff. All the more important that she get him to lunch on time . . . .

"Let's skip to the main event," she said. Because the *big* dish will knock your socks off.

When she next parked, Marcus, his eyes round, rushed from the car. Everyone did. She gave him time to take it all in: the world's largest birdbath, atop an intricate lattice pyramid, above a round trolley base with sixteen enormous wheels. In addition to a stand-alone trailer, a built-in shielded room high above the ground held many of the onsite controls. The instrument arm, jutting out from and over the dish, made the telescope that much more impressive.

"The Green Bank Telescope," she began, pointing up at the enormous paraboloid dish. "Completed in 2000, the GBT replaced the smaller big telescope that collapsed under its own weight from metal fatigue in 1988. The dish's signal-collecting surface measures one hundred meters by one hundred ten meters—longer in both dimensions than a football field. Only that's not *a* surface, but two thousand and four small aluminum surfaces. Automation tilts and warps each panel in real time as the structure moves, to compensate for sagging, thermal gradients, and wind."

"*Damn*, that's big. What happens if lightning strikes?"

"It happens about four times a year, without incident. The GBT weighs more than sixteen million pounds, about the same as nineteen loaded and fueled jumbo jets. When lightning does strike, that's a lot of metal, with all its metal wheels firmly pressed against the well-grounded steel track. The track is lots of metal, too: a circle sixty-four meters in diameter."

She resumed her script. "When tipped such that the instrument arm reaches its highest position, the GBT stands taller than the Statue of Liberty. This is the world's largest fully steerable radio telescope."

Hand to his forehead, shading his eyes, Marcus countered, "Surely Arecibo is bigger."

Because everyone knew the observatory at Arecibo, Puerto Rico. Filmmakers loved it. The first time she remembered seeing the Arecibo dish was in some old James Bond flick. *Golden Eye,* maybe.

Arecibo's dish was *three* hundred meters across, its aluminum panels suspended over a mesh of steel cables to form a single surface: way too massive to move. To aim the Arecibo telescope—to the extent it could be aimed—you positioned its suspended instrumentation module using the cables that spanned the dish. None of which mattered: if she failed, Arecibo would face the same problems as Green Bank.

Valerie limited herself to, "Bigger, but not fully steerable." She pointed at the GBT's base, where the mammoth wheels engaged the circular steel track. "As opposed to *our* big scope. This whole structure can rotate up to forty degrees a minute, versus one-fourth degree per minute needed to keep pace with Earth's rotation. The dish can tip up and down at as much as twenty degrees per minute. That instrument turret at the end of the arm holds up to eight independent instrument modules, each—"

"Back up," Marcus said. "Those tipping and turning rates. You're telling me that the GBT can track planets, asteroids, even close-orbiting satellites. Stars and galaxies only move with the Earth's rotation." She must have looked surprised because he added, "Remember who I work for?"

"Right. And sorry."

"Except asteroids and most planets don't emit radio waves. In the middle of the quiet zone, where my cell phone has no service and NRAO won't even permit digital cameras up close, I can't believe the observatory is pumping out radar pulses so you can read the echoes."

He was quick, which was promising, and he seemed engaged in what she'd had to show him. But around the eyes she saw a touch of . . . something. Suspicion? Was she that transparent, or was it something else?

"You're correct," she said. "Arecibo transmits and Green Bank reads the faint echoes. We *could* transmit ourselves"—she pointed up at the instrumentation arm—"by replacing one of the receiver modules with a transmitter, but that would hardly be radio quiet. My work involves radar mapping of Titan, and we partner with Arecibo to do it."

"Titan? Just how sensitive *is* this scope?"

"If there were a cell phone on Titan, with the GBT"—and lots of post-processing—"I could listen to the call." Barring other complications, and that topic was coming. "We need to move along, Marcus. The weekly science lunch is not to be missed."

Especially because *you* are on deck.

*   *   *

Patrick Burkhalter toted his cafeteria tray to the residence hall's second floor, where he found the social lounge half filled. Many of his colleagues were already seated and eating. Others surrounded Valerie Clayburn and her guest, meal trays in hand, intercepted before they could find a table. With maybe eight thousand people in the entire county, everyone welcomed new faces. But visitors and outsiders comprised very different categories, and after eight years here Patrick remained an outsider.

"Hey," he offered as he took an empty seat. Tamara Miller glanced his way, nodded, and went back to her conversation with Liam Harris. Something about intergalactic dust.

Patrick went to work on his country-fried steak, mashed potatoes, and gravy. His choices would do nothing for his waistline or his cholesterol, but who did he have to impress?

Or to live for? *That* was a thought depressing enough to make him set down his fork.

Their guest got perhaps two minutes with his lunch before Valerie began tapping her water glass with a butter knife. "Hi, everyone. We have a visitor, as you may have noticed."

Not to mention that she had put out the word to make sure the tech staff all came today. Would she get the outcome for which she so obviously schemed? In Patrick's experience, manipulating scientists and engineers worked about as well as herding cats.

"Hello," the chorus rang out raggedly, from around the collection of short, narrow tables arrayed in a U.

Valerie said, "Our visitor, Marcus Judson, works at NASA Goddard on the demonstration powersat project. I'm hoping he'll tell us about it."

Patrick refocused on his lunch while others murmured their encouragement.

Judson kept his response short, and Patrick approved. You didn't know you were today's featured attraction, did you?

"So what do you think, folks?" Valerie prompted. "How will powersats affect us here?"

And the games began.

"A powersat is a huge noise generator," Aaron Friedman said. "And because it's sky-based, that's noise from which we can't hide."

"The power beam is focused." Judson slid away his tray, the meal all but untouched, clearly perceptive enough to see what was coming. "The downlink won't come anywhere near here."

"Doesn't matter," Aaron persisted. "Well, aiming will help, but not enough. The satellite shapes the beam with phased-array techniques, right? So there are unavoidable side lobes to the main beam. That's basic math. Even sixty dB down, there'll be a lot of noise."

Engineers and astronomers set aside lunches to argue about phased arrays: their pointing accuracy and failure modes, the frequency distributions apt to show up within the noise, and whether sixty decibels was the expected attenuation for a side lobe. Of course even sixty decibels down from one gigawatt left a kilowatt of noise.

Judson kept thanking people for their comments. Mostly he let the staff argue among themselves, jotting notes on paper napkins—and looking ticked off.

This was not a mugging, exactly. More like an intervention, or maybe an inquisition. When Patrick tried to catch Valerie's eye, she looked away.

Patrick knew all about inquisitions by the tech staff. That had been his introduction to Green Bank, too, if for a different reason. Judson would go home with only bad memories to show for the day. Whereas he . . .

He still bore the scars. Patrick was more than qualified to coordinate routine maintenance and teach visiting astronomers to operate the gear, so it hadn't been *entirely* a pity appointment. More like an *I'll owe you one* arrangement between execs at the apex of Big Science.

After the *Jules Verne* probe went missing, JPL wanted Patrick *gone*. NASA did, too, but even more, they wanted to put a halt to the embarrassing publicity. No matter what anyone suspected, they could only prove that he had cut procedural corners to upload an emergency maneuver. That the distant probe went silent days later could have been pure coincidence.

And so Patrick had made clear what would keep him from giving interviews and suing for wrongful termination. He required ongoing access to a big dish—somewhere.

Without *too* much torture of the English language, Green Bank was somewhere.

And so he went in one not-so-easy step from the principal investigator of a major interplanetary probe to lowly observatory staffer. Training and maintenance offered plenty of opportunities to use radio telescopes without grant applications sure to be rejected.

He used the big dishes every chance he could get.

After the divorce—no *way* would Anna move here from Pasadena—what else did he have to do?

He had sworn to Anna that things would turn out all right. That maybe this had happened for a good reason. He would not have trusted him, either, especially given how little he had been able to explain, but it still hurt that *she* hadn't. More than anything, he missed the kids. He wondered if Rob and Clarissa would ever understand, or forgive him for the divorce.

When Patrick tuned back into the present, Judson remained in the hot seat. Only the objections varied: from powersats, miles across, getting in the way of observations, to the heat they would reradiate as infrared, to minutiae of RF interference. Some people argued for the joy of arguing. Par for the course here, but Judson could not know that.

Along the way, an admin slipped into the lounge and handed Valerie a folded sheet of paper. Another joy of life in the quiet zone: runners instead of cell phones. Valerie grimaced at whatever she found written, dashed off her own note and handed it to Judson, then rushed off.

By the time the hyperbole reached, "Powersats will mean the end of astronomy until"—yeah, right!—"someone builds an observatory on the far side of the moon," Patrick had had enough.

"There's more to life than astronomy," he snorted. Too bad Valerie had left. If anyone needed the reminder, she did. But for Simon, she might never go home. "And life takes power, people. Lots and lots of power."

Turning, Tamara gave Patrick an *Et tu, Brute?* stare, but from across the room a couple of engineers nodded.

"We learned to live with DirecTV," Ernesto Perez conceded.

To which someone snapped, "Yeah, by giving up listening on those frequencies."

Rekindling the debate, from which it took the tech director noisily sliding back her chair to bring a halt.

\* \* \*

At least, Marcus thought, tucking his notes from the lunch into his shirt pocket, one secret of the universe had been revealed. Town meetings were *not* the worst way to spend a day.

If he had correctly parsed Valerie's scrawl, she was retrieving a sick kid from school and going home for the rest of the afternoon. One scribble might have said "single mom," to explain her disappearance. It was too bad about her son, but Marcus was happy to make a quick getaway.

Only driving home, as much as he tried to enjoy the Appalachian scenery, he couldn't. Ellen's recent rebuke kept nagging at him: *Have you considered the possibility someone else might know something?*

If he could get past Valerie bushwhacking him, she had given him a lot to ponder.

arcus poked at a telecomm console, setting parameters for the upcoming conference call, and thinking: All meetings are not created equal. *He* was in a mundane conference room at Goddard, deep within suburban Maryland, but this call was out of this world.

Whatever grief the week might bring him, the progress review reminded him why everything else was worth it.

Landscape undulated over the conference table, sliding past as a distant camera swiveled on its post. Somewhere behind the camera, the full moon was about to set; Phoebe's hills and structures cast long, knife-edged shadows. To his right, in the tourist-bot preserve, the Grand Chasm gaped: a vast, inky blackness. The dazzling "star" just above the eerily close horizon was The Space Place, almost two hundred miles ahead of Phoebe in its orbit.

Ellen limped into the telecomm room, bearing Starbucks. Despite physical therapy, her leg kept bothering her. She set a cardboard cup on the table beside him.

"Thanks," he said, concentrating on the final link left to configure. "That said, you have no respect for tradition."

She laughed. "Okay, who confirmed for today's session?"

He gestured at the holo. "The usual folks on the far end, though Darlene Stryker is at the powersat. She'll call in from there."

"How far *is* the far end today?"

As distant as it could be. "As the neutrino flies"—right through the Earth, without noticing—"it's about thirteen thousand miles. Relayed through two geosynch comsats and then down to Phoebe, call it a half second."

She closed the door and settled into a chair. "Who's joining from on the ground?"

"Phil and Bethany." Phil Majeski was the prime contractor's program manager. Bethany Taylor was Phil's chief engineer. Both disdained SETA contractors. "Phil's netting in from corporate. Bethany called to say she's stuck at a subcontractor's facility. Resetter picketing, unrelated to us, something about shale-oil gasification in Wyoming. I'm linking her in now." Marcus waved a wireless key fob at the sensor in the comm console. The authentication LED blinked green. "Ready."

"Let's go."

Marcus shrank the Phoebe image to one-fourth size, then switched views from the surface to the base's little common room, where three men sat waiting. As they and Ellen swapped greetings, Marcus connected the other locations.

"Everyone have the agenda?" Ellen asked. She started through her list.

The comm console took notes, but speech-recognition software glitched under the best of circumstances. These weren't. Merely this many people in one conversation sometimes confused the software. With the comm delay between Earth and Phoebe, people spoke over each other as often as not, and echo suppression was less than perfect. Noise suppression filtered out the drone of Phoebe's ventilation fans, but not the random clatters of—well, Marcus did not always know what.

So Marcus took notes, too.

*Lots* of notes. Hydroponics yields in Phoebe's still experimental gardens. Performance data on the thrusters that would slowly lift the powersat, its construction now almost complete, to its operational orbit. Final integration tests on the microwave transmission arrays. Production data on Phoebe's automated factories, churning out solar cells (and in smaller quantities, other electronics), structural beams, and water and oxygen for the construction crew. Defect and repair rates. Assembly anecdotes—but not many, the process having become routine. Assembly statistics.

PS-1 had just topped two million pounds! How amazing was *that*? The late, unlamented International Space Station had massed only about one-third as much, and its on-orbit assembly had required more than a decade. But the ISS had been lugged up to orbit piece by piece, battling Earth's gravity all the way—for more than a thousand dollars for every pound. For a powersat fabricated on Earth, launch costs alone would rival construction costs for a coal power plant of equivalent capacity.

But most of PS-1's ingredients came from Phoebe's mines. And that was why—while there would never be another big tin-can space station—tens of powersats would join PS-1. Even combined, all those powersats would scarcely touch Phoebe's trillion-ton mass.

Motion in one of the four holos kept drawing his eye. Darlene Stryker, in her skintight counterpressure suit. She floated above the vast plain of the powersat, the nearest safety-and-inspection camera following her as she drifted at the end of her tether. As the camera tracked her, coworkers—most many-tentacled robots; one human and spacesuited like her—passed in and out of the background. He did not see any of the hoppers that shuttled workers the fifty miles from Phoebe to the construction site on the powersat.

Two million pounds was an abstraction. But two miles square, more or less: that was real. That he could *feel*. Marcus admired the plain of solar cells aglitter in the moonlight. PS-1 seemed to stretch on and on forever.

"Okay," Ellen said at last. "Good session, folks. Bethany, I'll look forward to your update on getting the backup water recycling system back to nominal. For next week's meeting?"

"No problem," Bethany said. "Chances are you'll have something in your e-mail by the day after tomorrow."

"Excellent." Ellen stood. "That should do it, then."

"One thing," Marcus said. The words just popped out. Something about PS-1 stretching into the distance. Something about defects, and big engineering, and his subconscious at work.

Phil Majeski scowled, putting his whole face to work: brow furrowed, eyes narrowed, lips pursed. Phil was no fan of support contractors.

"What is it, Marcus?" Ellen sounded surprised. He usually held any comments until after the meeting.

What indeed? Big engineering. What else was big? The solar farm he and Ellen had toured. Square miles there, too, of solar cells, plus the rectifying antennas newly added to receive the microwave downlink from PS-1. The Green Bank Telescope, the collection area of its dish a "mere" two-plus acres. Eavesdropping on phone calls out near Saturn.

Then he had it: the flip side of the powersat, from this vantage unseen. The microwave transmission arrays. No one had ever deployed such a large phased-array transmitter, whether using solid-state masers or tube-based amplifiers coupled to microwave antennas. Nothing ever built even came close. PS-1 incorporated both type arrays, each in several design variations. The separate arrays would operate standalone or in unison, allowing side-by-side comparisons. In every case, many thousands of transmitters . . .

"The failure rates on the klystrons and masers?" Marcus began cautiously.

"What about them?" Bethany said. "We *covered* that. They're all testing well within contract specs."

"Understood. But when won't at least one tube or maser be out of spec? Pumping out microwaves at unintended frequencies?" Because the focused, steerable power beam resulted from *exactly* controlling—individually and in real time—the many thousand transmitters. The math of phased arrays was a thing of beauty, the choreography of constructive and destructive interference among transmitters. Only waves at the wrong frequency would not interfere properly, would not aggregate into a controlled beam. Wrong frequencies were just . . . noise. "A single misbehaving klystron—out of thousands—is like a whole TV satellite transmitting on an unauthorized frequency."

"Which is why," Bethany snapped, "when a klystron goes out of spec, we'll power it down. Powersat-resident maintenance robots and spare parts, remember?"

And if, in the meanwhile, the interference obliterates an interstellar observation years in the planning, or the faint echoes of a radar beam bounced off Titan?

"Maybe the radio astronomers have a legitimate concern," Marcus said. "How soon will PS-1 detect and adapt to an out-of-tolerance transmitter?"

"Soon enough," Bethany came back, only without her usual cockiness.

Ellen heard the uncertainty, too. "As I recall, Kendricks signed up to a requirement to minimize RF interference with ground-based systems."

"We *all* have a schedule requirement," Phil rebutted. Schedule was the blunt instrument with which Congress beat up NASA, and NASA the contractor. But deadlines could work both ways. "Surely schedule takes precedence over hypothetical failure modes."

"And suppose that such a hypothetical failure occurs?" Ellen persisted. "What operational tests do you have planned to demonstrate PS-1's corrective action?" Pause. "Marcus, would you check that for me?"

"Sure, Ellen," Marcus said.

He was all but certain that the test-case database contained nothing relevant. And that Kendricks's award fee for the calendar quarter would take a hit if Ellen wrote up the finding as a critical deficiency. And that Phil, who as the Kendricks program manager got a slice of the award fee, would share the pain.

Phil sighed. "It won't be necessary, Ellen. Transmitter failure and response sounds like another set of simulations we should run."

"And also," Marcus added, "simulations with randomly spaced *pairs* of transmitters gone rogue at the same time." Twisting the knife, but also being practical. "Dealing in such large numbers, two near-concurrent faults are bound to happen."

Because what the hell. Phil hated him anyway.

＊ ＊ ＊

Toe tapping aimlessly (and, occasionally, kicking the Ethernet cable), Valerie pondered an empty screen. She was *so* tempted to roll up her datasheet, but at week's end the application window closed for observing time on the big dish. Miss the cutoff—or fail to make a strong case—and she would have to wait four months to reapply.

She and a few hundred other needy applicants.

By her side at the dinette table, Simon worked on a school assignment. Or, to judge from *his* fidgeting, not. At least while she sat there, the IM window on his datasheet remained closed. "How's the assignment coming?" she asked.

He countered with, "What's for dinner?"

Not encouraging while Simon still toyed with his midafternoon snack, and with a big stack of homework due the next day. "Want me to take a look? Need some help?"

"Nah." Fidget, fidget.

She looked anyway. The top window in his datasheet was a social studies unit called The Great Oil Shock. There had been, she read furtively, "an unexpected drop-off in production among some of the world's largest oil suppliers." Very PC: something had happened. Not something anyone caused to have happened.

Not that she would want to try explaining the Crudetastrophe to a nine-year-old, but it was no mere "drop-off," and someone had most *definitely* caused it. Even though who, and what had happened October 12, 2014, remained a closely held secret of the Restored Caliphate.

But far more was known than the sanitized children's lesson Valerie was surreptitiously skimming . . .

* * *

Oil prices surged in the weeks following Simon's birth. Valerie scarcely noticed, let alone registered that the jump supposedly was a big deal. With a colicky newborn to care for, who had time to sleep, much less to surf?

Or, for that matter, to drive? She had nowhere to go for the next few months, and work, when she did go back, was in biking distance. And hallelujah for teachers: Keith had the summer off, too. If the world chose to have a crisis—and when was it not on the verge of one?—she figured the world could muddle through without her. And, anyway, didn't energy prices yo-yo every few years?

The world *did* have a crisis without her.

That August the Caliph's Guard declared to the world that it had deployed atomic devices deep within the country's main petroleum reservoirs. To deter aggression by its enemies—variously: counterrevolutionary elements, apostate neighboring regimes, the Zionist entity, and hostile Crusader powers—the Guard vowed to deny their oil for all time if blasphemers impinged on the Caliph's holy sovereignty.

Still, she scarcely noticed. Simon was all of three months old. Keith was up to his eyeballs in last-minute lesson plans. After two years as a substitute, he had *just* gotten an appointment to teach economics at the Pocahontas County High School. She and Keith both struggled to make child care arrangements so she could return to work at the observatory. The few scattered minutes she could spare from family, if only to clear the cobwebs from her brain, she spent poring over the latest exosolar planet surveys.

If none of that had been happening in her life, she still would not have understood what insanity drove the Guard to trigger its nukes. To this day, perhaps no one knew outside the regime's inner circles. And maybe not even them. After the explosions, Guard factions had turned on one another, and on foreigners, in an orgy of blame, purges, and executions.

But however mysterious the Crudetastrophe's origins, its consequences were all too clear:

—Radiation tainted petroleum reserves measuring in the billions of barrels, the contamination spreading into neighboring states' oil fields. Whether the reservoirs were always linked deep underground or the atomic blasts had opened fissures between once distinct reservoirs—experts disagreed—petroleum exports abruptly ceased from across a wide area.
—Regional antagonisms erupted into open warfare.
—Oil-field destruction and shipping blockades spread far beyond the Restored Caliphate's borders. Economies collapsed across the Middle East.
—The price of petroleum tripled.

The supply and price shocks plunged most of the world into deep recession. Unlike the oil embargos of 1967, 1973, and 1979—their extent and duration limited, ultimately, by the suppliers' dependence on oil sales—the Crudetastrophe was irreversible. Many onetime exporters could not resume production, as fervently as they wished to.

China's and Japan's export-driven economies collapsed further and faster than most. Almost overnight, China and Japan were selling U.S. treasury bonds rather than buying them. Interest rates soared, currencies deflated, and countries reneged on their debts.

Stagflation, Keith called it. Stagnation and inflation together.

Nine years later, The Great Stagflation still raged. But not everywhere—

The Crudetastrophe explosions had not affected Russia's vast oil and gas reserves. Russia emerged from the crisis as a petro-superpower, controlling unprecedented wealth, snapping up American treasury bonds at fire-sale prices, and vying for global economic hegemony.

And as chaos spread across the Middle East, Keith's Marine Corps reserve unit was called up . . . .

\* \* \*

"Mom. Mom. Mom!"

Valerie shook off the old, sad memories to find Simon squinting at her suspiciously. "What is it?"

"What *is* for dinner?"

She was in no mood to cook. "Frozen pizza." As Simon beamed approval—not exactly a compliment to her culinary skills—the phone rang.

Life without cell phones was liberating. But only corded phones? Shaking her head at the primitiveness of it all, Valerie took the three steps to her ancient, corded landline phone. Simon was squirrelly today. If she took the call on her datasheet he would be out of his chair like a shot to mug for the webcam.

"Valerie?"

She could not place the voice. "Yes?"

"Marcus Judson." Pause. "Is this a bad time?"

In hindsight, she had not handled his visit very wisely. It was hard to imagine this call ending well. "Now is fine. What's up?"

"You and your cronies gave me something to think about. And the thing is . . . you're right. There might be a problem."

The well-stretched cord would reach well into the dining room. She went; Simon followed; she shooed him back. "Your assignment," she mouthed. "Go on, Marcus."

"It's not like I think we should stop work on the powersat, but there could be complications. There might be problematical failure modes we need to work around." When he started explaining phased arrays to her, she interrupted. "Remember who *I* work for?"

"Touché." He coughed. "I meant to ask, Valerie. How's your son feeling?"

"Thanks for asking. Simon has progressed to the malingering stage." And unless he is bleeding from the ears in the morning, he's going back to school.

"Okay, here's the thing. We never had our one-on-one discussion, and I'd also like to collect input from specialists there to fold into a failure-mode simulation. What if I come back out, say, Friday the twenty-eighth?"

"That would work." But there was something else in his voice. A hesitance. He wouldn't. Would he? "Was there something else?"

"Yeah . . . I wondered if I could take you out to dinner afterward."

Crap, he would. She hadn't dated but once or twice since Keith died. For the longest time, she hadn't been ready. After, Simon and work consumed her time. Anyway, she was content with things the way they were. Or was it resigned?

Had she wanted to, who was there *to* date, anyway? Coworkers? Uh-uh.

If she told Marcus no, then what? A sudden loss of interest in radio astronomy? He did not seem like the punitive type. Hell, *she* had sand-bagged *him*. Maybe he meant only a dinner of colleagues.

As her thoughts churned, the silence stretched.

"Or not," Marcus said. "I thought we might hit it off, but maybe you're seeing someone. Or whatever. Forget I asked. It has no bearing on my returning to Green Bank. I do need to talk with the experts."

"No," Valerie said, surprising herself, "asking is fine." Reassuring which of them? "And dinner does sound like fun."

Astronomers, engineers, and programmers wandered in and out of the Green Bank social lounge, where the atmosphere was more like an after-hours bull session than an inquiry. For long-scheduled observing time or to handle other commitments, Marcus told himself every time someone left. But despite the informality—or, perhaps, because of it—the notes file on his datasheet grew voluminous. His fingers ached from so much typing on its virtual keyboard. One thing this gathering was not: a D.C.-style, stultifying *meeting*.

Phil Majeski's simulation team would have its hands full in the coming weeks.

Valerie Clayburn was among the nomads, leaving Marcus to wonder how they would sync up for dinner. Whenever she popped in he treated her like anyone else—this was work, not a date, and her coworkers were all around, too—while second-guessing himself whether he was being too distant.

Why, but for a getting-back-on-the-horse-that-threw-you theory, had he asked her out?

Because Lindsey—the horse who *had* thrown him—was three months gone. Because life went on. Because Valerie was smart, intriguingly intense, and, despite her apparent efforts not to show it, *hot*.

". . . until they're in the way."

*They?* Marcus had let his mind wander. Again. "Say that again?"

"Are we going too fast?" Tamara Miller asked. "Moving targets. How will we know where they are until they're in our way?"

*Going too fast* would serve as an excuse. Marcus opened a datasheet window for the auto-transcription function. With everyone chiming in at will, the voice-recognition output was half gibberish, but half was more than he had processed over the past few seconds. He skimmed. Aha. *Migration.*

All powersats, not just PS-1, would be built near Phoebe and its mines and factories. After completion and checkout the powersats would be boosted—slowly, because they were so massive—to their final destinations. In geosynchronous Earth orbit, GEO, they would be all but stationary overhead.

"So your concern," Marcus inferred, "is the trek to GEO, with the powersat's orbit spiraling out till it arrives."

Tamara nodded. "Yeah. How will I know when and where it's going to get in my way? Or maybe *they*, if there may be more than one powersat migrating at once."

"Not just us," Valerie said, back again. "Optical astronomers, too. And pity the poor Earth-based infrared astronomers. A structure that's miles square soaks up a lot of sunlight."

"Kind of the idea," Marcus said, getting laughs. "But I see your point. You need a way to plan around the powersats even before they settle into geosynch. I can recommend an Internet application anyone can access for tracking and orbital predictions. And real-time position, too, as determined by GPS. Okay?"

"What about filing flight plans?" Tamara countered. "Shouldn't powersats be in FAA databases?"

Marcus took notes. "Probably a good idea." And around Phoebe and The Space Place, essential for safety, too.

"Real-time access," Ernesto Perez added, "so we can input the powersat orbital predictions into our scheduling software."

When Valerie disappeared again, around 4 P.M., Marcus thought maybe she had left to change clothes. (He planned to change, but after his first visit he had known to leave coat and tie in the car.) When she reappeared half an hour later, though, she still wore the same blue jeans and tan sweater. Even in sneakers, she was almost his height. He guessed she was about five foot ten.

She could wear a flour sack and be gorgeous. As for his coat and tie, they would stay where they were.

Five-ish, Aaron Friedman left with a parting shot of, "See you later, Valerie."

Marcus waited for her to correct her colleague. She did not. He thought he had asked Valerie out. On a date. Had *Can I take you out to dinner?* somehow changed meanings during his time with Lindsey?

Shit, he was not ready for this.

The two of them finally had the lounge to themselves. "Ready for dinner?" he asked.

She smiled awkwardly. "Sure. That'll be nice."

"I'll need you to suggest someplace to eat."

"Not hard." She smiled again, and this time it came across as genuine. "We don't have many places to choose among."

They headed in his car for Durbin, only slightly less tiny than Green Bank. Instead of making get-acquainted chat (not that he seemed to remember how), he focused on the narrow, twisty roads. The ten-mile—and thirty-minute—drive took most of his attention.

Unless dimness counted as a décor, the family restaurant and bar had none. Several people he recognized from today's meeting, including Aaron Friedman, occupied stools at the bar. Banter with the bartender suggested they were regulars. That was one mystery solved, anyway. As for Valerie's expectations for the evening? Time would tell.

Compared to the afternoon's free-for-all, the conversation once he and Valerie were seated felt stiff. His scars were too fresh. Her scars, whatever they were, seemed to run deeper. He called it a toss-up which of them felt more ill at ease.

Ruling out shoptalk might have been a mistake. What *did* people talk about on first dates? He couldn't remember. The short menus, when the waitress brought them by, offered few possibilities to eat *or* discuss.

"How old is your son?" he asked as they waited for their appetizers. "Simon?"

Getting the name right got him another of those too-rare natural smiles. "Simon. He's nine. Precocious guy, in a mischievous kind of way. Reminds me . . ."

Of Simon's father, Marcus filled in the blank. It felt too soon to ask. All he came up with, gracelessly, when enough time had passed was, "What have you read recently for fun?"

She named two novels he had never heard of, but he asked about them anyway. The waitress arrived with their entrées and the conversation trailed off again. This evening was a *disaster*.

* * *

Valerie told herself she should be home with her son. Only she knew that for a lie: Simon did just fine with babysitters, had more or less adopted Brianna as his big sister. Lying to yourself is never a good sign.

Her head was not in the game.

She found little to say when Marcus asked about favorite movies and music, or volunteered his own. When he launched into gadgets—about which, as an engineer, he was predictably enthusiastic—she shot down that, too. Sorry even as she said it, she disgorged some inanity about devices that would not function in the quiet zone or were a pain tethered to an Ethernet cable.

And when he unintentionally brought Keith to mind, she shut down even more.

She should have asked around about first-date topics. Clearly, she would not need to ask about second dates. "Will you excuse me? I should check on Simon," she said.

"Sure." Reflexively reaching for his cell, Marcus laughed at himself. (She liked that in a guy. Too bad she was such a failure at this.) "I guess the restaurant has landlines you can use."

"For regulars, the house phone. It's behind the bar." She stood. "I'll be right back."

She found Patrick Burkhalter holding down a barstool. The rest of the Green Bank regulars appeared to have left.

Patrick must not have shaved that day. She thought he had worn the same pants and shirt the day before. He was heavier every time she saw him, his clothes tighter, his gut bulging over his belt. The mound of buffalo wings in front of him would do nothing to reverse the trend. And he drank alone far too often. Poor guy: no one to go home to.

"How's the big date going?" Patrick asked her.

"Just colleagues," she said. After the fact, if not by original intent. "Hand me the phone?"

To judge by the giggling in the background when Brianna answered, Simon was doing fine.

Patrick was nursing a beer with one hand, prodding his datasheet with the other. An Ethernet cable snaked behind the bar from the datasheet. Something about Patrick tickled at the back of her mind.

Damn! Maybe she had gadgets to share after all. And they were wireless in a *big* way.

* * *

Black, sterile landscape hung in a shallow arc before Marcus. Up close, churned ground. In the left distance, a range of low hills. Straight ahead, receding into the distance, a pockmarked plain. In the right distance, rippled terrain that blended into more hills.

Phoebe, as he had never experienced it.

He and Valerie sat side by side on her living room couch, an ordinary game controller in front of each of them on the coffee table. "What do you think?"

Marcus hardly minded being invited inside after dinner—but he was more than a little surprised. She had insisted she had something to show him. What was this about? "Interesting," he offered neutrally.

"Give it a shot," she said.

He glanced down at his game controller. Landscape shifted as his head moved. Infrared laser beams shining into his eyes and sensors tracking eye motions from the reflections. He looked up and the landscape shifted again. "The hills to my extreme left and right look alike."

"Identical, in fact. The bot's full-circle view is compressed into ninety degrees, because you, unlike the bot, can't see three-sixty. To your far left and far right, about ten degrees of landscape overlap for continuity. You get used to it."

Marcus had never seen the attraction of the Phoebe tourist bots.

Moon bots: maybe. Over the years robotic lunar landers had deployed those to far-flung and quite varied terrain. The catch was cost: lunar bots were *expensive*. Once an armchair explorer sent a lunar rent-a-bot over a cliff or into a crevasse—that was that. And because of the comm delay to and from the moon, accidents did happen. And so, time on lunar bots did not come cheap.

Lose a bot on tiny, nearby Phoebe—much less likely, anyway, given the shorter comm delays—and often someone could retrieve it. Recoverability made armchair exploration of Phoebe affordable.

But Marcus "saw" PS-1 and Phoebe almost daily, with clearance to operate the surface-camera systems. (Not bots though. For security purposes, work bots could only be accessed with much higher clearance than he had, and then only from local terminals.) He had come to think of the rent-a-bots creeping about parts of Phoebe's surface—when, from time to time, they strayed outside the tourist zone—as so much optical clutter.

Still . . .

He swept a hand across his controller. Gesture-sensing logic read the motion—more clever processing of infrared reflections. With an all but imperceptible delay the landscape slid to his right as the bot turned. Motion somehow emphasized the duplicated scenery at the extremes of the holo.

If he recalled correctly, and the fast response suggested he did, Phoebe was all but overhead at the moment. He swept his hand back—and nothing happened.

"Hold your fingers together," Valerie said, "so you don't clutter the IR reflections. Fingers don't control individual tentacles."

Walking by gesture would be a great user interface. If his hand had eight opposable fingers. If the round-trip delay, ping-ponged through comsats, though far more manageable than in the lunar case, did not sometimes approach a full second. "Walking" involved a joystick and then only indicated a general direction. The bot's onboard nav software figured how to locomote across the landscape.

He swept his hand again, keeping his fingers straight, still, and together. This time, the landscape shifted as he expected. "I don't get it. Exploring Phoebe seems like the last thing that would interest you."

"Patrick, a guy I work with, was into these bots right after Phoebe rentals came online." She seemed about to say more, and to reconsider. "I tried to interest Simon in remote-controlled exploration. Any kid his age is going to spend time in VR, and this seemed much more civilized than the usual shoot-'em-ups."

"How'd that go over?"

"A mom's suggestion? About as well as you'd expect."

Marcus kept gesturing, the landscape swaying in response. "Am I ready for a stroll?"

"Uh-huh. Let's find a pair of bots somewhere interesting." She did something with her controller and a translucent pop-up materialized over the landscape. "Okay, here's an idle pair of bots near the Grand Chasm. You take bot three-twenty-seven." With a gesture, she changed the scene.

He had seen the Grand Chasm often enough, but never like this. Never so vast. What had changed?

The horizon was *way* too close.

"These bots can't be more than a foot tall," he said. "I'm used to watching from the safety cameras, atop eight-foot posts."

"Size isn't everything," she said. And blushed.

Marcus pretended not to notice, guessing the words had just slipped out. If Valerie was one for flirting or double entendres he had yet to see it.

He waggled a tentacle at her bot. "So, come here often?"

Laughing, she managed to make her bot shrug. "Only twice, both times long ago."

"Hmm. Maybe this can be our place." The line felt hokey, and yet like the first uncontrived remark he had come up with all evening.

They each arched a tentacle over the railing to peer into the abyss, where scree piles dotted the dark, undulating depths. He saw bots stranded partway down and the tentacle tips of others peeking out from beneath piles of rubble. Trapped before the barrier went up, or did tourists climb their bots over the railing?

The chasm sides looked unstable, but exactly how treacherous were they? Marcus needed several tries to grasp and drop a stray pebble over the railing. Under Phoebe's scant gravity, the rock more floated than fell. Finally, picking up speed, it struck a canyon wall and triggered a slow-motion rockslide.

Few people had ever entered the Grand Chasm, and—as much as geologists ached to explore Phoebe's most prominent feature—none had gone down very far. Too dangerous, the risk assessments always concluded. Even flying in, a hopper's exhaust could start an avalanche. Someday, perhaps, when mining was less of a priority, the staff could tunnel into the bottom of the rift.

Someday remained distant.

Marcus had long suspected an excess of caution after the early— and unrelated—incident during the establishment of Phoebe base. One geologist had already died on Phoebe, and NASA was determined not to lose another.

Now, in eerie silence, as the slo-mo rockslide went on and on, Marcus reconsidered.

Only how was he seeing this? Not sunlight—ever. Not earthlight, given the minimal comm delay. Phoebe had to be more or less overhead at the moment, deep inside Earth's shadow. Moonlight? The moon was just past first quarter. The light it cast would strike obliquely, the shadows pointing in one direction—only the shadows around the bots pointed every which way. That suggested artificial lighting, yet he saw neither lamps nor spotlights.

He gave up trying to work it out. "I'm confused. Where is our light coming from?"

"Not light. Not as you mean it, anyway. The bots use lidar."

Like radar, only based on laser beams. "So this is all computer-synth imagery?"

"Uh-huh." She stood and stretched. "I feel like coffee. How about you?"

"Sure." He followed her into the kitchen, where a pair of binoculars sat on the counter near the back door. "Wildlife?" he guessed, pointing.

"Stargazing." She finished putting up the pot of coffee and grabbed the binocs. "Come outside."

The night was cool and cloudless. After the moon, waxing gibbous as he had remembered, The Space Place, playground of petrocrats, kleptocrats, and the other superrich, was the brightest object in the sky. Only this was a sky unlike any he had seen in a *long* time. Far from big-city lights, the stars blazed. Thousands of them.

"Try these." She handed him the binoculars—

Through which countless more stars shone. And *there,* aglow in infrared from the residual heat of their last passes through sunlight, tiny shapes: an oval, a rectangle, and, the brightest of the three, a not-quite-round pearl. Phoebe's sunshield and PS-1, seen at a bit of an angle, and The Space Place. Phoebe itself was too dark and cold to spot even with thermal imaging.

Her hand was on his back, turning him. "Now look. No, up a little. A little higher."

"At what?"

"You'll know it when you're there."

The Milky Way *looked* like spilt milk—with a scattering of diamond chips.

"Wow," he said. "Thanks." He slowly turned, taking in the grandeur of the night sky. He eventually thought to offer Valerie her binocs. To the naked eye the night now seemed blacker than ever. "It's very dark out here."

"Oh, crap!"

Huh? "What's wrong?"

"You didn't plan to drive back tonight, did you? If you think it's dark here . . ."

Think how dark it will be in the forest, crossing the mountains, he completed. "Not a problem. I have a room for the night in the observatory residence hall. You don't need to chase me off just yet."

"That's good." A sudden, unexpected peck on the cheek suggested she meant it. "And if you'd like, how about you come by in the morning for breakfast?"

Turning, slipping his arms around her waist, Marcus said, "I'd like that a lot."

From the secluded anonymity of a black stretch limo, shared only with a longtime assistant, Yakov Nikolayevich Brodsky watched urban streets slip past.

He always enjoyed visiting Chicago. With its extensive expatriate community, he dined well here, on everything from blini to borscht to stroganoff. The finest elaborate banquet cost less than a passable snack in Moscow—

Because few here could have afforded Moscow prices.

And so, in a very different way he relished the signs of America's decline. The weed-choked medians. The empty stores and shuttered factories. The would-be day laborers milling about in a 7-Eleven parking lot. Most of all he enjoyed the waiting lines and per-gallon prices as they passed neighborhood gas stations.

What a difference a decade could make.

The limo sped downtown amid an escort of blue-and-white Chicago police cruisers. Lights flashing, they crossed under the rickety elevated train tracks that demarcated the Loop.

"We're almost there, sir," the driver announced soon after. "Five minutes."

A driver! How quaintly decadent. But doubtless the driver with whom he had been provided also spied on him. "Very well."

Yakov savored, too, Chicago's distinctive architecture. Perhaps his favorite example was the masterpiece that came into view as the motorcade turned onto Jackson Boulevard.

For decades the Chicago Board of Trade Building had towered over everything else in this city. From the speeding car, alas, Yakov could not fully appreciate the edifice's art-deco distinctiveness. He could scarcely even see the three-story statue of Ceres, goddess of agriculture, which crowned the building's peak.

*This* building projected a confidence and a presence, embodiment of a bygone era, of an American century. Not so the many modern glass-and-steel skyscrapers: their drab and boxy exteriors served only as metaphors for the hollowed-out American economy.

Police had cleared the street and sidewalk in front of the Chicago Board of Trade Building and were keeping scores of picketing protesters behind sawhorse barricades. AMERICAN GRAIN FOR AMERICANS many placards read. STOP BURNING FOOD another popular sign demanded.

Inwardly, he smiled.

As the limo pulled up to the curb, eight serious men and women in somber garb strode from the main entrance. Yakov waited for the driver to open his door.

"Welcome, Yakov Nikolayevich!" one of his greeters declared, a hand outstretched. "You honor us by your visit."

"Hello, Roland," Yakov acknowledged. Roland Johnston was chief executive officer of the CBOT. Yakov would deal with no one lesser.

"I trust your flight was satisfactory?"

"Very comfortable. Thank you." Washington, to which Yakov was posted as deputy trade representative, was only a short hop away. Shorter, in fact, than he would have wished. He so seldom found the opportunity to fly his Learjet. "My assistant, Irina Ivanovna Chesnokova."

"Ms. Chesnokova." Roland introduced his aides and hangers-on, and then, with a quick gesture toward the protest, suggested proceeding inside. "I apologize for the ruckus."

"Democracy," Yakov said. They could decide whether he intended sympathetic understanding or ironic dismissal. "Very good. I would like to see the trading floor." The pits of the original trading floor, alas, had been filled with concrete, the new area turned into mundane offices. A travesty, Yakov thought. "And the electronic trading facilities, of course."

"Naturally," an aide agreed. The corner of a folded datasheet peeked from a pocket of her jacket.

The Americans would give him the grand tour, fawn over his every word, then wine and dine him. When he completed his business, their limo would whisk him back to the airport. And between?

Between—to the certain dismay of the demonstrators outside, and countless others of similar opinion—his hosts would do everything in their power to expedite his purchase of corn and wheat. Two million metric tons of each, with intimations of yet larger purchases to follow.

They would bow and scrape and cut corners on his behalf, because he did not need their help. He could, he would suggest obliquely, shift much of his purchasing to the Canadians and Australians. His minions could quietly accumulate much of his stated need in smaller lots, through Internet trading and via pliant third parties, before anyone would see the pattern.

Only he wouldn't. Visibility, not secrecy, suited his purpose. That so rarely happened.

Ethanol substituted for gasoline. Higher grain prices made ethanol more expensive and less competitive. The mere specter of higher grain prices would spook oil markets around the globe. Whatever few extra dollars he might spend on grain—which, with great magnanimity, Russia would distribute to her friends in the Third World—would be more than repaid in higher energy prices.

Roland Johnston was by then extolling the virtues of some recent upgrade to his organization's electronic trading mechanism.

Yakov just nodded. If anything important came up, Irinushka could summarize later for him. She had already asked several probing questions about the measures taken to assure the integrity of data in their computer systems.

The men among Johnston's staff crowded around her, drawn to her classical beauty, vying to impress. Some must suppose she frowned in concentration at their wit or wisdom, or struggled with English jargon, for their speech had gotten louder and slower. And she, never giving any sign, would despise them for their vanity and condescension.

She had been born deaf. She had neither heard nor spoken until she was five, after receiving the cochlear implants masked by her long, flowing, red hair. When too many people spoke at once, or in chaotic environments like the trading floor, the din sometimes confused the implants' noise filters and speech-discrimination circuits.

Despite everything, she understood more than the fawning, self-important young men could imagine.

"Are you seeing what you wanted?" Johnston asked.

Yakov nodded. "This is a very worthwhile visit."

How strange it was to accomplish grand strategy by means as prosaic as buying corn. Because deputy trade representative was only his cover for his true position: a senior agent of the Federal Security Service.

Russia's interests often required methods more subtle—or far more dramatic.

**W**hat do you think, professor?" Eric the bartender asked.

Patrick looked away from the 3-V in the corner. "I think the Yankees will win in a blowout."

Eric laughed. "That's a given. No, I wondered if you were ready for another."

It was Patrick's turn to laugh. "No, *that's* a given."

"I like the way you think, professor. Be right back."

Three people sat along the bar and a few couples at scattered tables: Saturday night in Outer Nowhere. No families with children, thankfully. He still found families hard to take.

Eric reappeared with a fresh, foaming pint. "Your beer, professor."

"Thanks." Taking a long slow sip, Patrick returned his attention to the ballgame.

He took no offense at *professor.* Eric called anyone from NRAO that. In the winter, when this ski resort bar would be hopping, Eric's patrons were *sport.* Except any ski bunnies who Eric was hitting on. Them, he promoted to *sportette.*

Snowshoe was far enough from Green Bank to keep Patrick's co-workers to a minimum. Alas, because the resorts offered most of the area's finer dining, that minimum was not zero. As, captured in the behind-the-bar mirror, the approaching man and woman reminded him.

"Hi, Patrick," a familiar voice called cheerily.

Swiveling on his stool, Patrick thought Valerie Clayburn and her NASA friend made a cute couple. Both wore casual slacks and knit shirts: dressed up for her and down for him. "Hi, Valerie."

"Marcus Judson. Patrick Burkhalter." To Patrick, Valerie added, "You remember Marcus visiting us for a staff lunch?"

The name? That, Patrick had forgotten. But Marcus himself, after the reception she had arranged for him? No way. The wonder was that *Marcus* had gotten past it. Hopefully he had seen through to the good person underneath. Though maybe he just had eyes in his head.

Too much information. "Of course. Hello," Patrick said.

"Pleased to meet you. You're the guy who put Valerie onto Phoebe bots, right?"

Patrick shrugged. "You make it sound like I encouraged her."

Eric sauntered over, a napkin over his arm. "What can I get you, professors?"

"Two glasses of the house Merlot, Eric," Marcus answered.

"You've been promoted to a regular," Patrick said. And quickly: Valerie's ambush had been only four weeks ago. "Feel honored."

"Patrick is an astronomer, too," Valerie said.

"Astrophysicist," Patrick corrected.

Marcus rubbed his chin, brow furrowed. "There's a difference?"

"A big one." Valerie grinned. "Say I'm on a plane. If I feel sociable, I'm an astronomer. Everyone loves astronomy. When I want to read in peace, I'm an astrophysicist."

"Marcus, I'll get us a table. Patrick, will you join us for dinner?"

Which part of *astrophysicist* was unclear? "I don't plan to stay late tonight," Patrick lied.

Besides, Valerie did not need a chaperone. Patrick wondered if Judson would become a regular with her, too. Everyone would know when Judson stopped getting a room in the res hall for his weekend visits. Green Bank was a small town, and the observatory staff was even tinier.

"If you change your mind," Valerie persisted, then strode off for the dining room.

Eric ambled back, setting down two wineglasses. "I started you a tab, professor."

"Thanks." Judson picked up the glasses, took a step away from the bar, and stopped. "Tough break," he said softly.

The Tigers had just left two men stranded on base. "Jankowski is on fire this season," Patrick said. "ERA of what, around two-nine?"

"That's not what I meant."

"Aren't you on a date?" Patrick asked. He turned, pointedly, back to the Yankees-Tigers game.

If there was one thing Patrick could not abide, it was sympathy.

* * *

Valerie slid back her plate, pleasantly full. "That was excellent."

"That was a salad," Marcus said, as though disagreeing. *He* had had a sirloin with a loaded baked potato, and all that remained on his plate was a sprig of parsley. Maybe only half a sprig. "How about some dessert?"

He ate like a force of nature, but if she skipped dessert so would he. "I'd split one." One bite was splitting.

"What do you recommend?"

"Pretty much any of the desserts." As in: *You* pick. Because you studied the dessert choices before you ever looked at entrées. And because you're going to be eating most of it.

Why was dating so complicated?

"How about the death-by-chocolate cake, then. With a scoop of ice cream?"

"That sounds good." And maybe *two* bites.

"So, about Patrick."

She had wondered when Patrick would come up. "He's a planetary astronomer. I think you two would get along. He's not always so . . ."

"Cranky? Surly? Belligerent?"

"I was going to say gruff." The waitress came by to clear the dinner plates and took their dessert order. Valerie figured she could change topics. Patrick was so . . . sad. "Simon came home from school today with the funniest story."

"Hold that thought. I have a question about him. Patrick, I mean. What was with the disclaimer when I mentioned Phoebe bots?"

"Honestly? I don't know. It's odd. He used to rent bots quite often. But it's true that he didn't encourage me to try bots myself."

The waitress returned with their coffees, their dessert, and two forks. Marcus moved the plate into the center of the table. "What does he do at Green Bank?"

"Mostly maintenance, and some training of visiting astronomers. With authorization you can schedule observations over the Internet, but we don't give out those codes to anyone till they've trained onsite." Three bites, she decided, taking a fork. "Do you know his history?"

"Yeah." Marcus's eyes widened with his first bite of cake. "Not the kind of incident I would forget. Ex-JPL. Broke basic ops protocol, and in the process lost a deep-space probe."

"I think that's oversimplified." She fidgeted with her napkin, searching for the right words. Patrick had confided in her, just a little, once when she had really needed the distraction. "Suppose he had gone through channels, that he had submitted a proposed maneuver. Suppose that while he waited for a review committee to approve, the spacecraft got whacked by an oncoming rock." The inward-streaking pebble that, Patrick had said, could not be found in what remained of the final telemetry after his hasty upload. "Would that be better?"

"No one second-guesses waiting for channels." Marcus, wearing a sudden sour expression, set down his fork. "And when something was everyone's responsibility, that makes it no one's fault. Okay, I might have acted, too. More carefully, I would like to think. And without wiping the comm buffer afterward to try to cover my tracks."

"He's my *friend*, Marcus." And the loss of Patrick's family, career, and the respect of his peers was too steep a penalty.

Patrick had been in her office the day two Marines in full dress blues showed up. As Patrick had been there for her for long days after. Merely, quietly, *there*, not driven off, as were so many, by the embarrassment of not knowing what to say.

A good man hid beneath all that rancor. She felt Patrick's pain.

And in a rush, her own. She still missed Keith terribly. She wished her son could have known his father, taken away when Simon was just learning, stumblingly, to walk. But in an instant, a roadside bomb in Afghanistan had changed . . . everything.

What was she doing on a *date*?

Keith would want her to get on with her life, but she felt miserable. She tried to keep the turmoil off her face and knew she had failed.

"Sorry," Marcus said, looking confused at her mood swing. "Are you all right?"

"Just . . . distracted."

"Do you want to talk about it?"

"No," she insisted.

Marcus took the hint. "So Patrick doesn't observe anymore?"

She wrung her napkin some more. "Not officially." Because Patrick's proposals for time on the dishes seldom got approved. "But training involves targets, and he picks the aim points. His students end up tracking lots of objects in the outer asteroid belt."

"Outer belt," Marcus repeated. "Meaning?"

"Beyond the ice line. Distant enough from the sun that ice doesn't melt or sublimate."

"Listening for the beacon of the *Verne* probe, you mean. After, what, eight years?"

"Nine," she corrected. How absurd were the odds Patrick would ever hear it? Space was *big*. And who knew if the lost spacecraft even still functioned? "I know. It's sad."

"Poor guy."

The waitress topped off their coffees. Valerie wrapped her hands around her cup to warm them. Not that the room was cold.

"I think I should be getting you home," Marcus said. "You look . . . tired."

She opened her mouth, but an explanation refused to come. Dragging out the evening would not be fair to him. "You're right," she managed at last. "Sorry."

The drive home to Green Bank continued in awkward silence. She broke it by babbling about how in 1960 Green Bank hosted one of the first academically respectable SETI meetings. Search for Extraterrestrial Intelligence was one of Patrick's avowed passions, and she launched into describing the transmitter module—never installed, of course—that he had designed and built in his spare time for the big dish. He often puttered after hours in the electronics shop.

Only no one she knew believed Patrick gave a flying fig about SETI, or that he had spent months getting ready to send a reply to hypothetical aliens. What everyone understood—and no one would ever raise with Patrick—was the thing for which he *did* prepare: the day he detected the *Verne* probe's beacon. Each year, as that hope seemed more forlorn, he spent less time tinkering with the idle transmitter.

Her voice trailed off. She and Marcus completed the drive in uncomfortable silence.

They finally turned into her driveway. Light flickered in the windows, Brianna watching 3-V. Then a little figure bounded past the living room window: Simon, wide awake. Valerie fancied she heard little-boy engine noises. The dashboard clock, as she sneaked a peek, read 8:46 P.M. She was pathetic.

"I'm sorry," she told Marcus, yet again, as he walked her to her door. "I'm not fit company tonight. May I call you in the morning? Maybe we can go for brunch."

"Sure. I can stay till noon or so. Big meeting Monday to prepare for."

He didn't offer details and she didn't ask. The powersat, quite accidentally, had brought them together. It would not keep them together. It was, like Keith, a subject they did not discuss.

The two unmentioned elephants in the room.

On the porch, Marcus gave her a perfunctory kiss good night. "Will you be okay?"

"Sure." She forced a smile.

Someday.

**S**licing the tops off whitecaps, a sleek, thirty-foot hovercraft raced along the Santa Barbara Channel. In the distance, rugged and pristine, stood one of the islands of Channel Islands National Park. Santa Cruz Island, if Dillon correctly remembered the map. The sky was almost painfully bright. Sun sparkled off the waves.

"Southern California hardly counts as the tropics," Kayla Jorgenson shouted over the roar of the engine. Her tan Dockers, starched blue blouse, and L.L.Bean windbreaker might as well have been a business suit. She had pulled her hair back into a short ponytail. Only white knuckles as she clenched the handrail betrayed nerves. "This time of the year surface-water temperature only approaches sixty degrees, so the test bed won't reach the output levels the system would achieve near the equator. We still get a temperature differential, with respect to the bottom of the intake pipe, better than twenty degrees. The results we're measuring match our simulations quite well. That said, to unambiguously prove the technology, we would like to deploy a full-scale demo system somewhere warmer."

*If we get the money,* she managed to convey without uttering the words.

Dillon tugged his cap lower. Despite Ray-Bans and the cap's long visor, he squinted against the glare. He was a captive audience on the small boat, and Kayla was not one to waste face time. He remembered his first impression of her: focused.

They could have choppered to the demo site a lot faster, but after crisscrossing the country, flying from one cash-hungry start-up to the next, Dillon had opted for sunshine and sea breezes. His face turned toward the afternoon sun, closing his eyes, he thought tanned thoughts.

He was exhausted. Already that week he had toured a lithium-ion automotive battery plant in Saginaw, a superconducting cable company outside Chicago, a scale-model geothermal power plant in Nevada, and, only the day before, a Silicon Valley semiconductor design shop with some ideas for improving solar cells. The score so far for the week: dud, promising, dud, and *scary*. Cortez Photovoltaic used chemical dopants and industrial processes that made him nervous as hell. An anonymous tip to the EPA should slow that bunch for a while.

"Besides the convenient location," Kayla kept going, inexorably, "reusing the drilling rig really slashed our upfront costs. All we had to do was lower pipe, something any oil platform is already configured to do. If we extend this concept to . . ."

When Dillon next opened his eyes, the platform, which had been only a dot on the horizon, had swelled into a massive, looming structure.

Oil drilling in the Santa Barbara Channel: madness. Merely seeing this oil rig filled him with rage, but he bottled the anger. He could almost wish the Crudetastrophe had tainted the reservoir deep beneath his feet.

Like the drilling platform itself, ocean thermal energy conversion was an enormous undertaking. He felt the throb before he heard it. As they raced toward the old oil platform, the pulsing grew and grew.

"You'll want these," Kayla said. Her left hand came out of her jacket pocket with two pairs of earplugs. "Antinoise. They cancel repetitive low-pitched sounds like what our big pump makes."

Not much use to fish, porpoises, or whales. *They* were screwed. One of the staff engineers Dillon had tasked to vet Jorgenson's pitch had brought up the noise issue. Her guesstimate was that underwater noise from an OTEC plant would exceed ambient levels for a good mile from the platform.

The Santa Barbara Channel was summer home to about 10 percent of the world's blue-whale population. What about *them*?

But Kayla was right about the earplugs. The throbbing all but disappeared once Dillon had his pair in place.

She was still pitching OTEC when the hovercraft, settling into the water, coasted up to the platform's floating dock. The oil platform—an all-but-incomprehensible maze of girders and pipes, catwalks and steel plates—loomed over Dillon. High above, enormous derricks reached far out over the channel.

Twenty feet above the waves, where a spidery catwalk hugged one of the platform's massive support posts, a worker in hardhat and orange coveralls stood waiting. Projecting outward and upward, held almost vertical by taut steel cables, was what could only be a raised gangplank.

Kayla shouted out a string of numbers, and the roustabout released the brake of a winch. With a whirr of gears the gangplank pivoted and began to descend. The floating dock bucked and slued as, with a *thud*, the foot of the ramp struck.

"Nice drawbridge." Dillon gestured at ocean all around. "And one hell of a moat."

"We don't want uninvited guests, obviously," Kayla said. "We change pass codes daily."

As the dock's wobble dampened out, Coverall Guy loped down the gangplank to meet them. While he and crew secured the hovercraft, Dillon kept looking around. A wire-mesh cage bobbed nearby, buoyed by pontoons at the corners. Peering over the hovercraft's side, wondering what the enclosure was and how deep it extended, he was startled by dark, darting shapes within. They had to be two feet long, at least.

"What *are* those?" he asked, pointing.

"Alaskan sockeye salmon," Kayla said, grinning at his double take. "Some of the cold water we've lifted to the rig gets vented through the aquaculture units. That should be good for some extra income from the local seafood joints. We're thinking we might farm Maine lobsters in another cage."

While the chilled water spewing from the rig did what to the indigenous species? Fish farming was not the insult to nature of many ventures he saw, and the shadow of an oil platform was hardly a native habitat, but still the caged salmon saddened him.

Dillon followed Kayla up the gangplank, rising and falling with the floating dock, to the lowest catwalk. From there their route was hand over hand, rung by rung, straight up the massive pillar. When they reached the bottom deck he tried not to look through the metal grating to the surging waves far below.

The next visit, if there was one, he would take a chopper!

From the bottom deck they climbed endless flights of stairs, not stopping until the helipad level. Barrels and bulky gear lay scattered across the helipad. To deter unauthorized landings? "You really don't want visitors, do you?"

Kayla just shrugged.

He grabbed his cap as a wind gust snatched it from his head. Vibrations his earplugs would not let him hear crept up his legs, shaking his entire body.

The California coast sprawled in the distance. Kayla, who had saved her breath for the long climb, resumed her spiel. "Lots of oil platforms are like this. Near enough to land for easy resupply. In water deep enough to offer a significant temperature differential. Generating power by dropping pipe here is less disruptive than laying pipe from shore out to deep water."

Compared to some projects Dillon had assessed, this was environmentally sound. Sun would heat the surface waters no matter what. It would be better that obscenities like this platform had never been built, but at least with OTEC the platforms might contribute clean power.

Except that nothing built on a scale this monstrous could ever be benign.

"This pilot project will generate, if I remember correctly, five megawatts?" Dillon asked. "How do you deliver the power to where it will be used?"

"Converted to microwaves." She gestured across the helipad to a sturdy metal tower studded with antennae directed to points around the compass. "The small dishes will beam power to nearby drilling platforms, which will no longer need diesel generators to have electricity. The big dish"—which was not all that big—"will beam to the receiving antenna under construction on Santa Cruz Island. I guess visitors at the Nature Conservancy's research center aren't ready to give up supercomputers and hair dryers.

"The microwave tech isn't much different from how the NASA power-sat will transmit power to the ground, except that we aren't pushing the state of the art. We're dealing with megawatts, not gigawatts, and transmitting over a much shorter distance."

Powersats: the most mega megaproject of them all. If Kayla understood what mattered to Dillon—and, of course, she could not possibly—she would have picked a different example. Likening her endeavor to powersats had turned his stomach.

In her ignorance, she kept talking. "Of course not every OTEC facility will use beamed power. Where we lack a line of sight to land, and maybe for really large-scale generators, we expect to run marine power cables. You know, like the big offshore wind farms use."

And Dillon suddenly knew exactly what monkey wrench to throw into these particular works. "I have interests in a superconducting cable start-up." Even though the bunch in Illinois did not yet know it. They had been eager enough to get some of his money.

"Zero-resistance underwater cables to the power grid on shore. Of course, that would be great." Kayla hesitated. "At the capacities we'll need, superconducting cable is experimental at best. We've got a lot on our plates as it is."

"No, this could work," Dillon said firmly. "Look, I'll put my cards on the table. One-of-a-kind investments aren't worth my time. I look for synergies, win-win situations. Here we have one. The other bunch would get an impressive, real-world demonstration. You would get first crack at a more efficient way to bring OTEC power ashore."

"Does this mean my company has your backing? That you *will* invest?"

Dillon gazed out across the Santa Barbara Channel, saying nothing, the breeze whipping his hair. She could do the math.

She straightened, squaring her shoulders. "If you back Jorgenson Power Systems at the funding levels we've discussed, we'll assess our fit with your other company."

"That's all I'm asking."

Because commercializing technology of this scale would involve several more rounds of capitalization. Getting follow-on investments was all but impossible without the tangible endorsement—second-round buy-in—of the earlier investors. So: Kayla's people *would* factor the new technology into their plans. Just as, when Dillon called to dangle a bit of venture capital, the Chicago bunch would swallow hard and agree to a marine deployment—*despite* the complexities that would introduce—for their first big field trial.

With a few million bucks of other people's money, he would tie *both* ventures in knots.

CONVERGENCE | 2023

Monday, July 31

**T**he blasts of cold air began as soon as the mantrap door swooshed shut. Gusts tousled Marcus's hair and tickled his sock feet, and he shivered in a sudden draft as the isolation-booth air-return vent sucked up whatever molecular detritus the randomized puffs had dislodged. Chemical sensors sniffed for explosives. Magnetometers scanned for metal. Somewhere in Dulles International, he presumed, a TSA agent studied his full-body scan.

Short of administering colonoscopies, TSA could not be any more obtrusive.

A speaker crackled. "You may now leave the security station and reclaim your belongings. Have a safe flight." The door in front of him slid open.

As Marcus reclaimed his shoes and pocket gear, Ellen stomped—as best she could in stocking feet—to the carry-on inspection area. The security-booth air gusts had left her hair in disarray. A TSA screener had upended her purse into a tray and was sifting through the contents. She muttered, "Ah, the joys of modern air travel."

"Tell me about it." Marcus opened and reclosed his datasheet, which inspection had left more crumpled than folded. "At least we have time to get coffee before heading to the gate."

"There's that." She raked her fingers through her hair, slipped on her shoes, and repacked her purse. "I know *I* feel safer."

On cue, the airport PA system reminded them that the terror alert status had been raised to red. The week before, passengers on a Boeing 787 inbound from Dakar to Atlanta had subdued terrorists assembling a bomb in flight.

Oh, for the simpler era when color-coded security alerts had briefly gone away. What color would TSA proclaim after the next incident? Infrared? Microwave?

The terrorists (the Jihadi Alliance? The abortive attack had all the earmarks of their work, but no one was saying) had yet to admit how they had smuggled explosives aboard. Marcus guessed they had only to *say* they had carried the explosives internally to reduce air travel to utter chaos.

Infrared. That was when the colonoscopies would begin.

Cups of coffee in hand, he and Ellen rode the airport train to their gate. Marcus said, "Tell me again why everyone doesn't just network into this meeting? The off-worlders will link in whatever the rest of us do."

"It's too important. Sometimes you just have to be face to face."

"Then why don't they come to us?"

"I run an energy program," she said. "How would it look if I insisted lots of them travel so you and I didn't have to?"

"But bosses have prerogatives."

"I do." She grinned. "That's why you're getting on the plane with me."

As they exited the train and once again as they walked along the concourse, the PA reminded them of the alert level. And that unattended packages would be incinerated. Together with their owners, once identified. At least that was how Marcus chose to interpret the distorted announcement.

There was a blinding flash over the tarmac. Thunder, loud and rolling, rattled the concourse a second later. Marcus said, "We're not getting out of here anytime soon."

"I guess not." Ellen slowed to read an airport monitor, on which DE-LAY was suddenly very popular. "It's official. Our flight will be late."

He offered his best long-suffering expression.

"Seriously, this is an important review. Just between us, I *wanted* to hold it in California. Lots more opportunity that way to interact with the techies."

Without Phil Majeski stage-managing every conversation, she meant.

The Test Readiness Review *was* a big deal. If all went well, Kendricks Aerospace would get the go-ahead for preliminary operation of PS-1. Test beams sent to ground stations, starting at trivial power levels and stepping up. Device failures simulated to test autonomous repair by the onboard robots. Short-range maneuvering, exercising thrusters and the onboard navigation software. By year's end, barring some unpleasant surprise, PS-1 would begin its long boost to geosynchronous orbit.

In his mind's eye, Marcus pictured it: on station, motionless in the sky, streaming power on demand to converted solar farms across the country. The ultimate proof of concept, after which many more power-sats would be built. The first step to energy independence . . .

"Fair enough," Marcus said. "I admit it. Some things are worth a bit of travel."

Ellen flashed an enigmatic grin. "I'm glad you think so."

* * *

"The worst flight *ever*," Marcus groused. "Storm delay. Air-traffic delay at the far end. In between, mewling and puking babies. Crammed in like cattle."

Valerie let him vent, relieved he had called. "Did you get any dinner?" she finally asked. Body time, it was after 10 P.M. for him.

"Ellen's talking to her husband, and then she and I plan to head out. Tex-Mex, maybe. Anyway, I wanted to say hi first."

To let *her* know that his plane had not blown up. Terrorist bombs, even failed plots, struck way too close to home. And Marcus still had to fly home. "Go, eat. You must be starving, and I know you have several big days ahead of you."

"I am, and I do."

"Think you'll have time to talk after you eat?"

He grimaced. "Sorry. The jerk contractor uploaded drafts of several briefings while we were in the air. I should check them out."

"Understood. Maybe tomorrow night."

"Maybe," he said dubiously. "Good night, hon."

"Good night." Reluctantly, she broke the connection.

Their bots on Phoebe got to spend more time together than they did.

**D**illon slinked along corridors and down stairways, feeling heroic and a touch theatrical. At two in the morning, he was apt to be the only person awake on the former oil platform, turned OTEC pilot plant. R & D types did not work nights.

He certainly hoped he was the only one awake.

Stepping off the bottom deck onto one of the massive pillars that supported the structure, Dillon's mood crashed from self-conscious to terrified. A fall from the ladder to the ocean far below could kill him.

When Yakov had proposed this—mission?—it had seemed daring. Exciting. A stimulating change from Dillon's usual subtle, long-term sabotage. He remembered feeling flattered by the suggestion that he might be a man of action. He remembered how good it had felt to figure out how to sneak men onto the platform, how proud he had been of Yakov's praise.

But they had had those discussions by light of day, on solid land. Could he actually *do* something so bold?

Now, his heart pounding, Dillon wondered if he had been crazy to agree.

Or if maybe he had lost his mind long ago . . . .

\* \* \*

Years ago, after a really bad fight with Crystal, he had had to get away. It had been two weeks on a Harley, biking all over the Southwest, with only nature and his own thoughts for company. On good days, not even his thoughts had intruded. He had picked the Southwest for no deeper reason than that he had never experienced it. Flown over it, of course. Flown in and out of Phoenix and Albuquerque on business, ditto. But never explored the countryside.

At first he saw only wasteland, but after a few days a curious thing happened. He started really looking—

And found wonders. Here, yucca plants peeking above the dunes, their roots hidden deep below. There, stunted but stubborn, clusters of oak and juniper. All around, stretches of piñon pine, sagebrush, and chaparral.

When he got off the bike, he found animal trails. Oddest were the delicate footprints with two toes pointing forward and two back. Road-runner footprints, he learned, when he retrieved the datasheet from his saddlebag. And there were insects and animals, too, from tarantulas to armadillos to pronghorn antelopes. *Everywhere* he found a rich tapestry of life—

Except around towns.

Sodded yards, to his newly heightened sensitivities, were an abomination. So were the little yapping dogs, the thirsty ornamental trees, the swimming pools. And the big waterworks projects that made possible the other desecrations.

Camping one night in the desert, the gypsum sand ghostly pale by moonlight, the stars brilliant overhead, he had had an awakening. A revelation. An epiphany. If Gaia was a true deity, not just the embodiment of nature, then a religious experience.

And anyway, who was he to say who Gaia was or was not?

He had learned young how quickly a fool and his money were parted, and even earlier how many people, his parents included, could never manage to get any money in the first place. But from generalized contempt, he had awakened into a heightened realization.

Humanity was a plague on the planet, screwing up all that truly mattered.

He had returned from his road trip-cum-retreat a changed man. He apologized profusely to Crystal. They had not fought about her inability to have children, not exactly—but the tension *because* of it had strained the marriage almost to breaking. Now, he rejoiced. The last thing the world needed was more people.

But more—much more!—must be done. Only what? What could one man do?

Then, out of nowhere: the Crudetastrophe.

Finally, Dillon saw the way. Energy drove everything. Cut off energy supplies, and you starved the beast.

*He* would find ways to starve the beast, too.

* * *

Dillon shivered, chilled by the wind and spray. Back pressed against the immense post, hands clenching a railing, he felt that the wind could carry him off the catwalk at any moment. Twenty feet below, glimmering in the moonlight, the waters of the channel foamed and surged.

Subtle sabotage sounded better with each passing minute.

From the sea: a brief double flash, a pause, then a triple flash. A small boat, its engine muffled, emerged from the darkness.

Dillon released the brake that secured the gangplank cables. He cringed at the whine of the winch and, moments later, the thud of the gangplank against the floating dock, although he doubted either sound could be heard on the platform far above.

Three figures dressed in black and wearing black ski masks bounded up the ramp to his catwalk. Two wore tool belts; the third carried a clanking satchel. "Thanks, boss," the man in the lead said. "We'll take it from here."

Lower the gangplank. After the unannounced visitors did their work and sailed off, raise the ramp again. The three men would be in and out within the hour, and no one would ever know they had been here. Just as no one would know Dillon's role.

Only that another upstart energy technology would have gotten a black eye.

Tomorrow or the next day, when things went awry, Dillon would be as incensed as anyone. No, *more* incensed. And disappointed. And shamed. And compelled to pull the plug.

As for why direct action was so important at this particular time to Yakov? That, Dillon did not get.

* * *

Eve Moynihan sat in her bunk, flashlight in hand, sheet pulled over her head, reading a graphic novel on her datasheet. It was hot and stuffy under the covers, but Grandpa got up, like, a zillion times a night to go to the head. If he saw light under her door, he would tell her to go to sleep. That would not do: if she could sleep, she wouldn't be reading.

Thinking about the heat only made it worse. She clicked off the flashlight and threw off the sheet. It was *still* hot and stuffy. She was dripping with sweat.

As a nightshirt she was wearing one of Dad's old T-shirts. She peeled the damp fabric away from her skin.

Waves gently lapped against the side of the boat. Waves meant wind, didn't they? Maybe she could cool off on deck.

Or not. She was not much of a swimmer, and Grandpa insisted she wear a life vest whenever she was topside. Nervy, really, because he was not much of a swimmer, either. Mom, who swam like a fish, was a pretty good authority on the subject.

"I won't be falling off a boat," Grandpa had rebutted when Eve brought up the double standard. "On my boat, you follow my rules." Then he had ruffled her hair, like she was five years old or something, and added, "Captain's orders. You have to obey the captain."

So I won't fall of the boat, she thought. It was too hot to wear a life vest.

As hot as Eve felt, the doorknob was hotter still. Odd. With a hand wrapped in a hem of the T-shirt, she pulled the door closed behind her. In their cabin, Grandma and Grandpa were both snoring.

Up on deck, air was moving. The wind helped evaporate her sweat and she felt cooler—for a few seconds. Then she was worse than ever. She even felt hot inside, if that made any sense.

By the second, she felt hotter, and hotter, and *hotter.*

She was sweltering, roasting, burning up. The deck seared her feet. It was suddenly more than she could bear and she screamed.

Cool and wet, the ocean beckoned. With a wail of despair, dashing for the side of the boat, she grabbed for a life vest. The metal buckle burnt her hand, and reflexively she let go—

As her momentum carried her over the side.

Cold water jolted her to her senses. The current was carrying her away from the boat. "Grandma! Grandpa!" she shouted. As she treaded water, screaming, a wave surged over her and saltwater ran down her throat.

Somehow, coughing and choking, she stayed afloat. "Grandpa!"

Her head was so *hot*! Only when a wave broke over her, or she dunked her head, did she get a moment of relief.

There! People on deck. Grandma and Grandpa. They were screaming, too.

"Grandpa!"

He threw her a line. It fell far short. Another wave washed over her, and when she came up this time, he was fumbling with a life vest. He screamed even louder trying to buckle it.

She went under again.

Fighting back to the surface she saw Grandpa leap from the boat. The unfastened vest flapped as he fell.

Her head was *so* hot. She couldn't think straight.

Another wave washed over her . . . .

A day into the meeting, Marcus decided, the PS-1 test readiness review would put any three-ring circus to shame.

It was not that more than one presentation, demonstration, or closed-circuit 3-V inspection went on at a time. Ellen and Phil, seated side by side at the front of the Kendricks Aerospace corporate auditorium, in ongoing whispered consultation, kept the TRR on subject. But there was no way to avoid the multitude of viewpoints, offered by everyone from power-grid operators to aerospace engineers to radiation-health specialists from NIH and EPA.

As NASA's program manager, Ellen got the final word whether to proceed with on-orbit testing. But until the review board, the menagerie of outside experts assembled by the National Science Foundation, decreed PS-1 was ready—and safe—go-ahead was simply infeasible.

With almost three days of the review left to go, the notes file on Marcus's datasheet already seemed impossibly long. Still, he was exhilarated. Nothing major had come up. More than a meeting, this was a *milestone*. At the next coffee break, he had to give Phil Majeski full credit. No matter that Phil would take the compliment as sarcasm.

And then, during a presentation on RF noise simulations, an earnest-looking young man came scurrying up the auditorium's center aisle to whisper into Phil Majeski's ear. Phil's expression flashed from irked at the interruption to . . . what? Marcus could not decide. Nothing good.

Phil leaned over to whisper to Ellen, who nodded. "Keep going, Brad," Phil said when the engineer behind the podium trailed off. Phil and Ellen strode to one of the side rooms off the main auditorium.

What the hell? With Ellen doing—whatever—Marcus struggled to concentrate on the briefing. Kendricks engineers had come up with a way to detect and disable out-of-spec transmitters. Autonomous maintenance robots would be stationed all around the powersat anyway. With a software tweak and a minor electronics upgrade, the bots would triangulate the position of any malfunctioning transmitter and report it to the beam-control supervisory program. The program would take the failed unit offline, tweaking control parameters from nearby transmitters to compensate. Cheap, clever, and elegant.

If multiple transmitters went out of tolerance at the same time, to the point where triangulation failed, the supervisory software would shut off the beam. Transmitters would then be switched on and off in small groups and varying patterns until the individual failures could be isolated.

Pleased as Marcus was, and as pleased as he imagined Val would be, it was hard to maintain focus while wondering what kept Phil and Ellen away.

Then a real-time window flashed in his datasheet, with an IM from Ellen. *Join us.*

Bethany Taylor, folding her own datasheet, stood seconds after Marcus did. Summoned, too? They met outside the little side room.

"Do you know?" he mouthed.

Bethany shook her head.

The engineering presentation faded into an inarticulate murmur as Marcus closed the door. A vid, its audio turned low, hung over a datasheet that lay draped across the table. The Reuters icon glimmered in a corner. Major news, then. Behind the talking head, Marcus saw a rockbound coast and boats bobbing in a light chop.

What could this have to do with PS-1? Somehow it must, to pull Ellen and Phil away from such an important program review.

"Replay bulletin," Phil said.

"This is Theresa Wallace, in the Santa Barbara Channel." The camera panned away from the reporter to survey the backdrop. "We are anchored near Santa Cruz Island, off the Southern California coast. You don't see buildings, or roads, or any of the accoutrements of civilization. That's because Santa Cruz, like all the islands of the Channel Islands National Park, has been set aside to preserve irreplaceable natural and cultural resources. Only a few tourists and researchers visit this remote park each year, and the official population of Santa Cruz Island is just two."

Back to a close-up on Wallace: "And yet, incredibly, high-tech tragedy has struck here.

"Ralph and Mary Moynihan planned to show their granddaughter a bit of nature. They anchored offshore late yesterday afternoon." The viewpoint shifted, zooming in on one of the boats, its paint scorched. "And then, apparently as they slept, the Moynihan family was *cooked*."

Cut to a trembling woman in her sixties, her face red and severely blistered. Beside her, the inset image of a girl, perhaps eight or nine years old. "Eve's screaming jolted me awake." Her voice cracked. The crawl declared TWO BRUTALLY SLAIN. "Then I was scr-screaming, and so was Ralph. The pain was unbearable, like I was on fire and—"

"Stop playback." Ellen shivered. "I can't watch that again. I'm sure you get the idea, and you'll have no problem finding coverage if you want to see more."

With a tap on the datasheet Phil banished the frozen image. "Once was plenty for me, too."

"Cooked," Bethany said. "Microwaves?"

"Uh-huh," Phil said.

Marcus felt ill. "I remember reading something about beamed microwaves for nonlethal crowd control. The Army tried it in Iraq, I think, years ago, with truck-mounted transmitters. The microwaves induced painful heating in the skin, chasing people away before any permanent damage could occur." And the parboiled-looking woman on that report? And two—husband and granddaughter?—dead? *That* seemed permanent. "That was the theory, anyway."

Phil shook his head. "Not the Army. It comes out later in the report that some alternate-energy project in the Santa Barbara Channel was beaming power. Only a few megawatts, but short range. I'd wondered at first if extremists had hacked into the software that aimed the beam, but apparently not. The best guess is that vibrations on the platform loosened mounting bolts on the transmitting antenna."

Marcus had been wondering about Resetters, too, but carelessness was no more acceptable as an explanation.

"A horrible tragedy." Bethany shuddered. "This will sound terrible, but I'd bet we're all thinking it. The Resetters will pound us with this accident. If a few megawatts did this, they'll ask, what harm might PS-1 do with a gigawatt?"

Marcus *had* been thinking that, and Bethany's admission made him feel just a bit less callous. "And not only Resetter groups. The oil cartel will be all over this, too."

"Agreed on all counts." Phil sighed. "Nor will it be long until some-one at our review finds out, whether surfing or getting a call. We need to think about how to break the news—"

The sudden clamor in the auditorium suggested they were already too late.

**S**ushi?" Marcus said. "Sure."

He did not care for sushi—the Japanese word for bait?—but he liked even less the idea of eating dinner alone. Ellen had an urgent conference call to take that evening with the NASA administrator. Marcus figured he could guess the topic.

"Excellent," Savannah Morgan said. "A girlfriend told me about a *great* sushi place nearby. Follow me, gentlemen."

Marcus had met her and Carlos Ortiz the first day of the review, at which both were observers. She was a civilian cyber-security expert at Space Command headquarters at Peterson AFB in Colorado. Everything about Savannah was exuberant, from bright eyes to grand hand gestures. She wore her hair in a bun pulled so tight Marcus wondered if her forehead ached. Colonel Carlos Ortiz, her uniformed colleague, was short, barrel-chested, and very dark, with a gravelly voice. He was stationed nearby at Vandenberg AFB.

"Lead on," Carlos said.

They ducked out a back door to avoid Resetter picketers and the media circus at the Kendricks main entrance. Leaving air conditioning felt like stepping into a blast furnace. At a nearby cabstand they grabbed a ride. Savannah keyed in the restaurant's name and the auto-cab pulled away.

Carlos peered out at the boisterous crowd. "This is *not* a good turn of events."

"What happened near Santa Cruz seems to have been a freak accident," Marcus said. "The Resetters already hated PS-1. Won't this blow over?"

Carlos shook his head. "I don't see Resetters as your real problem. The Russians and their lackeys will have a field day with this. Powersats as WMDs."

"But powersats aren't!" Marcus snapped.

"But they *could* be," Savannah said. "Yeah, I heard yesterday's briefing about the interlocks and safeties. It's all very multilayered and sophisticated—and, hence, hard to get across to the public. The black hats only have to convey, 'Think how many pieces have to work right. Because when one of those pieces *doesn't* work or some safety mechanism gets turned off: death rays. Broiled while you sleep.'"

No one had anything to add to that.

Kendricks Aerospace employed thousands, most on government contracts. That made upkeep of the headquarters campus a reimbursable overhead expense, and the management did not skimp. A block away from the immaculately groomed office campus, though, the neighborhood turned seedy. Piles of uncollected trash. Panhandlers at every bus stop. Store doors wedged open, the whirring box fans glimpsed inside the entrances surely unequal to the task. Storefronts boarded up and spray-painted with graffiti.

Too much of the country, of the *world*, was this way, and the downward spiral could not be reversed without cheap, plentiful energy.

Someone was responsible for the Santa Cruz accident. Whoever it was, Marcus silently cursed them.

Their autocab passed a news kiosk scrolling teasers. Between bankruptcies and box scores, blackout reports and brownout schedules, something flashed by about sabotage at the Bay of Fundy tidal power plant. Like *every* energy disruption, the incident meant more money to the Russian cartel. Before Marcus could retrieve his datasheet and buy the download file, they were out of range.

The cab's console chimed to announce their imminent arrival.

"Sushi!" Savannah enthused. "That's not something you want to order in Colorado."

"So at home for seafood you go with the Rocky Mountain oysters?" Marcus asked.

He took her mimed gagging as a no.

Sushirama was three-fourths empty. Marcus told himself it was Wednesday night and unfashionably early, knowing neither was the reason. Washing down every mouthful with beer, unable to shake the day's awful news, Marcus mostly avoided noticing what he ate.

His new friends swapped stories about mutual acquaintances.

"So what do we *do* about this mess?" Marcus interrupted. "The PS-1 project, I mean, and Santa Cruz, and public opinion."

Savannah shrugged. "What you *are* doing. Test, test, test, then test some more. Make damn sure the safety interlocks work. Involve people like Carlos and me to make sure the system can't be hacked."

"Because you think it can?"

"You never know," she said. "Nothing Kendricks presented so far came across as problematical, but that proves nothing. The smallest oversight in implementation can be a security hole. You can be certain unfriendly hackers are looking."

"Last week's defacing of the White House website?" Marcus asked. "Russians?"

Carlos shook his head. "Too trivial for a hack sanctioned by a foreign government. You want my guess? The Chinese this time. Kids, trainees showing off for the props. But where an attack starts, let alone who's behind it, is nigh unto impossible to prove. When you know what you're doing, and the pros do, you work through long chains of anonymous relays."

"How often . . . ?" Marcus wondered.

"Don't ask," Carlos said. "If I told you, I'd have to kill you.

"The good news is I didn't see any gaping security holes in the PS-1 design. And kudos on one feature: I approve that core powersat functions like authorizing downlink sites *aren't* network-accessible. What you can't net into, you can't hack."

"Any other advice, guys?" Marcus asked.

Savannah laughed. "Yeah. *Illegitimi non carborundum.*"

Don't let the bastards wear you down? Easier said than done when geopolitics—or was it the excellent beer?—had Marcus's head spinning. "Is that it for the Russians?"

Carlos nibbled on maki, considering. "They'll pressure us to abort the project. They won't *do* anything."

"Because they can't?" Marcus said. It didn't seem plausible.

"Because militarizing space is expensive, with too much bad press for whoever goes first. And WMDs in space are illegal by international treaty. No, the Russians will keep claiming *we're* the ones taking that first, illegal step.

"And because the Russian space forces *do* understand your safeties and interlocks. PS-1 isn't a weapon, not as built. After today, my feeling is they don't even need to convince anyone PS-1 is a disguised weapon. It'll suffice to call PS-1 an accident waiting to happen."

"There has to be a way to make powersats more acceptable." Marcus picked at his food, wishing he believed himself. In all those town meetings, had he changed any minds?

"Cheap, reliable electricity. That's what people will understand." Savannah shook her head. "If we don't lose our nerve first."

* * *

Fish scraps swallowed whole did not a meal make, and if the Japanese had any concept of dessert, Marcus had yet to encounter it. Somewhere in Los Angeles a Snickers had his name on it. He was begging off an evening of barhopping when a call from Ellen made excuses moot.

"How'd your call go?" he asked her. She looked drained.

"Interesting," was all she would admit. "How soon can you get back to the hotel?"

"Once I get a cab, maybe twenty minutes."

"I'll be in my room."

He was at her door in twenty-five minutes, after a short cab ride spent surfing news sites. The death-from-the-skies narrative had already begun.

In person Ellen looked even worse than over the phone.

"Are you all right?" he asked.

"I've had easier days." She waved him inside. "Sit. I'll fill you in."

Marcus took a chair. Ellen sat on the foot of the bed. She said, "Not to keep you in suspense, PS-1 testing can proceed. If we get through this week's review without showstoppers. If we redouble our efforts at test and inspection before going live. If we, government and contractor alike, prove we take our responsibilities seriously."

"What's a showstopper? Who decides?"

"Our blue-ribbon review panel, for starters. And the administrator will review their findings. And behind the scenes, so will someone from the White House."

Marcus thought back to his unsettling dinner conversation. "And Resetter pressure? Foreign propaganda?"

"The official guidance is: Prove them wrong."

"Redouble our efforts." Marcus gazed out the window, trying to imagine what redoubling would entail. His imagination failed him.

"The administrator and I had a long talk after the conference call. He wants to send an independent inspection team. I'd been considering one anyway."

"An onsite—on *orbit* inspection?"

"Right."

"And Phil agreed," Marcus said dubiously.

"It's not his decision." Ellen sighed. "I'll miss having you around every day."

Huh? "You're *firing* me?"

He had immersed himself in this project. He had devoted three years of his life to PS-1. To become some sort of public sacrifice to show NASA was serious?

In his mind's eye, Sean leered. *You're a sucker, bro.*

"Fired?" For an instant, Ellen just stared. "Marcus! Of course not! I need a personal representative up there with the inspection team. Someone who knows the system inside and out. Someone I know I can trust.

"Who do you imagine I'd send?"

**T**hen the lobbyist says . . ." "The old goat doesn't have interns, he has a harem." "Lost their budget so fast they still don't know what hit them." "So the deputy undersecretary called over to Interior . . ."

Ah, Washington gossip.

Soaking it all in—the good, the bad, and mostly the banal—Yakov took his turn manning the grill. Earl Vaughn, friend, neighbor, and host, held court at the bar. People thronged the patio and deck and spilled onto the lawn. Someplace in the press of neighbors and other guests, wherever the conversation was liveliest, Yakov knew his charming wife would be found.

"Oh, crap. It's you."

*A hell of a greeting.* Yakov turned. "Good to see you, too."

They had a bit of playacting to go through. Tyler Pope, an analyst at the CIA, would pretend not to know Yakov was Federal Security Service. Yakov would pretend not to know he knew Tyler knew. An open question: whether Tyler knew Yakov knew.

Tyler said, "Every time I see a foreign national, it means filing another pain-in-the-ass contact report." His Texas drawl grated—if not as much as when he chose to practice his Russian.

"I am sorry to be such a burden." Yakov flipped a row of burgers. "Let me make it up to you. Have some barbecue. Grab a bun."

"Have you seen the form? My fingers will be bloody stumps before I'm done typing. Give me *something* to report."

"You can say I buy corn. But, Tyler . . ." Yakov leaned forward conspiratorially.

"Yes?"

"I think maybe I will continue to buy corn."

"Thanks a bunch, neighbor. Or should I say, a bushel?"

They exchanged a bit more such nonsense before Tyler went off with a burger. It was all comfortable and familiar. Safe and predictable, if you were logical and thought ahead.

Yakov thought *far* ahead.

As a boy, to be a chess grandmaster had been the limit of his ambition. He could have achieved it, too—of that he was certain. Instead, the Federal Security Service (in its Russian acronym, the FSB) recruited him first. It turned out they recruited many chess prodigies, especially those, like Yakov, also skilled with languages. Nations played their own games, with the entire world as their game board.

Nations had neither permanent friends nor permanent enemies, only permanent interests. But not even nations were permanent: Yakov had watched the Warsaw Bloc come unglued, the Soviet Union break apart, and America's own jetliners turned against her.

The game of nations was more challenging by far than chess, more interesting, and—unlike chess—still far beyond the capabilities of any computer.

Bureaucratic maneuvering was also a game, one at which Yakov excelled. He had climbed rapidly in the ranks of the FSB. With influence at home came his choice of postings abroad. Less patriotic master players chose Stockholm or Paris. *He* had chosen the hellhole that was the Restored Caliphate.

"Allowing" a few old Soviet nukes—rendered subtly unstable—to fall into the hands of the fanatics had been his boldest gambit.

A very successful gambit, too, after which Russia dominated world petroleum markets. Bolivia and Chile controlled the lithium essential for electric car batteries—and Russia could, as needed, coerce Bolivia and Chile. If America was not yet quite prostrate, time was on Russia's side. The game of nations should have ended with the Crudetastrophe—

Only the game of nations, unlike chess, dealt the occasional wildcard.

*Phoebe* was a wildcard. The dormant comet had come hurtling, quite literally, out of nowhere. For as long as the Americans controlled Phoebe and its resources, an escape from their dilemma existed for the Western powers.

The powersat project had to fail, and fail so spectacularly that no one would attempt it again. Not until the last drop of petroleum was under contract, and Russia was without rival, and it suited her to reintroduce the technology.

And so, for a little while longer, the game of nations would continue. Russia would still win. *He* would still win. Very soon now.

Allowing a neighbor to relieve him at the grill, Yakov headed for the bar. He felt like celebrating.

\* \* \*

Dillon sat in his parked car, windows open for the nonexistent cross breeze, sweating buckets. Only principle kept him from raising the windows and blasting the air conditioner.

*Damn* Yakov, anyway.

From a house down the street from where Dillon waited, fuming, happy chatter rose. A neighborhood get-together? He ached to crash the party looking for Yakov, but resisted. What he had to say to the bastard must be said in private.

Dillon turned on the radio. He watched and waited until, finally, singly and in pairs, people began emerging from the backyard gathering. A man and woman came Dillon's way. The woman was blond and fair, entirely ordinary. The man was dark and stocky, his features broad, his salt-and-pepper hair thick and unruly—almost like fur. Everything about him hinted at ancestors from the Eurasian steppes. Yakov, damn him, Brodsky.

Dillon got out of his car.

Yakov said something in Russian to the woman, presumably his wife, who nodded and went into a house. "I am surprised to see you here," Yakov said. "McLean is off your beaten path, I should think."

"I've been leaving messages for more than a week. You didn't return my calls." You bastard.

"I have been busy." Yakov gestured at his front walk. "Very well, come inside. I trust you had a pleasant drive from New York?"

Nothing about today could be pleasant. Giving no response, Dillon followed Yakov up the front walk, inside the house, and into a dark, book-lined study. A magnificent chessboard, black onyx and white marble inlaid into a mahogany tabletop, stood beside the desk. The wooden chess pieces, intricately carved, were lustrous.

With a flick of the wrist, Dillon disdained offers of a drink and a seat.

"As you wish." Yakov poured vodka for himself. "What is so urgent?"

"I thought we had a *partnership*."

"We do. A very productive one, to my way of thinking."

"Did, Yakov. We did have a partnership. Past tense."

The picture of nonchalance, Yakov settled into the leather wing chair behind the desk. His drink sat untouched. "My sources identify interesting start-up ventures. Your company gets my experts inside those ventures for a closer look at new technologies. Together we discourage . . . unfortunate . . . new infrastructure. The arrangement serves us both."

Amazing! The bastard dared to imply a moral equivalence.

They had—*had* had—a marriage of convenience. When they met, long ago, at a glitzy Manhattan high-tech expo, Dillon had thought himself *so* clever to have enlisted the resources of a Russian trade representative.

Too late Dillon understood who had recruited whom.

He said, "You want high energy prices out of pure greed. I want high prices to save the planet. *Someone* has to force people to reduce their impact on Mother Earth."

Yakov took a pawn and began rolling it between fingers and thumb. "As you say, we both aspire to high energy prices. I fail to see what troubles you."

"People *died*, damn it!" Only a few caged animals in the Nature Conservancy's wildlife research center were supposed to roast, and *that* had been difficult enough for Dillon to accept. True, he hoped humanity would develop the wisdom to let itself become extinct. That was a far cry from slaughtering a little girl. "Innocent people, Yakov."

"A few dead birds would not have served my purpose, so our people pointed the transmitter elsewhere. But be at peace. The man owned a yacht. How innocent could he be?"

A not-so-veiled threat? Dillon owned a yacht, too, and Yakov knew it. "You and I are through. Your engineers no longer work for me, no longer will have access to . . . anything I see. *That* is what I came to tell you. You can forget we ever met."

"I think not."

"It isn't for you to decide." Trembling with rage, Dillon turned to leave.

"You must see something before you go." Yakov smiled dangerously. "I promise. It will be worth your while."

Setting down the pawn, Yakov pressed a thumb against the sensor pad on his desk. Emitting a red laser beam, the computer—no mere datasheet—scanned his face, seeming to linger on an eye. The computer announced something in Russian and the beam disappeared.

"With certain information, one cannot be too careful." Yakov typed a long string of commands. Finally, he turned the display so that Dillon could see.

Video, but of what? The color balance was odd. Night vision? As the imagery jittered and bounced, Dillon needed a few seconds to parse a gigantic pillar rising from the sea and a man waiting on a spidery catwalk.

The vessel with the camera glided to a stop, and the image stabilized. The camera zoomed into a tight close-up of a face. *Dillon's* face. Sick to his stomach, he saw himself lower the gangplank and welcome three men dressed all in black onto the oil platform.

"Shall I fast-forward to the cheery wave with which you send off our colleagues, their mission accomplished?"

"You're bluffing." Dillon struggled to keep his voice steady. "You won't show that to the police because then I would tell them everything."

"An accessory to murder? I imagine you would cooperate." Yakov shrugged. "I am an accredited diplomat. Worst case, your government declares me persona non grata and sends me home. The only one interested in releasing this recording to the police is me."

Dillon stared. "But why would *you* . . . ?"

"Your task is complete, a timely reminder to the public of the dangers of microwave beams." Yakov reclaimed the chessman. "This is you, Dillon: a mere pawn. At this moment, by your own choice, a sacrificial pawn.

"Still, let us for a moment consider our options. You can go to prison, humiliate your wife, and destroy everything for which you have labored. Or you can trust me again and, pardon the terminology, be promoted to a queen. Stay with me and we will advance both our interests. You choose."

Knowing that he had no choice—and, too late, that Yakov could never be trusted—Dillon asked, "What do you have in mind?"

Valerie collected the scraps and wrappings from a very pleasant picnic lunch, while Simon rammed around nearby—up, down, and all around the nearest trees. "Look at me!" he shouted about every ten seconds.

"Wow!" Marcus answered every time.

After lunch he had stretched out on the blanket, a slight smile on his face, his eyes closed. He looked as relaxed as Simon was manic. Or maybe, after three sandwiches, epic quantities of deli salads, and two brownies, the man was going into hibernation.

"The amazing thing," Valerie said, "is that the running and climbing won't tire him out. I'm exhausted just from watching."

"Then don't watch. As long as he keeps up yelling, you'll know he's fine."

"Spoken like an engineer."

"Guilty as charged," Marcus said. "It's very nice here. It's as if we have the forest to ourselves."

Because they more or less did. "Green Bank does have its charms."

Sitting up, he gave her a quick hug. "It only needs the one."

The line was awkward, and she was awkward. To have someone in her life again—even though that usually meant texting and a nightly phone call—felt wonderful.

And scared the hell out of her. She shivered.

"I need to be up there," Marcus said. "Engineering is a contact sport."

Whereas astronomers only watched. Likewise guilty as charged, but she was still offended. And relieved that he had misunderstood her reaction, not that his upcoming adventure was much easier for her to discuss. "You *want* to be up there."

"That, too."

"Space is *dangerous*," she blurted out.

"It isn't just something I want to do, it's something I *have* to do, and I don't mean because Ellen asked. This is about the future. It's for you, me, and Simon. It's for the whole country." He sighed. "And Keith must have said much the same before he went overseas. Sorry."

"It's okay." They both knew it wasn't.

What a pathetic mess she was! After almost four months, they were hardly—together. Every time things got hot and heavy, she had pulled back. "I'm not ready," she had told him just last night. She guessed he was not quite ready, either. He had somehow seemed almost relieved.

So maybe they were both pathetic messes.

"Look at me!" Simon called.

"Be careful, hon," she answered without looking.

"I'll be fine," Marcus tried again. "Space is a tourist destination."

"Of spoiled, indulgent zillionaires." Oversexed zillionaires. Commercials for The Space Place were about as subtle as Viagra ads. Would zero-gee sex really be *out of this world*?

"You make my point, Val. Allowing any harm to befall a zillionaire guest is terrible for business, even before the lawyers get involved.

"Flying as a mission specialist, I'll get twice the training any tourist gets." Training for which he left tomorrow, a detail he neglected to mention. "And rather than being a tourist, gadding about playing space polo or whatever, I'll be on Phoebe or at the powersat the whole time, surrounded by old hands from NASA and Kendricks Aerospace."

That made perfect sense, damn it. Everything about him going made sense—except how the very idea tied her insides into knots.

No one was more committed than Marcus to the project's success. He knew PS-1 inside and out. His boss trusted him. He was qualified to train for spacewalks in the neutral buoyancy tank. (Learning to scuba had been Lindsey's idea—one more reason to resent the woman.) And even I, unwittingly, played my small part to make him a stronger candidate, as our bots explored Phoebe together.

"Look at me!" Simon called.

Something in Simon's voice was different than the last many shouts, and she did look. He was at least fifteen feet off the ground and still climbing! Her heart leapt to her throat. "Come down! This minute!"

He kept climbing.

"*Simon!*"

"We don't want to scare him," Marcus whispered. "Simon, you little monkey."

"Or to encourage him!" she hissed.

"It's okay," Marcus whispered back. "Monkey want a banana? Peel it with your feet?"

Simon stopped to look down at Marcus. "You can do that?"

"Well, *I* can. At least I used to be able to. Silly monkey, you won't find any bananas up there. The bananas are all in the picnic basket."

Simon considered. Making *eep-eep* noises, he started to climb down.

Whistling nonchalantly but moving fast, Marcus headed for Simon's tree—

And with an *oof*, caught Simon as he slipped and fell.

"I want a banana," Simon said, wriggling.

Valerie dashed over and took Simon, squeezing the boy so tightly that he squealed. "We're out of bananas, hon. We'll buy some on the ride home." Over Simon's head, she mouthed to Marcus, "Thank you."

"No problem," he mouthed back.

To see Marcus as a possible companion, maybe she had had first to see him as a possible dad. For whatever the reason, a lot of her doubt had just evaporated.

While her fears for him had redoubled.

**V**alerie had had it wrong. Space training was not dangerous. Some of the people in the zero-gee trainer just *wished* that they could die.

Not Marcus. Not, anyway, today. So far.

On his first flight, the training plane porpoising across the Gulf of Mexico, he had blown chunks. He had made lots of rookie mistakes. Skipping breakfast. Launching into aerobatics at his first opportunity, without acclimating first to the sensation of freefall. Turning his head during one of the high-gee pullouts. Thinking about how this worked: the plane tearing from steep, full-throated climbs, its turbofans belching black smoke, into great parabolic arc-overs, into steep dives, into screaming pullouts. Climbing and dropping ten thousand feet—over and over and over. And maybe the worst slipup of all, psyching himself out.

Every zero-gee training plane since the dawn of the space age had carried the nickname *Vomit Comet*. Knowing that hadn't help.

Feeling *great*, Marcus soared across the padded main cabin. All around, people in boldly colored flight suits drifted and hovered, twisted and darted, like so many tropical fish in a gigantic tank. Blue for the real astronauts and space workers in training. Green for NASA's guests: everyone prepping for the PS-1 inspection. Red, the most common color, for the tourists. In the spectrum of visible light—scientist humor—red was as far as possible from blue.

The sad truth was that red suits outnumbered blue and green, and the Cosmic Adventures training center—once the NASA Johnson Space Center—had been a shock.

His flight to orbit, like his training, would be commercial. Before arriving at the training facility, he had not internalized that. NASA Goddard's usual research was too esoteric to interest industry, and its campus did not offer enough unused land to draw speculators.

Approaching the cabin's back wall, Marcus tucked and rolled. A thrust of his legs sent him gliding back the way he had come: sixty feet to the opposite bulkhead. "It gets better," he called to two men and three women, their faces pale, belted into their seats and waiting for the misery to end. Both men and one of the women wore green.

The review team was limited by budget, schedule, security clearances, and, Ellen had intimated, acceptability to the White House. At least two of the team candidates would stay behind. He guessed there would be volunteers.

"Better?" one of the seat-belted men groaned. "Any time would be fine."

One of the seated women turned her head toward Marcus—and as quickly away, lunging for her airsick bag.

"Honest, it does," Marcus said, floating away.

Many of those loose in the cabin, while faring better, still flailed about unproductively. Swimming in air did not work well.

Marcus gave a shove to a woman (he guessed from the long, bobbing ponytail) stranded in midair. The recoil sent Marcus soaring on a new trajectory. He kicked off the wall, throwing himself into a corkscrew spin just for the fun of it.

Because it *was* fun. His parents, of the attitude that fun was all this was, had commended him on his government-paid boondoggle. Sean had mused aloud about the Seven Thousand Mile High Club—never mind that it would have been seven thousand kilometers—and whether Phoebe, like The Space Place, kept "escorts" on staff.

And Mom and Dad called *him* cynical.

"Feet down," a loudspeaker warned. Inside five seconds, gravity would return.

Marcus extended arms and legs to slow his spin. He twisted, getting his feet oriented, trying not to land on Savannah Morgan when he came down. Once *down* returned.

Of the onsite inspectors whom he would be babysitting (as Ellen would have it, with whom he would liaise), so far only Savvy had gotten her space legs. She and Marcus grinned at each other as they positioned themselves.

With a howl of the plane's engines, gravity returned.

Vomit spattered the floor and Marcus's flight suit as he landed steadily, if not yet quite gracefully. He stretched out flat as gee forces surged. Not that 1.8 gees at the bottom of the arc could compare to the four gees he had experienced riding the centrifuge, but *that* acceleration was steady. None of this up-and-down, on-and-off—

His stomach lurched.

So, okay, he did not entirely have his space legs.

Almost before he knew it, the engines were throttling back and the loudspeaker advised, "Going over the top." Zero gee came in not-quite-half-minute spurts, about one every minute.

*Spurt* was an unfortunate image, but he powered past it.

Zero gee returned with a feeling deep in his gut like at the top of a roller coaster, for an instant before the rest of his body caught up. Then he was up and away, turning lazy somersaults in midair, a bigger-than-ever smile on his face. He had just gotten a mind's-eye view of Simon Clayburn, space monkey, afloat in zero gee and peeling a banana with his toes.

When he called Val tonight, Marcus thought he would keep that picture to himself.

* * *

Bearing a loaded tray, Marcus surveyed the cafeteria's crowded dining area. He recognized faces, but saw no one he actually knew. Between the hectic flight-training schedule, futile efforts to stay current with PS-1 progress, and random summonses from the candidate inspectors, he had yet to achieve a routine.

Still, eating alone tonight had been his choice.

The would-be inspectors did everything together. He was not one of the group, not exactly, but still he would have to work with them. And so, often, he ate with them. Some evenings, though—and tonight was one of them—he was not in the mood to be treated, as some of them would, as the enemy. When push came to shove, Ellen had had very little influence over the composition of the team.

Maybe, he thought, if the *Vomit Comet* had tamed Olivia and Reuben. (Did he wish that on them? Not really. Not *very* much.) But to judge from their sniping that afternoon, his chief critics had recovered from their ordeal.

Olivia Finch, quick-witted and sharp-tongued, presumed that NASA and its contractors—*all* of them, including Marcus—would hide everything they could. Her skepticism was ironic, given how Phil Majeski and the rest of the Kendricks crew expected Marcus to hyperventilate about the most trivial variance. She was a quality assurance specialist from Caltech. And Reuben Swenson, for all his good-ole-boy affectations, was twice as sharp and almost as distrusting. He was a power systems engineer from the DOE Oak Ridge Lab.

The way Marcus's luck ran, he *knew* Olivia and Reuben would end up among the chosen.

Midday, pleading the press of work, Marcus had IMed Savvy—they had become friends, pure and simple—not to wait for him tonight at dinner. He could work 24/7 and still never catch up, so he had not even been lying.

But before even opening his message queue, Marcus had called Val at home. She had another long night ahead at the observatory. He had thought the appeal of radio astronomy was that you did not need to work nights, but the big radio telescopes were too expensive *not* to schedule around the clock.

They had talked for more than an hour. By the time she had had to dash to work and he had gotten to the cafeteria, the hot entrées had sold out. He would cope: as long as the grill line stayed open he would never go hungry. He could eat a cheeseburger and fries every day.

A table at the back of the dining area had two empty seats and he headed that way. The four men sitting there were deep in conversation.

Marcus had noticed them before. It was his impression they were bound for The Space Place.

"Are these seats taken?" he asked.

"Help yourself," one of the four said. "We're leaving." And kept talking.

Marcus ignored them, taken with the impulse to send Val flowers. His datasheet, only one-fourth unfolded, drooped off the end of the table. As he entered the stiffen-for-typing command, a shopping-bot icon started to flash. *Bargain found.* Tapping the icon revealed an unbelievably good price for the upscale 3-V set he had been coveting.

Had he been naïve enough to believe the offer, the urgent instruction that he needed to reconfirm his banking information stood to correct him. Damn! Another generation of agent software compromised.

Google confirmed the break-in. The Russian mafia was suspected. Or the infamous hacker, Psycho Cyborg. Or freelancing students from any of three notorious Chinese hacking academies. Or maybe organized crime in Botswana. The only element of the reports that Marcus found credible was that digital forensics folks were on a merry chase from computer to computer around (and around, and around) the world, hoping to track the exploit to its source.

Good luck with that.

Flowers would wait. First he had to shop—the slow, geezerly way, directly at the websites of a few trusted estores—for new agent software.

Three of his tablemates did, finally, leave; one offered an ironic-sounding, "Bye, boss." Their most solemn member stayed behind, seated catercorner to Marcus.

The straggler had a long, gaunt, almost ascetic, face, with a deeply cleft chin. He was wiry and even seated managed to seem athletic. His blond hair, worn short, had begun to recede. He squinted so much that Marcus could scarcely tell the man had blue eyes.

"Hi. Marcus Judson." He leaned close enough to offer his hand. "I'm headed for Phoebe soon." Anyplace else, *Where are you from?* or *What do you do?* were the standard icebreakers. Here, everyone opened with something about their upcoming flights.

"Dillon Russo. The Space Place." Dillon seemed awfully dour for someone going to the world's most exclusive tourist destination.

"Enjoying your training?" Marcus asked.

"It's been . . . interesting."

"That it is." Marcus searched his table in vain for a saltshaker. He snagged one from another table and sprinkled his fries, then took a big bite from his burger.

"You know, a meat diet consumes far more energy and generates more carbon emissions than eating vegetarian."

Uh-huh. And how much energy will it take to hoist your bony vegetarian butt and a week or two's supply of (shudder) tofu to The Space Place?

At least Dillon had left methane—cow farts—out of the discussion.

Marcus finished chewing, then returned to training. "What have you done here so far?"

"My med tests. FAA disclaimers and safety lectures. Got fitted for my counterpressure suit. A couple rounds up against the toilet trainer."

"Ah, the toilet trainer," Marcus sympathized. Step one on the instruction placard read, ACTIVATE CAMERA.

Going to space meant learning to shit while jammed, positioned *just so*, against a four-inch toilet opening. Peeing down a funnel into a vacuum hose was the easy part. Male docking *not* recommended . . .

"Good times," Dillon agreed, grinning. "But wait, there's more. The centrifuge. Flew the hopper"—barebones utility craft—"simulator, while some snag with my scuba certification got straightened out. Once it finally did, mostly I've been in the NBT."

Marcus had spent time in the neutral buoyancy tank, too. The tank was the world's largest and deepest swimming pool. It contained life-sized mock-ups of Phoebe base and several other key Phoebe structures, The Space Place, and a representative expanse of PS-1.

Neutrally buoyant objects, however massive, could be moved about in the NBT as though weightless. In a pressure suit, wearing weights to neutralize the trainee's own residual buoyancy, the NBT was the only way to mimic aspects of space conditions for longer than the half-minute at a pop that the *Vomit Comet* achieved. Real astronauts rehearsed in-space construction projects for days in the NBT before trying them out for real.

None of which made the NBT a good zero-gee training simulation. Try to move anything quickly in the tank and the water's drag—hardly a factor in space—interfered. The objects with which one practiced seemed weightless, but the swimmer himself did not. And the scuba divers all around, loitering lest some trainee got into trouble, shattered the illusion of being in space.

"I haven't seen The Space Place mock-up," Marcus said. There were not enough hours in the day, even if NASA would have paid his way to use that end of the tank.

"Nor I, beyond the preflight requirement." Dillon rubbed his chin. "I can see *that* once I'm up there. I figured, why not spend my time in the tank mock-visiting places I can't visit."

For someone who vacationed in space, extra NBT time probably cost only loose change from beneath the sofa cushions. It must be nice to be rich. Unless—

"One of the men here earlier called you boss. Do you do business on orbit?"

"We work together. I own an investment firm and The Space Place outing is last year's bonus."

"Business must be good."

"You have no idea." The words came across closer to a dirge than agreement.

Real astronauts, and Marcus knew a few, were far less serious. The old adage was evidently correct: The rich *were* different. Oh, well, he would have a zillionaire anecdote with which to regale Val.

"Done your freefall flight training yet?" Marcus asked.

"Tomorrow's my first flight." Dillon looked at his tray, the food picked over, and slid it away. "It's never too soon to stop eating."

"Today was my second time, much more successful than the first, so I'll offer you some free advice. Eat *something* in the morning, just nothing heavy or greasy. A dry bagel, say, or some cold cereal."

"Thanks." Dillon stood abruptly, shoving back his chair. "I've got work to do. If you'll excuse me?"

"Sure. Have a good evening." As his new acquaintance stalked off, Marcus guessed the man did not know how.

* * *

With a stack of hard-copy program listings under one arm, Patrick followed Valerie down Jansky Lab's second-floor hallway. She paused outside the observatory's main control room to tap at a wall-mounted keypad.

He had never been trusted with the access code. As a point of pride, he had observed closely enough, often enough, to know the code. As a point of honor, he had never used it.

With a soft squeak, the door opened.

"Hey, Ian," she called to the man on duty.

Ian Wakefield glanced up. He was chewing on the stem of an old briar pipe he had never been seen to smoke. Eight computer displays sat on the curved console that he had to himself. "Hi, guys. Shut the door."

Patrick looked for a clear spot to set the printouts.

All around, holos flickered and LEDs glowed. A row of electronics cabinets stood in the middle of the floor. More cabinets filled an interior nook, behind a glass partition. All that gear—supercomputers, signal processors, amplifiers, and an atomic clock—spewed RF that could bollix observations. Even the humble keyboard on which Ian pounded away emitted low-level RF as its innards ceaselessly scanned to detect keystrokes.

Unseen copper screening—behind painted wallboard, beneath well-worn carpet, and above the acoustic ceiling tiles—encased the room. Conductive glass in the windows completed the enclosure. Many a physics lab was a Faraday cage: a room whose metal sheath kept ambient radiation outside. The GBT control room was an inside-out Faraday cage, *trapping* radiation; this cage kept the emissions from all this electronic gear from reaching the exquisitely sensitive receivers of the big scopes.

"The door," Ian repeated.

Patrick set his printout stack on the floor and pulled the door shut. "Where do you want us to set up?" he asked Ian.

Ian gestured vaguely. "What are you two up to?"

"ASTRID upgrade," Valerie said. "We've got time reserved for testing on the forty-five-foot dish."

Ian called up the day's observation schedule. "Right, so you are. Okay, to install software you'll need sysadmin privileges. Valerie, I'll log you into workstation six."

There an emphasis on *you,* and a sidelong glance that Patrick ignored.

"It's a slick upgrade," Valerie said, talking fast. She blithered when uncomfortable, and slights like Ian's made her uncomfortable. "The dishes are always oversubscribed . . ."

Patrick wasn't uncomfortable, only sad. Misplace a billion-dollar spacecraft just once, and years later people still don't trust you. He arranged printed-out test cases on the console ledge as Valerie rattled on about the sky survey one of her grad students was doing, and that a dish slewing between approved observations could be observing while it moved.

The astronomer's integrated desktop, the observation-planning software more commonly known as ASTRID, did not plan between sessions. Yet. Patrick had helped Valerie code an upgrade to change that. The new code would take pending requests into account when planning how to redirect a dish. Rather than take the simplest path—rotate this far; tip that much—the upgraded software would optimize dish movement to seek out objects of interest along the way as it moved. The new software not only read the look-when-you-can list, it updated the list as it went. Suppose a scope were to look repeatedly at sky objects A and B. With the new software the dish would trace a different route, gathering different data along the way, each time. Yet another new feature reprioritized based on the real-time weather, because rain and snow blocked some wavelengths.

"Pretty cool," Ian conceded, gesturing outside at the heavy rain. "I could have used that last upgrade today. Okay. Test away."

"Thanks." She plugged a thumb drive into her assigned workstation.

"What do your hear from Marcus?" Patrick asked. He didn't care beyond calming down Valerie.

"His second *Vomit Comet* ride. He didn't throw up today," she said lightly.

Too lightly. Marcus's upcoming spaceflight plainly terrified her.

"Any day you don't throw up is a good day," Patrick said. "And what's Simon up to?"

"He's sleeping over at a friend's tonight." After a flurry of typing, she turned. "Okay, the software is installed in a test partition. Test sequence one, please."

As testing proceeded, Ian glanced over his shoulder every so often to give Patrick the fish eye. With traces of pity rather than distrust, Valerie checked on Patrick, too. Because, obviously, the new software also meant many more opportunities to hunt for the *Verne* probe.

Knowing Valerie meant well, Patrick pretended not to notice.

From within the claustrophobic confines of the spaceport mantrap, Dillon watched TSA screeners poke and prod his carry-ons. How interesting could shoes, a datasheet, and a bottle of aspirin be?

He imagined the various sensors at work, sniffing for explosives and scanning for metal. Beyond the already intrusive airport-type screening, he also got X-rayed. He might have had a bomb up his ass, and no one bound for space could credibly object to a few millirems on the ground "for everyone's safety."

The mantrap door slid open and the overhead speaker came on. "You may now leave the security station and reclaim your belongings. Have a safe flight."

As Dillon slipped on his shoes and tucked his few carry-on items into flight-suit pockets, Jonas Walker exited the mantrap. Jonas was senior among the three "employees" Dillon had been ordered to deliver to The Space Place. The others, Lincoln Roberts and Felipe Torres, had already cleared the security checkpoint and exited to the tarmac.

"Shall we, boss?" Jonas said. Only however deferentially he spoke, it was not a question. He gave the orders now, he did not take them, and it had been no accident that he, not Dillon, was the last of the four to pass through security.

Jonas was soft-spoken and poised, almost petite, yet with a creepy physical intensity: James Bond turned welterweight wrestler. He knew more about software than any five other people Dillon knew. Ditto Lincoln in electrical engineering and Felipe in communications systems. Tweedlesmart, Tweedlesmarter, and Tweedle-Effing-Genius. In simpler times, Dillon had been happy to have Yakov's experts at his company.

More naïve times.

"Are you ready?" Jonas prompted, this time with an edge to his voice.

"Sure." Dillon grabbed his bag. He wondered what hold Yakov had over Jonas and the others, but they no more responded to Dillon's subtle probing than he to theirs.

Maybe we're *all* trapped.

"After you, boss."

At the terminal door, held open by a smiling member of the ground crew, they were offered sunglasses. They walked out into a gorgeous late-summer day. Heat devils shimmered and shimmied over the tarmac.

One of the huge mother ships officially dubbed *The Space Portal*—and known to everyone as *Big Momma*—sat straight ahead, its white paint gleaming in the sun. Mother ship one or two? Dillon wondered inanely. And which of Cosmic Adventure's three shuttles?

As though he did not have enough to think about.

Beneath a hundred-fifty-foot wingspan, *Big Momma* appeared to have three fuselages, but only two were part of the plane. The central segment was the shuttle on which they would ride to orbit. Near the mother ship's cruising ceiling, the shuttle would drop free and light its rocket.

Dillon and Jonas started walking.

The shuttle was a fat dart studded with windows for the passengers. From the angle at which he approached, Dillon could not see the rocket nozzle. The entire back half of the shuttle was covered in frost condensed from the air by the frigid liquid-hydrogen and liquid-oxygen tanks. The rime weighed less than sufficient insulation to have kept the ice from forming.

Dillon first, they strode up the shallow ramp into the shuttle. A man and woman stood waiting inside, with big starburst logos emblazoned on their yellow flight suits. Pilot and copilot. Dillon did not know, or care, who was which.

"Welcome to Cosmic Adventures," the man said. He had a scruffy mustache and a crooked smile. "It's a great day to fly."

The shuttle accommodated six passengers, with three seats on a side, and the flight was going to be full. Lincoln and Felipe had taken the back row. Dillon thought he recognized the women, both raven-haired beauties, from space training. They sat in the middle seats, leaning into the aisle, speaking Spanish. He and Jonas took the remaining seats, in the front row.

Dillon immediately began fastening and tightening restraints: a lap belt and two shoulder harnesses. He would be damned if whoever came to check on the passengers would find anything to adjust on him.

Because the belts were something he *could* still control.

Mustache Man checked everyone's seat belts and double-checked the hatch seal before disappearing into the cockpit. The lock in the metal cockpit door engaged with a *clunk*.

"This is Captain Blackwell," a woman's voice announced. She had a touch of Southern accent. "Prepare for departure. Our ride is cleared for takeoff."

Dillon looked out his window. Though *Big Momma* blocked much of his view, he saw they were already, ever so slowly, creeping away from the terminal.

They trundled down the runway, the start of the trip to orbit eerily mundane. Using almost the entire long runway, the heavily laden plane more lurched than leapt into the air.

With the plane's top speed of only two hundred knots, Dillon had expected this phase of the "launch" would drag. Instead, as the ground receded beneath them—the Florida coast lush with life, the Atlantic waters a rich blue-green—he willed time to stop. A lump formed in his throat. So much beauty.

Too soon, *Big Momma* began leveling off and the next announcement came. "Approaching sixty thousand feet. Prepare for release and launch. Release in five. Four . . ."

At zero, Dillon's stomach fell out.

Faster than he could process *we've dropped* the shuttle's rocket roared to life. An elephant sat on him and crushed him into his seat. His cheeks sagged toward his spine. His eyeballs pressed into his head.

The shuttle tipped into a steep climb. "Ignition," the pilot reported, unnecessarily.

It was not a whole elephant, not even close. Max acceleration would be only three gees and Dillon had taken four gees on the training centrifuge without breaking into a sweat. But with the ship's growl and shudder, as the ground withdrew and the sky grew darker by the moment, it *seemed* different.

"Whee!" the woman behind Dillon half cheered, half grunted.

"Next stop, The Space Place," the pilot announced. "Is everyone comfy back there?"

Not even close, Dillon thought. But the gnawing in his gut had nothing to do with the roar of the engines.

\* \* \*

Thaddeus Stankiewicz watched his baby sister, grinning from ear to ear, sashay across a crowded living room. A dozen people must have waylaid her en route. "You clean up good," Thad said as she finally got to the phone.

"Thanks!" She twirled once for the camera.

In fact, Robin was gorgeous and dressed to kill in a short, low-cut, black sheath. Her hair, long and golden, was swept up into a fancy hairdo to which he could not put a name. He thought the dangly diamond earrings were new. Men in tuxes and women in cocktail dresses milled and murmured in the background.

"It's about time," she said. "I thought you'd forgotten."

"Never. And I hope you know I'd be there if I could. I wish I lived closer." I wish we lived on the same world. "In my defense, it's still early afternoon, Phoebe time."

"Well, it's almost eight in Stockholm. When *will* you deign to come down to—"

Twin girls, *so* like Robin at the same age, in matching pink party dresses, crowded the camera. "It's Uncle Thaddeus," one shrieked. Deborah, he thought. She was always just a bit taller.

"Hello, Uncle Thaddeus," the girls chanted in unison.

"Hi, girls," he said. "You both look very pretty. Are you taking good care of your mother on her birthday?"

"Uh-huh," Deborah said. Cynthia only nodded vigorously.

"My little darlings have been on their best behavior." Robin put an arm around each girl. "When will their favorite uncle grace us with a visit?"

"Soon," Thad lied. Beneath the camera's line of sight, he rapped the shelf of the comm console. He glanced over his shoulder at the locked door of his tiny room. "Sorry, kiddo. Duty calls. Enjoy your party." He leaned closer to the camera. "Bye, girls."

"Bye, Uncle Thad—"

He broke the connection before he lost self-control. "Take care, kiddo," he told the final, frozen frame.

For weeks after . . . the incident, Thad had awakened every day, when he slept at all, expecting, and dreading, to be called upon again. To get new orders. As much as he wanted to leave—to flee—the scene of the crime, he had not dared. But the call never came and he had learned, once more, to sleep.

He had dared to hope, as the months passed, that new orders would never come. That he was done. That he was *out*. That he could carry his shame and guilt with him to the grave. That Robin would never know what he had had to do to protect her.

When two years passed without contact, he had dared to apply for a job Earthside—and an anonymous e-mail advised that his assignment was not complete. Every day since, he had awakened wondering if today was the day.

Thirty minutes earlier, the long-dreaded message had come at last. The innocent-seeming words had etched themselves into his brain. Something compelled him to reread the text anyway.

*A great birthday party, cousin—too bad you aren't here. I wanted you to have some reminders of what's important. Enjoy. Jacob.*

Cousin Jacob was imaginary. *Yakov* was all too real. And Thad's master, these past long years.

Thad tapped the text's first attachment, a file named *Birthday 2023*. A holo opened: of Robin, beaming, wearing the cocktail dress he had just seen, her adoring husband at her side. She held out dangly diamond earrings, still in their little, black-velvet-lined case, for her guests to admire. The twins, in identical pink party frocks, grinning goonily for the camera, stood hand in hand in front of their parents.

Without question, the vid had been taken today. And Yakov had it.

The remaining attachment was labeled *Birthday 2014*. He remembered that birthday all too well.

Robin had been a wild kid: rebellious, often drunk, hanging with a bad crowd. He was ten years older, and she had always looked up to him. Had he been around for her, maybe he could have done something. Instead he had been in Afghanistan.

*Somehow we're always a world apart, kiddo.*

When Robin's high school expelled her, their parents, calling it tough love, had thrown her out, too. She was long gone—out of touch, out of sight—before he even knew. When his regiment shipped home, he had had no idea where to look for her.

By 2014, she was a druggie, hopelessly addicted, hooking to support her habit. On her nineteenth birthday, taking stock of her life, she chugged a bottleful of pain pills.

From the ER, Robin had reached out to Thad. "I can't do this anymore," she had said. "I can't take anymore." Gaunt, trembling, with tears streaming down her face, she had put herself into his hands. He had sworn never to do what their parents had done. He would never abandon her. He would never fail her.

Together—and with lots of therapy—they somehow worked through things. Robin detoxed, learned to stop hating herself, and got her GED. She went to college and met her future husband. Randall Brill came from old money; he proudly carried a "Fifth" after his name to prove it. Randy and his family believed her late start at college came of two years backpacking across Europe.

*I wanted you to have some reminders of what's important.*

If Robin's past were revealed, it would destroy lives across the family. Could she go on after that? Or would she try again to kill herself?

*I wanted you to have some reminders of what's important.*

Yakov had used Robin's secret once to bend Thad to his will. Yakov had needed "a man I can trust," on Phoebe. "A man with motivation, to perform a small, technical task."

And because no one could know about Thad's task, a man had had to die.

Three years after that . . . murder, Yakov was back in touch. What horrible thing did he want?

His hand shaking, dreading what the second attachment would show, Thad tapped the 2014 icon.

*File corrupted*, a pop-up proclaimed.

He found, as he expected, a message encrypted within the "corrupted" file: *Prepare the artifacts and await contact. Do not reveal yourself unnecessarily, but the success of the mission comes first.*

Artifacts, Thad understood all too well. His "small, technical task" of three years earlier. He trembled to think what type of mission required them, because the devices he had built could serve only one purpose.

I do it for Robin, he told himself. Whatever *it* was. Because he had no choice.

To keep his promise to his baby sister, he had long ago compromised himself beyond redemption.

\* \* \*

Beautiful beyond words, Earth receded in Dillon's window. While other passengers floated about, cavorting in freefall as the shuttle coasted toward their hotel, he remained in his seat. He could float just as well where they were headed, but Gaia's slow retreat was an almost religious experience.

Two clicks sounded on the loudspeaker. "This is Captain Blackwell. We've been flying tail-down so you can enjoy Earth. I hope everyone has appreciated the scenery. We're coming up to another quite spectacular view, though, so we'll be rolling over. If you might find that maneuver disorienting, you may want to buckle up. Regardless, stay alert and enjoy the show."

Jonas and one of the women returned to their seats.

"Commencing slow roll in sixty seconds," Blackwell updated, then gave a countdown from ten. "Commencing roll."

The men and one woman still afloat in the cabin seemed to rotate in the air, but it was the shuttle, not the passengers, that turned. The earthlight streaming through the windows slid up the wall. As Earth fell from sight, a holo opened at the front of the cabin. Three small, bright objects glistened in the image.

Blackwell's travelogue resumed. "I'm relaying our view from the cockpit. We're overtaking Phoebe and its sunshield. At the moment we're about five hundred miles apart. The bright oval is the sunshield. The shield is actually round, but we're catching it at an angle. We don't see Phoebe itself. It's behind the shield from us, and too dark anyway to spot easily.

"What looks like a rectangle is a square we're viewing almost edge-on. That's NASA's prototype powersat, PS-1, constructed mostly with raw materials from Phoebe." She spouted the usual bullshit about how great powersats would be. She rattled on how the onboard thrusters would lift PS-1, once its checkout was complete, to a stationary orbit above the Americas, while *more* such obscenities were built. "The powersat is dimmer even though it's about fifty miles closer to us than the sunshield. On to the third—"

"Why is PS-1 dimmer?" the still-floating woman asked.

The cabin must have had a microphone, because Blackwell answered. "The shield is white to reflect sunlight. The solar cells on the powersat are dark to absorb sunlight.

"On to the third object up ahead: the deformed-looking dot. It's both smaller by far than the other things we're seeing, and it's two hundred miles beyond the sunshield. That dot, ladies and gentlemen, is The Space Place. We'll be docking there soon. While we're busy in the cockpit, you're welcome to listen and watch on channel one."

Spacecraft docking patter turned out to be as dry and formulaic as airplane cockpit chatter. Dillon began surfing other options on the in-flight entertainment system and came upon an educational vid. At least he assumed it was educational: the animation showed Olympian gods looking down on Earth.

". . . was a Titan, a daughter of Gaia, whom some call Mother Earth. Phoebe was often described as 'golden wreathed' and associated with the moon. How appropriate then that Phoebe now *is* a moon."

He fast-forwarded, until the visual changed from animation to real imagery.

". . . still debate the origins of the object that became Earth's second moon. The orbit on which it was spotted must have been new, or the object would have been observed years earlier. Regardless—"

He fast-forwarded again. Animation, when it resumed, defied recognition at the speed he scanned. He went back to PLAY and the image resolved into a dark, tumbling blob.

". . . and without detailed knowledge of the object's exact nature, NASA's options were limited. The key question was: how solid and sturdy was the object? How hard of a shove could it withstand before shattering into an unstoppable hailstorm of debris? If, as turned out to be the case, it was a rubble pile, NASA would need to deflect it very gradually."

A stylized spacecraft zoomed into the animation frame, to hover, its thrusters blazing, above the tumbling blob.

"Enter the gravity tractor." The spacecraft graphic alternated twice with the image of an ordinary farm vehicle. "All objects in the universe attract each other. The object we know as Phoebe outweighed NASA's gravity tractor by about a million to one, but thrusters on the Rescue One spacecraft kept it from being pulled down to the surface. By maintaining with its thrusters a slight separation, the spacecraft exerted a very small—but very steady—pull on Phoebe.

"Just as an ordinary tractor uses a mechanical linkage to tow a plow, NASA's spacecraft used the pull of gravity itself to . . . slooooowly . . . over many months, move Phoebe into a more desirable trajectory. By the time Phoebe came within reach of a crewed mission, *Rescue One* had closely observed Phoebe for a year. NASA astronauts knew exactly where to set the thermal nuclear rockets that nudged Phoebe into its present orbit."

Someone tapped Dillon's shoulder.

"We're passing right *by* Phoebe," a female voice asserted. She had a charming accent. "Why can't we visit?"

Dillon looked up. The woman should have put her hair into a ponytail or something. As it was, she looked like Medusa. "Security," he said. "So I hear."

"Because I might conquer America's precious little moon with my nail file? Oh, wait. I don't have my nail file. I was told I had to pack it."

Across the aisle, Jonas snickered.

"Trust me," Dillon said, "I had no part in setting that policy."

The loudspeaker clicked again. "This is Captain Blackwell. We're cleared for final approach to the hotel. If you have not already done so, please return to your seat for docking."

Dillon had studied the brochures for The Space Place. He knew its major parts, how its systems operated, and just how big it was. But until then, he had not truly had a feel for it.

Outside his window: a pearl onion (pierced by a white toothpick) with an equatorial bulge. The pearl became a great bubble. The "toothpick" ends were docking stations, one projecting from each pole. The bulge resolved into two concentric doughnuts, the outer one spinning. Sun-tracking solar panels hung far enough from the hotel not to impede guests' views.

Closer still, more detail emerged. The struts that connected the solar panels to the main body of the hotel. Clinging to the bubble, two arcs of much tinier bubbles: emergency escape pods. Where too-bright sunlight would otherwise have streamed inside, the bubble material had been polarized, and from this angle was opaque. Elsewhere within the bubble, hints of interior structure.

Scattered specks—people in spacesuits—zipped about the hotel. The sphere's diameter was about forty times their height! The people jetted to one pole of the hotel as the shuttle coasted toward the other.

"Docking in five seconds," Captain Blackwell announced. The shuttle hesitated as bow thrusters engaged. "Four . . . three . . . two . . . one . . ." There was the faintest of vibrations as magnetic couplers engaged. "Welcome to The Space Place."

**F**eeling needy and manipulative, Valerie e-mailed a few recent adorable pictures of Simon. Then she waited for two days before she called her parents. Timing was everything.

She checked in with them more or less weekly, and every conversation was pretty much the same. The weather is crazy. Politicians are crooks. A catalog of aches and pains, "But what can you do?" For some hapless 3-V star, a slut-of-the-week award. A recitation of grocery sales in Danville.

This call was no different, and Valerie wondered if she would have to raise the subject. She decided to wait a little longer.

Mid-rant about Illinois's latest corrupt governor, Mom stopped. "Enough of that. I meant to thank you for the new pictures of Simon."

"You're very welcome. I hope you guys enjoyed them."

"Dad says Simon is growing like a weed." Pause. "The next time we see Simon, Dad says, we won't even recognize him."

Taciturn as Dad was, he did say things on occasion. More often, *Dad says* was code, Mom hinting at matters she did not care to raise outright. *Dad says* twice was a giveaway.

"We can't have that," Valerie said. "You guys should come for a visit. Spend some quality time with your grandson."

Mom blinked. "You're asking?"

"I'm asking." Hoping her jitters did not show, Valerie suggested, "How about this coming weekend?"

"*This* weekend? That's not much notice."

*I* didn't have much notice. "You and Dad are retired, Mom."

Mom tipped her head, considering. "I'll need to check with your father, but sure. We'd love to see you and Simon."

"And Mom . . ."

"What, hon?"

"Can you watch Simon for me at the beginning of your visit?"

"The fog begins to lift. Who is he?"

"Yes, I'm seeing someone. He asked me on a getaway weekend." And to the launch, to see him go *very* far away. It was all Valerie could do not to shiver.

Ever since Marcus had called from the training center to invite her, she had been putting off this conversation. Unless Mom came to watch Simon this trip could not happen, and scarier than seeing Marcus off was *not* to see him off.

What came next? "You're not married," perhaps. Valerie saw nowhere to go from there, beyond agreement. Or, "How well do you know this man?" Just five months, Mom, and mostly from afar, but if that is not long at all, it seems long. In a good way. Or, perhaps, "What are the sleeping arrangements?" Marcus, whether he was being gallant or sensitive, obtuse or still hung up on Lindsey, had offered separate rooms if Valerie wanted. She didn't know what she wanted!

And the scariest question of all: "Do you love him?"

She only knew with certainty that she had loved one man. He had gone to Afghanistan and never come back. Deep in her gut, experience warned: love equaled loss.

Did she love Marcus? Probably. Almost certainly. But love wasn't real until the word came out of her mouth—and out of his. And if love equaled loss—

Did part of her *want* Mom to talk her out of going?

For all the scenarios Valerie had imagined, she had missed one.

"Dad and I loved Keith, too," Mom said. "His death was a tragedy. But, hon . . . ?"

Valerie waited.

"Your father will be *so* happy you're getting on with your life."

* * *

The circuitously routed, many-times encrypted e-mail reached Yakov in his embassy office. Merely the message's origin on The Space Place, were the wrong parties to take notice, might raise inconvenient suspicions, but he did not worry. Russian programmers were among the best in the world, and the Federal Security Service engaged only the best of the best.

And she who personally handled his information security? She was the most skilled of all. Yakov trusted in her talents without reservation, no matter how very far removed infosec was from his own expertise. It was not only that at the highest levels of the Counterintelligence Directorate, her exploits were legendary. The CIA, MI5, and the Mossad all wanted dearly to nail the hacker they knew only as "Psycho Cyborg."

Boasts were cheap. Survival convinced.

Unwrapped and decoded, the message to Yakov read, simply, *P-K4.* Pawn to king four, in the classic, descriptive chess notation that Yakov still favored.

Pawn to king four: the opening move of many a game.

The Americans, oblivious, did not know they were in a game. Or that there was a game to be in. Or that, with his men in place, the game clock was running. Or that the stakes of the game were—the world.

Entering his own terse message, to Psycho Cyborg herself, Yakov took the next move. *It is time for things to get hot,* he wrote.

Very hot.

**M**arcus's flight from Houston and Valerie's flight from D.C. came into the same terminal. Good: He could meet her at her gate. To meet at baggage claim would be in no way romantic.

Their hug was satisfactorily *It's been* way *too long,* but in the accompanying kiss, passionate though it was, he sensed a trace of *But why am I here?* He hoped he was wrong.

"Baggage claim?" he asked. Not for him: Cosmic Adventures had checked most of his luggage through to Canaveral Spaceport.

"Only my carry-on. I like to travel light."

"One more reason you're a keeper."

A smile came and went. "Lead on."

They picked up their rental car and hit the road. His flight had been late, but hers later; he worried that they would not get where he wanted in time. Once they left the Interstate, palm trees and gated communities lined the roads. The traffic sucked.

"I'm still not seeing why you picked Tampa," she said. Because they would have a three-hour drive Monday morning to Cape Canaveral. She would have a two-hour solo drive back across the state to catch her return flight.

Not Tampa, just its airport. "You will." He hoped.

Making small talk and catching up, they drove the length of Cape Haze. The sun sank lower and lower, and his anxiety grew. At the little town of Placida, they took the bridge—with its unconscionable tolls, to discourage the riffraff —to Gasparilla Island.

"Any relation to sarsaparilla?" she asked.

"The perhaps fictitious Spanish pirate, José Gaspar, is big business in these parts."

"Huh. So our weekend has a pirate theme?"

"Arrr, matey." Though he still wondered if anyone would be shivering his timber.

As they began passing large private homes on ocean-facing lots, she looked surprised. He pulled to a stop on the shoulder. "Right: not a hotel. This is a friend's second home, and she's letting me use it." The sun peeked out *between* houses. There was just one way to make it. "Val, I propose that we go straight to dinner while we can enjoy the sunset. We can unpack later." And postpone the conversation about into which bedroom to set her bag.

"Sure. I mean, arrr."

The restaurant near the island's south end was unassuming—but oh, the view! Florida was not quite yet in season, and they almost had the place to themselves. They took a table on the patio, near the beach, and he ordered wine. The sun, red and fat, almost kissed the horizon. Long, slow combers washed up the sand. The breeze from the ocean was cool.

He asked, "How are your parents?"

"Good."

"They don't mind keeping an eye on Simon?"

"Let me put it this way. They may not notice that I'm gone."

"Simon sent me a note. Did you know that? Told me not to let you eat kiwi, that you'd blow up like a balloon."

"I can't have *any* secrets?" She sighed melodramatically.

They finished the carafe and started a second. Seagulls glided low over the waves while a brown pelican settled noisily onto a spray-slick boulder. The sun had all but disappeared, painting ocean and a rim of sky the color, somewhere between pink and red, to which he could never put a name. "Let's take a walk before ordering."

She nodded.

They slipped off their shoes to play tag with the waves. Hand in hand they strolled along the beach. By the time they reclaimed their table, the sun had gone and the stars were out. Gazing over the water, utterly relaxed, he said, "I could sit all night listening to the surf."

"Marcus." She sounded serious.

He turned as she took his hand. "Yes?"

"How would you feel about listening to the surf from the house?" And somehow imagining he could have missed her point, she clarified, "And not necessarily sitting."

After a weekend of intimacy, the ride across Alligator Alley was much too short. Valerie dreaded watching Marcus leave—

While he could hardly wait for his flight to begin.

Spotting the first Cosmic Adventures billboard, it hit her. This is it. He *is* going. But Marcus was *so* excited, and not just at the adventure. He truly believed in powersats as safe energy for everyone. In some measure, he even went to PS-1 to protect her work.

He chattered enthusiastically, while her spirits yo-yoed, the entire drive.

Of the early Space Age, only vestiges remained at Canaveral Spaceport. The Rocket Garden. The enormous Vehicle Assembly Building, in which Saturn V moon rockets and then space shuttles were once prepped for flight. A few launch complexes, including the pad reactivated in haste after the discovery of Phoebe.

Tourist attractions and historical monuments.

And diminishing it further: hotels, hangars and warehouses, and, finally, a low, garish terminal structure.

But it was his terminal. The gateway to his adventure. For his great cause.

With pride and fear, she walked Marcus to the departures counter. Kissing him bon voyage, she knew his mind was already far, far away.

* * *

Afloat in the cabin of the Cosmic Adventures shuttle, Marcus thanked his stomach for staying put. Savvy Morgan and Olivia Finch floated with him, but Reuben Swenson, clutching an airsick bag, remained belted into his seat. Earthlight—mostly the reflected blue of the oceans—did nothing for his pallor.

The loudspeaker clicked. "Commencing a slow roll in sixty seconds," Captain Blackwell announced, then gave them a countdown from ten. "Commencing roll."

Marcus took hold of his seatback. As Earth vanished, the cockpit camera's view popped up. Phoebe's sunshield came into view. PS-1 was a dark square beside it, The Space Place a brilliant dot beyond them both. He did not yet see Phoebe.

"Enjoy the view of the powersat while you . . ." Blackwell chuckled. "Sorry folks, habit. My standard patter. You're the ones who'll decide when PS-1 gets the go-ahead for GEO."

"No rush," Savvy said, grinning.

Reuben, contributing once again to his barf bag, seemed to differ.

"With such a knowledgeable bunch on my ship, maybe I should be the one asking questions." The captain paused. "No? Then maybe you have questions for me."

"What about solar flares?" Reuben asked. From his tone of voice, he hoped one might put him out of his misery.

"Good question," Blackwell said. "Sunspots run in eleven-year cycles, and we're near the peak of a cycle. We are apt to see more flares than usual. Flare radiation can travel at half or more light speed, so there's not a lot of warning.

"Earth's atmosphere blocks the radiation, but of course we're well above the atmosphere. That, and the short notice, is why space habitats have radiation shelters. The Space Place has the fancy kind: they can project a big electromagnetic field to deflect the radiation. Phoebe does it the easy way: a deep tunnel. This ship's metal hull is inherently a shelter, too, though not thick enough that you'd want to spend hours aboard during adverse conditions."

"And if a flare hits while we're at work on PS-1?" Olivia asked.

"Little metal closets," Marcus said. He wanted the inspectors in the habit of asking *him* their questions about PS-1. "Only for emergencies, though. With the typical warning, workers can get back to Phoebe."

"About that warning," Captain Blackwell said, "there are solar observatories for spotting solar flares and such. You'll always have several minutes warning, usually more. Plenty of time to get into a shelter. Solar astronomers can even sometimes predict a flare."

"How good are space-weather predictions?" Reuben persisted.

"About like weather forecasting fifty years ago," Blackwell answered cheerfully. "Enough about that. I need to get back to work, and you need to return to your seats."

Buckling up, Marcus studied the cockpit-camera view. Black on black, very faintly, a glob stood out against the darkness of space. Phoebe. He watched it grow.

Reuben leaned across the aisle toward Marcus. "And such?"

"And such *what*?" Marcus asked back.

"The captain. She said solar flares and such. What's *such*?"

"Coronal mass ejections. CMEs. In layman's terms, a radiation shit storm."

CMEs were among the space hazards with which PS-1 had to coexist, so Marcus knew a fair amount about them. The typical CME was a few billion tons of matter flung from the sun's corona, heated to plasma, traveling at a million or more miles per hour.

Given all the directions in which the sun *could* spit out CMEs, you hoped one did not come straight at Earth. When a major CME did, it fried electronics, garbled radio transmissions, and induced continent-spanning current surges powerful enough to disrupt, sometimes even crash, power grids. And that was inside an atmosphere to take the brunt of the abuse.

None of which, Marcus decided, would reassure Reuben. "But like flares, the space weather system monitors for them."

Reuben groaned. "Tell me again why I volunteered for this joyride?"

"Final approach," Blackwell announced.

A rocky mass emerged from the darkness, growing by the second. A sprinkling of lights marked the main base and its outbuildings. A necklace of strobing lights defined a landing zone. Distant from both sets of lights, glimpsed only in profile as a bite out of the star field: the automated infrared observatory. Blacker than black: the inky depths of the Grand Chasm.

Marcus had seen most of Phoebe on security cams and from rented bots—but never like this. Never in person. And in minutes, he would *be* on Phoebe.

Reuben Swenson looked like he still expected an answer.

"You volunteered," Marcus told him, "in a good cause."

The most fun to be had around Phoebe base involved flying a hopper to or from PS-1, but Thad could not shake a sense of impending doom. It did not help that Reuben Swenson, rather than trusting his seat belt or gripping the rear-saddle handholds, clung to Thad like a remora. Counterpressure suits, skintight, hid nothing.

Crescent Earth, mostly ocean and clouds, hung overhead. PS-1, straight ahead, glittered in the sunlight. To Thad's left and right, about forty yards distant, a hopper paralleled his course. Marcus Judson piloted on the left, with Olivia behind him. Savannah Morgan flew solo on his right, ideally not attempting, as she had joked, to "improve" the console user-interface software while on their way.

On Thad's command console, the PS-1 icon remained centered in the nav window. In his rearview camera, the compressed-nitrogen spray propelling the hopper dissipated over a very short distance from white fog to invisible. The hopper trembled as Reuben squirmed on his saddle. The wiggling was nothing their gyros couldn't sense or attitude jets manage—just annoying.

A console LED blinked twice as Thad's countdown timer, its digits green for *go* phase, broke sixty seconds. "Coming up on coasting phase," he radioed. "How's everyone doing?"

He got back a chorus of goods and fines. Only one response sounded insincere, but even Reuben, on the ass-end of the curve for acclimating to zero gee, had performed suit and hopper exercises to Thad's satisfaction.

And in a pinch Thad could activate the autopilots on any of the hoppers, fly one by remote control, even fly all three in formation. For now he only kept watch, the imagery from his hopper's sideways-looking cameras streaming into corners of his HUD.

"Are the hopper nav computers ever turned off?" Marcus asked hopefully.

"Not on purpose," Thad lied. "Pilots, watch your timers." At zero he cut off his hopper's thruster. Only a few seconds late—nothing the nav software could not handle—his charges did, too. On his console the timer reset to seven minutes, now in the yellow of the coasting phase, and resumed counting down.

"Thruster reversed," Savannah was the first to announce. "But for the record, I feel cheated."

"Not me," Marcus said. "I want to *see* myself arrive at PS-1, not back into it."

Amen to that, Thad thought. "Test reversal, everyone."

If anyone's gas valve had malfunctioned, they had time to pivot with their attitude jets. Savannah might get her wish. But every hopper gave a puff of thruster gas from its bow.

They coasted, while PS-1 grew and grew. Marcus and Savannah switched to a private channel, presumably to discuss an inspection protocol.

These were competent people, even (in other circumstances) likable people. Almost certainly, Thad had concluded after a day spent working with them, after finding some reason to be alone with each of them, they were not—not any of them—Yakov's people.

*Prepare the artifacts and await contact. Do not reveal yourself unnecessarily, but the success of the mission comes first.*

None of the newcomers had even hinted at another role, or shown awareness of what Thad had built—and hidden—so long ago. If he was not to hand off the devices, what had Yakov meant?

Flashing interrupted Thad's brooding. "Prepare for maneuver," he radioed. With better precision than on their earlier maneuvers, his apprentices started their hoppers decelerating. The timers had reset again, now decrementing in the red of *stop* phase. PS-1 loomed larger than ever. In fifteen minutes they would be docking.

*Prepare the artifacts and await contact. Do not reveal yourself unnecessarily, but the success of the mission comes first.*

His mind skittered around and around the same nasty suspicion. He wasn't delivering his contraband devices *to* a visitor. Did that mean he would be turning the devices *against* one?

How much longer must he wait for Yakov's mysterious contact?

\* \* \*

Dillon floated in the hotel's renowned Grand Atrium, a clear bubble more than two hundred feet in diameter. Many of the guests—and so, too, much of the staff—were outside, suited up and riding hoppers, playing or observing space polo. He hoped they would stay outside for a good, long while. He liked having this volume almost to himself.

After the past several weeks, he needed to relax—and at last he could. He had gotten Jonas, Lincoln, and Felipe aboard The Space Place, with no trace of a connection to Yakov. And accomplished it so smoothly Dillon could almost wish he had asked Crystal along.

Not that she would have come. The extravagance of his outing had made her furious, and he could not explain. Once he got home he would make it up to her. Somehow.

My job, thank Gaia, is done. And that means *I'm* done. Yakov had promised.

Air currents had wafted Dillon toward the hotel's north pole, giving him a great view of the hotel's rings. The outer ring spun as always at a stately two revolutions per minute. The inner ring (really, only three "elevator" cars connected by curved structural elements) was spinning down. He wondered who was entering and leaving this unspun central volume.

If the rings marked the hotel's equator, he was at around fifty degrees north latitude. (*Fifty-four forty or fight*, bubbled up from some deep recess of his memory. He had no idea what that meant.) Small bubbles, zero-gee private rooms (and, in the unlikely event of an air leak, shelters), ringed the atrium at thirty degrees latitude, both north and south. Hatches to the two arcs of escape pods lay at about sixty degrees south latitude.

Jonas, Lincoln, and Felipe disdained most zero-gee sports, so they would not be outside playing or watching polo. They were not enjoying the freedom and view here in the grand atrium. So where were "his" employees? After sports and zoning out, the main attraction here was freefall sex. Maybe they were to be found among the wobbling private bubbles.

If Yakov had had a reason for placing three deniable representatives aboard this hotel—and ruining Dillon's life to do it—he had yet to discern it.

* * *

A vast, dark plain hid half the sky. PS-1 did not *really* extend forever, but from where Marcus glided, a few feet above, the difference was not obvious.

"Be alert, people. We're coming up on a row of docking posts," Thad radioed.

Marcus's hopper had slowed to less than a slow walk. He switched his main display from nav mode to landing mode, then guided a targeting circle over the nearest docking post. The circle flashed. "I have target lock," he reported.

"Lock here, too," Savannah called.

"Go," Thad said.

Marcus double-tapped the console's touch panel and his hopper ejected its docking tether. The gas-propelled tip—guided by hopper sensors through the cable at the tether's core—wrapped itself around and around the post. With another few taps he turned off the hopper's main thruster and started the take-up reel. A spurt of gas killed his forward momentum as the last of the docking tether wound onto its spool.

"Touchdown. The crowd goes wild," he radioed.

From the adjacent post, Thad said, "We'll call it a two-point conversion if you dismount without floating away or putting a boot through the solar cells."

Marcus and the rest had practiced dismounts in the neutral buoy-ancy tank in Houston and again on a mock-up on the surface of Phoebe; this was *not* the same. The surface that glittered a few feet beneath his boots was fragile and wafer thin. A typical expanse of the powersat (moved to the Earth's surface) would have weighed a fraction of an ounce per square foot. By the time he had reached the annular plat-form at the base of the post, he was soaked in sweat.

Olivia clambered down beside him. "Wow," she mouthed.

"You said it." Only *wow* did not begin to express his feelings. Maybe no words could.

They had docked about halfway out from the powersat's center, near a diagonal. Guide cables and catwalks crisscrossed the delicate sur-face. A primary computing node, where Savannah would do much of her inspection, was a mere few hundred feet away. Beyond the comput-ing node, Marcus spotted the array of connectors, most still unoccu-pied, where robotic spacecraft would someday dock to designate new downlink coordinates.

Here and there, metal closets: radiation shelters. At risk of freezing off your privates, they were outhouses, too, because the closets stocked urine collection devices. Bleed oh-two into a shelter and you could safely open a counterpressure-suit fly. Only be *really* careful about resealing the fly before opening the shelter hatch . . . .

He scanned more systematically. All around, scuttling robots. A pair of human workers removing a solar panel to access the klystron-and-antenna array on the satellite's other side. Farther still, along the powersat's closest edge: some of the many thrusters that would—if this inspection trip went well—lift PS-1 to GEO. And in the distance, back the way they had come, two hoppers flying in tandem, towing a loaded cargo pallet. Midsurvey, when he turned his back to the sun, his visor automatically depolarized.

One by one, everyone descended their docking post and checked in. "All right," Marcus said. "Everyone has their assignments for today—"

Text popped up on his HUD. *Incoming call from Earth.*

Huh? This was not a public link. "Going private for a moment," he told everyone. "Take the call," he told his suit. "Hello?"

"Hey there, spaceman," Ellen's familiar voice greeted him. "It's Wednesday."

So? "We just docked with PS-1. We're about ready to get to work."

"How does it feel?" Ellen asked. "Having status to *give* at a weekly meeting? And from PS-1, not our dreary conference room?"

It felt great!

*　*　*

Thad went off to lend a hand to some Kendricks workers. Savannah settled down by one of the powersat's four primary computer complexes; its open access panel cast a faint shadow by earthlight. Olivia and Reuben meandered across the vast structure, taking measurements and capturing vids as they went.

Marcus waited to be called upon.

Every so often Reuben removed a solar panel and the transmitter panel beneath, sticking his head through the hole to study the powersat's other side. He and Olivia went on and off their own private channel, dictating their detailed findings, but once, while within an expanse of microwave antennas, with only his legs showing, Reuben forgot to switch channels. "Like God's own horn section," he muttered.

For a while Marcus trailed after the pair. But that was silly; he could not lose them. Counterpressure suits used the same color-coding as flight suits. The green-suited figures together were Reuben and Olivia. The green suit by itself, other than Marcus's own, was Savvy. (Thad, in blue, having joined a crowd of Kendricks workers, could have been anyone.) If Marcus did manage to lose track of a colleague, the helmet-cam views relayed to his HUD still showed everything he could need to see. If he wanted to look from other angles, he had plenty of experience remotely accessing PS-1's onboard cameras.

He stopped following them.

To Savvy's tuneless humming he watched bots transfer concrete structural elements from a recently arrived pallet to a parts depot. Amazing stuff, that concrete: a blend of dust, carbon nanotubes, and glue, every ingredient mined and manufactured on Phoebe.

All around him bots scuttled about clutching instruments, tiny tools, and spare parts: measuring, adjusting, replacing. Many bots moved alone; others worked in teams to manipulate objects much larger than themselves. He played a game with himself, trying to guess which bots were guided by onboard programs and which obeyed the dictates of human operators. Logic said most bots had to be autonomous: one unit per ten thousand square feet did not seem like much, but across the vastness of PS-1, that came to more than ten thousand bots.

It was enough tiny pliers, screwdrivers, and whatnot for ten Santa's workshops. He tried to imagine little elfin hats and tiny, upturned slippers on all those bots.

He monitored the remote readouts of the inspection team's oh-two. He unplugged and removed a random solar panel (freakishly thin!) and the microwave-transmitter panel beneath, peeking through in an impromptu inspection of his own. Unlike the solar-cell side on which, for their own safety, everyone worked, the transmitter side was uncluttered: no shelters or depots or guide wires or *anything* that might scatter microwaves. He put the panels back in place, careful not to chip the strong-but-brittle Phoebecrete struts.

He glided hand over hand along one of the guide cables, just for the practice, to a catwalk far across PS-1. The powersat was too vast and thin to be mechanically rigid, and as Marcus flew along he sensed the immense structure bending and flexing. But that was impossible; the perception was—had to be—in his mind.

To form and focus power beams required knowing *exactly* the relative positions of all the many thousand microwave transmitters. Sensor arrays detected PS-1's every flexure and tremor. Electro-elastic fibers constantly tensed and relaxed under real-time software control, synchronized by any of PS-1's four atomic clocks, to maintain precise alignment by damping out any vibration. And just in case the anti-trembling system failed, transmitters turned themselves off—not that PS-1 *was* transmitting—if independent accelerometers ever indicated that flexing had gone out of tight tolerance. It was another complex set of functions that Savvy would be testing another day.

Another day in which he would be on call, floating around and watching. He wondered if the workers might let him help . . . with *something*.

A robot labeled 3056 waited nearby, inert. Marcus tapped command codes into the wireless keypad strapped to his left forearm, but 3056 did not stir.

"Thad," he radioed. "Why can't I get a construction bot to move? We're all supposed to have sysadmin privileges for our inspection. That authorization should be more than adequate." Because there *isn't* any more privileged level.

"You'd think." Thad sighed. "I created new accounts for your buddies, but you already had an account up here. I never got around to upgrading your authorization. Sorry. Give me two minutes. Once that's done, you'll need to jack into a local comm node."

"Okay, thanks. And I should have remembered about using the local terminal." Because these are serious bots, doing serious work, not toys like Val and I use to stroll about Phoebe. The wireless links to *these* bots were heavily encrypted.

Marcus linked his forearm keypad to a nearby comm node with a fiber-optic cable from his tool kit. This time when he gave an order, 3056 scuttled away from him. He lined up four idle bots and sent them off onto a hundred-yard dash. Controlling them with codes was less natural than with the game-controller interface he and Val used with the Phoebe bots, but still easy enough. With his helmet camera he shot a vid of them scrambling, and mailed it to her. *Thinking of you,* the accompanying note read.

On his return trip across the powersat Marcus peeked into supply depots and counted oxygen tanks, water bottles, and charged batteries. He sampled the pap—both varieties were foul—from his helmet dispensers. He tried and failed to perceive the functioning of the attitude system, thrusters cooperating to keep PS-1's solar cells facing toward the sun. With a grin every time he looked overhead, he savored the ever-changing panorama that was Earth.

After a couple of hours, he was bored.

"Savvy," he radioed. "Private channel three." For no special reason, he waved at her. She waved back. "How's it going?"

"I'm still poking around, but so far, no surprises. As advertised, several critical functions for aiming the beam are hardware controlled. Beaming only works if the designated collection point radioed to PS-1 matches—in hardware—lat/long values preconfigured in a control-module port. And the powersat's failsafe handshake with an aiming beacon at the authorized downlink point is all done in hardware, too."

"That's all good, isn't it?"

"Outstanding, if it holds up. I haven't yet emptied my bag of dirty tricks. Even though I've confirmed aiming is hardware controlled, there's still *some* access from the ground. There has to be. To choose from among the authorized downlink sites. To start and stop transmissions. To initiate and read out onboard diagnostics. To control thrusters for orbital station-keeping and the eventual boost to GEO. I need to make sure that when using—or misusing—those few ground-accessible functions, I can't get into anything else."

"To do what?" he asked.

"Just let me do my job, okay?"

A priority alert started blinking on his HUD, but he figured he could finish the discussion. A comm emergency override took that decision from him.

●  ●  ●

Dillon's stomach gurgled and he thought maybe he would head to the gravity ring soon. Some guests spent their whole stay in freefall, but Dillon did not see the point in eating from a squeeze tube when minutes away there was a four-star restaurant at one-third gee.

Soon, but not yet. Except for Maria Portillo, one of the women who had been on his shuttle, he had the northern hemisphere to himself and that hardly ever happened. Arms and legs fluttering, expending more energy than he cared to, she did slow laps through the air. With flippers on her feet, her long black hair loose and flowing, she brought to mind a mermaid.

The only distractions were distant oofs and grunts. While the northern hemisphere was one wide-open expanse, nets and taut ropes ran every which way through the southern. Once you acclimated to zero gee, you could get a hell of a good gymnastic workout there; until then you could make your way through as though on monkey bars. Not coincidentally, arriving passengers disembarked their shuttles through the air lock at the hotel's south pole.

Earth shone through the wall. Dillon found it inexpressibly calming. If only everyone could experience Mother Earth this way, surely many more would fight the good fight to protect her.

Whenever air currents nudged him to face south, the polo game came into view beyond the clear, curved wall. Hoppers darting. Tethered onlookers maneuvering with gas pistols to keep out of the players' way. The strobing red balloon "ball" sailing hither and yon, now and again scoring through the illuminated goal loops sited at three points of the game triangle. Had another few people chosen to play, there would have been a fourth goal, defining a tetrahedron.

The stupid polo game would not last forever. With a sigh, Dillon reached for the small gas pistol clipped to his belt—and his hand bumped someone. Twisting around to see whom sent them drifting apart. "Sorry, Maria."

"My fault." Her English had a charming Latin accent. "I should watch where I am wafting."

"Where's Adriana today? Outside?"

"What happens in The Space Place stays in The Space Place." Maria gestured at the nearest private bubbles, some of them set opaque. "Your colleagues, too?"

"Maybe." He changed the subject. Maria and Adriana had turned out to be high-ranking marketing execs at Bolivian National Lithium Company. He could handle getting some cartel money invested into Russo Venture Capital Partners. "I was about to head out for lunch on the ring. Care to join me?"

"That would be very nice."

He offered a hand. With gentle puffs of his gas pistol he delivered them to the equator, to the webbing beside a door. She stowed her flippers in a mesh pouch. The inner ring was despun and they went, feet first, through the connecting tube onto an elevator car. They slipped their feet through loops on the car's back wall. He pressed the panel marked OUTER RING.

The inner door closed. Unseen circuits activated. Electromagnets in the elevator cars pressed against Earth's much larger magnetic field, and the inner ring began to spin. The wall to which they had attached themselves became the floor. A progress bar on a wall display tracked their gradual spin-up.

"After hours adrift, gravity feels odd," she said.

And it was not even *much* gravity. At max, on the outer ring, the spin simulated one-third Earth's gravity. Spinning any faster, the Coriolis effect would have made many people ill.

"Ding," he announced, in unison with the elevator, evoking a smile. A floor panel slid open, and they stepped down the ladder in the connecting tunnel to the outer ring. What had become a ceiling panel slid shut, and a door opened in their tunnel. They walked out onto the central aisle of the outer ring.

"Coming through," a woman's voice called.

"Good day, Captain Aganga," Dillon said, no matter that *captain* was a pretentious title for a hotelier. The long-term staff lived and, when they could, worked on the outer ring, where gravity helped maintain their bone mass. They still had to exercise, though.

Their hostess was jogging toward them, in an odd gliding pace adapted to the low gravity. She was very tall and very dark. Sweat soaked her hair band, ran down her neck and face, and glued her T-shirt to an admirable physique. She blotted her face with a towel as she went past. "Mr. Russo. Dr. Portillo." And then she was past them.

"On to lunch," Dillon said. He and Maria walked in the opposite direction to the captain, past machine shops, supply rooms, and engineering sections, toward the dining room. They encountered Jonas, wearing a sweatsuit, a towel draped over one shoulder, leaning against a doorjamb, phone in hand. Catching his breath, Dillon supposed.

"Hello, boss." Jonas saluted. Mockingly? "Maria."

"Hello," they said.

Maria followed Dillon's lead and kept walking.

Farther down the hall, they found Felipe also standing, also dressed to jog and holding a phone. "That's two of you. Where's Lincoln?" Dillon asked.

Felipe made a crude gesture. "Occupied."

"Show some manners," Dillon snapped, appalled.

He and Maria came to the dining room. Chamber music played softly. Mozart, he thought. Something smelled wonderful. The maître d' came scuttling up—

And sirens began to wail.

*　*　*

In the tunnels of Phoebe and in the chambers, large and small, of The Space Place, loudspeakers came to life. Aboard every ship and within every spacesuit—around PS-1, too—every radio receiver flipped to its emergency channel. Everywhere, sirens wailed.

Then the recording began, identical in every location.

"Alert. Alert. This is not a drill. The Space Weather Prediction Center predicts a major solar event. Report at once to the nearest radiation shelter. Alert. Alert . . ."

illon and Maria swam from the elevator into the Grand Atrium—and chaos.

"First things first," he told her. "Spacesuits."

"Right."

They pulled themselves along ropes to the southern row of rooms. In the bubble next to him, the wall rippled and vibrated, frantic rather than erotic. Dillon said, "The fastest way to change is with a partner." He followed her to her room and helped her into her counterpressure suit. In his room, she returned the favor. Each stripped naked in the process, and there was nothing erotic about that, either.

The loudspeakers blared, and he recognized Captain Aganga's resonant voice. "All guests are to put on vacuum gear and proceed to the southern air lock. This is not a drill. The elevators will cease operation shortly, once supervisors confirm evacuation of the outer ring. Proceed as quickly as you safely can to the south-polar air lock. Staff there will check your suits. Once outside, other staff will guide you . . ."

The polo players and observers were mostly still outside. Through the clear walls of the Grand Atrium, Dillon saw a freefall scuffle break out over a stash of oxygen bottles, even as a hopper approached towing a fresh supply.

"I don't *understand*," Maria said. "Why are we going outside into lethal radiation? I thought the hotel has electromagnetic shielding, that the whole place is a radiation shelter."

That had been explained, but he knew he hadn't internalized all the bad news. He guessed she hadn't, either. "I heard the captain say the shield generator has failed. We have to evacuate."

"To Earth?"

From more than four thousand miles up? Anyone evacuating by escape pod would get a fatal dose of radiation long before reaching the ground. And—sudden intuitive flash—their safe evacuation to Earth could do nothing to advance Yakov's plan. Whatever the hell that was.

"I don't know," Dillon lied. "We need to get going."

Captain Aganga had been drenched with sweat from her jog, but Felipe and Jonas had been fresh and dry. Because rather than catching their breaths, they were lookouts. They had been keeping watch for Lincoln, the electrical-engineering wizard. Had EM SHIELD been a placard on a door between the two men? Dillon was almost sure it was.

By the south-polar air lock, people had queued up. Some carried bags, small suitcases, or even, in one case, a backpack. Most, like he and Maria, had only the spacesuit they wore.

He thought, We look like refugees.

Aganga continued directing the evacuation. "There are too few staff to pilot all the hoppers. Any guest qualified to fly a hopper is invited to identify herself to the staff inside the air lock. Hotel personnel will as-sign guests to hoppers for the flight to Phoebe."

"Phoebe!" Maria shuddered. "That's *far*. And off-limits."

Two hundred miles. "The depths of Phoebe are the only possible radiation haven we can reach. They have no choice but to accept us."

And that must have been Yakov's plan! Somehow. Part of it, anyway. Dillon no longer flattered himself he understood his erstwhile "part-ner."

How could even *Yakov* plan for a CME to come shooting at Earth?

Someone in staff livery came speeding by, and Maria grabbed his sleeve. She said, "Hoppers? Why not the escape pods?"

"Sorry, ma'am. The pods do one thing: return to Earth if something goes catastrophically wrong." (Something *had* gone catastrophically wrong, Dillon thought. As always, people had anticipated the wrong catastrophe.) "To keep the pods simple and reliable, that is all they can do. Once lit, the solid-fuel retrorocket runs till it burns out. The pods will deorbit; they cannot be used to maneuver *in* orbit. If you'll excuse me?"

"But I don't want—"

"That's just how it is, ma'am." Shaking off Maria's hand, the hotel worker rushed off.

* * *

By the time Thad's charges had regrouped at their docking posts, the evacuation of PS-1 was well underway. "We have plenty of time," he had assured them, hoping he was right.

They had the good sense to keep chatter to a minimum, or at least to use private channels among themselves.

Forty tourists? Twenty hotel staff? Phoebe's population was about to quadruple. It was going to be cozy in the shelter.

Oxygen and water for the extra people would not be a problem; Phoebe produced those for The Space Place in the first place. But what else might they need in the shelter? Food. First-aid kits. Blankets. Flashlights and a battery assortment. Datasheets, because the CME could take hours to stream past. Critical spare parts for—he was not sure what, and hoped someone had had time to think that through. Counting only the staff, the number of toilets in the shelter was marginal. So: bunches of urine collection devices, and fresh piddle pads for the ladies.

A CME could fry satellites and much of Phoebe's surface gear. The bigger the structure, the more susceptible, to both charge buildup and induced currents. In theory, PS-1 had been designed to handle a CME. He guessed they would find out.

The hopper garage was crowded by the time Thad got to Phoebe. Waving the inspection team toward the main air lock, he advised, "In you go. Anything small you guys may want with you in the shelter, get it now."

"Is there time to change into clothes?" Reuben asked.

"Is there time to check messages?" Marcus asked.

"You figure that out," Thad said. "Just be inside the shelter in fifteen minutes." Because in not much longer, the first wave of the Phoebe evacuees would descend on them. Soon after that Phoebe would emerge from behind Earth.

Soon after *that*, the leading edge of the CME would burst over them.

After cycling through the air lock, they grabbed Velcro slippers from the wall rack and scattered. Thad joined them in flouting the rule about keeping spacesuits near the entrance. He dashed to his own room to find the message-waiting light blinking on his comm console. Not forwarded while he had been out, he supposed, because the recall had put local networks into overload. He tapped DISPLAY NEXT.

*Take care of yourself. Cousin Jonas is coming. Your cousin, Jacob.*

This is not happening! Thad told himself.

He yanked open the deepest drawer in his small dresser and flung the clothes from it into his hammock. With a nail file jammed into the crack he pried up the drawer's false bottom. Beneath lay the parcel hidden for *so* long. He stuffed the parcel and fresh batteries into a tote bag, covered everything with a clean jumpsuit, and put the false bottom and wadded clothing back in their places.

Then he sped to the main air lock. "Cousin Jonas" would be among the soon-to-arrive tourists.

*       *       *

*Do not reveal yourself unnecessarily.* The words gave Thad hope Yakov's other agents would not reveal him if he cooperated. He might yet come through . . .

Through what? He had no inkling, beyond *something bad*.

Just inside the main air lock he found a frightened-looking crowd, all wearing red or yellow counterpressure suits: tourists or hotel staff. Helmets in hand, borrowed Velcro slippers crammed over their boots, they shuffled down the station's central corridor into the station. Here and there an evacuee carried a suitcase or a pitiful satchel.

Thad noticed three men in red at the rear of the procession, looking all around. Why had they caught his eye? Because they looked more composed than the rest?

The chief had put on a fresh jumpsuit for the occasion. "This way," he urged, waving evacuees down a cross corridor. "I'm Irv Weingart, station chief on Phoebe. Our deep shelter is this way. This way, people. I'm . . ."

The shortest man among the trio fixed his eyes on Thad. "Cousin Thaddeus?" The man managed the Polish pronunciation, something Thad had only heard from a great aunt. "Is that really *you?*"

Yakov's contact. "Yes, it's me. Small world, Jonas."

The three men angled over to Thad. "Where are they?" the short one hissed.

"Follow me," Thad whispered. He ushered them into a nearby pantry.

The pantry was empty—not only of people, but with many of its shelves cleared. Thad reached into his tote and delivered the parcel and the sack of batteries.

Jonas tore open the parcel, nodded approval, and put everything into his satchel. "These better work."

"They will." Thad opened the door. "We have to get into the shelter."

"In a minute." Jonas seemed oddly indifferent to the CME racing their way. "Now give me user ID and password for a sysadmin account for the powersat."

"It's useless. Sysadmin log-on only works from hardwired terminals on PS-1 itself." And going there *now*, with the CME about to strike, would be insanity. Thad could not get his mind around what these men thought to accomplish. "We have to get to the shelter."

"Indeed we do." Jonas smiled enigmatically. "Our mutual acquaintance told me that the magic word is 'Robin.' "

Thad flinched. "All right." He recited his log-on codes. "Now can we go?"

"We three will go. You have to disable long-range comm first."

"I *can't* turn off comm," Thad protested. "We have people still on the surface. They're shutting down and securing the observatory, solar-cell factory, nuclear power plant, and anything else they can get to in time."

"Long range," Jonas repeated. "As in, reaching Earth. But I said *disable*, not turn off."

"The long-range radio is already switched off as protection against the CME. If I turn it back on, the CME will get it."

"This isn't up for discussion." Pause. "Remember Robin."

"All right." For Robin. "Let me take you to the shelter before someone gets suspicious about us."

"We wouldn't have it any other way," Jonas repeated.

The surface crew, still in their vacuum gear, emerged from the main air lock as Thad shepherded Jonas and his companions toward the shelter. "Stragglers," Thad explained.

When they reached the entrance to the shelter, lights blazed inside. He wondered if anyone had thought about pumping out the heat from so many extra bodies, or to bring in extra fuel cells.

"*There* you are." Irv looked relieved. He stood beside an open hatch. "Cutting it close, don't you think? Go on down. I'm going to make one final sweep of the station."

Pausing on the ladder that led down a shaft into the shelter, Jonas shot a dark look over his shoulder.

"I'll check things out, Chief," Thad said.

"Station chief's prerogative."

"Our visitors have met you," Thad said, desperately. "You keep them calm while I do the run-through."

Irv shrugged. "Okay. Don't tarry."

Tarzan-swinging toward the command center, Thad tried to imagine an innocent-seeming way to disable comm. He could not just pop the circuit breaker or jiggle loose a socketed component. After the CME had passed, someone might get to the command center before him. But when the CME came through, all sorts of electronics would fry . . . .

He found heavy-gauge wire in a parts cabinet and snipped off a length. Gripping the wire with insulated pliers, he shorted the high-voltage terminal of the power supply to components inside the main radio console. Sparks flew. On circuit boards, devices went *pop*. Smoke erupted. For good measure he fried the diagnostic subsystem, too, then closed the cabinet doors.

By wrapping his hand in a handkerchief, he managed to coil the wire—still hot, its insulation bubbled and blackened—without doing harm to the fingers of his counterpressure suit. He rushed to his tiny room to cram the coiled wire under the drawer's false bottom. It would not do for anyone to find the wire.

He found Irv pacing outside the shelter entrance. "I was about to come looking for you."

"Ye of little faith," Thad said. "Let's go down."

*   *   *

Dillon stood in the shelter, obsessively looking around, obsessively checking the wall clock. The CME was almost upon them.

Welded aluminum panels lined the shelter, a volume hollowed out deep beneath Phoebe's main base. Phoebe's mines offered many minerals in abundance, but not metals. Those had to be lofted from Earth, and that happened only for a good reason. Such as providing a few key parts of PS-1. And a sturdier storm cellar . . .

A stranger (a woman, he thought) had shoved a drink bulb into his hands. Someone in a blue flight suit, anyway, so he or she was one of the Phoebe personnel. He had half drained the bulb before it registered that he had burnt his mouth on hot coffee. Tuning out the discomfort, he checked the clock again. Another minute had passed.

The shelter was full, but more people kept crowding inside. Dillon recognized maybe half the faces in the shelter, from among hotel guests and staff. A few others looked familiar. He guessed he had seen those people, in fact, remembered having had a dinnertime conversation with one, at space training in Houston.

That was another world. Literally.

Maria, reunited with Adriana, stood across the shelter speaking rapid-fire Spanish. At least Dillon thought it was Spanish. With so many people talking at once it was hard to tell.

Jonas, Felipe, and Lincoln were in a huddle near the entrance. They, like many of the evacuees, had blankets draped over their shoulders. Of the three, Dillon could see only Jonas's face. He looked tense.

Why the hell *not* look tense, Dillon thought. He still shook from the long hopper ride.

Jonas saw Dillon watching. "Join us," Jonas mouthed.

They were smart and tech-savvy. They would understand what was going on. As Dillon edged through the crowd to stand with them, more people came in. One gave Jonas a nervous, sideways glance.

Dillon flinched at a sudden loud booming. Looking toward the noise, he saw the station chief rapping on the still-open metal door. People turned, and some quieted down. More rapping and booming. The crowd gradually fell silent.

"May I have your attention?" Weingart said. The station chief's hand had moved to the metal door's simple latch handle. "According to forecasts, the leading edge of the CME will reach us in five minutes. It's time we close ourselves into the shelter to wait it out."

"Is everyone accounted for?" Jonas asked. "From Phoebe, the hotel, and PS-1?"

"Yes," Weingart said.

"Here, inside this room?" Jonas persisted. "Everyone."

"Yes." Weingart repeated impatiently. "It's time we—"

"Excellent," Jonas said. "My friends and I will be leaving."

"I cannot allow that," Weingart said. He began pulling the door. "We'll be all right."

"I'm afraid I must insist." Jonas threw off his blanket and dropped his bag. He held—a *gun*! So did Lincoln. Felipe had a gun in each hand.

At least the devices looked like guns. They had handgrips and outward-pointing metal rods. But unlike any gun Dillon had ever seen, the "barrel" was solid rather than hollow and was wrapped in wire coils. A metal doughnut, smaller in diameter than the coils, hugged the barrel at its handgrip end. A battery sat beneath the barrel.

"What is this?" Weingart asked. "Whatever you have in mind, forget it. It's about to become lethal out there."

"Nevertheless," Jonas said. "Felipe, give the boss his gun."

One of the odd guns was shoved into Dillon's hands!

At some level he must always have known Yakov would never let him go free, for an eerie calm washed over Dillon. He could stop thinking, stop speculating what he might do or should do or could do. He could not possibly disassociate himself from whatever was about to happen.

His only hope of a future lay in joining these men. A future in Russia, under the Russian equivalent of a witness-protection program, even if everything worked out—but still, a future. He wondered if Crystal would join him.

"It's suicide to go out there," Weingart said. "A very messy suicide. The radiation won't kill you immediately, but you'll get many times a lethal dose. I can't let you go."

Jonas waggled his gun. "You can't make us stay. Now back away from the door."

"I don't know what kind of Tinkertoy gadget you have—"

*Zap!*

Weingart gaped at the red, bloody hole in his thigh. For a moment, he looked stupefied. Then he crumpled, collapsing in slow motion.

In the sudden hush, Dillon heard the high-pitched whine of a circuit recharging.

"It's called a coil gun," Jonas said conversationally. He thumbed something on the handgrip. With a *click,* a new metal doughnut emerged and settled onto the barrel. "It uses electromagnets to accelerate a metal washer. Does anyone else require a demonstration?"

No one spoke.

Jonas smiled. "Good. Stay inside and you might live through this."

Felipe, Lincoln, Jonas, and Dillon backed out of the entrance, closing the hatch behind them.

* * *

The hatch slammed shut.

The *boom* of finality jarred everyone from their stunned silence. Around the shelter there were sudden shouts, and tears, and knots of whispered consultation.

Marcus shivered. He knew those men. From the training center. The one they called boss was—Marcus needed a moment to retrieve the name—Dillon Russo.

Phoebe's doctor was struggling through the crowd toward Irv Weingart. One of the hotel evacuees, shouting, "I'm a doctor," was pushing that way, too.

"*Quiet!*" Thad yelled, louder than anyone. "Everyone move against the walls, please, as best you can. Let the doctors through."

Marcus sidled backward, doing his part to clear a path, then twitched as someone grabbed his arm. Savvy.

"Those bastards trained with us!" she said. "I'm sure I saw them in Houston."

"I remember."

How *much* did he remember? One evening he had taken an empty seat at their table. All but Dillon had left. He and Dillon had discussed training, of course. But hadn't there been something else? Dillon had criticized Marcus for . . . eating meat.

Vegetarianism was not what bothered him. That was a lifestyle choice, and it did not mark someone as an extremist, let alone a terrorist. But Dillon had not criticized the animal rights aspect or the health benefits of a meat-free diet. He had complained that raising beef expended too much energy. The pieces fit.

"Shit!" Marcus said. "Almost certainly, the four of them are Resetter extremists. They'll be after PS-1!"

Thad must have heard. He pushed through to Marcus. "Tell me what you know."

Marcus told his story, ending with, "We have to stop them."

Thad tapped his wristwatch. "It's too late, unless you have a death wish."

No, but Dillon and his buddies must have one to expose themselves to a CME. Marcus wondered: Did the CME somehow figure into their plan?

The work crew had left PS-1 with its systems shut down, like unplugging a TV before a lightning storm. A CME washing over the powersat would still do some damage, but robots and spare parts staged inside metal sheds would handle any necessary repairs. Unless—

Marcus said, "If those guys reactivate PS-1, the CME damage will be bad. Very bad. Maybe start-over-from-scratch bad."

Thad looked conflicted. "They're out there, willing to die for their cause. We're in here. If *you* are nuts enough to leave the shelter, they're armed."

Marcus started unfolding his datasheet.

"What are you doing?" Savvy asked.

"Maybe we can net to the command center from here." Only the shelter walls were lined with metal. A Faraday cage. If they opened the hatch a crack and tossed out the datasheet, it could transmit a message to the command center. "Call down to NASA. They can order PS-1 into safe"—inert—"mode."

Thad shook his head. "Won't work. Our long-range comm is off for the CME."

"We have to do *something*." Marcus glanced over to where doctors still worked on Irv Weingart's leg. He looked zoned out on painkillers. "Who is in charge? I need to talk to him."

Thad smiled sadly. "With Irv out of commission? The sorry truth is, I'm in charge."

CONFLAGRATION | 2023

**Y**ou know what we know," said the man at the Space Weather Prediction Center.

Valerie heard exasperation in his voice, but suspected that she was projecting. She had been monitoring the news—for anything and every-thing about spaceflight—since sending off Marcus. It seemed impos-sible that it had been only three days since his launch, and only three hours since the break-off of comm from orbital facilities. Her gut in-sisted something was wrong.

"Then you don't know when this CME will be past?" she said.

"Nor how long the magnetosphere will take to settle back down after the CME has left us. That's what I'm telling you." And what he kept tell-ing her, no matter how many ways she rephrased her questions. "Unless there is something else?"

"You've been very kind," she told him. If not very helpful. "Thank you."

He hung up before she could reconsider.

Valerie clicked through the CME alert warning on the weather cen-ter's home page to pore over the latest data in their public databases. The instrument readouts she found all suggested that the ion flux had yet to peak. She went back to the home page to subscribe to any updates. This once she wished she could have news texted straight to a cell phone.

She tipped back in her chair, searching her office for inspiration. And found none. She rechecked NASA's space weather alert. It had not changed in two hours. She surfed, promising herself she would work Real Soon Now. She found no inspiration on the net, either.

She had tried and failed at a hurried breakfast to explain CMEs to her parents. But however esoteric solar outbursts were to Mom and Dad, CMEs were part of her job—in the way hecklers were part of a comedian's job. When the eruption of plasma that was a CME barreled into the solar wind, the interaction could blast out radio noise.

Interference. Disrupted observations. PS-1 and Phoebe. Marcus. *Damn!*

She stomped down the hall to Aaron Friedman's office. He was a solar radio astronomer. Maybe *he* could offer a useful forecast on the CME passing.

"Did you hear this CME coming?"

"Good day to you, too. No, I didn't." Aaron shrugged. "They aren't all noisy."

Because if you could hear them all, it would be too easy. Nor could you see them all. Not, anyway, the ones you would most *want* to see: those racing straight at the Earth. The sun's glare washed out their faint glow until, all too close, oncoming CMEs appeared as dim halos around the solar disk. To spot an onrushing CME was especially hard now, at the peak of the sunspot cycle, while the solar disk was pocked with sunspots and coronal holes, while it teemed with prominences and filaments.

So it was not too surprising that *this* CME had gone undetected until its leading edge of ions washed over the early warning spacecraft stationed a million miles sunward from Earth. It was not the first CME to almost reach Earth before it was detected, nor would it be the last.

Then why—besides fear for Marcus, besides something to distract her until communications could be reestablished—did this CME bug her? The sheer bad timing?

"Is that all you wanted?" Aaron asked, channeling the young man at the Space Weather Prediction Center. Or, at least, his exasperation.

She wanted Marcus, safe on the ground. Safe in her arms.

"How bad *is* this CME?" she asked.

"It's a whopper, but not bad. Not so far, anyway. I haven't heard of outages that don't have other, more mundane explanations."

Nor had she, in her recent surfing, seen any incidents to blame on a CME. That was odd. So what, other than mess with anything electrical, might a CME do?

She vented at Patrick in *his* office for ten minutes before having a constructive idea. "Do me a favor? Find me an aurora webcam."

He tapped away, and a holo popped up over his desk. "Here's a feed from Norway."

Leaning one way then the other, she studied the streaming video: a handful of flickering, glowing green tendrils in the sky. Pretty, but she had seen far more impressive specimens of the northern lights. "Okay, try somewhere else."

A second vid opened. "Alaska," he said.

She saw only blue sky in this image. Daylight sometimes washed out the northern lights, but still . . .

Unasked, he offered her a third view. "From the bottom of the world, McMurdo."

"Is it just me?"

"I don't get it, either. The CME should be whipping up huge auroras, even if it isn't messing with electrical systems on the ground." He tapped his desk with a pencil. "So where *are* the spectacular auroras?"

"That's the question," she said.

The young man still on duty at the Space Weather Prediction Center—for all that he clearly wished Valerie would stop phoning—had no explanation, either.

* * *

Everyone looked to Thad for guidance, and he had none to offer. He had to struggle to manage monosyllabic grunts. He watched as others dispensed food and water.

I'm going into shock, he thought. Or could someone with the presence of mind to diagnose shock be in shock?

Irv Weingart lay stretched out on the floor, his leg bandaged and the bleeding stopped, loopy with painkillers but breathing easily. The remainder of the shelter was standing room only.

At least, Thad thought, they could stand forever without tiring. On Phoebe's surface the bulkiest person among them might weigh a pound. Here, deep within the tiny world, everything and everyone weighed even less than on the surface.

You could not hang someone in Phoebe's feeble gravity. Almost, he laughed. Almost, he cried.

As time passed, the mood within the shelter grew angrier and angrier.

"We've got to get this man to the infirmary," the hotel doctor said. "Will the CME have passed yet?"

"Not necessarily," someone answered. "The infirmary isn't as far belowground as the shelter, but it's still underground. Maybe it would be safe there."

Thad roused himself. "And when you poke your nose out the door, and they shoot you? How safe is that?"

"Whatever they meant to do, by now they've done it," Marcus Judson said.

"Uh-huh." Thad gestured at the hatch. "You certain enough to go first?"

The doctor and Marcus exchanged glances. Neither moved for the door.

Thad breathed a sigh of relief. "That's showing good sense."

Maybe, just maybe, if he could keep everyone inside the shelter long enough, the radiation would kill Yakov's people before one of them found a reason to expose him.

And if, in the meanwhile, Irv died?

Irv for Robin, Thad told himself. As, once, it had been Gabe Campbell for Robin. Even as Thad bargained with himself, he wondered what Jonas and gang were up to.

And how many more would die.

*　*　*

Clasping a hopper by one front and one rear handhold, Dillon lifted. With excessive force: the hopper sailed over his head. As his arms reached their full extension, the hopper jerked his elbows and lifted him bodily off the garage floor. Just above the garage floor, his tethers brought him to a safe halt—and the hopper delivered a painful yank to his arms.

Felipe, standing nearby with another hopper in hand, guffawed.

The utility craft weighed only about as much as Dillon did: call it three-quarters of a pound. But while an object's weight varied with gravity, its mass did not. He had to handle massive objects with care to avoid injuring himself.

Gravity, what little there was, and the tension on the tether slowly returned him to the garage floor. He set the hopper back down and, with practice, mastered moving it about. Only then, with an extra forty feet of tether unreeled, did he tote the hopper out the garage door. Depositing the hopper on Phoebe's dark surface, he turned around for another load. Phoebe's garage was filled with the hoppers flown over from The Space Place. He had many trips ahead of him.

"How are you guys coming?" Jonas radioed on a private channel. He and Lincoln had hoppered to the infrared observatory to scavenge parts, and Dillon had no idea why.

"Fine," Felipe said.

"Coming along," Dillon said. "But *why* are we doing this?"

"Because the rodents might come out of their burrows."

So that no one could pursue them to PS-1, Dillon interpreted that. Until a shuttle came up from Earth, the four of them would be free to wreak havoc on the accursed powersat. *He* would have spent their limited time dismembering Phoebe's factories, to keep more powersats from being built, but perhaps Yakov was right. Destroying PS-1 itself would be more dramatic.

Yakov's mysterious orders—secret, anyway, from Dillon—did not involve drastic action against the prisoners themselves. Thank Gaia for small favors. Eve Moynihan and her grandfather already burdened Dillon's conscience.

And his own death? "No CME?" he prompted Jonas.

"Again, I *told* you. There is no CME. Never was. If you don't trust me, just think about it. A real CME would be playing havoc with our helmet-to-helmet chatter. That's why I broke the particle monitor. So the rodents won't find out."

Wonderful, if somehow true. By every account, radiation sickness was a horrible way to go. But what if Jonas lied? To judge from the casual way he had shot the station chief, Jonas would not scruple to speak convenient fictions.

And so, Dillon labored on, fearful at every crackle, hiss, and pop of his helmet speakers that he was a dead man walking.

Yet a part of him could not help but marvel at events. Like secret agents on 3-V shows, they had codes: the encryption software Jonas had uploaded, as soon as they left Phoebe's shelter, into everyone's helmet comm. And exotic weapons. Recalling TSA's near strip search, Dillon could not imagine how Jonas had gotten the guns.

With many laps yet to go, Dillon tried to tune in audio from a DirecTV downlink of today's Indians-Tigers game. He got only static. Duh: comsats were offline. Proactively, because of the fiction of a CME, he told himself, desperate to believe.

Passing Felipe outbound, Dillon returned to the garage for yet another hopper. They each had another two utility craft to move. Dillon radioed, "When do we head over?"

"Shouldn't be long," Jonas said. "We're almost done here."

Jonas and Lincoln had each taken a hopper. Dillon and Felipe would each take another.

With a gleeful hoot, Felipe flung the first of the extra hoppers into space.

* * *

The shelter was packed.

The inmates—their floor space limited, virtually without gravity—more crept than paced. Lines formed and circled for food, water, and the two toilets. Fans roared and air scrubbers labored to handle so many people in the small space. Lost to sight within the crowd, someone sobbed.

Marcus paced as unsuccessfully as everyone else. He worried about the base commander, whom the doctors said had lost a great deal of blood. He worried about Valerie, who would be frantic with worry about *him*. He worried about Thad, who seemed overwhelmed. He eavesdropped on wild speculations about what the terrorists could want enough to die horribly for, and how the damage they were surely wreaking could best be undone.

As the hours passed, as he could *do* nothing, it was all Marcus could do not to scream.

The particle monitor on Phoebe's surface was not reporting; it or the comm link to the shelter must have been knocked out by the radiation. The particle monitor in the shelter, though its counts bounced around, never detected any significant influx. As reassuring as he found those readings, it meant their inside monitor would be useless for telling them when the storm had passed.

After ten hours, Marcus had had enough. "It's been plenty long. Everything I know about CMEs tells me it's safe to come out."

"What do you know about suicidal fanatics?" one of the hotel evacuees snapped back.

Savvy said, "Suppose they are dead. What's our signal to leave the shelter? When we run out of food or water or oh-two?"

Alongside Irv, the hotel doctor cleared his throat. "The bullet has to come out. It's deep in the leg; I'd rather not go after it with only a first-aid kit. It would be much better for the patient if we can get him to the base infirmary."

Marcus bellowed at the hatch, "We need to bring this man to the infirmary!"

"Pipe down," Thad yelled back. The din in the shelter quieted a bit. More softly, he said, "I'm in charge here, remember?"

"So what's the plan?" Marcus countered.

"We wait for rescue. People will wonder when they don't hear from us."

"How long will that take?" Savvy asked. "NASA is apt to assume at first that the CME damaged our comm. They'll wait a bit for us to bring it back online. And when people *do* come, why would they come armed?"

"We wait," Thad repeated.

The hell with *that*, Marcus thought. "Dillon Russo! Dillon's colleagues! Two of us will be bringing out the man you wounded. We need to get him to the infirmary."

From beyond the hatch: silence.

"Do *not* do this," Thad warned.

"Don't shoot!" Marcus shouted. He grabbed the hatch latch, but it did not budge. He yanked harder. Nothing. He braced a foot against the jamb and, putting his whole body into the effort, heaved.

In shock and dismay, Marcus said, "We're trapped in here."

•  •  •

Descending a docking post, Dillon tried, and failed, to take in the immensity that was PS-1. The powersat's straight lines and foreboding blackness could not have stood in starker contrast to the achingly beautiful orb that hung overhead.

The hubris to build this monstrosity left him speechless, almost in tears.

When he regained his composure, he would help his colleagues to destroy this evil.

•  •  •

From his perch beside a docking post, Dillon turned, trying to take in everything.

Jonas floated in arm's reach of a gaping access panel about halfway from the center of PS-1. Felipe flew back and forth across the powersat's vast surface as though plowing a field, his hopper puffing gas all the while. For all Dillon knew, the man was joyriding. As for Lincoln, the only evidence was the tether that snaked through the gap opened where he had removed solar panels and whatever structure lay beneath.

Here, there, everywhere: little octopoid bots. The little automatons had come tumbling out of shelters, dispersing to do . . . whatever it was they did, when Jonas canceled the CME shutdown. Maybe they would be tasked to help with the disassembly.

Dillon radioed, "I'm ready. Where should I begin?"

"What do you mean?" Jonas asked back.

"This thing is *huge*. As fulfilling as it would be to rampage and smash, I can see that's not realistic. We have to concentrate our efforts on what's most important, what will be hardest to repair, before NASA sends up a ship. If we're to destroy this abomination while we have it to ourselves, we have to work smart."

"I'm not following," Jonas said.

"About how to destroy it?"

"No," Jonas said. "About why you think that's our purpose. That's not at all what Yakov intends us to do."

*　*　*

Yakov sat in his study, the rain drumming against the windows. The night sky, were he to step outside, would be a uniform, ominous slate gray. As much as he wished to see the signal with his own eyes, that was impossible. His night-vision binoculars would stay in their case.

Trusted men and women were in place, waiting, around the world. It would suffice for them to forward their observations. He would know soon enough.

Sipping hot tea, he waited for the phone.

At last, it rang. After idle pleasantries, Arkady Vasilyev said, "You will never guess what I spotted on my last hike. A rose-breasted grosbeak! We hardly ever see them in California."

Above Los Angeles, unlike Washington, the sky was clear tonight.

"You are sure of what you saw?" Yakov asked.

"I am positive."

"Then I envy you. I would like to have seen it."

"I understand, my friend."

They discussed other rare birds they had seen, or heard, or wished to—and it was all lies. What Arkady Vasilyev—not his real name—had seen with *his* night-vision binoculars was far more remarkable than any bird sighting: a slightly cooled stripe across the sun-warmed surface of PS-1. Someone from Jonas's team was cooling the area with gas sprayed from a utility craft.

And so, without any radio transmission from the powersat to attract American notice, he knew his team was in place.

After several minutes of such prattle, Yakov excused himself. With Psycho Cyborg's expert assistance, he, too, had secret messages to deliver.

* * *

Blades spun lazily in the stiff breeze over the Pacific. The windmills were enormous: their blades spanning two hundred and fifty feet, their pedestals rising two hundred feet above the ocean. When the wind blew fast enough, each windmill generated almost two megawatts of power. A hundred windmills stood spaced across a few square miles.

One by one, in a hundred electrical generators, copper coils fused and melted. Power output sagged and surged on the high-voltage transmission lines that ran to the coast. Distribution substations ashore overloaded.

In cascading power failures, Yokohama, Tokyo, and Osaka ground to a halt.

* * *

Venezuela's greatest triumph ringed the harbor and sprawled along the coast. A jumble of storage tanks brimming with petroleum, diesel fuel, gasoline, and liquefied natural gas. The modern refinery with its capacity of three hundred thousand barrels per day. Pumping stations. A cat's cradle of pipeline, moving vast quantities of fluids about the complex. More pipeline, snaking out to the oil fields. Lighters shuttling fuel to supertankers too huge to enter the harbor.

Much of the rambling facility was just coming back online after a preemptive shutdown in the face of the coronal mass ejection. Everything was checking out fine—

Until explosions ripped through the night. The fires soon raged out of control.

Fortunately, disaster struck on the third shift. The dead and unaccounted for remained, just barely, below four hundred.

* * *

Like colossi, mighty pylons bestrode the desolate plain.

High-capacity, high-voltage, superconducting cables swooped from one pylon to the next, to the next, to the next . . . across thousands of miles. And so, vast solar farms in the Outback fed their gigawatts into the power lines that spanned a continent—

Until, deep within the desert, stretches of the cable flashed white-hot before exploding in a spray of metallic vapor. More slowly, like candles in the sun, nearby metal towers melted.

And a continent away, Melbourne went dark.

* * *

Dillon had taken his turn at the console, obliterating a few of the grotesque, counterproductive, hubristic constructions of "civilization." And proudly, even giddily, so: every target they destroyed with the powersat's microwave beam had been an outrage against Gaia.

But the adrenaline rush had passed. Beyond some point—and how could they not already have passed that point?—the destruction *they* inflicted was equally an affront to Mother Earth.

"I think we have everyone's attention," Dillon said, desperately.

Except for the smudge of black smoke off the Venezuelan coast, the effects of their activities could not be seen from this altitude, even with visors set to full magnification. The rest he had fleshed out from Jonas's matter-of-fact descriptions and his own—ever more appalled—imagination.

So much death and destruction!

"I imagine so," Jonas admitted.

"Then *use* it." Dillon gestured at the nearby radio antenna. The transceiver meant for routine operation of the powersat was in no way constrained to that purpose. "Send them our"—Yakov's!—"demands, so that this slaughter can *stop*."

"Demands," Jonas echoed. "We have demands?"

**V**alerie sat up with a start.

She remembered reluctantly turning off the 3-V, because her folks would not go to bed until she did. Not that staying up past two had accomplished anything, because the only news from Phoebe was: no news. Formless dread had kept her tossing and turning until—the latest she remembered checking the bedside clock—after four.

Her bedside clock read 9:12 A.M. Maybe *now* there would be information. But turning on the bedroom 3-V, she found she had awakened into a new nightmare.

There was a knock on her door. Without waiting for a response, Mom came in wearing a nightgown, robe, and slippers. "Go back to bed, hon. Everything is closed today. I'll wake you if there's any word about the people on Phoebe."

"Everything is closed." Valerie gestured at the 3-V, in which a refinery blazed, while the crawl scrolled a litany of other disasters. The headline: TERRORISTS STRIKE WORLDWIDE! "Because of this? What *is* this?" She threw off the blanket. "Did you get Simon to school?"

Mom shook her head. "Simon is in the yard, tiring out your father. Hon, everything but essential services is closed. The president declared a national state of emergency."

"I've got to get to work."

"It's *closed*."

"Regardless, Mom, I have to get to the observatory."

When Valerie pulled into the parking lot, twenty minutes later, she saw bikes and cars. She wasn't the only staffer unable to just sit home.

Patrick found her in the break room, as she paced waiting for coffee to brew. He took one look at her and gave her a hug. "Any word from Marcus?"

She shook her head.

"If you insist on being here, I'm working from your office. You shouldn't be alone."

"Thanks." The pot finished brewing and she filled their mugs. "I was thinking. Suppose the CME fried Phoebe's main base transmitter. Could happen, right? They'd still have low-power stuff. Like spacesuit helmet radios."

Remember when we met, Marcus? I said I could eavesdrop on a cell phone on Titan.

"And we have a big receiver. Good thinking."

"Now if I could only find a bit of free time on the big dish . . . ."

"You know? I seem to recall an anomalous reading the last time I ran diagnostics. I'll be taking the big dish offline real soon, now."

This time, she hugged him. But as long as they tracked Phoebe, they heard—nothing.

✴ ✴ ✴

Footsteps in the Jansky Lab corridor were nothing unusual. These footsteps were. Too fast. Too soft. Like people sneaking up . . .

Valerie twitched as someone shouted, "Clear!"

Turning, she saw two men wearing camo, flak jackets, and helmets. Carrying *guns*! Shuffling noises in the corridor suggested others.

Nodding to the soldiers, a tall, ruddy-faced man in a rumpled blue suit walked into her office. He had thinning, close-cropped brown hair and a bristly mustache gone gray. He could have been the father, maybe even the grandfather, of any of the soldiers.

But the sight of a grandfather did not ordinarily send a chill down her spine.

"Dr. Clayburn?" the older man asked.

Patrick stood. "Someone's serious about giving us the day off."

Ignoring the gibe, the man in the suit offered his ID. A holo logo shimmered above it. "Valerie Clayburn. May I have a minute?"

"That's me," she said, although he seemed already to know that. "And what the *hell* is this about?"

"My name is Tyler Pope, and I'm with the CIA. You placed an interesting call yesterday to the Space Weather Prediction Center."

"I'm an astronomer, Mr. Pope. We're interested in space."

"Don't talk to him," Patrick said. "Not without a lawyer."

"Thank you for your opinion, Dr. Burkhalter. Don't look so surprised. I told you I'm CIA. You're still in the room because you were also on that call."

"And why is the CIA interested in space weather?" Patrick asked.

Pope said, "Dr. Clayburn, you're in no more trouble than the rest of the country, but unfortunately, that's a great deal. Lawyers can't help us. So will one of you please explain that call?"

"My friend is on Phoebe." She shivered. "I *hope* he's on Phoebe. The last contact I had, a short e-mail, he was at work on the NASA power-sat. But because of adverse space weather, a radiation hazard, he would have been evacuated to Phoebe. The problem is, there's been no communication from Phoebe since just after the weather alert."

"And your call to the space weather people?"

Patrick gestured at the muted 3-V. "Don't you have a crisis to attend to?"

"Who says I'm not?" Pope turned back to Valerie. "Your call?"

She had made three calls, the first two routine. "You mean when I said that yesterday's CME—sorry, that's coronal mass ejection— wasn't acting like a CME. No auroras. They couldn't explain it."

"But your question stuck with them," Pope said. "Here's the thing, Valerie. May I call you Valerie? The thing is, there *was* no CME yesterday."

"I reviewed their data, and I'm qualified to make sense of it."

"I'm sure you are, given accurate data."

"I hardly think you're trained to—"

Pope cut her off. "Because of your questions—for which, thank you—a staffer at the Space Weather Prediction Center took the initiative to double-check their records. I'm told data from the early-warning spacecraft downloads through NASA's Deep Space Network. So this young man went back to the DSN, and in the buffer DSN keeps to diagnose any problems in recent communications they found . . ."

"No trace of a CME," Valerie completed. "So what *did* I see in the weather center's database?"

"Except for time stamps, the supposed readings for yesterday's event turn out to duplicate a CME from 2019. When the security folks at the weather center reinstalled their intrusion-detection software, they found they had been hacked by experts. That's when they called the DOD Cyber Command."

"But how . . . ?" She trailed off in thought. Suppose one wanted— never mind why—to fake a CME. Could it even be done? "People interested in flares and CMEs go to the official repository, and that's the Space Weather Prediction Center. When an alert goes out to subscribers, the hundreds of satellites that a CME might clobber get put immediately into standby mode. When satellites reawaken undamaged, people just think how fortunate they were. Any independent scientist trying to measure the CME's ground-level effects, when she doesn't detect any, is apt to run diagnostics, check calibrations and the like, before questioning the official alert."

Pope nodded. "You're very sharp, Valerie."

"Still," Patrick said, "those ground-based measurements will eventually check out. It can't be a matter of more than days."

*Hiding* a CME to destroy satellites might appeal to the sorts of fanatics who blow stuff up, Valerie supposed. Why do the opposite? Why fake a CME? And why bother if questions were sure to be raised after a day or two?

Then an even stranger question struck her. "The Russians have a space weather system, with independent data sources, run by their Space Research Institute. That weather center also shows a CME. Were they hacked, too?"

"Or," Pope said, "are the Russians showing bad data on purpose? Do you begin to see why the CIA is interested?"

\* \* \*

All very intriguing and bizarre, Patrick thought. But relevant, how? "What does this have to do with Valerie, or our armed guards?"

"Look outside," Pope suggested.

Opening the window blinds, looking down into the parking lot, Patrick saw a Pocahontas County Sheriff's cruiser.

"I asked the local police to keep an eye on you until I got here," Pope said. "The people I'm investigating have bigger ambitions than hacking the Space Weather Prediction Center. *I* found out you were asking perceptive questions. Someone else might."

"I'm in danger?" Valerie asked, incredulous. "If I am, what about my family?"

"I don't think anyone is, but I won't take chances." Pope gestured at the troops. "I'm leaving these men behind. Your family will be well protected."

"*They* will. Where will *I* be?"

"With me, I hope. You spotted something important before anyone else. A government crisis team is gathering, and we need your kind of insight."

"I need to be here, where my friend can reach me."

"We're working to reestablish communications with Phoebe, too. Trust me, we have resources you cannot begin to imagine."

With Marcus unaccounted for, she was *so* vulnerable. Patrick could see her wavering. "Do you want to do this? And would you like me to come along?"

"I don't recall inviting you," Pope said, glowering.

Patrick refused to react. Of *course* Mr. CIA had seen his government files, and judged Patrick unworthy of trust. Bastard.

"Will you keep an eye on Simon and my parents?" she asked.

"Of course." Patrick hesitated. "So you're going? You're sure."

"I have to," she said.

Because if the CME was imaginary, then why had Phoebe base gone silent? And how could any of this, as Pope had hinted, relate to this morning's terrorist attacks? By joining this task force, Valerie might find out—and about Marcus, too.

"I understand," Patrick told her. "Do what you have to do."

"I'm glad that's settled," Pope said. "If we can be going, Valerie, time is of the essence. We have a chopper waiting."

*　*　*

Wooded, rolling countryside vanished behind the helicopter. Overwhelmed by events, Valerie had scarcely noticed when they took off from Green Bank's tiny and seldom-used airstrip, but from the chopper's shadow their course was east-northeast. Except for the pilot, she and Tyler Pope had the aircraft to themselves.

"Are you all right?" Pope asked her.

"Truthfully? I'm too numb to know."

"Sorry to whisk you away like this. It *is* urgent. And there are things I couldn't share around your friend."

"He's a good man!" she protested.

Pope shrugged. "I don't doubt that. Good and well suited to a crisis are very different."

Such as losing the *Verne* probe by acting in haste. Taking Pope's point did nothing to assuage her pangs of guilt.

"Valerie."

She turned to look at him.

"Contrary to what you've seen on the Internet and 3-V, the attacks aren't bombings. Governments are sitting on the real story for a little while, so the bad guys don't know we know."

"Who *are* the bad guys?"

"Unclear." He sighed. "But I have my suspicions."

"The Russians, you intimated. Their space weather center could have been hacked, too."

"Maybe. Russians involvement doesn't mean *all* Russians."

"If their space weather center isn't complicit," she said, "then how does any of this involve the Russians?"

"Consider the targets. Most are alternate-energy-based power generation and distribution facilities. The one petro facility to be hit is the main export hub in Venezuela. The Russians haven't been happy with Petróleos de Venezuela shipping way over its cartel-approved quota.

"Did you happen to check the price of oil futures today?"

The Crudetastrophe had taken away Keith. Now another oil-related crisis? She could not *bear* to think about losing Marcus.

"Valerie. Valerie, stay with me."

"What?" she said, woodenly.

"The nonbombings. The attacks come from space, using a microwave beam from PS-1. *That* is why everyone is suppressing the true nature of the threat. Until the news gets out, no one will question NASA and Cosmic Adventures sending a relief shuttle to Phoebe, to repair whatever has gone wrong with their comm and to bring back anyone needing evacuation." Pope glanced at his wrist. "They should be taking off right about now."

Maybe Marcus *wasn't* doomed! "A rescue mission!"

"Indirectly," Pope said. "The shuttle will carry a squad of special-ops folks, trained for combat in space. At the last minute they'll veer to retake control of PS-1."

* * *

Patrick accompanied the soldiers to Valerie's house. Mr. and Mrs. Yarborough had not struck him as the kind to take well to the military descending on them. Then again, who did?

He settled into Valerie's home office, ready to intervene for her parents if the need should arise. A 3-V droned in the living room. Whenever they cranked up the volume, it meant another terrorist attack.

His impression was of attacks all over the place and he did not see the logic. He hunted around until he found an Ethernet cable with which to net his datasheet. After plotting the attacks on a globe, he *still* saw no pattern.

Maybe another of the day's mysteries would somehow shed light on the situation. A fine idea—except that he had no idea how to plot a counterfeit CME.

There was yet another mystery, the one that had Valerie frantic. Why was there no news from Phoebe? Patrick expanded his plot, draping his holo globe of Earth in a broad sinusoidal band. Little pennants stood here and there within the band.

Every one of the terrorist attacks had happened in view of Phoebe and PS-1. And every attack had taken place while PS-1, if not always the target, had been in sunlight.

"What have I done?" he whispered.

\* \* \*

*Big Momma* lumbered down the Cape Canaveral runway. The plane lurched—its engines laboring, as always, under the weight of a fully fueled orbital shuttle—off the tarmac into a cloudless blue sky. Glowing gases, 2,700°F hot, streamed from the turbofan exhausts.

High overhead, a sensor once a part of the Phoebe infrared observatory homed in on the heat source. Powersat controls designed to maintain focus on a surface location—despite the powersat's orbital motion and the Earth's rotation—maintained a lock on the target.

At the appointed time and altitude, *Big Momma* released its cargo. Lighting its main engine, spewing 6,000°F exhaust, the shuttle shot skyward. The sensor redirected its attention to the brightest infrared source in its field of vision—

And an intense beam of microwaves lashed out.

Shuttle electronics shut down, overloaded, and arced. Liquid oxygen and hydrogen in the shuttle's fuel tanks flashed into vapor—and vapor pressure burst the tanks.

In an instant, the shuttle became the heart of a fireball.

For a time the fireball was the hottest thing in sight; microwaves continued to pour down on it. But the fireball burnt out. The debris dispersed and cooled.

And the distant sensor redirected the ravening microwave beam onto the blazing exhausts of the fleeing aircraft, *Big Momma.*

By the West Virginia standards to which Valerie had grown accustomed, Mount Weather was not much of a mountain. Not that she had gotten much of a look: the chopper had swooped in low to the ground, skirting the little town Tyler Pope had identified as Berryville, Virginia. Hustled from the helipad into a sprawling underground tunnel complex, she had been left waiting, all alone, in a small, sparsely furnished meeting room.

Her mind clung to irrelevancies because she could not bear to think about the worldwide terror, or the disastrous rescue attempt, or Marcus's uncertain fate. *She* was supposed to help the CIA? The idea was ludicrous. She couldn't help herself.

Other than a table and six chairs, the room offered only a 3-V and some rolled-up datasheets. Cans of tepid soda, forlorn, waited on the table. The institutional gray walls were windowless and bare.

She searched in vain for an Ethernet cable, then laughed at herself. She was beyond the quiet zone. This shelter must have wireless service.

For a while she watched the news, much of it dealing with aircraft worldwide diverting to the nearest airfield lest they, too, be swatted from the sky. But since the destruction of the shuttle and its mother ship, the terrorists had returned their attention to stationary targets. She turned off the 3-V when coverage cut to the Philippines. Something about a geothermal power plant being reduced to slag. . . .

By shoving chairs against the table, she cleared space to circle the room. What kind of people would do such terrible things? Had killed . . . how many? By now, perhaps thousands. What would such people care for the lives of a few score civilians in orbit?

She did not notice the door opening.

"Excuse me," a woman said, closing the door behind herself. She was tall, clearly Asian, maybe Japanese, and wore thick, round glasses.

"Yes?"

"I'm told we're the red team." The woman laughed nervously. "Let me back up. My name is Ellen Tanaka. I'm with NASA, from the power-sat project."

Marcus's boss! "Valerie Clayburn. I'm a radio astronomer. I questioned the CME alert, and for that lapse in judgment the CIA brought me here."

Ellen cleared her throat. "Shall we acknowledge the obvious? You're seeing Marcus, and I'm the one who sent him up. I hope you don't hate me for that."

Did she? Valerie thought of the last time she had seen Marcus, *so* eager to begin his adventure. "Had you sent anyone else, he would have been disappointed. And if you don't know it, he likes and respects you. A lot. So, no, I don't hate you. I don't blame you, either."

Ellen pulled out a chair and sat heavily. "I wish I could say the same."

Valerie did *not* want to dwell on Marcus going away. "What's a red team?"

"Surrogate bad guys. We're to try to think as the people controlling PS-1 would, with luck anticipating what they'll do before they do it. I think the term comes from Cold War war games, when red teams stood in for the Russians."

"And still do?" Valerie asked.

"So I'm told. Right or wrong about who, though, PS-1 is the problem. Where shall we start? With how the bad guys are doing what they're doing?" Ellen popped the tab on one of the warm sodas. "Mind you, the person we *really* need is Bethany Taylor, the contractor's chief engineer. She was in the air, though, and her flight got diverted to Fargo. So far no one's been able to set her up with a secure enough connection to link into this facility. Bethany knows way more about the powersat than, well, anyone."

"If also something of a bitch on wheels."

Ellen grinned, and the mood lightened. "I can guess where *that* comes from."

Not that Ellen had disagreed, Valerie noted. She grabbed a datasheet and handed Ellen another. "Okay. Let's get to it."

* * *

They worked.

Ellen, despite her modest disclaimer, knew a great deal about PS-1. Valerie had retained more than she would have thought possible from Marcus's enthusiastic descriptions.

An orderly delivered food and coffee. They must have eaten, because sandwiches disappeared and the carafe went empty, but Valerie could not have said how or when it happened.

Checking e-mail, she found nothing from Patrick. Adages be damned: no news meant only no news. She hoped. She sent a note, asking him to hug Simon for her, how Mom and Dad were coping, and would he keep listening in on Phoebe?

Ellen kept trying to access security cameras on PS-1. The subsystem rejected her reactivation requests: *Unauthorized command.* "I should be able to do this," Ellen muttered. "Viewing is not a sysadmin function. Not supposed to be, anyway."

"Can you contact a sysadmin to do it for you?" Valerie asked.

"Any I can reach, the ones on rotation to the ground, can't help. As a matter of security, sysadmin functions can only be executed from hardwired terminals on PS-1 itself."

"What access do you still have?"

"None." Ellen sighed. "Someone up there must have changed authorizations to require sysadmin access to do *anything*."

The more attacks, the better their chance of spotting patterns. They turned on the 3-V for any breaking stories that might be instructive.

Instead they got the Russian president, in full-throated, lectern-thumping rage. In translation he condemned the U.S. for building a powersat. "This so-called power satellite must always have been intended as a weapon of mass destruction. Or are we to believe that within hours an innocent electrical power plant can be converted into a terrible weapon? The world is not so naïve. Nor do we fail to notice that the facility that all were told would hang stationary in the skies over the Americas instead threatens our entire planet four times each day. And to compound its earlier deceptions, America now claims to have 'lost control' of its illegal weapons platform to Resetter fanatics. It is a matter of criminal negligence at best, a matter of—"

Ellen hit mute and set down the remote. "This isn't helping us."

"Why blame Resetters?" Valerie asked. "Have the terrorists identified themselves?"

"From the selection of targets, I would guess. Most are alternate-energy projects, the sort the most extreme Resetters oppose."

"Only it took Russian connivance to get the terrorists, Resetters or not, where they are."

Faster than either of them could react to a quick double knock, the door swung open. "How's it coming in here?" Tyler Pope asked.

"I don't get the point of these attacks," Ellen said.

"Me, either," Valerie admitted. "Or why whoever controls PS-1 hasn't—apart from the shuttle—touched the U.S."

"Was that a question?" Tyler waggled the coffee carafe, deemed it empty, and set it back down. "Oh, the U.S. has been hit, and it's insidiously clever. The anger from around the world comes right back at us. Powersats are fast becoming more untenable than the alternate-energy systems being so openly targeted."

"The Russians took over PS-1!" Valerie shouted. "That's what you said."

"I believe that more than ever," Pope said. "NSA wizards have looked over the computers at the Space Weather Prediction Center. I'm told that the intrusion and the code left behind have all the earmarks of a Russian pro hacker who goes by Psycho Cyborg. Still, the evidence for Russian government involvement is entirely circumstantial."

NSA? *No Such Agency,* Keith used to translate that, mockingly. As though a huge federal agency with vast resources could hide in plain sight. Such as the big complex at the north end of the quiet zone: she knew no one who believed the Navy's claim of ownership. Not a lot of call for naval facilities in the middle of a landlocked state. Or any obvious reason for the Navy to operate antennas to rival Green Bank's.

Valerie had met parents at Little League games who did not work at the observatory but asked *damned* perceptive questions about the telescopes. National Security Agency, surely. It stood to reason the country's premier eavesdroppers would also have computer whizzes on staff.

"Which leaves us where?" Valerie asked.

"It leaves us, as far as world opinion is concerned, with an American weapons platform constructed in space in violation of international treaty. Worse, a weapon the control of which we carelessly lost to terrorists. Or, according to a fair chunk of the blogosphere, the pretense of lost control, there being no proof whatever that the U.S. does not still control PS-1."

"*Are* there terrorists? And are they Resetters?" Ellen asked.

"Hell, yes, there are terrorists," Pope said. "But as for who they are, that's a tougher question.

"A lot of intel work is looking for patterns. The past few hours, *legions* at the CIA have been digging into the background of anyone who could have been involved.

"So here's a pattern for you. Remember the microwave incident early last month in the Santa Barbara Channel? The company whose beamed power killed that little girl and her grandfather?"

"All too well," Ellen said. "The accident generated tons of bad press about beamed power and PS-1."

And if that accident had never happened? Marcus would still be on the ground. Valerie couldn't help thinking that, but kept it to herself. *If only* wishes helped nobody.

"The company was a start-up," Pope said. "Its lead investor was Russo Venture Capital Partners. Reviewing passenger manifests from Cosmic Adventures, guess who showed up? Dillon Russo. Also three of his employees, all engineers. All on The Space Place when it had to evacuate to Phoebe."

"Quite the coincidence," Ellen said.

"No coincidence," Pope said. "I just can't prove it yet. Regardless, people who vacation in space are rich and well connected. Names are already coming out. I won't be the only one to make the Dillon Russo connection.

"So what's your choice, ladies? American terrorists or American agents pretending to be Resetter terrorists? In either scenario, the U.S. becomes competitively stronger as power plants and energy resources go boom in other countries. Of course while all this happens, *everyone* is being weakened in absolute terms." Pope grimaced. "Everyone, that is, except the Russians."

The universe could be subtle, but it was never devious. The universe didn't know how to lie. Not only did Valerie have no answers, she did not even know the questions. Except one. "What about everyone else from Phoebe and The Space Place? How do the conspiracy theorists explain that no one can contact them?"

"Hostages. Coconspirators. Irrelevant. Take your pick." Pope rubbed his eyes, looking exhausted. "We have experts out the wazoo to analyze the politics, but not for PS-1 itself. So back to work, you two. We don't have much time to find the powersat's weak point."

*　*　*

The air inside the shelter was stuffy and dank, reeking of sweat, urine, and fear. People milled about, murmuring, shivering.

A fortunate few slept. Thad wondered how they did it. He tried to rouse himself to remember it would not be only himself dying.

No one could ever have anticipated spending more than a few hours in the shelter, especially not crammed in like commuters on a Tokyo subway. Their air scrubbers were failing under the load. And it was *cold*; to conserve fuel cells, he had dialed down the thermostat to fifty degrees. For all the densely packed humanity, Phoebe sucked out the heat through the insulated walls. They would asphyxiate or freeze to death before food or water became an issue.

Thad tried the hatch. Again.

Still jammed. Whatever Yakov's team had done to the door, it was stuck but good.

Marcus pushed through the crowd to make yet another protest. "We have to get word out," he insisted. "Or else we're going to die in here."

And in a whisper: "We've been out of touch for close to two days. NASA may already think we're dead."

"I'm open to new ideas," Thad said.

"All I have is the old idea we have yet to try. Look, we're stuck inside a Faraday cage. So we cut a hole in the wall. Shove through a radio sending an SOS. Patch the hole."

The idea was not only old, but useless. Of course no one but Thad knew the main base radio was fried. It would never relay anything. "It's wishful thinking that the base radio and computers will have come back up on their own. And a datasheet has a range of what? A couple hundred feet?"

"I've refined the plan a bit. We pull the radio from someone's helmet. Helmet radios are good for miles, right? I mean we could talk with a helmet radio between PS-1 and Phoebe."

"Relayed through big antennas on Phoebe and PS-1," Thad said.

"Be realistic! What do we have to lose?"

"Air! Heat!"

"For how much longer?" Marcus shook his head. "Here's something you have no reason to know. The woman I'm seeing is an astronomer. A *radio* astronomer. Val once said she could hear a cell phone on Titan. So maybe she'll hear a helmet radio from a few thousand miles."

The plan was still daydreams and moonbeams. "The wall panels aren't made of tin foil. How do you expect to cut through one? And do it leaving a clean cut you can seal over."

"I've been working on that, too. Savvy still has her tool kit from our PS-1 outing. We'll start by scraping with the blade of a screwdriver. If that wears out, then other tools, then belt buckles. We'll *make* it work."

"And to seal the hole once the radio is outside the wall?"

Marcus rapped on a supply cabinet. "We undo the hinges if possible, break them if not. The door is a flat piece of rigid plastic. We'll make our hole somewhere the wall is flat. Set the door over the hole, and suction alone assures us a decent seal with the wall. The hotel people are all still in counterpressure suits, so we'll have plenty of leak patches to tape the edge of the cabinet door. From a datasheet in the shelter, we'll be able to network through the plastic cabinet door with the radio on the outside. So if *it* connects to anything . . ."

Such misplaced optimism. Thad tried, and failed, to remember the nature of hope. "Suppose you get your scavenged radio outside without killing us all. We're still beneath the base. Your signal will be absorbed by tons of metal. No one will hear squat."

"Phoebe is whipping around the Earth," Marcus persisted. "Sometimes the signal path will be through the dirt. It won't always be upward through the base."

Thad permitted himself to believe. "Okay, Judson, we'll give it a try."

*  *  *

"But how can the beam be so *dangerous?*" Ellen burst out. "Marcus and I traveled the country swearing up and down the system was safe. That the beam just isn't that intense."

But the powersat dealt with immense power, Valerie thought. A *gigawatt* of power, more than enough to do enormous harm. *How* you beamed that power made all the difference. Perhaps abducting a radio astronomer had not been such a bad idea. Especially a radio astronomer who had spent weeks debating the system end to end with Marcus.

Whoever controlled PS-1 had changed the beaming optimization. Defocused the beam? Refocused it? She would have to commit serious math to figure the best way to intensify localized hotspots. But *could* she wring out hotter—*much* hotter—hotspots, by constructive interference among the thousands of transmitters? Absolutely.

Valerie said, "PS-1 isn't dangerous, not as you built it. The story changes if someone doesn't care about efficiency or beam uniformity or power dribbling out in side lobes. Then parts of the beam can be made very intense."

"Lethally intense?"

"It'll take me some time to run the numbers, but yeah." Setting aside that hundreds, maybe thousands, dead already gave them the answer.

Tyler Pope stuck his head into the room. "Ready to dazzle?"

"Give us ten more minutes?" Valerie asked, fingers skimming the datasheet's virtual keyboard.

"That was a rhetorical question. Your presence is required in the war room."

\* \* \*

Valerie did not know what to expect of a war room. Giant wall screens. Lots of men and women, many uniformed, seated around an enormous conference table. Flags. Was that all too *Dr. Strangelove*?

Not really.

Perhaps the resemblance should not have surprised her. On the flight in, Tyler Pope had told her Mount Weather first opened in the depths of the Cold War.

She and Ellen were introduced to forty or so people, about half in the room and the rest netted in because planes remained grounded. Valerie did not try to retain names, struggling just to catch the organizations. In uniform: lots of military, mostly Air Force and NSA. In dark suits: CIA, FBI, Homeland Security, the State Department, and White House aides.

And here *she* was wearing blue jeans and a Hard Rock Café T-shirt.

One of the White House aides asked, "What does our brain trust have to suggest?"

Ellen said, "PS-1 is *meant* to beam power. Directing a beam takes only three things. A beacon on the ground target. Lat/long values aboard PS-1 that match the beacon's coordinates. A correctly formatted 'go' signal from the ground. Someone on PS-1 can update the permissible target list and input the 'go' code locally. I think the dependency on beacons is the weak link."

"We've sensed beacons at some of the targets," a woman in an Air Force uniform said. (A colonel, Valerie was almost certain. Keith had often had her quiz him on rank insignia before weekend call-ups.) "Elint picked up some signals just before attacks. Where we didn't detect a beacon for an attack, it may be because we didn't have a bird in position."

"Elint?" Valerie asked.

"Electronic intelligence. Nonvoice eavesdropping. A spy satellite, to keep it simple."

Ellen nibbled on her lower lip, thinking. "We built PS-1 to stop beaming if the beacon went off center. This new, intensified beam must fry the beacon entirely. Does the beam keep going after the beacon stops?"

"It does," the colonel said. "The elint birds see ongoing backscatter from the ground."

Ellen squirmed in her chair. "More software bypassed, just like reshaping the beam to make it more intense. Another bypass for which the bad guys would have to be *on* PS-1."

Someone asked, "But the beacons still serve as initial aiming points. Can we use that?"

The colonel shook her head. "Energy infrastructure is big and distributed and often in the middle of nowhere. Our best guess is that the terrorists remotely activate beacons by cell phone or radio when it's time for a strike. Bottom line: It's not safe to go in after spotting the signal. Two special-ops teams sent to suppress newly spotted beacons got . . . caught in the downlinks."

Cooked, the colonel meant.

Ellen shrank into herself. "It wasn't supposed to be a weapon," she whispered.

"Placing beacons . . ." Valerie hesitated, her question not yet clear in her mind. "Is that why attacks come only every hour or two? Too few bad guys on the ground to place beacons?"

"Unknown." Pope turned to a CIA colleague, a petite African-American woman. "Any luck getting patrols to catch the people setting beacons?"

"Every ambassador has been tasked to put out the word. That'll take time. So will deploying patrols."

"And we could be dealing with offshore wind farms or thousands of miles of pipelines and power cables," the Air Force colonel reminded them. "It's impossible to guard everything."

"Or they could change targets," a White House aide said glumly, "to damn near *anything.* What if they aim at cities?"

"They?" someone else challenged. "Is anyone still up there?"

"Someone is," an NSA guy answered. "We pick up their helmet chatter, although we have yet to break the encryption. Statistical analysis suggests they're speaking English. If so, another statistical analysis says they're using Russian intel-grade encryption. Which we have never broken."

"Let's get back to basics." Pope turned to Valerie and Ellen. "The shuttle and mother ship were moving targets. No fixed lat/long values to target. What does that tell you about how the bad guys compromised the lat/long matching function aboard PS-1? And if we're certain a plane or spaceship is free of beacons, does that make it safe to fly?"

The CIA *hadn't* been crazy to bring in an astronomer. "The warmer the telescope, the more thermal noise it generates. To do infrared astronomy, you want your instrument kept *cold*. Hence, there's an observatory on Phoebe."

"Meaning?" Pope asked.

"Meaning any bad guys on Phoebe had access to very good infrared sensors."

Pope said, "Whoever the bad guys are, they *were* on Phoebe. That faked CME brought together everyone in the neighborhood."

"That tears it," a two-star general said. "That's how they got the shuttle this morning. Infrared tracking. And if they can track a shuttle launch, they can track an inbound missile, too."

"You would destroy PS-1?" Ellen said. "We have to *save* it. We have to use it as it was intended. If not, then I've spent years building a horrible weapon. . . ."

Suddenly Ellen was on her feet, ashen, lurching from the room. Pope whispered to his colleague and she followed.

Smash the damn thing to splinters! Valerie thought. Then we can send help to Phoebe.

Someone—Valerie did not notice who—suggested, "What about launching from out of sight, sometime when PS-1 is over Asia?"

"Just a *great* time to be lobbing a missile in the direction of Russia and China," a man from Homeland Security said, fidgeting with his necktie.

The general stared down the civilian. "Russian early-warning satellites will spot any launch, and if Pope is correct, I imagine they'll relay the information to PS-1. There's no way we can know. And unless the payload loiters in orbit for a long while, making the intercept that much harder, I suspect it will retain enough heat for this astronomical sensor to lock onto against the cold background of space."

"For much of every orbit, the sun will warm your payload," Valerie said.

"I have a question," a man from the State Department said. "Why did we send up that shuttle in broad daylight? A solar-power satellite can't be much of a threat at night."

"It's not that simple," Valerie answered. "Earth's shadow narrows with distance. I can't do precise trigonometry in my head, but PS-1 is in full shadow less than one hour out of every six-hour orbit. Can you get a warhead to that altitude in less than an hour?"

Glowers and murmurs gave Valerie her answer.

"Then what's left?" a White House aide demanded. "Waiting like so many fish in a barrel, while the terrorists render us more dependent by the hour on Russian oil?"

The general shook his head. "If we can blind the IR sensor with ground-based lasers, a missile might get through. If the powersat hasn't already been networked into the Russian early-warning system. If that's the case, our only option may be launching so many missiles we overwhelm it."

That evoked lots of esoteric discussion about what and how and when to launch, about different payload options whose code names meant nothing to Valerie. Get *on* with it, she thought. Why the hell have missiles, if not for our own defense?

Looking a bit less pale, Ellen returned. She listened, frowning, shaking her head.

"What's the matter, Ellen?" Valerie asked.

"A missile will punch through PS-1 like a bullet through a wet tissue. Aside from the small hole, the structure is going to remain intact. Probably operational."

Several junior officers spoke at once about explosives, and momentum transfer during a collision, and multiple warheads, and—

Suddenly red in the face, Ellen shouted them down. "Do you not get how *big* PS-1 is? Two million pounds. A wafer-thin square two miles on a side. Every essential component is fault tolerant, and then many times replicated. Most everything is highly distributed. The powersat is *designed* to keep on working past failures, even to repair itself.

"To stop PS-1 you must *obliterate* it. Using lots of missiles or, God help us, a nuke."

For long seconds after Ellen's outburst, no one spoke.

"Christ," one of the White House people said. "That's been someone's effing brilliant plan all along. Let America waste years gearing up to mass-produce powersats. Let us commit to powersats as our way out of the post-Crudetastrophe box. Then convince the world we built an illegal WMD. Leave us no choice but to blow PS-1 to bits to stop the mayhem. Two million pounds of shrapnel: it'll be decades, maybe centuries, before anyone uses that region of space or the resources of Phoebe."

"What about the *people* on Phoebe?" Valerie asked. "If our missiles blast the powersat to space junk, how will we rescue them?"

No one would meet Valerie's eye. Not even Ellen.

At not quite 8 A.M., the day was already steamy. New Orleans, at least in the French Quarter, remained mostly asleep. Sitting in the shade of an awning, sipping an iced coffee and nibbling still-sizzling beignets, Dillon was at peace. Apart from indigents and hungover revelers sprawled out on park benches, Jackson Square was deserted. Seagulls and clanging channel buoys made the only sounds.

Crystal sat across the little wrought-iron table, sipping her own iced coffee, looking as content as he felt. They had the café almost to themselves. The breeze over the levee kept toying with her hair. After each gust she tossed her head, just so, to settle her bangs back in place. The maneuver never worked; somehow that made it even more adorable.

Setting down his cup, he reached over to pat her hand. "I could stay here all day."

Only somehow she was out of reach. Far away. Slipping away. Fading. A speck glimpsed through a reversed telescope. On another world.

He lunged—

Heart thudding in his chest. Dillon snapped awake. His knuckles, although he wore gloves, smarted where he had cracked them against the closed door of the little shelter. He *was* on another world.

He unstrapped his helmet from the side of the shelter. The interior of the helmet glowed, but to read the time from the HUD he had to slip it over his head. Fifteen minutes before he had to stand his next watch.

No point in trying to return to sleep. He used the primitive sanitary facilities, ate an energy bar—wallpaper paste would beat the slop from the helmet nipples—before sealing suit and helmet.

He vented oh-two from the shelter so that the hatch would open, and carefully swung himself outside. The splendor that was Earth brought a tear to his eye. Then a black, inchoate blot on that beautiful orb *really* made him want to cry. In his HUD's digital zoom, dark smoke from the refinery in Venezuela blended with smoke billowing from the bigger-than-ever oceanic burn-off. Burst tanks must still spew petroleum into the azure Caribbean.

"Enjoy your nap?" Felipe asked, only there was a ragged hint of strain under the surface cheerfulness. He waved from the open door of a nearby oh-two depot.

"All things considered, I'd rather be in The Space Place," Dillon said. "What's been happening?" Not that he thought he would like the answer.

"The usual, boss," Jonas answered. "An ethanol distillery here. A tidal generator there."

But where was Jonas? Dillon did a slow turn. He spotted the team's true leader at the open hatch to one of the powersat's main computer complexes. Taking aim now at what?

In the heat of the moment, awash in adrenaline, Dillon had struck his share of blows. But overnight—did night apply? In any event, as he had slept fitfully—the enormity of their actions had overwhelmed him. How many more lives must now weigh on his conscience?

"When does it *stop*?" Dillon asked.

Jonas shrugged. "Not up to me. Nor you, either."

"But it *is*," Dillon insisted. "By now, we must have made whatever point Yakov wanted made. If we agree among ourselves that something prevents us from continuing—say, that we've run out of oh-two reserves—who is to know otherwise?"

"What do you suggest?" Felipe asked.

"We take hoppers back to Phoebe or The Space Place. Take escape pods . . ." Dillon trailed off, wondering where they could go. Not home, ever again. Not anywhere with extradition. "I know we can't steer the pods. Time our departure to land in Russia." And then? Witness protection, maybe, or secret identities. He had begun to appreciate the vast scale of this operation. Yakov must have great influence in Russia to have pulled it all together.

Maybe, someday, through a trusted third party, contact could be made with Crystal. Maybe she could be convinced to join him.

"You were right, chief," Felipe said. "Insufficiently committed."

"Then as we discussed," Jonas said.

Dillon looked around wildly. The hoppers were docked across the powersat. Between him and escape were two men with drawn coil guns.

"Back into your cubbyhole," Jonas ordered. "I won't ask twice."

"Why don't you just shoot me?" Dillon screamed. "What's one more death?"

"Whatever you believe, I don't enjoy killing. Especially up close. So don't make me."

Dillon made his way to the nearest shelter. The tiny door shook with finality as someone slammed and latched it from outside.

\* \* \*

Ambassador Anatoly Vladimirovich Sokolov had furnished his private retreat at the Washington embassy more like a dacha than an office. A dacha fit for a czar, to be sure, but still a dacha. Sofas and chairs were all made for relaxation. Hot and cold dishes lined the long buffet table. The disguised freezer offered only vodka bottles.

Behind the ambassador, the room's true windows overlooked the embassy's central courtyard. Floor-to-ceiling displays on the other walls could show anything. When the ambassador worked, Yakov supposed, these walls would seem book-lined or darkly paneled. Today the holos offered deserted Black Sea beaches. Comfortable on a leather sofa, Yakov approved of—everything.

Dmitrii Federovich Aminov, FSB station chief and Yakov's nominal superior, sat at ease on a great leather wing chair. He was the ambassador's only other guest.

"To our success," the ambassador said. They were several rounds past long-winded toasts. He raised his glass.

They downed their shots and the ambassador poured refills. Everyone nibbled from the buffet, one zakuska or another to buffer some of the free-flowing alcohol.

In address, as in setting, formalities had been waived. They were here to celebrate. "Thank you, Anatoly Vladimirovich," Yakov said. "The operation indeed goes well."

"You are too modest." Sokolov smiled. "The president himself asked me to extend his congratulations."

President Khristenko, clearly. Not the hapless, clueless occupant of the White House.

Yakov nodded. "I am honored." And I trust that soon I will receive such thanks in person, in Moscow.

"A thing of beauty," Dmitrii Federovich said. "Alternatives to petroleum set back for years. Greedy partners unwilling to limit their exports will now do well even to meet their production quotas—with no one to blame but the Americans." He raised his glass. "To the Americans. Our customers for as long as the oil lasts."

They drained their shots, and Dmitrii poured the next round.

"If I might," Yakov began.

"Naturally, Yakov Nikolayevich," the ambassador beamed. He picked up his glass for the expected toast.

"A suggestion," Yakov said. "The American authorities are trying to blame everything on some cabal from The Space Place. Hoping to shift the blame."

Because the FBI, at least after the fact, was not entirely inept, and investigators had seized Dillon's condo and business. Had they not made the association, Yakov would have arranged the anonymous release of video of Dillon bringing saboteurs onto the OTEC platform.

"Anatoly Vladimirovich, when you next speak to the press, perhaps you might remind them that every flight to The Space Place originates from the United States. That every item of cargo delivered to the hotel or to Phoebe is both X-rayed and hand-searched. That every passenger, too, was X-rayed. So unless the Americans wish to implicate their own TSA . . ."

"As either fellow terrorists or criminally careless." The ambassador roared with laughter. "Excellent."

Yakov raised his glass. "To the TSA."

Exhausted, her brain reduced to mush, Valerie had reluctantly checked out the quarters assigned to her. Tyler Pope had spirited her away only that morning—but it already seemed a lifetime ago. Mount Weather was like another world from Green Bank.

The room looked comfortable enough, but despite the late hour she knew she could not sleep. She checked e-mail with the datasheet she had been using. A short note from Patrick: Simon and her parents coping okay; no signal detected from Phoebe. Telemetry had resumed from The Space Place, he supposed from a normal automatic reboot. No other comm detectable from the hotel; guests and staff presumed still absent.

Military satellites had reported the same reboot, with analysts making the same inference about The Space Place.

She sent Patrick a thank-you e-mail. She sent a short, *Be good, and Mommy misses you,* note to Simon. She switched on the 3-V but lasted only a couple minutes: every channel showed news and the news remained appalling. She checked out toiletries in the bathroom and clothing in an array of sizes in the closet and dresser. Apparently anyone staying beneath Mount Weather was expected to have arrived on a moment's notice. A faded scribble on the bottom of a dresser drawer declared: *Dick Cheney slept here.* She tried to remember who that was.

She went to bed, only to toss and turn.

Several times that day, she had asked about plans for a rescue. Haranguing or cajoling, bargaining or pleading, the method made no difference. "We'll discuss that later," devolved into stony silence.

Giving up on sleep, she prowled her room some more. One drawer had a "guest services" booklet, as though this place were a hotel. She began flipping through. The tunnel complex, called Area B, comprised almost fourteen acres! Rather than a hotel, it was a small town.

She located a twenty-four-hour dining room on the Area B map. She navigated through deserted halls to the eatery, got coffee and a stale scone, and carried her snack to an empty table.

Ten minutes later an Air Force major exited the cafeteria line. He saw Valerie, hesitated, then came her way. She thought she recognized him from one of the brainstorming sessions. To save her life, she could not have said which meeting. Garcia, she thought his name was.

"Dr. Clayburn, right?" he asked. "May I join you?"

"Sure, Major."

"It's Walt." He sat. "How are you holding up?"

"Swell. Oh, and call me Valerie." She broke tiny pieces off her scone.

"Waiting is hard." Walt glanced around the room. To see who might be listening? "No one asked, but I'm going to be the voice of unpleasant reality. Because facts are facts.

"Since the attacks from space began, PS-1, Phoebe, and the hotel have all been monitored. From Earth. With space assets. There's encrypted radio chatter on PS-1. No one has overheard a peep from Phoebe. No one has seen anyone stir." And very reluctantly, "Not a single escape pod has been used."

Because if anyone could, doubtless someone would have bailed by now from Phoebe. That no one has—you naïve woman—means they are all dead. So no one sees any reason to put lives at risk in another rescue mission.

She would be damned if she would acquiesce. "So what's the big plan, Walt? To conclude from an *absence* of evidence that they're all dead? That no one need waste a thought on them?"

"I don't know," he said. "Honest. But a lot of smart people are working on it."

*Not a single escape pod has been used.*

"I'm not ready to give up on them." On Marcus.

Walt would not meet her eyes.

"I'm *not!*"

* * *

Marcus looked around. Maybe two-thirds of the people wore helmets and counterpressure suits. The rest, those without suits in the shelter, had collected across the room. Of course putting on vacuum gear was only a precaution.

Famous last words?

Taking turns, Marcus, Savvy, and Dino Agnelli had scraped a more-or-less round hole through a wall panel's inner layer of aluminum. The insulating foam beneath had scooped right out. Savvy had just finished scribing a circle in the outer layer. The way the aluminum flexed, whatever lay beyond was less than rigid. Good: it would be faster to excavate.

The hole-in-progress sucked heat from the shelter.

Dino studied the ragged gap. "We're getting there," he declared.

Agnelli was a Kendricks employee, an electrical engineer, and one of the Phoebe old hands. He had the sort of open, honest face that people instinctively trusted. Marcus knew him from PS-1 telecons, had always liked the guy, and was glad finally to have met him.

Not so happy about the circumstances.

"Agreed," Marcus said. "Everyone ready?"

"Go for it," Thad said.

In a crouch, Marcus reached into the opening. Savvy knelt beside him, ready to do her part. From above, Dino shone a flashlight into the gap.

The screwdriver in Marcus's hand, the one with which they had started, had worn down to more of an ice pick. He stabbed.

Air whistled as he pushed and pried, then pulled back to bend up a tongue of aluminum sheet. "Go!" he shouted to Savvy.

People had, in theory, secured loose papers, food wrappers, and the like. Plenty still swirled about, pelting Marcus and getting sucked onto the little hole. His suit heater kicked on as Phoebe sucked more heat from the room.

Savvy brushed aside detritus to grip the metal tongue with insulated pliers. She tugged, cursing as the pliers slipped free.

"Slow and steady," Marcus said.

She grabbed hold again and, more slowly, peeled back a strip of metal. The whistling swelled. In the shelter, a couple of people moaned. "Back to you," Savvy said.

Marcus hacked with the screwdriver at the ice and grit behind the panel. Chunks broke off and shattered. He had to scoop the area clear, because the out-rushing air tried to hold the debris in place.

"Looks big enough!" Savvy called.

Hands reached over Marcus's shoulder. He grabbed the scavenged helmet radio with its improvised antenna and maneuvered the equipment into the opening. Damn! The hole was not yet deep enough. He handed back the radio and, in a frenzy of overhand stabs, made a deep puncture into the frozen dirt for the antenna.

The whistling had ominously faded.

"Try again," Marcus said. With the antenna nestled into its deeper hole, the radio fit. Scavenged fiber-optic cable trailed from the radio back into the shelter. "Cover!" he shouted, kicking away from the wall. Savvy kicked away at the same time.

Two women whose names Marcus had forgotten lowered the cabinet door—till suction ripped it from their hands. It slammed into the wall. As best Marcus could hear through his helmet, the hole was plugged, but people kept slapping pressure patches around the edge of the door. A bit of paper he held pinched between his gloved fingers wavered, but that might be only from people moving around.

"I'm releasing some oh-two," Thad called out.

"Shall we try?" Savvy asked. She had a datasheet under her arm, and had taken off her helmet.

"Do it," Dino said.

Savvy jacked the dangling end of the cable into her datasheet, then tapped away on the virtual keypad. "I'm connected to the outside radio," she announced to cheers.

"What's *it* connected to?" Dino asked.

"Nothing yet," she said.

Welcoming her optimism, Marcus could not help but wonder how long—especially after the oh-two that had just gushed out—they had left.

"It's going to work," Marcus told everyone. Himself included.

•   •   •

Boulders and dirt patches. Gravel fields, glints of ice, and twisty crevasses. The stark landscape undulating in the familiarly peculiar perambulation of a Phoebe tourist bot. Only Valerie felt nothing familiar in this trek, and not merely for exploring without Marcus.

The bot corral had returned to service, just as The Space Place and other satellites by the hundreds had roused themselves from standby mode or awakened to commands radioed from Earth. And why wouldn't they have returned to operations? The supposed CME had not been real.

Making the ongoing silence from Phoebe base all the scarier.

"*Faster*," she snarled at the dark holo that hung over her datasheet. Her words, like her frustrated hand gestures, did nothing. Once she had mastered the keyboard commands with which she had to make do without a game controller, she had pushed the bot to its fastest pace.

And that was a crawl.

On the other hand, her quixotic search could not hurt. Then why *not* attempt it? She squirmed in her chair, then fidgeted, then (succumbing to the habit she would have thought broken decades ago) gnawed on her nails. Gradually the scenery changed. A long, taut cable came into sight.

She typed a new order to the bot, setting it on a course parallel to the cable.

Toward Phoebe base.

•   •   •

Huddled together beneath blankets most people in the shelter slept, or at least they tried. To move took more energy—hence, more oxygen—than to remain still. To sleep used the least oxygen of all. To sleep took some of the load off the overtaxed air scrubbers.

Thad kept turning down the heat to save energy for the scrubbers. Marcus guessed the shelter's temperature was somewhere in the thirties, because his breath hung in a white cloud. He told himself he should try to sleep.

Instead, obsessively, he watched Savvy's datasheet for some sign— *any* sign—of life.

*   *   *

More gravel, boulders, and dirt.

Snatches of conversation penetrated walls and came through ventilation ducts. Did Mount Weather ever sleep? Valerie guessed not. Though it was three in the morning, she kept expecting a knock on her door from someone demanding her expert opinion.

The gaping pit of an ice mine. A nexus of pipes. Lots more dirt.

Finally, bright "lights": an array of corner-cube reflectors. The optical devices sent any incident light back in the exact direction from which it had come. These exploited the ever-scanning (and eye-safe) ultraviolet laser beam of her bot's lidar to mark the border. Beyond this point be intensive mining operations and the NASA base. Trespass and risk revocation of rental privileges.

Striding between markers, she kept going.

The top of an ice distillery peeking over the horizon was her first glimpse of Phoebe base. She cursed at her bot to speed up, even though that would drain its battery faster. Then, as the bot stumbled to a halt, as the imagery stuttered, she cursed herself for a sleep-deprived fool.

She had had her pick of bots in the corral, to which all must have been recalled for safety during the "CME." The rental company had only one broadcast facility on the little moon; the radio-controlled bots, spread out across the tourist zone, relayed messages among themselves in an ad hoc network. Only with all bots but her one still inside the corral, there *was* no network.

She needed bots to daisy-chain a connection from the corral to the NASA base. She rented six—every bot with fully charged batteries— and sent them scampering toward the base. An ad hoc network opened and her forward scout resumed its many-legged scuttle.

The leading bot reached a packed-dirt plain scuffed with boot treads. She paused to look around. Nothing about the area seemed noteworthy. She resumed "her" progress toward the base and, coming over a low rise, saw a deep cave.

Only its surfaces were all planes. Every intersection was at right angles. The opening was man-made, not a cavern.

Scuttling closer, she saw coiled hoses and metal canisters along the walls. She could neither discern canister colors nor, if she were to sidle closer—not unless the labels had been written in ultraviolet-sensitive ink—read the descriptions. As natural as the grayscale holo appeared, it was all computer-graphic wizardry: the bot "saw" with lidar. The process of reconstructing images from reflections of a scanning beam was like the radar maps she so often worked with—as from-a-whole-past-life as mapping Titan now felt.

But color blindness did not matter, any more than did the mechanics of bot "vision" with which she was obsessing. Only physics was easier to contemplate than what *did* matter: that she had found the base's hopper garage—and it was empty.

Where could everyone have gone?

Almost, Valerie abandoned her search. She was at a dead end. The hoppers gone meant the people had gone. Doubtless she should tell someone what she had discovered. Tyler Pope, maybe?

And then what?

Maybe she couldn't bear to accept that Marcus and the rest had set out. If they had, all too likely their intent was—somehow—to retake PS-1 from the terrorists. If they had, there was nothing more she could do.

Maybe she couldn't bear the thought of more waiting.

Or maybe, she had a choice to make. She could take action, or she could defer to the debating society and hope they did something. She felt sudden empathy for poor Patrick, so many years ago. And she knew how Marcus felt about committees.

With her pathetic squad of tourist bots, she continued her search.

\* \* \*

Valerie pounded on the flimsy wooden door. It rattled in its frame, and the knocking should have awakened Lazarus.

"I'm coming!" came the cross reply from inside. The door opened inward and Ellen Tanaka, bleary eyed, peered out. She was dressed (for the day, or, like Valerie, had she never gone to bed? Valerie guessed the latter). "What is it?"

"I'm not sure. Maybe Marcus and the others. Grab a datasheet, let's find an unoccupied office or meeting room somewhere where we can spread out, and I'll explain."

At the end of an isolated corridor they found an empty room with a long table. Valerie plugged in her datasheet, pulling up a holo of Phoebe base's surface structures. She said, "Watch closely."

"I don't see—"

"There," Valerie said. "Did you catch that stutter in the image?"

"Ye-es. Wait a minute. How are we seeing this?"

"From a tourist bot I marched across Phoebe. The rental center has an independent uplink to comsats, I imagine so sightseeing doesn't compete for bandwidth with NASA business. The bot company's link rebooted after the faux CME. Now keep watching."

The image hiccoughed three more times.

Valerie said, "Now I'm switching to another bot." The glitches continued. "Another." More hiccoughs.

"Interference?" Ellen asked.

"I think so. And when a bot backs away even a little, the interference is no longer noticeable. I'll bet we're picking up a weak signal from inside the base."

* * *

Marcus had a pounding headache. He was exhausted, short of breath, and a little sick to his stomach.

He was succumbing to hypoxia.

A month's supply of oxygen waited in storage tanks outside the shelter's sturdy metal hatch. Ice to electrolyze into yet more oxygen lay beneath the floor and behind every wall of the shelter.

Breathing as shallowly as he could, Marcus hated the irony.

**P**atrick rapped on the sturdy door of the Green Bank Observatory control room. He could hear music from inside. Half a minute passed without response, and he knocked harder. Still nothing.

He resisted admitting himself with the access code he was not supposed to know. Revealing he knew the door code was no way to put off guard whoever was on duty inside.

The observatory remained officially closed for the emergency, and Patrick had his choice of nearby empty offices to call from.

"Control room," a man answered. Over the phone, the music was recognizable. Jazz, with wailing sax.

Patrick recognized the voice. If it had been anyone else, maybe he could have talked his way into what he needed. Not with Ian Wakefield. No matter how long they knew each other, Ian would never get past Patrick's reputation.

"Hey, Ian, it's Patrick. You drew the short straw?"

"Taking my turn."

Because the big dish was too precious to go unused. Someone had to baby-sit the controls and monitor the readouts, even though observation requests could be submitted over the net. This emergency was being treated like the average blizzard.

"Would you let me in, please? Some status messages from the big dish look odd to me. I came in to review the system logs."

"Okay." *Click.*

Patrick returned to the locked door. The music had stopped; this time Ian heard the knock. One of the control room's many computers streamed 3-V and showed a talking head. Audio was muted, but the crawl said plenty.

"New attack?" Patrick asked.

"Attacks. Tidal generator in Scotland. Several ethanol distilleries in Brazil."

"Bastards."

"Yeah."

Patrick waved at the curved console. "Where do you want me?"

"Station six. Which system log?"

Patrick named it.

Ian frowned. "That's nothing privileged. I would've mailed a soft copy to you. You don't need to be in the control room."

"The world is going to hell. I feel like company today, if that's all right."

"Sure. Sorry." A burst of typing. "Okay, you should have your log now."

Someone needed to take action. Patrick had once flattered himself that he was a man of action. And by the actions he had taken, made everything *so* much worse.

He had to fix things. He *had* to.

A real man of action could have intimidated or coerced or just convinced Ian to provide the sysadmin password. But overweight, out-of-shape, middle-aged him? No way. *He* could not intimidate anyone.

But he could be devious.

After scrolling through the log file for a while, Patrick printed off a page—only what he printed came from a file he had tweaked on his office computer. He handed Ian the sheet, saying, "Something's screwy here."

"The dish appears to be acting fine."

"Maybe so, but the telemetry and this log don't agree." Patrick slipped his hand into his pocket to activate the homemade device inside. It emitted a short clatter like jangling keys: auditory camouflage. He rolled his chair next to Ian's. "You see?"

Ian scratched his head. "Odd. Any idea what might cause the mismatch?"

"I once saw something like this with the forty-five-foot dish. It turned out that the diagnostic server was missing an operating-system patch."

"Which data are correct? The telemetry or the detailed logs?"

Patrick shrugged. "I need to see the executables to know what patches are installed. Log me in?"

Ian turned back to his keyboard and pecked away. "There you go."

Patrick spent ten minutes scrolling through binary files, making an occasional *hmm* for effect. "Everything looks fine, patch-wise. I'm going home to cogitate. Log me off?"

"Sure."

Back in his office, Patrick took the recorder from his pocket. It collected the faint RF emissions of keyboard electronics scanning for keystrokes. It was sensitive enough to pick up keystrokes from twenty feet away—only not through the control room's shielded walls. The keystrokes immediately after Patrick had activated his recorder were what Ian had typed to log in Patrick.

He had Ian's sysadmin-privileged user ID and password.

●   ●   ●

"So are you ready to be a good little terrorist?" Jonas radioed.

Dillon was ready to be damn near *anything,* if it would release him from the claustrophobic shelter. "I won't interfere," he answered cautiously.

"Good. Make sure you're sealed up, and I'll let you out."

Dillon double-checked his suit. "Confirmed." The hatch opened, and he stepped outside. "Where are Lincoln and Felipe?" Dillon asked.

"In shelters, taking a break."

Overhead, Earth was at about half phase. They were over Central Asia. With his visor set to magnify, ominous black clouds dotted the Middle East. New petroleum fires?

"Our doing?" Dillon asked.

"Excellent choice of pronoun. We're in this together. And yes. Plus assorted other strikes that do not declare themselves so visually. A special today on ethanol distilleries and wind farms."

No matter that Dillon had resisted many such projects, seeing them destroyed was worse. The world was a funny place. "Explain something to me: How much longer can this go on?"

"That's the big question, isn't it?" Jonas laughed mirthlessly. "While we can. Till someone loses patience and blows apart our home away from home."

"You make this sound like a suicide mission."

"You should work on your reading-between-the-lines skills. If only you had the time."

Dillon shivered. "Why would you agree to such a thing? I certainly didn't."

"Have you ever said no to Yakov and made it stick?" Pause. "I didn't think so."

"Look," Dillon said hastily, "don't get me wrong. I hate big engineering projects like, like . . . what we're standing on. Over the years, in my own way, I've held back lots of so-called progress. But resistance is one thing and"—he gestured overhead—"*that* is quite something else."

"Missing your luxury suite already, boss?" Jonas's hand rested on the coil gun that hung from his tool belt.

Dillon edged away. "You don't want to die. I can feel it. We can all run and . . ."

"Right. Have Yakov sic the Russian intelligence apparatus on us."

"We're dead if we *stay*. You said it yourself."

"If the Russians don't nab us, the CIA will. It's not like either side's radars could fail to notice escape pods setting off or reentering the atmosphere. If we aren't quietly executed, or with a tad more formality sentenced to the chair, then what? Guantanamoed for life? After what we've done, how long would that be?"

"We have nothing to lose by trying," Dillon protested.

"*We* don't. Our families do. If we don't follow Yakov's script, how do you think the world will treat our loved ones? They'll be associated forever with what *we* did. Disgraced. Ostracized. Hounded by reporters, the curious, and revenge seekers. And by the way, our wives will be left penniless after our victims' families sue.

"Accept it, boss. There is no way out. We keep attacking until PS-1 is blown apart. Then people can suspect whatever they choose. No one will be able to *prove* who was responsible."

Hope of a sort, if only for Crystal. Dillon sought comfort in that, but a new implication shook him. Everyone on Phoebe had seen them. "So the people in the shelter on Phoebe . . . ?"

"Collateral damage." Jonas said. "Once the missiles come down our throats, no one will be up here for a *long* time. Debris will make it too dangerous."

"And if no one blows us up?"

"Oh you innocent fool." Jonas turned away. "There are oil-shale mines across Canada. Why don't we see if a bit more vigor will put us out of our misery a little sooner?"

●　●　●

"We have no choice but to destroy PS-1," a White House adviser insisted. She had teleconned into Mount Weather from the District.

Tyler Pope could not retrieve the woman's name. He found these political geeks as interchangeable as Rosencrantz and Guildenstern, Frick and Frack, the Olsen twins, Eng and Chang, Shemp and Curly Joe—

Stop that, Tyler ordered himself. It was not only that he thought the woman was flat-out wrong. Which she was: As essential as it was to stop the attacks, it had to be done another way. A way that would not plunge the country back into its Day After the Crudetastrophe hopelessness. And, damn it, he did not care how launching missiles played with focus groups in Peoria.

He was not the only one struggling. At the front of the conference room General Rodgers had pressed her lips so thin, the wonder was she hadn't cut someone with them. It was no secret *she* wanted to take out PS-1 with an overwhelming salvo of missiles.

After frantic efforts in a dozen missile silos, finally they *could* launch. ICBM guidance systems had been reprogrammed. Nuclear payloads too heavy to lob up to PS-1's orbit had been swapped out for muscular post-boost vehicles fitted with lighter high-explosive warheads.

Had throwing nukes at PS-1 been doable, they still would not want to. Nukes in space would violate the Outer Space Treaty—as if America was not already living a public-relations disaster. And nukes released electromagnetic pulses. Unlike the recent, imaginary CME, an EMP in space *would* fry satellites.

But the missiles would not launch until President Gibson ordered a launch. And the president had requested another review of his options, because, "We need to be sensitive to world opinion."

Was world opinion so difficult to read? Death and destruction rained from the skies! If it came to using strategic missiles to end the slaughter, what rational person could object?

But for as long as they debated they were not launching a slit-their-own-throat assault on PS-1. A stupid reprieve remained a reprieve.

As the discussion dragged on—and as new reports of attacks from PS-1 kept trickling in—even Tyler began to waver. Because no one, least of all him, had had an alternative to offer. He was among the most senior analysts in the Agency's Russian section, and his failure stung.

At some point waiting for a new option to turn up became the stupid plan. At some point they would have to cut their losses, even at the cost of destroying the powersat and losing access to Phoebe. And they *had* to act before another government shot down PS-1, making the U.S. look impotent and paralyzed.

"To continue," Rodgers said. Without raising her voice, some trick of voice quality compelled obedience, and the White House aide then posturing trailed off. "Presume the decision is made to send missiles against the powersat. Our analysts have assembled several attack scenarios." Rodgers pulled up a PowerHolo chart that summarized a number of options. "In overview first, our launch options include . . ."

None of the civilians—Pope included—was qualified to make a choice.

A few friendly governments claimed to accept American protestations of innocence in the attacks. No one doubted PS-1 was the instrument of destruction. Everyone blamed America for building the powersat, and blamed her again for not ending the attacks. While Russia sat back and gloated . . . .

Major Garcia leaned over and whispered, "Where is your brain trust this morning?"

"I let them sleep in," Tyler whispered back. Because, really, what benefit could have come of them sitting through this bombast?

"Good call," Garcia said.

*   *   *

A quick walk-through suggested Patrick and Ian were the only people in Jansky Lab. The control room was on the second floor, so Patrick picked a random office on the first. Before touching anything, he put on latex gloves. It would not do for the authorities to find his fingerprints here. The authorities would be here soon, looking.

The workstation came up, as it was meant to, with a log-on screen. He rebooted, this time interrupting the start-up sequence with the keyboard combination that forced the computer to run from a flash drive. He installed a telephony application that would, at the appointed hour, phone out for him.

As of that moment, the clock was ticking.

He opened the window, the better to locate this office from outside. When he found the open window, he trampled the grass beneath it. Then he tossed a rock through the glass. Whoever investigated the bomb-threat call would think a stranger had reached through the broken glass to unlatch the window.

*   *   *

Patrick backed his pickup truck to the testing shed where he had long stored his "SETI" transmitter. The transmitter, a toolbox, a spool of heavy-duty power cable, and a two-wheeled hand truck were on the truck's flatbed, tied and padded for their short trip, by the time his ro-bodialed call went out.

At least he *hoped* the call had gone out. If he had screwed up that, he had already failed.

"I have placed a bomb in the Jansky Lab," the computer-synth voice would have told the Green Bank 911 operator. "You need to evacuate the building at once."

There was no bomb, of course, but Patrick needed the control room empty so no one could follow what he was doing. He needed a few hours unsupervised—and searching every nook and cranny of Jansky Lab would take hours. Computer gear, souvenir gadgets, electronics memorabilia, and esoteric paraphernalia littered every office, storeroom, closet, and lab. Boxes and crates lined the hallways, old stuff due to be carted away and new stuff yet to be unpacked.

At the first faint wail of a siren, Patrick sped toward the big dish. When he came to the interior gate he circled around it off-road rather than use his access card. A mile down the road, he backed his truck up to the Green Bank Telescope's ground-level elevator.

The sirens were much louder now.

Ironically, he had never intended, nor expected, his transmitter to be used. But to make the interminable make-believe credible—to convince everyone that he had no idea where the *Verne* probe had gone—he had had to work on the transmitter doggedly and diligently. He had had to convince really smart Ph.D. physicists and radio astronomers that he thought his transmitter would work.

It *would* work.

And that was damned fortunate. He saw no other way to mitigate what he had done.

Patrick stacked everything on his hand truck and rolled it to the elevator. The dish was tipped, tracking . . . whatever. Leaving the hand truck by the elevator, he let himself into the nearby trailer. With the purloined sysadmin password, he took local control of the GBT. Ian would have evacuated the control room by now.

With the local controls Patrick suspended the observation schedule and ordered the dish into its maintenance mode: stationary, the dish in its birdbath position, one end of the L-shaped instrument arm pointing straight up. He walked back to the GBT itself and rolled his gear into the elevator car.

The car doors opened about two hundred feet above the ground. The wind whistled through his hair. Grateful for the handrails, trying not to look down, he rolled his gear along the walkway in the instrument arm's presently horizontal segment. Another elevator took him straight up the instrument arm's now-vertical segment to the receiver room.

Only when his work was done, *receiver room* would be a misnomer.

The turret on the room's roof could house up to eight modular receivers. Any receiver could be rotated into position at the dish's secondary focus. The modular bays in the turret implemented a common interface, to which all receivers were designed and built. Standardization made it easy to plug in units designed to receive at new wavelengths.

Standardization had let Patrick design a *transmitter* to mate with a bay in the turret.

Climbing a stepladder Patrick poked his head through an access panel on the receiver-room ceiling—almost five hundred feet above the ground. A mile away, vehicles surrounded the Jansky Lab. Emergency lights pulsed red on the fire trucks, blue on the Pocahontas County Sheriff's cruisers.

So far, so good.

He climbed down and started unplugging and removing a receiver module. By the time he had installed his transmitter module and rotated it into focus, he shook from exhaustion and dripped with sweat.

He had to rest before continuing. He unfolded the datasheet in his pocket and used a fiber-optic cable to tap the receiver room's network access. He found the bastards on PS-1 still at it; on their current pass over North America, they were destroying Canadian oil-shale facilities.

There was no time to rest.

The turret's modular bays, for all their general-purpose flexibility, were limited in one respect: they were meant to accommodate receivers. They provided a correspondingly modest amount of electrical power.

He needed to transmit, and with lots and *lots* of power. For that he had to drop power cable down the instrument arm to the telescope's six-hundred-kilowatt, diesel-powered backup generator.

There was no time to rest.

At last he finished. He rode down to the ground and retreated to the ground-level trailer, in the shadow of the big dish.

Marcus had been as good as his word: PS-1's orbital parameters and real-time position as determined by GPS were both available online. Trying not to think about Marcus, Patrick input the data into one of the observatory's smaller dishes.

The powersat was unmistakable. Harmonics, or side lobes of the power beam, or individual transmitters out of tolerance? Patrick wasn't sure and didn't care. Valerie would know. He tried not to think about her, either.

Only Patrick *couldn't* not think about Marcus and Valerie. Not when Valerie was Patrick's best friend, when sometimes she seemed like his only friend. While the big dish slewed into position, Patrick dashed off a mea culpa to Valerie. Just in case . . .

When the dish settled into position and began to track PS-1, Patrick initiated transmission.

An intense microwave beam, focused by the world's largest fully steerable antenna, blasted skyward.

The beam shut off!" Felipe shouted, from where he sat tethered by a main computer complex.

Dillon twitched. "How can that be?"

"Haven't a clue. Go wake Jonas."

"I'm awake," Jonas radioed from one of the tiny shelters. "I'll be out in a minute. And I'll wake Lincoln. The problem could be electrical."

Earth was at full phase, meaning PS-1 was between Earth and sun. The four of them—the four terrorists—were on the solar-cell side of the satellite, in direct sunlight. Dillon could only see a bit of Earth, glimpsed between his boots through a small view port. Palls of smoke stained western Canada, from the attacks on oil-shale mines.

Only Dillon could not bear to think of himself as a terrorist. Saboteur seemed a nobler way to resist "progress." The powersat's beam had failed? Great!

Jonas emerged from his shelter and sped hand over hand by guide cable to join Felipe. Studying the console, he muttered under his breath.

"What's the problem?" Dillon asked.

"The controls say damn near every transmitter on the platform went out of tolerance. Some safety system cut the beam."

"This is a test bed," Dillon said. "I guess it failed the test." We've done what we can, so let's get out of here!

*"That's* interesting." Jonas did not sound as though he was responding to Dillon. "This bears looking into."

"What's interesting?" Felipe asked.

Jonas pointed at the console. "The uplink monitor. Someone is beaming at *us.*"

Dillon winced. "Is it our turn to be cooked?" He had resigned himself to death, or so he had told himself—but not to dying *that* way. Poetic justice be damned.

"That's the funny thing," Jonas said. "This new beam carries only a tiny fraction of the power that PS-1 emits. *Could* emit. Still, from the timing, this new beam must have something to do with our beam cutting out."

"The incoming beam drowns out any beacons?" Dillon guessed. Because if so, maybe they were done up here.

"That's not it," Jonas said. "Well, okay, an incoming beam *might* prevent us from hearing ground beacons. But the targeting beacon is the first thing to go up in smoke. I had tweaked the beam-control code first thing to capture the exact lat/long of the beacon before we open fire. After the beacon's gone, we keep aiming at the associated lat/long.

"When our beam stopped a few minutes ago, the target beacon was already gone. It'll be trivial, just not quite as accurate, to work entirely by entering target lat/longs up here."

Lincoln had finally emerged from his shelter. He must have been listening to the conversation. "That's a lot about what's *not* our problem. So what is?" he asked.

"I don't know," Jonas answered. "Yet."

●  ●  ●

In a cacophony of beeps and ring tones, and a dozen aides bursting into telecon rooms across the country, the presidentially ordered strategy review shuddered to a halt. Because:

—The NSA's primary East Coast telecomm eavesdropping station—euphemistically the Navy Information Operations Command—had gone deaf. Or, rather, someone had begun shouting too loud for NIOC to hear anything else. The prelude to an attack? An attack by PS-1?

—Because PS-1's latest assault, on a Saskatchewan oil-shale mine, had stopped abruptly before inflicting any significant damage.

—Elint satellites reported that PS-1 had cut off its power beam! Another, far weaker, power beam appeared to be scattering off and penetrating through the powersat itself. From a hasty analysis of the scattered microwaves, probable beam strength: a half megawatt. Probable origin: West Virginia.

"Where is NIOC?" Tyler Pope demanded. He had to shout to make himself heard.

"Sugar Grove," an NSA guy called back.

"And where the hell is that?"

"West Virginia. Middle of the National Radio Quiet Zone."

In other words, not far from Green Bank. Pope called Valerie's room. No one answered. He called Ellen's room, and no one answered there, either.

His chair crashed as he leapt to his feet. On his way out of the room he caught General Rodger's arm. "Make sure the Pentagon and White House know the attacks have halted. Tell them someone found a way to suppress the beam from PS-1." Only who the hell *was* that someone? "Make sure they know we can delay a decision on a missile attack."

"Understood," she said. "Where are you going?"

"To find an astronomer."

\* \* \*

For long minutes, Dillon basked in the inactivity. Maybe PS-1 had been disabled. Maybe the worst of the horror was past. Maybe—

"Aha!" Jonas said. "PS-1 has sensors to pinpoint out-of-tolerance transmitters. The beam from the ground is saturating the sensors, which misread the situation as lots of our transmitters crapping out. That's why software cut our beam. Once we're over the horizon from the transmitter, we should be able to restart."

"Three hours later, we'll be back in line of sight of whoever figured out how to jam us. And for all we know, *another* transmitter waits just over the horizon, ready to keep us neutered. What then?" Felipe asked.

"Still reading code," Jonas said. "I can't answer yet, but this looks useful. The shutoff code is in a recent overlay to the control program, not very integrated. If I can bypass it . . ."

"We'll be back online, even on this side of the world," Felipe said. "So then do we ignore this beam from the ground?"

Jonas said, "In the long run, soaking up these microwaves can't be good for us or PS-1."

Because it's healthier to take a missile down the throat? Dillon thought hysterically. "With no beacon to aim at wherever this signal comes from, I don't see that we have any choice." Other than taking the hoppers back to Phoebe and grabbing escape pods.

"Oh, we'll have a choice," Jonas said, "as soon as I tweak some other code. The *beam* will be our beacon."

*   *   *

Thad stared at a piece of safety apparatus that had always terrified him. The chemical oxygen generator would run 600°F hot, releasing oxygen for as long as it burned. Unless the candle had the least bit of contamination, in which case it was as apt to explode as to burn.

But his head was pounding, and he was exhausted.

So: Light the candle, or in a few minutes they would all slip into comas from the lack of oxygen.

Gritting his teeth, Thad struck the firing pin in the igniter module.

Blessed heat and oxygen began to flow.

They would live a little while longer . . . .

*   *   *

"What in the world?" Ellen muttered from across the room.

Valerie looked up. Ellen's bot's eye view showed a stretch of dark plain dotted with light-shaded . . . Valerie could not guess what she saw. In the image reconstructed from lidar scans, light shades denoted surfaces that were comparatively reflective of UV light. Scattered patches of exposed ice?

"Move closer to one of the things," Valerie suggested.

The bot sidled closer, and the blobby shape in the foreground became, maddeningly, almost recognizable. Other objects came clearer, too, and she recognized a clipboard and, yards away, a pen.

"This looks like a wad of cloth," Ellen said.

Laid flat, the object was a T-shirt.

"A blowout!" Ellen said. "This is bad."

Terrified of what she would find, Valerie sent two bots racing toward the base's main air lock—

Where inner and outer hatches gaped, exposing Phoebe base to vacuum.

* * *

Through bots' eyes, Valerie stared in dismay.

With Ellen's guidance, Valerie had—somehow—maneuvered two bots into the depths of the base. Rather than figure out how bots could— *if* they could—descend a ladder, she had run them into an open shaft, sending them into slow-motion falls. After a second tumble, she had two bots on the shaft floor outside the radiation-shelter entrance.

Another two bots, one at the top of the shelter's access shaft and the second in the main corridor, daisy-chained toward the ad hoc network that reached across Phoebe back to the bot corral and its high-powered, comsat-linked, radio transceiver. Two more bots waited at the air lock, one inside, one out. The moment the hatches closed, Valerie would lose her tenuous connection.

The bots outside the radiation shelter stared up at a latch jammed with a pry bar. The pry bar did not look heavy, or difficult to remove. Only a bot could not reach the latch . . .

One bot standing on another *still* could not reach the latch. Could the bots find stuff to drag here, with which to improvise a ramp or staircase? Conceivably—if, first, they did not have to somehow climb the human-scaled ladder to find the stuff. And if the bots' batteries were not almost out of juice. Nor were there more bots to send: she and Ellen had dispatched every bot with any significant charge in its batteries.

In desperation, Valerie jumped a bot. It *had* no jump mode, but by contorting its tentacles and then twitching them, she got a sort-of leap that lifted the bot a few inches above the floor. As it floated like a dandelion puff in Phoebe's insignificant gravity, she wanted to scream. Instead, while the first bot drifted down, she fine-tuned her technique with the second. It leapt perhaps a foot into the air. The first bot landed and she jumped it again—

And landed it on the latch!

"Are you ready to close the air lock?" Valerie asked Ellen.

"Just say when."

Valerie edged the bot into position. Four limbs coiled around the latch itself. Three grabbed the pry bar. The remaining tentacle pressed against the jamb beside the hatch, for alignment. She heaved.

Nothing.

Loosening her grip she wiggled the bot into another position. The pry bar shifted! She changed her grip and pulled again. And again.

*　*　*

There was nothing left to try.

Here and there, people sipped dregs of oh-two from counterpressure-suit tanks by taking turns with the helmets. Most people hunched over paper or datasheets, recording their last thoughts, wishes, and wills.

Marcus had written notes to his parents and brother. He had written to Ellen, assuring her he had come to Phoebe by his own choice, and thanking her for her many kindnesses. He had written Lindsey, wishing her well, because life really was too short to carry a grudge. And because he really needed the closure, the better to say good-bye to someone truly special.

If Valerie felt as he did—and he thought she did—their brief time together was about to morph into trauma. He was about to become another man who made promises he could not keep and then did not come home.

Marcus shook his head, trying to clear his thoughts. Was there a noise beyond the pounding in his head? A grating, rasping sound?

He edged through the crowd, toward the noise. Toward the hatch. He was so short of breath, he could hardly walk.

*　*　*

The bot teetered on its perch on the latch, the pry bar removed and still in its grasp.

How could she get the attention of the people inside? On Earth, dropping the pry bar to the floor would raise a clamor. Here? As the tool gently landed, it would scarcely make a sound.

Valerie swung the pry bar against the closed hatch. From the bot's precarious perch on the hatch, she could pull back only a couple inches. How much noise could it even make inside?

She swung it again. Again. Again. Again . . .

*   *   *

Patrick knew the instant his luck turned: the lesser telescope with which he kept watch on the powersat had just gone blind.

PS-1 had resumed beaming. At Green Bank, it would seem.

He had failed—again.

The safest place for him was in this control trailer. The quarter inch of steel plate all around that shielded the big telescope from the trailer's electronics would shield *him*. But like a metal spoon in a microwave oven, the steel plate could absorb only so much energy without melting or arcing.

He told himself the telescope itself, sixteen million pounds of metal, would absorb most of the beam. He reminded himself that the telescope absorbed lightning strikes several times a year. He told himself that, before long, orbital motion would drop PS-1 behind the horizon.

He might yet survive his latest failure.

Creaking came from the direction of the big dish. He imagined metal softening. Warping. Bending. Sagging.

Then: piercing squeals. The tortured shrieks of Brobdingnagian motors, gears, and bearings seizing up.

He jumped at a tremendous *bang!* Diesel fuel vaporized, the tank exploding? With a crackle and a shower of sparks, power in the trailer died. In utter darkness, he felt . . . hot. He told himself the sensation was only his imagination.

Renewed creaks and groans, louder and more ominous. Tearing sounds.

Then a rumble like the end of the world. Only it got louder and louder and louder and . . .

*   *   *

The rasping stopped—or, more likely, had never existed in the first place. Marcus pondered staying where he was. But then, faintly, he heard tapping. He resumed walking. He was gasping by the time he reached the hatch. Definite tapping.

"Hello?" he called.

A few people looked up at him, puzzled. Most did not stir. No one answered, inside the shelter or out.

"Hello?" he called again, louder.

Not quite rhythmic: continued tapping. Like someone torturing a nail.

Everyone was about to die in here. Someone was out there. Although the hatch had *never* budged since Dillon and his people left, Marcus tugged on the inner latch.

The hatch blasted open.

And all the dank and fetid air in the shelter spewed out after it.

CONQUEST | 2023

The gale blew Marcus from the shelter.

People screamed. Papers, datasheets, emergency-ration wrappers, and drink bulbs pelted Marcus, then whipped past him up the access shaft. As the wind lifted him, too, but more slowly, the hatch rebounded from the shaft wall to slam into his side and send him spinning.

Someone shoved him aside to clamber up the ladder into the station. Someone in a blue counterpressure suit and helmet.

Suddenly air gushed the other way: down the shaft. Toward the shelter.

Marcus crashed into a wall. Debris swirled about. As did an eight-legged something. A silvery tourist bot.

"I knew you would hear me," he told Valerie. And passed out.

*　*　*

"So what shall it be, hmm?" Jonas floated above a terminal, hands poised. "I see beacons lit for a solar farm in Cuba, a garbage-fueled municipal power plant on Aruba, and a tidal power plant in the Azores. What's your pleasure?"

Dillon shivered. Pleasure? "You know how I feel."

"I'll take that as a vote for something dramatic, something to get this over quickly." Jonas studied his terminal. "More than cigars will be smoking in Cuba."

"You really think that's necessary?"

"I do indeed, boss." Something changed in Jonas's voice, and his customary mocking tone vanished. "Because if we *don't* get a response soon we'll have to up the ante. None of us want that."

"Up the ante?"

"Uh-huh," Jonas said flatly. "Population centers."

* * *

"Shit, shit, *shit!*"

Abandoning a systematic search, Tyler Pope dashed toward the sudden, heartfelt curse. Valerie Clayburn did not strike him as the cussing kind, but these were not ordinary times and the pissed-off voice sure sounded like hers. He found Valerie and Ellen Tanaka in an out-of-the-way meeting room.

"There you are," he began. Then he noticed—in grayscale, the shading somehow offending his sense of nature—a holo of what must be Phoebe and its base. At the heart of the image, an air-lock hatch ajar. And obstructing much of his view, a white-on-red blinking banner that shouted: *Bots lost. User account frozen pending investigation.* "What's going on?"

The women exchanged anguished glances. Ellen nodded.

"First things first," Valerie said. She opened another holo to show a hatch in an interior room or shaft, the door latch jammed with a pry bar. "People were trapped inside the Phoebe radiation shelter. Ellen and I had marched tourist bots across Phoebe to see what we could learn. This image was taken a few minutes ago."

"Were trapped?" Tyler echoed.

Frowning, Valerie opened a third image: a blurry, canted, still shot of someone emerging from the hatch. "This is from maybe a minute before you joined us. I think the bot that took the picture is spinning in midair, knocked off the hatch latch from which it had removed the pry bar. But thin air, because we found the station in vacuum. The shelter hatch exploded open."

"And what's happening now?" he asked. "How are the people doing? What can they tell us about events on PS-1?"

"I don't *know*," Valerie said. She gestured at the original holo and its flashing disconnect banner. "Closing the air lock broke the radio connection to the bots inside the base. I've gotten myself blacklisted for seeming to have lost rentals."

"This I can fix," Tyler said, squinting at the logo in a corner of the images. "Out of Body Tours."

As he reached into a coat pocket for his cell, it rang. "Pope."

"It's hitting the fan again," Charmaine Powell said. By dashing off in search of Valerie, he had left his protégée doing the honors for the CIA in the war room. "General Rodgers wants you back, pronto."

"Meeting still flailing?" he guessed.

"The attacks have resumed."

"Okay, keep me informed. I'll be back as soon as I can." He hung up, surfed to Out of Body Tours, and rang the tech-support number.

"Out of Body—"

"National emergency," Tyler interrupted. "Your CEO, now."

"What's the nature of your prob—?" the tech-support guy began, squirming in his seat.

"Forget your script. The CEO, *now*. Homeland Security authorization code . . ." Tyler needed a moment to recall the string of digits. "You *do* know what's happening in the world?"

"A . . . a moment, sir. I need to put you on hold." Click.

"Homeland Security?" Ellen asked.

Pope shrugged. "I get fewer questions and more cooperation that way." Because cooperating with *Homeland* Security might mean saving your own hide.

The frozen image on the phone dissolved into a puzzled-looking blond woman. "Regina Foster. What's this about, Mister . . . ?"

Whether it was playing the national emergency card or his government expense account, in three minutes Tyler had the CEO's promise to transfer the entire bot operation on Phoebe to Valerie's control. Everyone on tech support would be at her disposal.

"But I don't know for how long we can keep it up," Foster said. "I want to help, not that I understand what's going on, but our Phoebe facility is running off backup batteries. We buy power from NASA, and their nuke hasn't returned to service since the CME."

Tyler's phone gave a call-waiting chirp, and the name on his caller

ID should *not* have been coming up. It wouldn't unless yet more shit had hit the fan—and it was that kind of day.

He said, "All the more reason to make things happen now. Work it out with Dr. Clayburn. I'm transferring the—"

"I don't *have* a cell," Valerie interrupted.

He transferred the bot lady to Ellen's phone and took his incoming call.

"Sorry to interrupt, sir," said a soldier in combat gear: the leader of the squad left to watch over Valerie's family.

Valerie must have recognized the sergeant, too. "Simon! My parents! Patrick! Are they all right?"

• • •

"Your family is fine, ma'am," the soldier said. "They're still at your house, with half my squad. Dr. Burkhalter left this morning."

Valerie stared, her heart pounding in her chest, hearing disaster in the young man's carefully flat and expressionless voice. "Why aren't you with my family?"

"Mr. Pope, sir?"

"Go ahead, Sergeant," Pope said. "What's going on?"

"Yes, sir. While watching the doctor's house, I monitored the police bands. The county sheriff received a bomb threat . . ."

Methodically, dispassionately, the soldier reported. Then he said, "Sir? I can't begin to *describe* this next part. May I show you?"

"Go ahead," Pope said.

The sergeant disappeared, replaced by sky and woods. The image swung crazily, then zoomed. But at what?

"Where was this vid taken, Sergeant?" Pope asked.

"From the top of the NRAO water tower, sir."

Valerie squinted at the jumble of white arcs, lines, and crumpled white . . . paper? The heap had no meaning to her without some indication of scale. Only as she stared, a squat white *something*, peeking out from beneath the rubble, caught her eye. Tiny: like a shoebox. And she saw something black, even smaller, in a trough of the rubble pile. The black whatever-it-was reminded her of something.

The cab of one of Simon's many toy trucks, likewise squashed.

The scale clicked in.

"The Green Bank Telescope has collapsed," she said in awe and horror.

"Yes, ma'am," the soldier said.

"The bomb?" she asked. Why would anyone . . . ?

"No, ma'am."

Pope helped her to a chair. "I came looking for you because someone was beaming microwaves *from* the quiet zone. Somehow, the beam stopped the PS-1 attacks . . . for a time."

Valerie shivered. "Until, *this*."

"So it appears," Pope said.

That "shoebox" was the onsite trailer for maintenance control of the GBT. She knew that trailer very well. And she knew someone who drove a black pickup. Who, her heart told her, would be found inside that crushed trailer. Beneath many tons of wreckage.

"Oh, Patrick," she whispered. "What have you done now?"

**T**hose *assholes*, Thad thought every few seconds. The curse, un-bidden and unhelpful, returned no matter how urgent the mat-ter to which he attended. To restart the base was complicated under any circumstances, and he was pretty damned sure no one had ever had to undertake a restart after a blowout. Or with dozens of tourists underfoot. Or with the station chief in the infirmary, doped up to his eyeballs.

*Assholes*. Jonas and his buddies had left almost eighty people to smother in their own fumes. It hadn't been enough to strand everyone by taking away every last hopper?

"Hey, Thad," someone radioed.

With his head still throbbing from a hypoxia-induced migraine, Thad needed a few seconds to place the voice. "Go ahead, Chuck."

"The power plant restarted without a hitch. I'm ready to send some juice."

"Excellent," said Dino Agnelli. He was flat on the floor, his head in-side the main comm console. "Then we can get some heat in this place."

"Let's not take any chances," Thad radioed Chuck. "Start at ten percent."

"Ten percent. You got it."

And Thad's status board said they did. "Good job, Chuck. Stay there for a bit, in case there are any snags."

Because there *would* be snags. The assholes.

Thad routed power to central heating, then shut down the emergency fuel cells with which he had restarted the base.

Dino inched out of the console. "Main comm is a total loss, Thad. They did a real number on it. Sorry."

What if anyone found out *they* was *me*? Thad shivered, and it had nothing to do with the station's chill. "Can you fix it?"

"I'll have to assemble a new transceiver from scratch. In theory, we have spares of everything." Dino stood. "With luck nothing that I need blew out the air lock."

"Assholes," Thad answered.

"You got that right. We're damned lucky not to have lost anyone. You want the good news?"

"Absolutely."

Dino settled into the command center's second chair and did something at its console. ". . . continue to rage out of control. Spacecraft and, with few exceptions, aircraft remain grounded worldwide. Meanwhile, in breaking news, powersat attacks have resumed after an unexplained brief hiatus. Joining us live from Havana, BBC correspondent—"

"Turn that off," Thad ordered. "How the *hell* is that good news?" Or even *news*? From the moment crew had stepped outside after their escape, people had been tuning into the radio and 3-V reports streaming down from broadcast satellites in higher orbits.

"I wired a spare helmet radio to the main antenna," Dino said, clicking off the newscast. "By good news, I meant only that now everyone inside can know what's going on. If they want to know." A long pause. "So are we going to live through this?"

"Yeah." Thad even half believed what he said. "With the nuke running, we have power for years. That means we have oh-two and water for years."

"Not food for years, though. Especially not with so many guests."

Because no one would be coming to get them. Not while PS-1 . . . *Assholes.*

Thad checked the work board. Five crew and Marcus remained outside. What, exactly, Marcus did, Thad did not know. But had Marcus not heard, or hallucinated, the tapping at the hatch, they would all have died in the shelter. If the man intuited that his girlfriend would have left something useful on the surface—even though he had no idea what that might be—it was worth taking a look. Meanwhile, every moment of spacesuit chatter told folks listening groundside that people remained alive on Phoebe.

But who *was* listening, using a hefty enough dish to hear them? NASA, of course. But Yakov—in any event, some part of Russian intelligence—would be, too. Yakov, whose last-minute message had ordered: *Do not reveal yourself unnecessarily, but the success of the mission comes first.*

And Robin and her family remained forfeit.

Everyone working topside had been directed to limit their conversation to getting stuff up and running. Whatever they transmitted might be intercepted, and helmet "private" channels lacked military- or intel-grade encryption. Thad and Savannah Morgan had argued (doubtless, for very different reasons) that they leave it to NASA—and to someone they *knew* at NASA—to ask for any report. NASA and military comsats could reach Phoebe as readily as had the commercial broadcast satellites.

*Do not reveal yourself unnecessarily, but the success of the mission comes first.*

The mission. Thad now knew what it was. And that *he* had made the mission possible. How many thousand deaths were on his conscience?

And how many deaths were yet to come?

\* \* \*

Marcus stood near the base's main air lock, tethered to guide cables, looking about. But looking for what? *Valerie, give me a sign.*

He saw the brilliant star that was The Space Place—without hoppers, unreachable. He saw base workers reactivating gear from the CME shutdown. All around the air lock and leading off to mines, distilleries, and factories, he saw the endlessly scuffed, scraped, and scarred surface. He saw work bots scuttling about on chores of their own.

And one bot, well out toward the too-close horizon, gamboling.

Transferring tethers to a guide cable that led toward the strange bot, he set off for a closer look. Halfway there, he could tell the bot was a tourist model. As if the bot saw him, too, it ceased its odd behavior. When he reached it, the bot was motionless.

He muted his helmet mike. "Val?" he asked, feeling foolish. "Valerie?"

The bot extended a limb to scratch at the surface. Ice glittered where it scraped away the asphalt-dark coating. A circle. Two dots.

A smiley face!

Because via the bot, through his visor, she had recognized his face? Read his lips? It could be.

The bot resumed drawing . . . no, writing.

He mouthed, "What do you want me to do?"

The bot continued its scratching. As it wrote, Marcus captured pictures with his helmet camera. He thought he understood what she had in mind. No way did he have the computer skills to implement what she proposed.

Very methodically, he obliterated the message with his boot tip.

*　*　*

With four people inside and its hatch closed, the base command center was full, if still nothing like the erstwhile crowding in the radiation shelter. With only a blinking cursor on the main screen, Marcus found the wait unbearable. And then—

Letter by letter, a message formed: *We have visual. Test audio.*

"This is Stankiewicz," Thad said. He had taken one of the room's two chairs. Marcus and the rest stood behind him.

*Loud and clear.* Pause. *This is Valerie Clayburn, radio astronomer and designated keyboarder. With me are Ellen Tanaka, NASA, and TLAs.*

Thad said, "With me on this end are Marcus Judson and Dino Agnelli, both NASA contractors, and Savannah Morgan, civilian with the Air Force."

"TLAs?" Marcus whispered.

Savvy whispered back, "Three-letter agencies. CIA and NSA, most likely. I suspect NSA wizards helped implement your friend's clever idea."

A clever idea Dino and Savvy had had to implement unaided at this end. Comm protocols were hardly Marcus's forte. He gathered that the link involved tunneling a covert connection through the Out of Body Tours wireless network, then bot by bot across Phoebe to the base. With the nuclear plant once again feeding power to the bot corral, they had bots to spare.

Whatever privacy they had on the link came of subtlety, not security. It was a Catch-22 situation. Without mathematically robust, NSA-blessed, encryption software *on* Phoebe, anyone on the ground had no acceptable way to send such software *to* Phoebe. All that Savvy hoped to achieve with standard Internet encryption was to deter curious employees at Out of Body Networks.

The uplink from Earth had to hide inside the bot command stream. To indicate, for example, "Turn twenty degrees clockwise and walk forward," entailed very few bits. Only text messaging, painfully slow, fit within the low-bandwidth uplink channel.

The downlink to Earth, however, got to hide in the high-bandwidth streaming video from bot "eyes." Bots normally streamed video with thirty-two bits of grayscale depth. Val's improvisation took grayscale video of the surface and overwrote the three least significant bits. Three bits sufficed for audio and a grainy, slow frame-rate video of the command center. Only a very discerning eye—and a suspicious mind—would notice anything amiss in the composite image.

A picture might or might not be worth a thousand words. What was not open for debate was that a decent picture took thousands of times more bits than words required.

Letter by letter, text crept across the command-center display. *Where's the station chief?*

Thad said, "Irv is in the infirmary, but he's stable. Shot by the bad guys."

*Who \*are\* the bad guys?*

"Dillon Russo," Marcus said. "I met him at the Cosmic Adventures training center in Houston, and I'm almost certain he's a Resetter. And the three guys who trained with him. Russo said they all worked for him."

*Thanks. TLA says that for other reasons, we thought those four were the culprits.*

*New topic: NORAD is tracking a few dozen new objects in Earth or-bit, not launched from the ground. Big things: about ten feet long. Preliminary analysis shows their orbits buzzing Phoebe. Any ideas?*

"My guess?" Thad said. "The hoppers the bad guys didn't need for themselves. We know the hoppers were missing from their garage, just not where they had gone."

The groups brought each other up to date. When matters reached the attacks from and on the Green Bank Telescope, Val's typing went to hell: missing letters, extra letters, transpositions.

No one commented on the glitches, but Marcus worried. In weeks of texting with Valerie, he had never seen typos like this.

*       *       *

Thad had little to say, reticent less as a matter of strategy than in dread of what, in his fear and guilt, he might blurt out.

He answered direct questions but volunteered nothing. Asked about the IR observatory, he radioed for someone on the surface to check it out. The pillaging of the observatory seemed only to verify existing TLA suspicions. He confirmed the base no longer had hoppers. No one admitted to knowing how the terrorists got guns to Phoebe, so his pleading ignorance fit right in.

*We doon't know why the GBT attaked..*

"This spy versus spy shit is fascinating," Thad snapped, "but suppose we get real."

The typing stopped. Marcus glared.

"Let's get to the basics," Thad continued. "You can't send a relief ship with supplies or to get poor Irv to a hospital. You can't stop the attacks from PS-1. Nor, even if someone here is crazy enough to go up against armed terrorists, can we. Without hoppers, we can't get to PS-1.

"So while you TLAs think your grand thoughts, here is what's on *my* mind. With Irv out of commission, I'm responsible for the sixteen people stationed here and the four inspectors. It's not official, but I also feel responsible for fifty-six evacuees from The Space Place. And while I could fret about how soon we'll run out of food, what *really* scares me is getting stranded. Once you blow PS-1 to hell—and for all our yakking, I don't see what choice anyone has—ships won't come up here, maybe ever."

That had to be, ultimately, Yakov's plan: the destruction of PS-1. It would sell Russian oil. It would set back American attempts to use less oil. And yet . . .

Yakov's goal and Thad's had converged. Once PS-1 was gone, the killing stopped. Once orbital debris rendered Phoebe unusable, he became of no value to Yakov.

*What do you suggest?*

"Evacuate! Get away while we have the chance!" he snapped back.

"We don't have enough escape pods," Dino said. "We have five four-passenger pods for the staff, plus a spare unit. That's nowhere near what we'd need."

No one suggested leaving anyone behind. Not yet.

Thad said, "That's four people per pod in deceleration couches. How many people can we shoehorn in"—or stack, like cordwood, in layers—"if we remove the couches? And maybe there is more nonessential equipment we can rip out."

"Without couches, people would get mashed," Dino said.

"You'd prefer starving to death?" Thad countered.

*Oxyggn for extra people?*

"We have counterpressure suits," Thad said. "If needed, we'll bring aboard oh-two tanks. Ellen, NASA has the pod specs. Can you research that for us? And any tweaking the reentry software might need to correct for unplanned mass in the pods?"

*SHe saidd yes.*

Marcus cleared his throat. "While you're looking, Ellen . . . I know it's a long shot, but see if we can modify the pods to use locally."

*Solid fule. Can't starrt and stop.*

"Right," Marcus said. "Sorry. It's been a long few days."

*Herre too.*

"Back to practicality," Thad said. "Pretty damn soon, someone will launch missiles. Don't bother denying it—we're not stupid. We're fifty miles from what's about to become a two-million-pound shit storm of shrapnel. How many escape pods will we lose if we wait till then to evacuate?

"I'm going to get people started stripping out the couches. Can you give me twenty-four hours? Or a few minutes warning?"

*If poxsible.*

That meant no. The TLAs would not trust this kludged comm channel enough to transmit a warning. And almost certainly, that a launch was imminent.

"Then let's get to work," Thad said.

*   *   *

Stankiewicz had it right, Tyler decided. The acting station chief *should* be focused on saving seventy-six innocent bystanders. Taking back PS-1 by a sneak attack from Phoebe was counterproductive daydreaming.

Tyler said, "Does anyone see a reason not to let these people get to work on getting down?"

No one did.

Ellen shoved back her chair and stood. "I've got my assignment. Keep the link open for when I have something to report."

*Meeting's ovrr,* Valerie typed. *Someone stay pn the line.*

"I'll hang around," Marcus Judson volunteered from Phoebe base. "Val, would you stick around, too?"

*Sure.*

"Everyone else, take five," Tyler announced. "Then we talk strategy."

People filed from the room, here and—according to the big display—on Phoebe. Valerie had not budged; she looked too drained to move.

Tyler felt the same but did not dare give in to it. From the first empty office he found, he called his partner. She had choppered to Langley to call in favors among Agency data-mining gnomes. It was a short flight, and PS-1 was below the horizon for a few hours. "Give me something I can use."

Like maybe a magic carpet. At this point, nothing less than magic would avoid stranding a bunch of good folks in space. Or more hours of presidential dithering.

From his cell phone, Charmaine Powell grinned. "Oh, I have something. Are you sitting?"

"I'm tough. What have you got?"

"E-ZPass records. Care to guess the when and where of Dillon Russo's last road trip?"

"This isn't the best day for playing twenty questions, Char."

"Be that way. On August twelfth, that's a Saturday, if you wondered, Dillon Russo's BMW jaunted from New York to McLean and back."

"McLean, as in Virginia?" McLean, as in just down the road from CIA headquarters? Because if Russo was another CIA source who, in fact, was a double agent, Tyler might *scream*.

"The very same. And there's more."

Something about that date nagged at him. Seven weeks ago. "Hold on for a moment." He paged through the calendar on his phone. For August twelfth he found a neighborhood barbecue—and a reminder to write up a contact report.

He returned to the call. "Russo came to see Yakov Brodsky, didn't he?"

"I can't prove it, but yeah. E-ZPass brings the car to the outskirts of your neighborhood. From the exit ramp, traffic cameras show him entering and leaving the neighborhood. Late afternoon."

Right after the party, for chrissakes. "And soon after, Russo buys four tickets to The Space Place and gads off to Houston for training."

"I thought you would find that trip interesting. As for Brodsky himself, he has only been back and forth between home and the embassy since Russo and friends ran amok."

Tyler said, "Let's put surveillance on Yakov. But *obvious* tails." Because if the NSA could listen in at Yakov's house or the embassy, they would be doing it anyway. "Maybe we'll rattle him. And have your data gnomes dig up what they can about his diplomatic and FSB career."

"You don't much care for your neighbor, do you?"

"I'm from Texas. How could I possibly like someone who burns my burgers and refuses to distinguish between barbecue and grilling?"

*   *   *

Valerie had the conference room to herself. Oh, how she wanted to talk to Marcus—but not like *this*.

On the big display, Marcus had settled into a chair. He said, "Val, are you still there? And are you all right?"

*I'm finne,* she typed. Why add to his worries?

"No, you're not," Marcus said.

*I'm fine,* she typed, this time getting it right.

"I know you better than that."

Typing slowly and deliberately, proofreading and correcting before she hit RETURN, she managed to get out, *Okay. You caught me. I'm worried about you.*

He ran splayed fingers through his hair. (She knew him pretty well, too, and that was one of *his* nervous mannerisms.) "When the GBT collapse came up, you began typing as if with ten left thumbs. What aren't you telling me?"

*I'm just tirred.* The typo went out before she noticed it. *Come down and we'll discuss it.*

A troubled look flashed across his face. Questioning whether he would survive to make it down? "Is your family okay?"

It was all she could do to send *yes.* If the microwave beam directed at the GBT had veered only a couple of miles, it could have hit the town. It could have hit—

What had Patrick been *thinking?*

"You know and I know something is on your mind," Marcus said.

He had too much going on already, and this could wait, but somehow she was typing again. *Patrick is dead.*

"The attack on the observatory? I'm so sorry, Val." He frowned. "His 'SETI' transmitter, wasn't it?"

*I assume so.* And again, her fingers ignored her better judgment. *He left me a message.*

"I'm so sorry, Val. I truly am." Pause. "If it will help, tell me about it."

Repeating foolishness could not help. But her hands were once again moving, and no longer making mistakes. *He wrote, "I'm doing my best to undo my last big mistake. It's the best way I know to honor my promise to look after your family."*

It made no sense. No sense at all.

"Patrick's last big mistake," Marcus said. "Losing the *Verne* probe? I don't understand what he meant. Do you?"

*Get down here and we'll figure it out together.* Or, at least, get down here.

The least popular spot in Phoebe base, no doubt for the awful memories it evoked, was the radiation shelter. Marcus shared those memories, but he could not sleep and he needed an empty area to pace.

Why even try to sleep? In two hours, he would be back in an escape pod, taking another turn at dismembering deceleration couches with a cutting torch. The couches were *not* designed to come out.

And so, his thoughts churning, Marcus trudged back and forth along a Velcro floor strip. It seemed impossible that a week ago he and Val had been together. Or that within that week, PS-1 had changed from his life's work to a WMD, and that thousands had died. Or that among the dead, his final words an enigma, was a close friend of Valerie's.

*I'm doing my best to undo my last big mistake. It's the best way I know to honor my promise to look after your family.*

Marcus stopped, turned, and began pacing in the opposite direction. *He* had not done well by his promises, either. He had promised roomfuls, thousands, of people that powersats were safe and good. He had promised Valerie that he would be safe going to Phoebe and PS-1, that he would be home before she knew it.

So much for good intentions.

Was that how Patrick felt? That his good intentions had all gone bad?

From everything Marcus knew, Patrick had spent years trying to find the *Verne* probe. Whether noble or nuts, what did Patrick's quixotic attack on PS-1 have to do with undoing his last big mistake?

Marcus skidded to a halt—or tried to. The abrupt motion tore him free of the Velcro floor strip and sent him airborne. He scarcely noticed. Suppose the *Verne* probe was not Patrick's big mistake.

Suppose *Verne* was never lost at all.

\* \* \*

"What about Phoebe drives everyone nuts?" Marcus asked. As far as he knew, he spoke to an empty room. Minutes earlier he had awakened someone left to baby-sit the Mount Weather end of the jury-rigged comm link. Their parting shot: *Getting your people.* "Totally crazy."

*Marcus, it's me. Ellen's here, too. What's crazy?*

"Sorry to wake you," he said. At least he hoped he had. By Phoebe and Eastern time alike, it was closing in on midnight.

*As if.*

"What about Phoebe drives you nuts, Val? Professionally."

*That it gets in my way.* A pause. *You wouldn't have tracked me down to ask that.* A longer pause. *Where it came from.*

"That's the one. If it had always been in the orbit where NASA discovered it, it should have sublimated long before people knew to look for it." Before there were people *to* look.

*Until recently, what became Phoebe must have orbited out past the ice line. Something perturbed its orbit.*

"Just as something perturbed its Earth-threatening new orbit so that we could capture it?"

Another long pause. He wished he could *see* them: talking it over. Yawning. Just for who they were, and how important they both were to him.

*Not the same. My money is on Jupiter.*

"Why not the same?" Marcus persisted.

*Ellen here. A gravity tractor is a spacecraft. It hovers over an asteroid, or whatever. Gravity pulls the rock and the probe toward each*

*other. As the spacecraft moves, that attraction tows the rock. The force
between the two is tiny. To shift a rock's orbit noticeably can take years
and a spacecraft carrying fuel for years.*

"Who is to say it didn't?"

*The gravity tractor wasn't launched until Phoebe was discovered by
NASA.*

"Understood. But the *Verne* probe was."

＊　＊　＊

In a remote corner of the twenty-four-hour cafeteria, over desperately
needed coffee, Valerie explained things as clearly as she could. This
was *important,* damn it.

No matter that the implications terrified her.

Either she was too fried to explain or Pope was not buying, because
he said, "This is not the time to commit astronomy. Everyone on Phoebe
needs to focus on getting *down*. Before . . ."

Before the missiles launch. No one would tell her how soon that
would happen. Neither she nor Ellen had any security clearance, let
alone clearances at that level. Her impression was that once some international coordination finished—a missile salvo could so easily be
misconstrued—the missiles *would* launch.

"It's not astronomy, damn it," Valerie said. "It's . . . an option."

Pope sighed. "Okay, try it again. With fewer, smaller words, please."

"Forget astronomy and think history," Ellen said. "In 2014, the
Crudetastrophe. In 2018, Phoebe is captured, a permanent base
established on it, and the PS-1 project begins. A busy four years, no?

"Back to October 2014 and the Crudetastrophe. All we knew at first
was: We're screwed. But a year later, an ongoing NASA survey, watching for space rocks that could endanger Earth, spots something that
ought not to exist, not in that orbit. However tough things have become,
suddenly there's hope.

"Then, in round numbers: a year, at crash priority, to build a gravity
tractor; a year to fly the intercept mission; and a year of infinitesimally
weak gravitational nudging. End to end, from the Crudetastrophe to
the reconfiguring of Phoebe's orbit, four years."

"I still don't see—"

Valerie cut him off. "In October 2014, *Verne* had just reached the outer asteroid belt. Right where objects like Phoebe belong. A month after the Crudetastrophe, *Verne* went missing. A year before NASA spotted Phoebe on its inexplicable Earth-threatening orbit. Do the math, Tyler."

Pope rubbed his chin thoughtfully. "Long enough—by analogy, anyway—for *Verne* to have changed Phoebe's orbit. You're saying that Burkhalter *threw* Phoebe at Earth?"

Valerie's eyes misted up. "I'm saying Patrick threw us a lifeline."

"Give me a second." Pope's eyes narrowed with concentration. "Burkhalter's note referred to his 'last mistake.' You're guessing that mistake was bringing Phoebe, and so the construction of PS-1, and so making possible the attacks from PS-1. That whatever he was doing with the Green Bank Telescope was trying to somehow make things right."

"It fits, doesn't it?" Ellen said.

Pope said, "When he spotted Phoebe, why didn't he just tell JPL or NASA—"

While *Verne* continued on its planned course deeper into the asteroid belt. While Phoebe and Earth diverged on their very different orbits. While an energy-starved civilization fell into pieces, and committees—and nations?—debated.

While the laws of physics dictated now or never.

Patrick would not have waited. Marcus wouldn't, either.

But Pope wanted it short. Valerie said, "Patrick saw the opportunity and he took it, because that was who he was. After that, would *you* want anyone to know?"

"I suppose not." Pope glanced at his wristwatch. "But how can this matter now?"

"I'm getting to that." Valerie swallowed hard. "*This* part is so sensitive none of us dared speak openly on the link. Suppose we're right. Then the big question becomes, where is the *Verne* probe now?"

"Why would I *care*?" Pope asked. He glanced again at his watch.

Valerie said, "Because there is a good chance *Verne* is on Phoebe. Able—if we can find it, if it's in decent condition—to ferry a few people to PS-1. If, by then, there is still a PS-1 to reach."

Pope grabbed for his phone.

A synthesized representation of Phoebe, slowly spinning, floated above the base command center's main console.

If Marcus squinted hard enough to perceive Phoebe as a sphere, its radius was little more than a half mile. A true sphere of that radius had a surface area approaching five square miles. Double the area to account for hills and valleys? Ten square miles seemed far beyond what he could search in a few hours. But did the entire area require searching? This little moon had been inhabited continuously for five years.

If *Verne* was on Phoebe, why hadn't someone, or some bot, spotted it?

He pondered the globe. He added overlays highlighting the little world's mines, factories, and various surveys. Any terrain NASA and its contractors and their bots had not crossed a million times, tourist bots must have explored.

What about beneath the surface? He retrieved surveys done with ground-penetrating radar. They only reminded him that Phoebe was not a world so much as a rubble pile, a loosely bound community of rocks, agglomerations of dust and hydrocarbons, seams of ice, and vacuum gaps. The Grand Chasm was impossible to ignore, but nothing else leapt out at him.

Three possibilities, Marcus enumerated, yawning, struggling to organize his thoughts. One: *Verne* is nowhere on Phoebe. It can't be found. Two: *Verne* is here, but Patrick hid it. Or three: It's here because Patrick lost control and it crashed.

Only Patrick could not have lost control. He didn't *have* direct control at the end, lacking access to a big radio transmitter. Presumably, Patrick had uploaded new commands to *Verne* via the Deep Space Network while he retained access as *Verne*'s principal investigator. He erased the upload from the comm buffers to cover his tracks, not because he panicked. After that, the *Verne* probe, repurposed, had to watch out for itself.

"What did you do, Patrick?" Marcus asked a holo.

The holo volunteered no more than Patrick ever had.

Marcus leaned back in his seat, hands behind his head, fingers interlaced. Patrick had no control. The spacecraft was on its own.

*Verne* pulled Phoebe, just as Phoebe pulled *Verne*, the gravitational attraction between two bodies simple to calculate. By maintaining a constant separation, *Verne* transferred the miniscule force of its thrusters to moving Phoebe. No impact or hard shoving to risk scattering the rubble. No landing to hazard.

Marcus stared at the most recent deep-radar survey. It stared back, hinting at something he was too tired or obtuse to see. Taunting him. A not-round, not-at-all-uniform rubble pile.

A nasty suspicion struck him. "Savannah Morgan," he paged on the base intercom. "Come to the command center."

Savvy showed up after a couple of minutes. She had dark bags under her eyes and darker smudges on her jumpsuit. "What's up?"

"I need a software engineer's insight." He gestured at the Phoebe holo. "Autopilot for a gravity tractor. Easy or hard to program?"

"Balancing act, right?"

"Yeah. Thrusters offsetting gravitational attraction between the two bodies."

"So the closer to Phoebe's surface the tractor hovers, the stronger the attraction. You would want to keep the probe in close."

"As I understand it."

Tipping her head this way and that, she examined the holo. "That being one of the bodies?"

"Yeah."

"Tumbling?"

Like its much bigger sister moon, Phoebe had one face tidally locked to Earth. But in the depths of space, remote from any large mass, why wouldn't Phoebe have tumbled? "I assume so."

She said, "Then, yes, a big deal. Because Phoebe was tumbling and is irregularly shaped, the force of gravity between it and the tractor would have varied continuously. Ditto because Phoebe's mass distribution is far from uniform. Obvious example: whether the Grand Chasm is near or far from the tractor."

"So how——?"

"How would I program such an autopilot? Adaptively. Using lidar or radar—*Verne* has one of those, right?—to monitor real-time separation. Constantly fine-tuning thrust to maintain separation within a narrow range. And if I want the tractor to hover just over the surface to maximize attraction? That means very little time to react when some inhomogeneity pulls in the probe.

"Or maybe I'd put the tractor into orbit around Phoebe. Any thrust from the spacecraft insufficient to break orbit would nudge the bound system of *both* objects. I figure a close orbit in that case, rather than a close hover, so I could apply more thrust. The probe's orbit would be changing *constantly,* both from the engine thrusting and Phoebe's inhomogeneity. Again, very little time to react whenever real life trumps maneuver calculations."

She took a deep breath. "For many reasons, that's far from the type of software I would care to write on the fly, let alone have to sneak into an unauthorized upload and splice into code designed for another purpose."

"A complex balancing act, then. And yet, it worked."

"Yeah." Savvy examined the holo some more. "Dollars to doughnuts, at some point it ended like most balancing acts."

"In a crash?"

She nodded. "Just don't ask me where."

\* \* \*

It took two hours for another mystery to insinuate its way into Marcus's conscious ruminations.

"Someone awake down there?" he called over the surreptitious downlink.

*Define awake.*

"I need someone to dig through the rental records for tourist bots."

*I'll get Dr. Clayburn. One minute.*

"Sure," Marcus said.

*Valerie here.* There was a pause Marcus read as, "You look terrible, but it won't help for me to point that out." *What do you need?*

"Suppose Patrick didn't just happen to develop a hobby driving Phoebe robots?"

*Why would I suppose that?*

"If *Verne* is on Phoebe, Patrick wouldn't want anyone to find the wreckage. Not after he had kept its hijacking secret all these years. He would want to hide *Verne*. Physically bury it."

*Yeah. I had wondered about that. Out of Body rental files show check-in and checkout times. Nothing about where a bot happens to wander.*

"It was a thought." He drummed fingers on the console counter. "Say, Val? Could you check the files for lost and stranded bots?" Because if you failed to return your bot to the corral before its batteries ran dry, you paid for its retrieval.

*Just a sec.* After a minute, she wrote, *Good call. Patrick got billed to replace several bots. But the records don't indicate locations.*

"Replace, not retrieve?"

*Yeah. Why?*

"Remember seeing any lost bots? On a very unorthodox first date?"

*In landslides. In the Grand Chasm.* A long pause. *Could it be?*

"Well, we know that *something* hit Phoebe."

F inding *Verne*, knowing where to look, could have been easy. Peer into the Grand Chasm with a high-sensitivity IR sensor: the spacecraft's radioisotope thermoelectric generator, powered by the slow and steady radioactive decay of plutonium, would still be warm. Or survey the chasm from above, towing a metal detector behind a hopper.

If only the terrorists had left them with IR sensors or hoppers. Or if there had been some reason to stock metal detectors on a world devoid of metal.

Instead Marcus made do with the nine volunteers game to join him in the chasm—and twenty less adventuresome types willing to man safety tethers to pull people out as they got stuck. Everyone entering the chasm carried a quick-and-dirty homemade metal detector, little more than an ac oscillator, a couple wire coils, and a voltmeter. Each volunteer had a stretch of canyon about two hundred feet long to search.

Straightened out, the chasm would have run about a third of a mile—beyond grand for a world not quite four miles in circumference. The rift varied in spots from a few feet in width to almost a hundred feet.

Marcus stepped into the abyss, his rate of descent at first scarcely perceptible. Weighing less than a pound, he easily arrested his fall with his gas pistol. Lateral motion was trickier; practicing, he almost crashed twice. The second time, his boot scraped a furrow along a shallow slope, setting off a slow-motion avalanche.

*Verne*'s arrival might have been like that: a slow, glancing, bouncing blow. He pictured rock and dust collapsing into subsurface voids. And he pictured something his boot could not imitate: plasma exhaust from *Verne*'s thrusters flashing ice to steam. Newly coaxed sunward, much of Phoebe's subsurface ice would have been primed, cometlike, to explode.

Maybe the spacecraft had cartwheeled from one end to the other of what would become the Grand Chasm, triggering steam eruptions and setting off majestic collapses. A blast of steam might have blown *Verne* away. Or *Verne* might lie buried deep beneath the chasm floor, crushed and inaccessible. Or the long-lost spacecraft might be just below the surface, unharmed by the slow-motion rain of dust.

And in just such a shallow hiding place, one of the volunteers found it.

*   *   *

Six men carried the *Verne* spacecraft into the abandoned hopper garage. Three men on a side. Like pallbearers. The remainder of the work party, like mourners, lagged behind.

"We're looking at history," Marcus said. But was the probe any more than a relic?

The probe's big dish antenna, once twenty feet across, had crumpled on impact like a paper cocktail umbrella. And like bumper and fenders collapsing on a car, the antenna had absorbed much of the kinetic energy of the crash, protecting what was behind. Once they removed the crushed ruin of a dish, the rest of the spacecraft looked more or less whole.

True, the sensor cluster was battered. Behind it, the flight-computer canister was dented. But at the rear of the spacecraft, the thruster, similar in operation and configuration to the thrusters on PS-1, appeared intact. And between . . .

PS-1 generated enormous amounts of electrical power from sunlight, but *Verne* relied for its power on a radioisotope thermoelectric generator. A spacecraft-scaled solar panel could not begin to drive a magnetoplasmadynamic thruster—not in Earth orbit, let alone in the outer belt, where the sunlight was much dimmer. Marcus was relieved, but not surprised, to find *Verne*'s RTG intact. NASA built every RTG to stay together—and contain its load of plutonium—even if the rocket that carried it exploded on the launchpad.

"Digging out this probe may have been the last mining anyone ever does on this world," someone lamented.

"None of that," Savvy said. "Let's check it over."

"I think I'll see how efforts are faring on the escape pods," someone else offered.

Others agreed, and the funeral processional became a recessional. Soon Marcus, Savvy, and a base mechanic named Jarred Finnegan had the garage to themselves. They switched off their radio transmitters and jacked their helmets together with fiber-optic cables.

The RTG still provided electrical power. Three argon tanks had split—but that left one fuel tank intact. The main thruster worked, magnetic fields accelerating ionized argon to very high velocities. Most of the little compressed-gas attitude jets worked, too. Power, engine, attitude control, and fuel: they had the basics.

At full thrust, had they not strapped *Verne* to a bolted-down workbench, their testing would have blasted the old probe into a garage wall. On Earth, the low-thrust, long-duration engine could not have lifted one-tenth the probe's weight. The exhaust of ionized argon glowed faintly, an eerie white-pink.

"But can you steer this thing?" Finnegan asked.

Savvy patted the dented electronics canister at the spacecraft's midsection. "With this? I won't even try. But to navigate the short hop to PS-1? If I can't code that on a datasheet in twenty minutes, I *deserve* to get lost."

"You mean you're volunteering?" Marcus asked.

"I was sent to look after PS-1 security, wasn't I?"

*   *   *

The same damned command center. The same four people crammed in. The same insecure link to the ground. But a whole new level of insanity, Thad thought.

"We have to do this," Marcus said.

*Cn you trrust it?* the ground asked.

To judge from the typing, Thad guessed Marcus's girlfriend again had the groundside keyboard. And that she was no fan of Marcus's proposed adventure.

Not that anyone on Phoebe had shared with anyone on the ground what Marcus proposed, lest someone else overhear. What if, Thad considered, I "accidentally" blurt out some details? But that could expose me with no guarantee Yakov and company would get the message. So, no.

"A walk in the park," Marcus said.

*With lionns and tigrs and berrs.*

"Some parks are more interesting than others," Marcus conceded.

"As I recall this park, the bears are armed," Thad said. And *I* provided the guns. He wanted to curl up and die, but that was not an option.

"The idea is to avoid and outwit the bears, not confront them," Savvy said.

"With luck," Dino added, "they won't see us coming. Or see us there: it's a big park."

Because Dino had also volunteered. Best guess, four people could hang on to what remained of the probe for its final flight. Marcus's plan called for four people.

What if, against all odds, they made it to PS-1? Everything Thad knew about the powersat said they had a chance to disable it.

"Another two hours, and we'll be ready to bail," Thad said. "All of us. That's been the plan, remember?"

*Still is.*

"For most people," Marcus countered, stubbornly.

*TLA sort-of agrees, Marcus. Do you have a fourth?*

Doubtless, someone among the base crew would volunteer. And if they succeeded? Then *he* would remain Yakov's puppet. Or "Cousin Jonas" and the others might be taken alive and expose Thad's role in this catastrophe. This insane attempt had to fail. Whatever it took.

For Robin.

Thad took a deep breath. "Station chief's prerogative. If we're doing this, then *I'm* number four."

* * *

It came down, Tyler decided, to trust. Did he trust Marcus Judson, a man he had never met, to execute a plan that he dare not describe? If yes, the crisis might yet end without blowing up PS-1, without denying America access to Phoebe and its resources. If yes, Tyler should do whatever it took to get the White House to postpone the missile strike for a little longer.

Even as the slaughter and the destruction continued.

Maybe nothing could convince the White House. The pressure to act must be enormous. PS-1's latest strike on the Trans-Mediterranean Power Co-op distribution system (the fourth such attack? The fifth? Tyler had lost count) had just severed Spain from the vast North African solar farms. A hundred gigawatts lost in an instant . . . it had blacked out Spain and Portugal and sent brownouts rolling across France and into Belgium, the Netherlands, and Germany.

*Did* he trust Judson?

"What's your opinion?" Tyler asked Ellen Tanaka.

"Hardly anyone knows PS-1 as well as Marcus. It's clear that *he* believes there's a vulnerability he can exploit. If he believes it, I believe him." Ellen smiled sadly. "I'm proud of him and terrified for him at the same time."

"And what do you think?" Tyler asked Valerie.

"Beyond wanting everyone on Phoebe safely on the ground?" She brushed back a tear. "That people don't come more tenacious than Marcus. And that if we don't tell them to try, we'll wonder for the rest of our lives: What if?"

"What about you?" Tyler asked General Rodgers.

The general fixed him with a hard stare. "Think about *what*? We have no idea what they intend to try. I'm just waiting for a launch order."

On the room's main display, Marcus asked, "Hello? Are we still online?"

"Tell him, yes," Tyler said.

"Yes, we're still here?" Valerie asked.

"Yes, go for it," Tyler said. "And then I have to go." Because he was *almost* certain no one would order a launch within two hours of evacuating Phoebe base. In thirty minutes by chopper, he could be at Langley. Where he would learn if the director would trust the opinion of an intel analyst he scarcely knew to trust the unknown plan of an engineer Tyler did not know.

And whether he had just sent four brave people to ground zero.

**T**had, Marcus, Dino, and Savvy emerged from the hopper garage, each tethered to a ground-staked guide cable and to *Verne*. With one hand grasping the spacecraft and another on the cable, they dragged themselves away from the base.

All the while, Thad's mind churned. It would be so simple to drop his end of the probe—but it would not help. Objects on Phoebe fell so glacially that the others would catch it. And after raging against this mission, wouldn't it raise suspicions if *he* were the one to drop it? Just as he could not "accidentally" break their little group's radio silence without raising suspicions.

Bright light spilled from the garage entrance and an array of post lamps on the surface. To his right the last few people queued up for the escape pods. On the common radio channel, people spoke in hushed tones, nervous, relieved, and afraid all at once. *Their* misery—after a harrowing ride—might soon end.

Grunting with effort, dragging their boot tips, the four of them managed to stop just before the cable's first piton. Like them, *Verne* weighed next to nothing. Unlike them, it massed six thousand pounds; with the corresponding inertia, it resisted starting and stopping. One by one, very carefully, they got to their feet, settled into a crouch, and unclipped their carabiners from the guide cable.

Thad and Dino held *Verne*'s aft end, Marcus and Savannah the bow.

Thad watched Marcus and Savannah touch helmets. They talked about *something* for a good thirty seconds, but unable to see their faces, Thad had no idea what. They finished their tête-à-tête and turned toward Thad and Dino.

"Ready?" Marcus mouthed.

Or, for all Thad knew, Marcus had shouted it. Their mikes were off lest they be overheard. Later, when they were in position, they would jack their helmets together with fiber-optic cables.

"Ready," Thad mouthed back.

The other two nodded.

About fifty feet away, four people scooted along another guide cable, two to the side. They held aloft, rather than a spaceflight relic, a fifth person. Thad did not want to think about forcing Irv's wounded leg into his counterpressure suit. Or about the gee forces of reentry squashing that leg. There were not enough drugs in the world.

Mostly, Thad wanted not to think about the gun that had shot Irv. Or who had built it.

Minutes later, the final escape-pod hatch closed.

"Talk about a ringside seat," Marcus said. And then—

An unseen ejector flung the first escape pod into space. Even as the pod receded from the surface lights, unseen puffs of gas from its attitude jets were orienting it. Within seconds it had traveled too far to be seen by the base lighting. And then—

The retrorocket blazed.

One after another, escape pods set off. Three. Four. Five.

Light erupted from Phoebe's surface. "Mother of God," Dino whispered.

Anyone observing Phoebe would have seen five pods launch and one explode. But the blast came from mining explosives, not the sixth and final escape pod. A bit of misdirection. And, just possibly, disguising a way down to Earth if the four of them survived the next couple of hours. Not that Thad foresaw that happening.

"On zero," Marcus mouthed. "Three, two . . ."

On zero, they leapt.

*  *  *

As Marcus jumped—once again fighting *Verne*'s inertia—every muscle and joint screamed in protest. Still, spacecraft, crew, and their bit of gear together weighed almost nothing. They sailed into space.

And, floating, he turned his head to watch Phoebe recede.

*Verne*'s thruster had more than enough oomph to have lifted them from the tiny moon, only there had been no safe way to stand the probe upright to climb aboard. And if they had had the time to build some kind of launch stand, what might the backsplash of plasma from the surface have done to the passengers? No matter that his back ached, jumping free had been the safe choice.

Setting aside how ridiculous an adjective *safe* was for any aspect of this joyride.

Jostling one another, they reoriented themselves parallel to the long axis of the probe. Marcus jammed his boots into two of the cloth loops, improvised stirrups, they had attached.

After getting into position, they unfolded and wrapped a dark gray blanket around themselves, covering their brightly colored counterpressure suits. While they drifted, any unwelcome observers might mistake them for a chunk of the exploded "escape pod."

Marcus turned toward a tap on his left arm. Thad offered him a fiber-optic cable. Marcus nodded, took the end of the cable and jacked it into his helmet. "Thanks," he said. He and Savvy repeated the process, and so on, until a fiber-optic ring around *Verne* connected everyone.

"Everybody comfy?" Dino asked.

"Just fine," Thad said.

Savvy muttered something unintelligible.

"What's that?" Marcus asked.

"Just fat fingers," she said. She poked at the datasheet with which she had replaced *Verne*'s crunched flight computer. "Okay. Everything's good."

"So, Savannah," Thad said, "what were you and Marcus whispering about just before we jumped?"

"Simply two friends wishing each other luck," she said.

True as far as it went, Marcus thought. He did not add anything, just watched Earth as they continued to drift.

"Ready, gentlemen?" Savvy asked.

Even as they agreed, Marcus felt the probe shifting, felt faint vibrations from the attitude jets. The stars seemed to swing. The lights of Phoebe base fell from sight. With renewed trembling, the attitude jets arrested the spacecraft's turn.

"And, *go*," Savvy said.

* * *

Were they accelerating? Maybe. The sensation of weight was so subtle Marcus had to convince himself. Even at full throttle, they would accelerate at less than 1 percent of a standard gravity. But that acceleration would go on, and on, and on . . . .

The faint glow of the thruster exhaust was unconvincing. But in dimness lay safety: if someone on PS-1 did not know to look, and precisely where to look, *Verne* should be invisible.

A timer, a simulated speedometer, and a simulated odometer shone in separate corners of his HUD. In a few minutes, they had reached a brisk walking pace. PS-1 glittered ahead, larger than when they had set out. Even with his visor in image-enhancement mode, he could not yet make out the details.

Just four days ago, he had flown a skeletal, compressed gas–propelled hopper from Phoebe to PS-1. That had been exhilarating. That had been *fun*. Now, his heart pounded. His hands shook. Because this time he rode a hastily salvaged wreck?

Or because murderers with guns were at the other end?

"How are we doing?" Dino asked Savvy, sounding as edgy as Marcus felt.

"You mean, are we lost? No."

Marcus kept his eye on the virtual instruments. Sixteen minutes. At around seventeen minutes, they reached fifteen miles per hour. They had come almost eighteen miles. Well, they had come thousands of miles—they, and Phoebe, and PS-1 all whipping around Earth at miles per *second*—but only the rate at which they closed on PS-1 mattered.

"Engine shutdown coming," Savvy announced. "In ten, nine . . ."

At zero, the elusive sensation of weight vanished. The faint glow of the thruster exhaust vanished.

"Swinging us around," she announced.

They had allowed not quite seven minutes, thruster turned off, to flip the spacecraft end for end. In that time, they would coast another fourteen miles.

This time, as the stars swung, it was PS-1 that disappeared from sight. Marcus fixed his eyes on the Earth, seeming near enough to touch. And yet Valerie felt so very far away.

Their trembling, slewing motion abruptly became a tumble.

"Oh, crap," Savvy said. "Lost an attitude jet. I can compensate with some of the others. Only . . ."

"Only *what*?" Thad asked. He had hardly spoken the whole ride.

"Only it may take a little longer than we budgeted to complete the flip."

Meaning, Marcus translated, too little time to decelerate once the flip was complete. Meaning they would come hurtling into PS-1.

*　*　*

As soon as he was airborne, Tyler radioed Langley.

"Powell," Charmaine answered.

"It's me, inbound. Help me out? Get me onto the director's schedule, stat."

"He's not here," she said. "He was called into the White House."

"Good. They'll both want to hear this."

*　*　*

A Sunday afternoon summons to the embassy was out of the ordinary, but these were far from ordinary times. Still, as Yakov drove into the District, he wondered what this was about. When he arrived, he found he must speculate a while longer. The ambassador had been called away.

A secretary brought Yakov to the private office. He found his boss, the FSB station chief, there ahead of him.

"Good day, Dmitrii Federovich," Yakov said. Were you also summoned?

"I am unconvinced of the day's goodness, Yakov Nikolayevich."

Not a very confident attitude, Yakov thought. "If I may ask, where is the ambassador?"

"Called to the White House."

"That could be good or bad," Yakov said.

"As may this." His boss tapped an open but dormant datasheet. A holo popped open: five sparks in a shallow arc. "Titov"—the military's Chief Center for Testing and Control of Space Assets—"saw escape pods launching from Phoebe. Five successful launches and one explosion."

Of six pods, total. "Evacuations before a launch against PS-1, perhaps," Yakov said.

Because people had been ordered to leave, via some comm channel yet to be identified? Or because the people on Phoebe had intercepted news broadcasts and had had the sense to bail out while they could? It did not matter which.

Dmitrii Federovich said, "But also repatriating those who witnessed the seizure of the station. Witnesses to the identity of *your* agents."

"Soon to be sacrifices," Yakov corrected. "Silent sacrifices."

The door opened. The ambassador, his expression giving away nothing, crossed the room to take the seat behind his desk. "It is good that you have both arrived."

"Ambassador," Yakov answered cautiously, although something about Sokolov's stiffness seemed off. As much as Yakov wanted to hear about the White House meeting, he did not presume to ask.

"I asked you here to express my growing concern," the ambassador said. "Yesterday's interruption of activity from PS-1 was most disturbing. So was the attack thereafter on West Virginia. It risked a touch of world sympathy for the Americans."

Whose plan had it been to further anger the world by leaving American territory unmolested? Yakov answered only, "Our experts surmise it was necessary, for the powersat to continue in its task, that the West Virginia transmissions be disabled."

*Our*, meaning FSB experts. *Our* as a reminder to Dimitrii that they were in this together.

But Dimitrii said nothing.

Yakov assured himself that he had taken every variable into account. The meddlesome radio observatory had delayed the endgame, but success must come, and would come . . . soon.

The most difficult variable to control was the nerve of his superiors.

"That brings us to another concern," the ambassador said. "At some point, the powersat's operations become counterproductive. Economies too weakened will buy less oil. You had assured us, Yakov Nikolayevich, that before we reached that juncture, PS-1 would cease operations—by ceasing to be."

Suddenly, the ambassador grinned. "But all those misgivings were before, my friends." He opened his disguised freezer and removed a bottle of vodka.

"Before?" Yakov echoed.

"Before a summons to the White House, so that President Gibson could advise me in person of the imminent missile launches."

＊　＊　＊

Four days in vacuum gear, with only short stints in the closet-sized shelters for respite. Four days with only emergency rations to eat. Four days without weight, and with precious little sleep. Four days of murder and mayhem. Four days of revulsion at the insults to Gaia, and shame for one's own contribution.

Four days waiting to die.

Dillon had imagined things could not get worse. Once more he had been wrong.

". . . NASA confirms reports of escape pods sighted leaving Phoebe. Transmissions from the pods indicate a complete evacuation, including the tourists and staff evacuated from The Space Place earlier in the week. At this time, no more is kno—"

He could switch off the broadcast but not his mind. The last shred of hope keeping him going was for Crystal. And what a sad, forlorn hope: that *when* he died, his part in this waking nightmare would remain uncertain, unknowable. That Crystal would not suffer for his failures.

Even that last, pitiful hope had now abandoned him. Among the evacuees on their way back to Earth, many knew who had left them to die.

＊　＊　＊

"One hour," Charmaine Powell said. "For your grand gesture, in-person plea, you got an entire hour's delay."

"And maybe early retirement." Out the chopper window, Tyler watched the White House recede. He tried not to dwell on the death toll an hour's postponement would cost. If he was misguided in his trust, it was not the type of mistake a person could easily live with. "'Only they know the plan, but they're smart and resourceful,' is a tough sell."

"I imagine so," she said. "Where to next?"

"Home, if I still remember my way." Also, just minutes from CIA Langley. "How about you? Any update about my neighbor?"

"Tails are in place. And here's something interesting. When the nukes went off, your friend was posted to the Russian embassy in the Restored Caliphate. He was expelled, persona non grata, right after. Several Russian nationals, in the meanwhile, were torn apart by mobs, blamed for the mess. People he knew, but no one definitively linked with him."

People loosely linked to Yakov. Sort of like Dillon Russo? "What else you got?"

"A Russian hacker, famous in certain geeky circles. The Guard was looking for Psycho Cyborg at the same time as your future neighbor got himself ejected."

Psycho Cyborg, who was behind the hack of the space weather center. Hmm. Pope said, "None of that is evidence, Char, but I admit it's very suggestive. Do you think our guy was involved with the Crudetastrophe?"

"I'm pretty sure the Guard thinks he was involved." She sighed. "I'll keep digging. It's something to do for the next hour."

\* \* \*

Traffic on the George Washington Parkway was light. Part Sunday afternoon, part overcast with steady drizzle, part ongoing crisis, Yakov thought. For whichever of those reasons, people were staying home, not driving.

It would have been difficult under the circumstances *not* to notice the boxy gray sedan that stayed a couple hundred feet behind him, slowing when he slowed, alternating lanes but seldom passing. Despite the overcast, the driver and passenger both had sun visors down. As though hiding their faces.

When Yakov invented an errand and exited the parkway early, a white van that had stayed two vehicles behind the sedan sped up to exit, too.

He shook the tail, wondering who the amateurs were and what they wanted, then continued home.

As *Verne* emerged from shadow, Earth transformed in an instant from a dim presence glimmering by moonlight into a brilliant arc of light. Earth's crescent, from tip to tip, dwarfed the full moon. Seconds later, the powersat emerged from Earth's shadow. The expanse of PS-1, less than a mile away, seemed larger even than the Earth.

We couldn't miss PS-1 now if we tried, Thad thought. And diving out of the sun, no way can Jonas or his people see us coming. If they somehow do see us, we're barreling straight at the solar cells: the side from which they can't beam microwaves. The timing could *not* be better for this mad scheme.

The four of them had shed their blanket, removed their boots from the stirrups, and untethered themselves from the spacecraft. Each held a gas pistol in one hand, and gripped *Verne* with the other.

"Here's a vote for dumb luck," Savannah said cheerily. "I hope our trusty ship hits someone."

"Amen," Marcus said. "On zero, gently. In three. Two. One."

At zero, as they separated, the fiber-optic cables tugged free of helmet jacks.

And Thad, rather than shove off gently, thrust as hard as he could.

•  •  •

Dillon blinked in the sudden glare as PS-1 emerged into sunlight. His visor darkened.

"Back to work," Jonas said. His voice sounded ragged. "When will those lame-assed, incompetent, indecisive chickenshits on the ground *do* something about us?"

What would be their next target? Dillon wondered. A power plant? A transmission line? It hardly mattered.

"Target locked," Jonas said. "And beaming . . . begins."

Would this horror never end? Dillon stared into the distance, across the plain of PS-1—

At a walking pace—missing Jonas and the computer console near which he floated by no more than twenty feet—a slowly turning *something* crashed through the powersat.

*  *  *

Marcus's gas pistol was fully engaged, and squeezing its trigger harder only made his hand ache. Hurtling straight at PS-1, he couldn't *not* squeeze for all he was worth.

He *was* slowing. When, obsessively, he turned his head every few seconds to check on *Verne*, it was nearer than he to the powersat. But one of the four of them must have dismounted clumsily, because the spacecraft had drifted off course and gone into a slow tumble. The old probe was going to miss the aim point.

It doesn't matter, Marcus told himself. PS-1 had three other main computing complexes. The crash was a diversion, no more. When *Verne* crashed through PS-1, maybe the bad guys would think *that* was the attack.

When the old probe almost brained a terrorist, Marcus cheered himself hoarse.

*  *  *

"What the hell?" Jonas screamed.

Dillon did not answer. It was part shock, part the ripple racing from the impact point. Before the wave reached him, he had to make sure his tethers were secure! By the time the ripple got to him, bots already swarmed to survey the damage.

Something hopper-sized had hit them. Maybe it was one of the hoppers he and Felipe had flung off Phoebe. The notion vaguely cheered Dillon. Still it had not looked like a hopper.

"Everyone up!" Jonas shouted. "Lincoln. Felipe. We're under attack. And the beam is down."

* * *

Marcus glided to a stop no more than fifty feet from a corner of PS-1. That was *way* too close for comfort. With the briefest of puffs from his gas pistol, he inched across the remaining distance. *Someone* was chattering on the radio. It was all encrypted, alas.

He was clipping his second safety tether when a faint surface ripple reached him. The wave swept past him, reflected from the powersat's edges, then returned, bound inward. PS-1 greatly outmassed *Verne*, but their encounter was not like a fly meeting a windshield. More like a rock hitting a two-mile-square, very thin window. Until the powersat's anti-trembling system damped out the vibrations, the microwave transmitters would cut themselves off. He had bought Earth a respite, no matter what happened next.

He pulled himself along a guide cable, low to the surface. Glancing across the plain, he saw scattered part and supply depots, hoppers at docking poles, other guide cables, and bots. Toward the center, two spacesuited figures emerged from shelters.

Had Savvy, Thad, and Dino landed safely? If they hugged the surface as Marcus did, he didn't think he could spot them from miles away. He crept along the cable to a junction and switched tethers to the intersecting cable, this one heading to his destination.

To shape and steer the power beam entailed very specific interactions among the powersat's transmitters. There must be constructive interference among some transmissions and destructive interference among others—and the solution changed continuously as PS-1 sped along its orbit and Earth spun beneath. To calculate the required signal phase for every transmission required knowing precisely the relative positions in three dimensions of all the many thousand microwave transmitters. *That* took real-time control to detect and counteract every twitch and tremor anywhere within the enormous structure. Any of

four atomic clocks, one at each corner of the powersat, could synchro-
nize the real-time sensing and controls.

Four visitors, unsuspected, one at each corner, would disable the four
clocks. When the last clock failed, the powersat would lose its ability to
maintain rigidity—and so, to form beams. And once PS-1 lost its ability to sense and control wobbles and flexures, the accelerometers integral to each transmitter would *keep* it from emitting.

Flexing would be most pronounced near the edges. Marcus defied
the little repair bots to maintain their grips—much less repair or replace broken clock modules—under those conditions. Trained specialists would have to make those repairs.

Marcus bargained with the universe: Let us knock out the clocks.
After that, it doesn't matter how clever the bad guys are. After that, the
military can launch a shuttle of troops to retake the powersat.

Let us knock out the clocks and it's game over.

* * *

Hand over hand, Thad sped along a guide cable toward the powersat's
center. He could have saved precious minutes by landing closer to the
middle—but one of the others disembarked from *Verne* might have
noticed. Looking innocent was hard.

When a spacesuited figure ahead seemed to turn Thad's way, Thad
pushed away from the powersat, floating to the end of his tethers and
waving his arms. As the stranger approached, Thad reeled himself back
to the guide cable and set off to intercept.

As the gap closed, the stranger took out a coil gun. In the direct glare
of the sun, his visor, like Thad's, was all but opaque. The label on the
red counterpressure suit read WALKER.

Squeezing the cable, Thad brought himself to a stop. He tapped his
own nametag, his helmet antenna, shrugged, then lobbed a fiber-optic
cable, one end already jacked into his own helmet.

Keeping the coil gun centered on Thad, the man inched forward.
He connected the free end of the cable. "And why are you here?" he
asked.

Thad knew no one named Walker, but he recognized the voice. It
was Cousin Jonas.

"I came with three others," Thad said quickly. "We're each to disable one of the atomic clocks. If that happens—"

"I know," Jonas said. "Where are the others?"

Thad pointed back the way he had come. "That was my corner, and I didn't touch its clock. So every other corner. But we all planned to make the circuit in case someone had a problem."

＊　＊　＊

Dillon goggled as Jonas returned from an unexplained errand—with a newcomer. From Phoebe, to judge from the stranger's blue counterpressure suit. Another of Yakov's agents, somehow.

As reluctant an agent as me? Dillon wondered. Not that it mattered.

Then Jonas had his coil gun in hand. "Sorry, boss," he said. "Too busy to chance mixed loyalties. Handgrip first, give our visitor your weapon."

Gingerly, Dillon complied.

Jonas gestured with his gun. "Now into a shelter."

They were all going to die here. Why not die in the open, with Earth resplendent? Dillon considered refusing.

But to die by gunshot and explosive decompression? Dillon was not prepared for that. He grabbed a guide cable and pulled himself to the nearest cluster of shelters.

Felipe, just emerging from one unit, shut Dillon inside.

＊　＊　＊

*Unexplained,* accused the text on Yakov's cell.

The single word, out of context, would mean nothing to anyone intercepting it.

But from the moments-ago news bulletin on his car radio, Yakov could guess the context: the abrupt halt, without destroying its target, of PS-1's latest attack.

No explanation for the cessation. So: no radio waves scattering from PS-1, as in the radio-observatory incident. Military satellites would have detected that. Not breakup of the powersat—that, too, would have been seen.

Hence: the second unanticipated countermeasure in two days.

Ambassador Sokolov had been advised of an imminent missile launch. Had the American president lied?

Something fluttered in Yakov's gut. He needed a moment, and some unwonted introspection, to put a name to the odd feeling.

The stirrings of doubt.

* * *

"Ride with me, Thad," Jonas said as the four of them went for the hoppers.

"Okay." Thad pulled back from reaching for the fourth hopper, and swung himself into the saddle behind Jonas. They had three raiders to handle; taking three hoppers was not unreasonable. Jonas had given him a gun and uploaded encryption software for his helmet computer. That would not have happened if there had been any trust issues.

As opposed to control issues. Thad had far more experience flying hoppers than any of these men possibly could. *He* should be piloting.

Jonas pointed over the bow of their hopper. "We'll take this corner. Felipe, the corner to my left. Lincoln, my right. Keep me posted."

With an unsteady takeoff, Jonas lifted the hopper off the powersat. Squads of maintenance bots, carrying solar panels and maser arrays, already scuttled toward the hole punched by *Verne*.

With some altitude, Thad quickly spotted the raiders, one each at every corner but the one assigned to him. No one yet had headed for that corner.

Jonas had spotted them, too. Opening the throttle, he called, "Tally-ho."

* * *

With a grunt, Marcus ripped the atomic clock from its housing and flung it into space. The recoil sent him flying backward over PS-1. Tethers pulled him up short.

He reeled himself in, clipped his tethers to a guide cable running in a useful direction, then set out for the next corner clockwise just in case Dino had had a problem. As Dino, hopefully, was already on his way to another corner, to backstop Thad. As Thad should be on his way to backstop Savvy, and she on her way to check on Marcus's assigned clock.

Motion above PS-1 caught his eye. A hopper! Racing straight toward him. He had been spotted; almost certainly, the others had been, too.

He tapped his forearm keypad, reactivating his mike. "Company coming. Mine's done. Be quick." He unclipped his tethers and his gas pistol, hoping to avoid capture for a little while.

The hopper kept accelerating. Planning to ram him? Knock him into space? With a squirt from the gas pistol, he dodged.

The pistol barely sputtered enough to waft Marcus off the powersat. Hurling away the empty, useless gas pistol reversed his drift, sending him slowly back toward PS-1. He raised his hands in surrender.

* * *

"Company coming. Mine's done. Be quick."

"Damn," Savannah Morgan muttered at Marcus's warning. She had destroyed her assigned atomic clock by snapping its circuit boards in half, but scarcely started toward the nearest main computing complex. Just possibly, she had had a bright idea.

Speeding hand over hand along a guide cable, she glanced up. A hopper was heading her way, tiny with distance, bearing two colorful dots. Red counterpressure suit in front, piloting. Behind—a blue suit.

Thad or Dino? That either man helped the terrorists made her ill. And whichever had betrayed them would not have disabled his assigned atomic clock.

She *had* to get to the computer.

From the hopper's vantage point, they could not miss seeing her bright green suit. A tarantula on a dinner plate would have had a better chance of hiding. Her only hope was speed.

Unclipping her tethers, she jetted ahead. Thad or Dino, whoever was on that hopper, had had enough propellant to land. Massing less than either man, her gas pistol should have propellant left. Ideally enough for her to start *and* stop.

The hopper veered: they had spotted her.

She slammed on the brakes with a long blast of gas. As she drifted over the computer complex's access hatch, she managed to grab the handle.

Her body kept going. *Damn* momentum. She screamed as her entire mass wrenched her arm and shoulder—but she did not let go.

The hopper was perhaps a quarter mile away and closing fast.

She popped the access panel, clipped tethers to the metal rings inside, and reeled her lines tight. The upright hatch seemed a flimsy shield. Back on Phoebe the bad guys had had guns!

Did they suspect she had a sysadmin login? Some among the Phoebe crew had to know the inspection team had gotten privileged access. Thad definitely knew.

"Be careful. We don't know who we can trust," Marcus had whispered to her, radios off, helmet touching helmet, just before the four of them leapt off Phoebe. "Someone from the base may have armed the terrorists."

"After I clobber my clock, I have an idea," was all she had dared to say. If someone on Phoebe *had* helped the terrorists, that someone might be . . . anyone. Even one of the men watching, wondering what she and Marcus were discussing in private.

As, it turned out, it was.

Peeking over the hatch, the hopper was maybe a tenth of a mile away. It was not slowing down, either. Planning to run her over? To shoot her as they passed? She had a minute, maybe, to do what needed doing. On an open radio channel she hoped still linked back to Phoebe, she shouted, "Look sharp." She did not dare to hint any more clearly. If the bad guys understood, they would undo what she was attempting. "Either Thad or Dino is helping the terrorists."

She logged on, found the screen she needed—

Sparks from the top edge of the panel. They were shooting at her!

Hunkering down, she typed frantically.

*   *   *

"What's he doing?" Jonas asked.

"She," Thad said. That would be Savannah, if everyone had landed at their assigned corners. "And I don't know."

A fine time to remember he had given the inspectors sysadmin access. Thad wracked his brain, trying to imagine what she might do.

Seconds later, she was shouting on the Phoebe-and-powersat common channel, in the clear, denouncing him for the entire world to hear. Spysats *would* be listening.

"Look sharp," Jonas repeated. "What's *that* about?"

"Haven't a clue."

Jonas fired a couple of rounds. One must have struck near her, because she scrunched lower behind the hatch. "I can't run her down without plowing through the surface and setting off more waves, or without slowing way down," he muttered.

"Do you have a full gas pistol?" Thad asked.

"Yeah. Why?"

"No time," Thad said. "Hand it over."

"If you can reach it, take it."

Leaning forward, Thad managed to unclip it. "Brace yourself."

As they shot past the open hatch Thad reached backward to pull on the hopper; with his other hand, he shoved off against one of Jonas's oh-two tanks.

The push-pull somersaulted Thad down the back of the hopper, into the hopper's aft gas jets. The spewing jets kicked him in the chest, killing most of his momentum. With a short blast from the gas pistol, he brought himself to a halt.

Savannah worked too close to the screen for him to see what she was doing. She might not even have seen him dismount. He clipped the gas pistol and took out his coil gun.

On the common channel, he said, "Hands off the keyboard. Move away from the computer."

Her helmet, like his, was opaque, but he felt her eyes burning into his nametag. "Why, Stankiewicz? Why betray your country?"

For family: the purest of reasons. And yet at the end of the day, he had just made things incomparably worse. For Robin, too, now that Savannah had exposed him. "Get away, *now*."

"Give me a minute to finish, Thad, and this nightmare will be over."

Only the nightmare would never be over. Trying to hate Savannah, but only hating himself, he said, "Hands off the keyboard this second, or I shoot."

Moving slowly, she unreeled tether and pushed off.

The screen listed PS-1 computer accounts and their authorization levels—and very few names still showed sysadmin access. Working down the list alphabetically, she had not yet reached Stankiewicz—the account Jonas and his cronies used.

Keeping an eye on her as she drifted at the end of her tethers, Thad revoked sysadmin privileges for both her and Marcus. Dino had never had sysadmin access.

Thad closed the access panel, waiting for Jonas to come back.

\* \* \*

As much as Valerie had come to hate the Mount Weather war room, she could not bring herself to leave. Not while everything hung in the balance. Not while Marcus and a few others attempted—

She had no idea what they imagined they could do.

PS-1 filled one of the wall screens, the image crisp. Adaptive optics, she thought, inanely. Real-time adjustment for atmospheric distortions. She could not tear her eyes away. Here and there people talked in hushed, purposeful tones.

Valerie had cheered with everyone else when something—the *Verne* probe?—burst through the powersat, and louder when Major Garcia announced, "Beaming has stopped."

If the beam *stays* off, the White House would have to abort the missile strike. Wouldn't they?

She would feel more confident of that if Pope were here.

Ellen gave Valerie's hand a comforting squeeze. Valerie squeezed back, too choked up to speak. Be safe, Marcus, she thought.

Minutes later, in a far more sober voice, Garcia announced, "Beaming has resumed."

*Be safe, Marcus.* With every passing moment, her hope seemed more futile. Until, relayed from an NSA satellite—

"Company coming. Mine's done. Be quick."

Valerie shivered at Marcus's calm but hurried warning. So much for *a walk in the park.* So much for the notion he had found someplace vulnerable to crash through, and was already on his way to The Space Place and its escape pods. PS-1 might have had a design flaw, a failure of replication, something that everyone else had overlooked.

From his warning, it did not sound that way.

But Marcus had finished his task—of *whatever* it was that the four of them intended. If he could finish his part, maybe they all would. Maybe the beam would stop for good. Maybe—

"Look sharp." That was Savannah Morgan's voice. "Either Thad or Dino is helping the terrorists."

While others listened on, Valerie had to turn away.

"Look sharp?" Ellen whispered. "Do you understand that?"

If only they could look more closely at things happening up there! Valerie froze. "He told Savannah to move away from the computer. What would she be doing on PS-1 at a computer?"

"I wonder . . . ?" Ellen tapped at her datasheet, and a close-up video of the powersat popped up. "Look at this!" she shouted.

"Where is that feed coming from?" General Rodgers demanded.

"PS-1's onboard safety system." The view cycled from one panning camera to another to another, as Ellen kept keying. "To give me access, my PS-1 account has been upgraded to sysadmin privileges, and the code restricting sysadmin access to onboard terminals has been bypassed. It has to be Savannah Morgan's doing."

"As sysadmin, can you kill the beam?" Rodgers asked.

"Sure, but they'll see. They'll just restore the beam, and they'll know to look for whoever gained access. They'll revoke my authorization."

"Not if you revoke *their* authorizations first," Valerie said. "Cancel everyone's privileges but your own. Can you do that?"

"Yes!" Ellen grimaced. "No, damn it. Not to make it stick. Stankiewicz can reboot from an onsite backup, with his sysadmin log-on still valid."

"Why bother giving us access?" someone snapped. "Just so we can watch?"

And as they *did* watch, two people in green suits were herded toward the center of the powersat, and relieved of tool kits, gas pistols, everything.

"I don't *know* why," Ellen admitted.

"Revoke their privileges and shut down PS-1," Rodgers ordered. "For as long as it remains offline, someone on the ground isn't getting cooked."

"No," Valerie insisted. "There's a better way to use our access."

Turning off Chain Bridge Road, nearly home, Yakov saw another gray sedan in his rearview mirror. No, the same gray sedan. The driver and passenger had traded seats.

Coming up to a yellow traffic light, Yakov floored it; the sedan came through the intersection on red.

Running red lights was not unusual in the city, even without diplomatic license plates. But drivers and passengers did not usually exchange worried looks.

Persistent, Yakov thought. And inept. He wondered who they were.

The sedan did not follow him into his neighborhood—as though his tails knew the neighborhood had only two entrances, and a white van waited near the other. Likely, then, this was not the first time he had been followed, and he had been too preoccupied to notice.

Yakov arrived home to find Valentina's car gone from the garage. He had just found her fussily neat note, *Gone shopping*, when his cell rang.

An embassy number. "Brodsky," he answered.

"Good afternoon, Yakov Nikolayevich," the ambassador said jovially.

Never mind *unexplained*. Something had changed again. Something must have gone right this time.

"Anatoly Vladimirovich, you honor me by your call. How may I be of service?"

"I called to pass along kind words about your recent wheat purchase. President Khristenko himself is very pleased."

"The president is too kind," Yakov said. "I hope sometime to have the opportunity to thank him."

"Oh, I believe that is quite likely, Yakov Nikolayevich. Until tomorrow, then."

"Until tomorrow."

Kind words about wheat meant nothing of the sort. Not as soon as Yakov would have expected, to be sure, but the Americans *had* launched.

* * *

Marcus floated at the end of his tether. At the end of his rope. Savvy floated nearby. Dino, apparently, had not made it. *Damn* it.

Three men hung nearby, all holding guns. The fourth was at a computer console. Visors darkened against the sun rendered all of them faceless.

"Sorry I got you into this," Marcus radioed.

"We had to try," Savvy said.

"You failed," a terrorist declared. "PS-1 remains operational, and while it does, we *will* continue to use it. Sooner or later, someone will cram missiles down our throats, but until then, we're too busy to watch you.

"So choose how you want to die. You can simply unclip and float away. Who knows? That might be very peaceful. Or go quietly into one of the radiation shelters, and we'll lock you inside. You'll survive just as long as we do."

"I don't care for either choice," Savvy said.

"Or I can shoot you," the talkative terrorist said. "Honestly, I'd rather not."

Behind the three terrorists, along the plane of the powersat, something stirred. Something? Or many somethings? It was as though the surface . . . writhed. Facing into the glare of Earth swollen to quarter phase, Marcus could not decide what he was seeing.

But he had a guess . . .

"Or you could surrender to us," Marcus said, "and maybe we can all forego getting killed."

"Funny man," the talkative terrorist said.

*  *  *

You can do this, Valerie lectured herself.

Too bad she could not believe herself. Engineering was the contact sport, not astronomy. But if not she, then who?

Then three terrorists raised their guns.

"Die, damn you!" Valerie screamed.

*  *  *

A soft gasp. From Savannah?

That was all Thad heard, but it made him glance over his shoulder.

Hundreds—no, thousands!—of bots, charging out of the earthlight. They sparkled, the light glittering not only from silvery carapaces, but from the tools in their grasps. As he stared, hundreds of bots swarmed Jonas at the computer console.

"Behind us," Thad shouted.

But Jonas shrieked louder. Tentacles built to grip guide cables now clutched arms and legs and helmet instead. The bots pounded. And tore. And stabbed.

Suddenly, over the radio: air whistling. From Jonas's helmet?

"Behind us," Thad screamed once more. He fired his coil gun again and again. The bots kept coming, too numerous to stop. Maimed bots, too, trailing shattered limbs.

Now Felipe and Lincoln were firing, too.

Bots swarmed up Felipe's legs. *He* screamed.

Dillon—ironically safe, for the moment, in the latched shelter—shouted to be released, to be told what was happening, and, finally, in inarticulate fear and rage.

Jonas's scream morphed into a burbling, choking death rattle.

The coil gun twitched impotently in Thad's grasp, its ammo spent.

Not only his: Lincoln, cursing, hurled his gun at the bots teeming at his feet. Too late, Lincoln jumped. Tens of bots already crawled over him, their limbs and tools flashing. Red fog spurted from tiny rips and punctures in his suit.

Thad leapt from the powersat.

From twenty feet above the powersat, he saw that bots had avoided Marcus's and Savvy's tethers. To protect the two? Maybe he was safe here, too.

It was a nice thought for the few seconds it lasted.

Whoever controlled the swarming bots had evidently designated only those specific tethers off-limits. Bots clambered up Thad's tether. He brushed them off with the barrel of the coil gun. More bots rushed up the tether, and he brushed them off, too—until one grabbed the gun.

He flung gun and bot away as forcefully as he could, as more bots started up the tether.

Throwing the gun had sent him into a rapid spin. There were bots all around, still inrushing from the farthest reaches of the powersat.

Detouring for a good three feet around Marcus's and Savannah's tethers.

Thad cast off the reels of both his tethers, to drift away from the bot hordes. With a gas pistol, he started jetting to the docking posts. He could take a hopper to Phoebe, grab the remaining escape pod there. Maybe he would be gone before the missiles hit, or the debris would take a while to disperse.

To do what? To go where? He had nothing to live for.

"I'm sorry," he broadcast on the common channel. "For all the deaths. For the shame I've brought my family. For everything."

Then he turned off his radio and his heater.

As the cold became all, as his thoughts, like his blood, thickened to syrup, he welcomed blissful oblivion.

* * *

"Are you okay?" a tremulous voice asked. It was the last voice Marcus expected to hear just then. *Valerie's* voice.

"Just shaken up," Marcus radioed back. And still shaking. He kept that to himself. "Do you control the—"

"You look okay." She had hardly paused, not waiting for his answer.

The Earth/comsat/PS-1 latency being, well, whatever it was at this moment, she might not yet have heard him. "I need you to jack into the main computer. It will be a secure link. Oh, and yes. I control the bots. I've sent them the order to stop swarming."

"On my way," Marcus said.

He reeled himself in, and saw Savvy doing the same. The bot army dispersed as he and Savvy made their way to the console. On nearby posts, cameras turned to follow their progress.

A body, tethered into place, floated just above the access panel. The helmet visor had cracked. Pain and fear had twisted the dead man's face, and his eyeballs bulged.

An unfamiliar voice, a woman, said, "Keep the bodies."

Gingerly, Marcus and Savvy moved aside the body, still tethered so it would not float off. They used fiber-optic cables to jack in.

"*Is* this secure?" Marcus asked.

"As secure as is anything up here," Savvy said. "When I was testing, that seemed secure. Of course four days ago, none of us trusted the network security enough to allow sysadmin access from the ground."

"We're glad you took the chance," Valerie said.

"This is General Rodgers, Air Force," the other woman introduced herself. "We don't have much time. Is the powersat secured?"

How could they be sure? Marcus wondered. "Four terrorists shut us into the shelter on Phoebe. All from The Space Place, and we have three bodies. We saw Stankiewicz jump off; we can, just barely, still see his suit, drifting. I'm not eager to go check him out."

"Our sensors say the body is cold." Rodgers paused. "And we see another body floating a little farther away."

"Poor Dino," Savvy said.

"That leaves one unaccounted for, possibly armed, and just the two of you," Rodgers said.

"General, you've *got* to call off the missile strike," Valerie said.

"It's not my call," Rodgers answered softly, "but I can't recommend it. Not with a terrorist unaccounted for."

Savvy said, "General, *we* control the beam. And we control the bots."

"We've suspended the beam," Rodgers said.

"If the last terrorist shows up," Savvy said, "we still have the bots."

"Maybe there *is* no fourth guy," Valerie said. "Wherever he is, he's not visible to the surveillance cameras."

"About those missiles?" Marcus asked. "Any second now Savvy and I will hopper back to Phoebe for the last escape pod." Because any chance is better than no chance. "We've saved the powersat, General. Dino Agnelli died to save it. Do not waste that sacrifice. Do not surrender the potential to build hundreds more like PS-1."

The silence stretched awkwardly.

"General, we're leaving," Marcus said.

"Wait," Rodgers said. "If I'm not back in two minutes, run for it."

And for almost two minutes, no one said a word. Marcus scarcely breathed.

"Stay put," Rodgers said. "If you watch very closely, you may see payloads zipping past. They'll arc by you, then splash down harmlessly in the South Pacific. That said, can you two hold out for a day? Where you are, not going to Phoebe or The Space Place?"

Marcus remembered checking onboard supply depots, killing time while the others inspected. Four days ago, Savvy had said. It felt like a lifetime. Any one depot held more than enough oh-two, water, and batteries. "Yes, General, we can do that."

"Agreed," Savvy said.

"Good," Rodgers said. "Within twenty-four hours, expect company: a shuttle of Special Ops folks. They'll secure the powersat and Phoebe. Their shuttle will bring you down."

"Thank you, General," Marcus said.

"No," Rodgers corrected. "Thank you."

**T**his is a very rushed op," Charmaine said. "You sure about this?"

"Concur, and yes," Tyler said.

He could almost appreciate how delicately she hinted that his last field op had been twenty-three years and two heart attacks ago. The action would be all of a five-minute walk from his own front door—and he would be driving to the op.

None of which mattered. To succeed, the op demanded his personal connection, and he damn well meant it to succeed. Anyway, Yakov would be far more rushed than he.

Tyler said, "And not that I'm superstitious or anything"—she snorted—"but things, finally, seem to be breaking our way."

"That they are."

Agency phones were as secure as cell phones could be, but that did not keep them both from speaking in circumlocutions. He said of the recaptured powersat, "Still behaving?"

"And still functional."

"Excellent," he said.

Not secured, though. To secure PS-1 required putting troops up there and, until less than an hour ago, it had been impossible to safely prep a shuttle launch.

Even if the Russians had failed to decrypt the latest radio links to

PS-1, they knew—the world knew—the U.S. had launched a missile salvo. Anyone with a decent pair of binocs could see that PS-1 remained intact. Any country with a decent early-warning system knew the missile payloads had been allowed to soar past PS-1.

So: hurried American announcements aside, the Russians knew who, however tenuously, controlled the powersat. They could not be happy about the reversal. The next few hours, until the U.S. could scramble a shuttle, were crucial. Until then, what was to stop the Russians from launching their own shuttle to, heroically, secure—and take occupation of?—the powersat?

The heat-targeting capability their agents had demonstrated against a Cosmic Adventures shuttle just two days earlier.

"Okay," Charmaine said. "If I don't hear from you within the hour, I'll come looking. Good luck."

"Thanks." Tyler hung up, hoping matters did not come down to luck.

* * *

Yakov grimaced in concentration, trying to digest the latest setback—and the ambassador's fury. Yakov drummed his fingers on his desk. He rocked in his chair. Vodka was not helping his mood any more than the Shostakovich symphony that pounded from the stereo. How had his operatives lost control of—

The doorbell rang.

Through an exterior security camera, Yakov saw a pizza van parked at his curb. A guy in a baseball cap and garish red company vest stood at the front door holding an insulated pizza carrier.

Yakov had not ordered anything; the man had to have the wrong house. As Yakov pressed the intercom button, the pizza guy tugged on the pizza carrier, lifting its flap to reveal a note: *Look at me.* The driver removed his cap, ostensibly to scratch the top of his head.

The "pizza guy" was Tyler Pope.

"Be right there," Yakov said. He hurried to the door. "Come in while I get my wallet."

The moment the door closed, Pope removed the hat and vest. He said, "You don't have much time, Yakov."

"I don't understand—"

"Playing charades has been fun, but not today. You are FSB. I'm CIA. Okay?"

"Okay," Yakov conceded.

"I don't know what the Restored Caliphate has against you, but I do know that the Caliph's Guard has a team in country set for a snatch. In town, actually. Yesterday and today the chatter ramped *way* up. My bosses are very unhappy with you, with very good cause, and I've been told to look the other way.

"But scumbag that you are, I can't get past that you have diplomatic immunity. So get the hell out of Dodge. The tower at Reagan National is primed to clear a diplomatic flight. You keep your plane prepped, right?"

"But Valentina—"

"Has three Agency people keeping an eye on her. Your wife will be fine." Pope set down the pizza carrier. "Have you noticed any new surveillance recently? You *must* have, because these guys are more enthusiastic than skilled."

The gray sedan. The white van. And if the Caliph's Guard had come for him . . .

"What do you propose?" Yakov asked.

Tyler offered the cap and vest. "Put these on. Take the pizza van. Get to the airport."

Yakov's antennae tingled. "And leave you—"

"Yeah, yeah, you keep secret papers or whatever here." Pope took plastic wrist ties out of his pocket. "The clock's ticking, damn it. Bind me to a chair or whatever. Valentina, when she finds me, can call the cops or your embassy."

"Right." He bound Pope's wrists behind him, arms around one of the sturdy floor-to-ceiling decorative columns that separated the foyer from the dining room. "I owe you one, Tyler."

"Then owe me two. Consider it my final neighborly favor. Is your Psycho friend local?" Pope laughed. "I know you won't tell me. But the chatter involved Psycho Cyborg, too. Who, I imagine, has no immunity. Because what the Caliph's Guard will do . . ."

Yakov shuddered. "Point taken." He slipped on the vest and cap.

"Don't forget the pizza carrier. Keys for the van are in the vest."

"I won't forget this," Yakov said.

"Good to know," Pope answered.

Yakov sauntered to the van, warning himself not to look too casual. Turning out of the subdivision, he spotted the gray sedan by the side of the road. Two people still sat inside.

He phoned ahead to the airport. And using the must-flee code phrase, he texted Irinushka to meet him at the general aviation terminal.

Psycho Cyborg deserved the same warning Pope had given him.

*　*　*

Dillon's universe had shrunk to a small closet. It would have been crowded for one. With ghosts, too . . .

If only the end would *get* here already. Instead the awful screaming echoed and reechoed in his brain.

And the dreadful *hissing* when Jonas's helmet had—well, Dillon was not sure quite what. He wasn't sure of anything, except the awful screams, then death rattles, and then eeriest of all, the silence.

He had screamed, too. He had pounded on the shelter door. No one could hear it, but he couldn't *not* pound.

What had happened? What *could* have happened?

After he had screamed, and moaned, and bemoaned his fate, a fragile clarity returned. Maybe the stranger who had shown up with Jonas was not who Jonas expected. Maybe the stranger had turned on Jonas. And if one stranger had arrived on the powersat, why not more? Was that not, in fact, likely?

Dillon switched from the mission frequency to the common, unencrypted channel. And people were chattering! A man and a woman. Another woman, her responses so delayed that she must be on Earth.

To have been trapped in this shelter proclaimed, if not Dillon's complete innocence, at least his reticence. Especially if Jonas and the rest were no longer alive to contradict him.

"Hello? Anyone?" Dillon called. "Anyone here on PS-1?"

"Who *is* this?" the man asked. "Where are you?"

"My name's Dillon. The . . . terrorists made me come with them. They shut me in a radiation shelter."

"Hold on a second."

The newcomers must have switched to a private channel for a while. A long while. Dillon wondered if they meant to leave him in his closet. If they did, he could not blame them.

"I know who you are, Dillon. And I saw you holding a gun on Phoebe."

"I was blackmailed to bring those men to The Space Place. At that point, I think they decided I knew too much about them. That's why they gave me the gun. I couldn't stay on Phoebe once everyone there believed I was one of the terrorists."

Skeptically, "Hold on."

"Wait! I'm low on oh-two."

Another pause. "Okay. I see a shelter with its latch jammed. I'm guessing that's you. Hit the door."

Dillon pounded, the door flexing beneath his fist. "Here! See me?"

"Yeah. Did you hear what happened to your cronies?"

He shuddered. "Yes."

"Remember that. When I give you the word, come out *very* carefully." The inside latch wiggled. "Very slowly."

Dillon opened the door just enough to show his hands, empty, then grabbed an exterior handhold to swing himself out. Two people in green counterpressure suits—MORGAN and JUDSON, their suit labels read—watched as Dillon tethered himself to the nearest guide cable. Judson inspected Dillon head to toe, front and back and took his tool kit before Morgan offered an oh-two tank.

Hundreds of bots all but surrounded them. If Dillon's eyes did not deceive him, some of the bots were flecked with red.

He shuddered. "Thank you."

"Don't thank anyone yet," a new voice answered. "I'm Pope, by the way. You and I are going to have a chat. As soon as you're jacked in."

Dillon's new captors gave him a long roll of fiber-optic cable. Long enough to hang himself, he thought. A deranged cackle escaped him.

"You find this situation funny?" Pope demanded.

"No!" Because Dillon had to wonder: Why question him here? Why not wait a few hours till he could be properly—interrogated—on Earth? Unless they had not yet decided whether to bring him. "No," he repeated, detesting the quaver in his voice.

"Good. Now tell me about your cronies."

And Dillon babbled. About how he met Yakov. About their arrangement, and the brilliant engineers Yakov had provided. About the OTEC platform.

That he could discuss the Santa Cruz incident, and that little girl, without as much as a catch in his throat made Dillon ill. The last few days had made him . . . callous? No, numb. How could he mourn one child and her grandfather with the blood of hundreds, maybe thousands, on his hands?

"And Yakov is getting away, scot-free," Pope said. "Skipping the country. Flying away. Not that we could touch him anyway. Diplomatic immunity."

*Diplomatic immunity.* Pope made the words sound obscene. Like some horrible miscarriage of justice. Or maybe, Dillon thought, that's how *I* feel.

Through the view port at Dillon's feet, beautiful Earth was just past full phase. Only Earth was not everywhere beautiful: the inky smudge of the Venezuelan disaster tore at his heart. By daylight, the spill and smoke was the only damage he could see. Not like the night-visible rolling blackouts that had surged back and forth across Europe. . . .

And then it hit him: Pope had volunteered information. Why?

"Skipping the country," Dillon said. "How?"

"On his private jet, speeding across the Atlantic. The only plane in the air for thousands of miles. Doubtless laughing his ass off at us."

At that instant, Dillon understood what Pope wanted. What could not be put into words. The price of Dillon's ticket to the ground.

He braced his feet against a guide cable. Even as he yanked great lengths of tether free from his reel, he leapt. He soared over the bot hordes, and then the tether pulled him up short. He began arcing down.

Toward the nearest main computer complex.

＊　＊　＊

Yakov had flown many times across the Atlantic. He had never before seen the radar screen empty. It was uncanny.

Irina Ivanovna sat in the copilot's seat, noise-canceling earphones shielding her cochlear implants from the drone of the engines. "Where will we go?"

"Moscow." Where else? "As disappointed as I am that the Americans did not destroy PS-1, the operation remains a tactical success. American extremists used an illegal American weapons platform to terrorize most of the world. In the process, we made everyone more dependent than ever on Russian oil."

"Will everyone see things as you do?"

"In Moscow we will make our case," he assured her.

"So why are you nervous?"

He was *not* nervous, he told himself. But then why was he sweating? He wiped his forehead with his sleeve. "Contemplation of the Caliph's Guard will do that to a person."

Irina was sweating, too. "Does the Guard know? I mean *know*, not just suspect?"

They could not know. No one in the FSB could have been so stupid as to reveal what he had done. But secrets escaped for reasons beyond stupidity.

Yakov's mind spun off into wheels within wheels, and paranoid fantasies, about who might have been coerced, or corrupted, or a double agent, or . . .

"Why is it so *hot*?" she demanded. "Can you turn down the heat?"

"Of course." He reached for the console—

The metal panel burnt like fire. As he stared, incredulous, at seared fingertips, the console erupted in sparks. His instruments went blank.

Irina screamed. Her face twisting with pain, she threw aside her earphones, also sparking, to slap at the smoke spewing from behind her ears.

"We won't be going to Moscow," Yakov said. Because the universe had, if not a sense of poetic justice, then a dark sense of humor.

Not that Irinushka could hear him anymore.

The Learjet's left engine burst into flame, and then the right. The plane went into a sickening plunge. Black smoke filled the cockpit. He felt himself charring, blistering, roasting. He felt he must explode into a bloody cloud of steam.

Well played, Tyler.

The instant of immolation when the fireball erupted was a sweet release.

EPILOGUE | 2023

**T**his is about Dad, isn't it?" Clarissa asked, tugging and twisting a lock of hair.

"I don't know, hon. I just don't know." Anna Burkhalter put an arm around her daughter and gave a hopefully reassuring squeeze. They sat side by side on their living room sofa.

"What exactly did they say?" Rob asked from his college dorm room.

As Rob *kept* asking, with only the slightest variations in wording, as though some secret truth waited to be teased and coaxed out of the cryptic request. Summons. Command.

Anna looked around the room with embarrassment. She had been on the verge of replacing the battered tables, the worn-shiny fabric of the sofa, the dated carpet, the cat-tattered curtains. She had been on the verge for years. More urgent uses for the money had always intruded, even before the divorce.

"Only that we make ourselves available for this call. Just the three of us. You *are* alone, aren't you, Rob?"

"*Yes*, Mom."

"I think we have to prepare for the worst," Anna said.

Because they had not heard from Patrick for a month. No one had. He would never go this long without calling or e-mailing the kids—if he could.

Because whatever else Anna had to say about Patrick, he was a good father. As good, in any event, as the kids let him be—and that they did not always allow him was probably her fault.

Forget *probably*. She vented about him too much, complained too much, and the memory made her feel like dirt. Because when rescuers got to the bottom of that mountain of wreckage, she just knew they were going to find Patrick's body.

"I know," Rob said softly.

A message-waiting icon began to blink. "Hold on, guys," Anna said.

"This is the White House," a stern-faced woman announced. "Mrs. Anna Burkhalter?"

"This is she," Anna managed. "And my son and daughter."

"Please hold." The woman was replaced by the presidential seal. And then—

"Thank you for taking my call," President Gibson said. His voice was firm and resonant, his manner grave. The massive wooden desk was familiar from a dozen presidential addresses. To one side, a flagpole stood. Behind him, the window wall had a pronounced curve.

"Mr. President," Anna stammered. She had not believed, not really, not until she saw him, saw the Oval Office, that this was not all some huge mix-up or cosmic irony.

"Mrs. Burkhalter, Mr. and Ms. Burkhalter, I have sad news to deliver."

"We understand." Only Anna understood *none* of this. Presidents did not make condolence calls.

"The rescue team in Green Bank completed its work this morning. As we all feared, Dr. Burkhalter is dead." The president paused. "You knew him as a father and former husband. You knew of him as a scientist. I want you to know that Patrick Burkhalter was also a great patriot. More than once, with great personal heroism and at a great personal cost, he performed deeds of critical importance to the nation. He was not at liberty to discuss his actions; his personal life—and yours—doubtless suffered for it. On the slight chance it will ease your loss, I wanted to tell you myself about his sacrifice."

"I . . . I don't know what to say," Anna said.

Because she did not understand any of this, except—with deep shame—the part about great personal cost. After that accursed spacecraft went missing, after Patrick had thrown away his career, he had told her that things happened for a reason. He had promised her that things would be all right. But rather than follow her husband, rather than *trust* him, she had spurned him. Taken the kids away from him.

She fought back the tears for a more private moment, even as Clarissa wept beside her.

"There is no need to say anything," the president replied. "But if mere words ever have the power to comfort, I offer these: We honor Patrick and recognize our debt to his memory.

"Beyond words, know that a place of honor is being held for Dr. Burkhalter at Arlington Cemetery. A suitable memorial in his name will be forthcoming."

"Sir?" Rob asked, his voice quavering.

"Yes, son?"

"My dad . . . he did okay?"

The president smiled. "Son, you cannot begin to imagine how well your dad did."

*  *  *

Isaac Kelly could neither hammer nails without bending them nor saw straight. Offered an electric nail gun, he became a hazard to himself and others. Even his measurement skills were suspect. For a supposedly brilliant and educated man, he had found he had rather limited talents.

Still, he could carry lumber and shingles around a worksite, clear away the scraps, run errands to the hardware store. He could see to it that the men and women with real abilities ate and remained hydrated. And so, one house at a time, for as long as the Habitat people would have him, he meant to do what he could. To do his penance.

Not his only penance, of course. Every morning, under the tutelage of experts, he searched his memory for the smallest details about his past life. The subconscious was an amazing thing, and he had noticed more, about many things, than he could have imagined. Even when his interrogators badgered and berated him, as they challenged the smallest gap or inconsistency in his answers, Isaac wanted to thank them.

There was much to be gleaned from what could be reconstructed about past associates whom the CIA experts could never question. They obviously drew conclusions from Isaac's recollections, conclusions they did not share with him.

And the former associate dead by his own hand? *That* death Isaac did not regret.

Isaac started up a ladder, carrying cold sodas for the men busily shingling. From the top rung he could see a bit more of the town, even catch a glimpse of the High Plains desert beyond. Vantage point was everything. Like the view from—

*Earth all but filling the sky. The spreading stain of oil in the Caribbean. Invisible death lancing downward—*

With a shudder he banished the mental images. The daily debriefings were more than often enough to relive those memories. Not to mention every night in his dreams . . . .

As he handed out cans of cold soda, the man who had been Dillon Russo—a man the world, and Crystal, must (happily?) believe dead— could not help but wonder.

What did the CIA *do* with the information he provided?

Friday, November 3

**W**hite House briefings were scary. In the course of his career, Tyler Pope had gotten himself hauled in front of the National Security Council often enough to know. But briefing the president? One on one? *That* had been gut-wrenching.

Now Tyler hung around to *de*brief the president, and the wait was even worse. Observing the telecon would have made the debriefing far easier—but mere analysts do not sit in on calls between heads of state. Not even volunteering to translate.

It's merely the fate of the world, Tyler told himself. Nothing to concern myself over.

He had the West Wing first-floor reception area to himself. He had not expected to come alone, but the director of Central Intelligence had been preempted at the last minute by business he had deemed, "less Earth-shattering, but more time-sensitive." Not that the suspense would have been any easier to bear while sitting with the DCI.

So Tyler could also look forward to updating the DCI on his impression of how things had gone.

Finally, the president's personal secretary appeared. "He'll see you now, Mr. Pope," she said. She saw Tyler into the Oval Office and closed the door on her way out.

President Gibson waited on one of the two facing couches, a highball glass of ice and amber liquid in hand. Scotch, if reports of the president's tastes were to be believed. Gibson rose as Tyler entered. "Care for a drink, son?"

"No, thank you, sir," Tyler said. He wanted his head clear. And he wondered if the president's drink was celebratory or boded ill.

"Sit, please."

They sat.

"Pavel wasn't very happy," Gibson offered.

Pavel, as in Pavel Borisovich Khristenko, president of the Russian Federation. The knot loosened in Tyler's gut. If all had gone well, Khristenko *should* be unhappy. Tyler asked, "Could you tell me how it went, Mr. President? From the beginning?"

"We started with the usual platitudes. Wives, families, we should talk more often." Gibson paused for a sip. "Then he allowed as how we had matters to discuss."

An acknowledgment of the obvious, Tyler thought. Nonetheless, an acknowledgment.

"Pavel commented on the recent terrible events, and the many economic disruptions." Gibson chuckled. "He seemed loath to move past that."

"To admitting Russia's role?" Tyler asked.

Gibson shook his head. "That's not how these things work. Our conversation was about what Pavel will do to avoid being forced into such an admission."

More than enough evidence existed to force the confession. Because the moment the hostages on Phoebe reestablished communication with Earth, Yakov's whole—brilliant—scheme began to unravel.

There was Dillon Russo's ongoing debrief, of course. Analysts digging into the backgrounds of Jonas Walker, Lincoln Roberts, Felipe Torres, Thaddeus Stankiewicz—and Russo, too, whom Tyler trusted about as far as he could throw—had uncovered plenty of links to Yakov. There were the days of helmet-to-helmet chatter and the occasional downlink from a Russian intel satellite, all intercepted by the NSA and all so much gibberish. With encryption software and security keys recovered on PS-1, the NSA had decrypted everything. And the most damning of all: things Yakov had nervously or carelessly revealed as he fled. Tyler had bugged the "pizza van," the pizza vest, and Yakov's plane.

"What does Khristenko have to say about my former neighbor?" Tyler asked.

"Oh, that's an interesting point," the president said. "I believe Pavel's biggest worry is that Yakov Brodsky and Psycho Cyborg *aren't* dead."

"Khristenko actually believes we kidnapped an accredited diplomat, albeit an FSB agent?"

"Is that harder to believe than that we might allow an accredited diplomat to be killed?" Gibson looked straight at Tyler.

Tyler said, "Our witnesses on PS-1 *both* saw Russo turn the microwave beam on Yakov's plane. And we have Russo's confession."

There you have it, Mr. President. Plausible deniability.

Never mind that we could have cut off the beam from the ground.

What if Russo had not taken the hint? Tyler wondered. Would I have ordered the shoot-down?

"Understood," Gibson finally said. "Regardless, the nagging doubt that we might have splashed a decoy and been as ill mannered as to snatch and interrogate two of their prized assets has made Pavel uncharacteristically . . . flexible."

Tyler relaxed, if only a bit. "Just how 'flexible' is he, sir? In any tangible way?"

Gibson set down his highball glass, empty but for some ice. "Russian oil spigots will be fully opened. And Russia will 'suggest' to its fellow cartel members that they do the same."

Expanded supply to meet the increased demand. If the spigots truly came wide open, perhaps even a touch of price relief. In the short run, the cartel might rake in more money than ever.

"Respectfully, Mr. President, that's not enough," Tyler said. "Not after the havoc the Russians caused."

"Patience," Gibson said, pointedly. "I observed that after the recent wanton destruction, every resource for generating electricity is, and will be, required. I proposed to Pavel that he very publicly embrace new technologies, anticipating the day the oil runs out. And in regard to powersats, in particular, I 'advised' that certain unfounded accusations, expressed in the heat of a terrorist incident, would best be retracted."

Take *that*, Pavel Borisovich. "I'll bet it felt good to twist the knife."

"You have no idea," Gibson said. "That brings me to our final topic. I told Pavel what I will soon declare to the world. That the military relief mission on Phoebe is the vanguard of a permanent American military garrison. That our outpost will have the resources to quickly deploy to and defend PS-1 and our many powersats to come. Further, that we will be putting Phoebe under the jurisdiction of American law.

"Should any international treaty seem incompatible with these actions, we will work vigorously to amend it. If necessary, we will withdraw from any such treaty. Anarchy on the high frontier is demonstrably too dangerous."

With PS-1 as recently modified standing ready to defend the outpost. Tyler supposed that nuance would have gone unarticulated.

"How did that go over, sir?"

"At the beginning of the Space Age, the nations of the world somehow convinced each other that we would leave behind our earthly interests, our earthly natures, when we sought to use the vast resources of space. It was wishful thinking, pure and simple. We ended up reproducing the lawlessness of the Wild West—that was your analogy, son, and I thank you for it—and relearning, the hard way, that peace and safety on the frontier require a sheriff."

"And?" Tyler prompted.

Gibson frowned; prompting apparently crossed some line. "Pavel had a number of objections. To which I observed that a few years ago lawlessness had led to . . . undesirable outcomes in the Restored Caliphate."

"And if he believes we hold Yakov, and Yakov is talking . . ."

"Let's just say that Pavel, who had become very stoical, suggested that perhaps bygones should be bygones, and something about not waking up trouble while it sleeps quietly."

"That's the Russian version of letting sleeping dogs lie."

"In this case," Gibson said, smiling, "it was Pavel's version of surrender."

Quid pro quo. Dirty secrets *kept* secret, and acts of war buried, because open conflict with Russia would be a terrible thing. Hostilities between Russia and the Restored Caliphate, although they would likely avoid American casualties, would still starve the world of oil.

Tyler had imagined himself subtle and saw how naïve he had been. Heads of state elevated subtlety to a very rarified plane.

Too bad, he thought, he could never share with Marcus and Valerie the extent of what they had accomplished. But even if he could, Tyler gathered the two of them had other matters on their minds.

**V**alerie paced and prowled her living room. When that palled, she straightened compulsively. Then she prowled some more.

She spoke with Marcus every night, texted with him several times daily, loved him without reservation. She had only actually *seen* him, been with him, twice in the month since he had been back on Earth. The first time had been more CIA debrief than reunion. The short while they had had alone together, they had spent in the moment, without any thought to the future. The second occasion was Patrick's funeral.

Marcus had had to stay in the District; she got that. Coordinating the repair of PS-1 and expediting the many powersats to follow had to come first. New responsibilities thrown at him, support contractor no longer, reporting directly to the NASA Administrator. *She* had gone home to Simon and Green Bank, to a shattered observatory, traumatized colleagues, and an uncertain future.

And so, the necessary, crucial, life-altering conversation had yet to happen. Did Marcus even know what they had to discuss?

But the delay was almost over, Marcus due any minute. So that they could talk, Simon was at a friend's house for a sleepover.

And then headlights turned into her driveway. They were in each other's arms, once more lost in a passionate *now*, the moment not yet arrived for words.

But eventually . . .

They had dressed, and had a snack, and settled onto the living room sofa. Valerie cuddled at Marcus's side, his arm around her. *Now* was bliss.

And ephemeral. "We need to talk," she said.

"Four words that never go anywhere good."

She shrugged off his arm, edged away so that she could see his face. "The thing is . . ."

"What is it, Val? Straight out."

"The observatory. My job. With the big dish destroyed, many of us have been given notice."

"That's awful." He reached for her hand. "And?"

And? Men could be so obtuse.

She would move in with him in a minute. In other circumstances, she would (she told herself) propose it herself. But not these circumstances. Not unemployed. Not appearing desperate rather than committed.

Would Marcus ask? Did he even want to ask?

"NRAO runs several observatories, not only Green Bank. I was offered a position at one of them, the Very Large Array, in New Mexico." She hesitated: having, and hating, to justify herself. Somehow she held her voice steady. "I need to take care of Simon."

Over to you, Marcus.

*        *        *

New Mexico?

Something had been on her mind for weeks, but Marcus had not known what. Okay, maybe he had been too busy, too preoccupied to ask. In his defense, he was not preoccupied solely with powersats.

New Mexico? Not if *I* have anything to say about it.

He said, "It seems like ages ago, but I remember promising I would always come back to you. Do you remember?"

"All too well."

"I couldn't have kept that promise without you."

"What are you saying?"

That we make a hell of a team. He would get to that. "Will *you* always come back?"

She began to cry. "I'm not talking about a trip, Marcus. It's a *move*. Cross-country. Maybe forever."

"You and Simon should come live with me. Or I'll go with you—if you'll have me, that is. Only maybe there is someplace you'll be traveling. I'll want you to promise to come back."

"Of *course* I'll, we'll, come live with you." With the sudden sunny smile, her tears were a lot easier to take. "But what are you *talking* about? What travel?"

"Remember the day we met? That little surprise you sprang on me? Simon wasn't feeling well. You had to leave early to pick him up from school."

"I remember." She sighed. "I was awful to you that day. I'll never understand why you came back for more."

"After you left, one of your colleagues, I forget who, said something like, 'powersats will mean the end of astronomy until there's an observatory on the far side of the moon.'"

"A bit dramatic," she said.

"Patrick thought so, too. He told the guy, basically, to get a life."

"Poor Patrick." She began sniffling.

Marcus handed her the box of tissues from the coffee table. "You don't see where I'm going with this? Truly?"

She wiped her face and blew her nose. "You asked me to move in with you. Where but Virginia would I be going?"

"The country is claiming the high ground," he said. "And it won't be only Phoebe. Think lunar resources."

"A far-side observatory? Really?"

He answered her question with a question. "Why rebuild the big dish in what's going to become a noisier and noisier neighborhood?"

"And you're saying that I . . . ?"

"That *we* have the president's gratitude. And, as it happens, also his promise. Who better than you and I to be the chief scientist and the chief engineer of the Patrick Burkhalter Lunar Far-Side Observatory? The president will announce the program next week."

"I can't be going to the *moon*. Simon is only—"

"Not to worry." Marcus had seen this one coming. "After the previous big dish collapsed in 1988, it took, what, twelve years to construct a new one? I think you can count on Simon being in college or out on his own before any big dish on the lunar far side is ready to use."

Valerie stared at him, looking . . . what? Sad, maybe. Confused. Conflicted. What the hell?

"What's wrong *now*?" he asked.

"I forced you into asking me to move in. While *you* were getting me a wonderful opportunity and even thinking ahead about Simon."

"You feel like you forced my hand. You can't be sure that I truly want us to live together."

"Uh-huh." Sniffle. "It's all so messed up."

Women could be so obtuse.

Marcus went to the hall closet to retrieve the little box from his coat pocket. He had carried around that box for two weeks, in the so far vain hope that proximity would inspire the right words.

The contents could speak for themselves.

"Well," Valerie said, on finding the diamond engagement ring, "I *might* be mistaken."

# AFTERWORD AND ACKNOWLEDGMENTS

Stories often sneak up on me. Not this one. I know exactly how and when this novel began: at a dinner three years ago with Tom Doherty, my publisher. Tom threw out a challenge for novels focused on energy issues and alternate-energy resources; I countered with the Crudetastrophe and the first notion of what became *Energized*.

Thanks, Tom.

At another level, perhaps *Energized* was destined. Once upon a time I was a physicist and computer scientist. I've seen, up close and personal, how government contracting—and in particular, NASA contracting—works. Along the way, I toured a satellite factory, flew the space-shuttle training simulator, wandered around the space-station trainer, and backed out, in dismay, from the space-toilet trainer. (In those primitive days, step one on the toilet's instruction placard read, *Load film in camera.*)

That background did not relieve me of doing research. Quite the opposite: it helped to show how much I needed to investigate. Technothrillers are not at all like writing about a galaxy long ago and far away. For this story, I wasn't free to make up the tech or the background.

NASA's Near-Earth Object (NEO) Program has, as of this writing, cataloged more than eight thousand NEOs. More than eight hundred NEOs measure at least a kilometer across. It has been estimated that a one-kilometer asteroid strike would kill up to a billion people. (The rock believed to have doomed the dinosaurs is estimated at ten kilometers across.) But as the story just concluded shows, NEOs can also provide precious resources.

Either way, what can humans do about a NEO that has our names written all over it?

Attending the 2008 Asteroid Deflection Research Symposium in Arlington, Virginia, gave me lots of useful background. Experts came from the government (NASA, the Air Force, the National Science Foundation, and other federal entities), academia, and industry—and most participants stressed that their presentations and comments reflected personal opinions and not the official viewpoints of their organizations. Without naming anyone, I'll thank . . . everybody.

I attended the symposium as a member of SIGMA, a group of SF authors providing futurism consulting, pro bono, to the federal government. So, thanks to the Department of Homeland Security, Science and Technology Directorate, for sponsoring me.

Gravity tractors are among the technologies in serious contention for deflecting a NEO. But, ugh: what a mundane name. Before I hijacked a spacecraft as my unauthorized gravity tractor, I pondered names for a long while. The only spacecraft named for Jules Verne is an orbital automated transfer vehicle—an unmanned cargo ship—built by the European Space Agency. Sorry, that's not good enough. The *Verne* should do something great. If only in fiction, now it has.

In 2009 I contacted the public affairs office at the National Radio Astronomy Observatory in Green Bank, West Virginia, to request a tour and perhaps meet a radio astronomer or two. They more than obliged. One highlight: The technical staff not only welcomed me to their weekly group lunch, they spent their lunchtime brainstorming about science and technology for the novel. (We'll chalk up to hard times post-Crudetastrophe Marcus's adversarial first encounter with the Green Bank technical staff.) To everyone at the observatory: thank you.

If you're ever in the neighborhood, I suggest that you drop by for the public tour. The Green Bank Telescope must be seen to be believed.

For input to the novel's medical aspects, I'd like to thank cardiologist and science-fiction author Henry G. Stratmann.

On to powersats . . .

Science-fiction author Geoffrey A. Landis is, in his day job, a NASA scientist who has published several papers about powersats. Geoff graciously answered many questions for me. He also reviewed and fine-tuned my preliminary concepts for PS-1, Phoebe, and the mechanics of capturing such an object. Thanks again, Geoff.

Speaking of Phoebe . . . when, someday, humanity does snag another satellite for Earth, I fear that all the good classical mythological names will have been taken. The major moons of Saturn, for example, are named after the titans of Greek mythology. Including "golden-wreathed Phoebe," the daughter of Gaia traditionally associated with *the* moon. Phoebe fit my purpose, and I'm sticking to it. In this instance, whatever my astronomer friends may think.

It's impossible to major in physics or to be a lifelong science-fiction aficionado without absorbing some astronomy, but I had never studied the subject systematically. This book has lots of it. (Case in point: When your turn comes to play space tourist, a surprise coronal mass ejection *is* worth worrying about.) So: I was pleased to attend Launch Pad 2009. Launch Pad is a NASA-funded astronomy workshop for writers, run by SF author Mike Brotherton, aka University of Wyoming astronomer Michael S. Brotherton. Thanks for having me, Mike.

Where the novel gets the details right, thank the experts. As always, responsibility for extrapolations, errors, simplifications, and fictional license lies with the author.

My appreciation also goes to Bob Gleason, my editor, for his encouragement, and to Eleanor Wood, my agent, for her support.

Last but certainly not least, I thank my first and favorite reader: my wife, Ruth. This book kept me more preoccupied than most, so thanks also for bearing with me.

—Edward M. Lerner
January 2012

## ABOUT THE AUTHOR

EDWARD M. LERNER worked in high tech for thirty years, as everything from engineer to senior vice president, for much of that time writing science fiction as a hobby. Since 2004 he has written full-time, and his books run the gamut from techno-thrillers, like *Energized,* to traditional SF, like the InterstellarNet series, to, with Larry Niven, the grand space epic Fleet of Worlds series of *Ringworld* companion novels.

Ed's short fiction has appeared in anthologies, two collections, and many of the usual SF magazines. He also writes the occasional nonfiction technology article.

Lerner lives in Virginia with his wife, Ruth.

His website can be found at www.edwardmlerner.com.